SHADEBRINGER

BOOK ONE

THE LAND OF IRGENDWO

GRAYSON W. HOOPER

This book is a work of fiction. Names, characters, businesses, organizations, places, events, and incidents are either a product of the author's imagination or are used fictitiously. Any resemblance to actual persons, living or dead, events, or locales is entirely coincidental.

Published by River Grove Books
Austin, TX
www.rivergrovebooks.com

Distributed by River Grove Books

Design and composition by Greenleaf Book Group
Cover design by Greenleaf Book Group
Cover Images: Silhouette of soldier by Fernando Blanco Calzada, Forest in autumn morning mist by DavidTB, Jungle Dream by Tino Lopes, used under license from Shutterstock.com

Publisher's Cataloging-in-Publication data is available.

Print ISBN: 978-1-63299-468-4

eBook ISBN: 978-1-63299-470-7

First Edition

For Pops, family, and the lads

CONTENTS

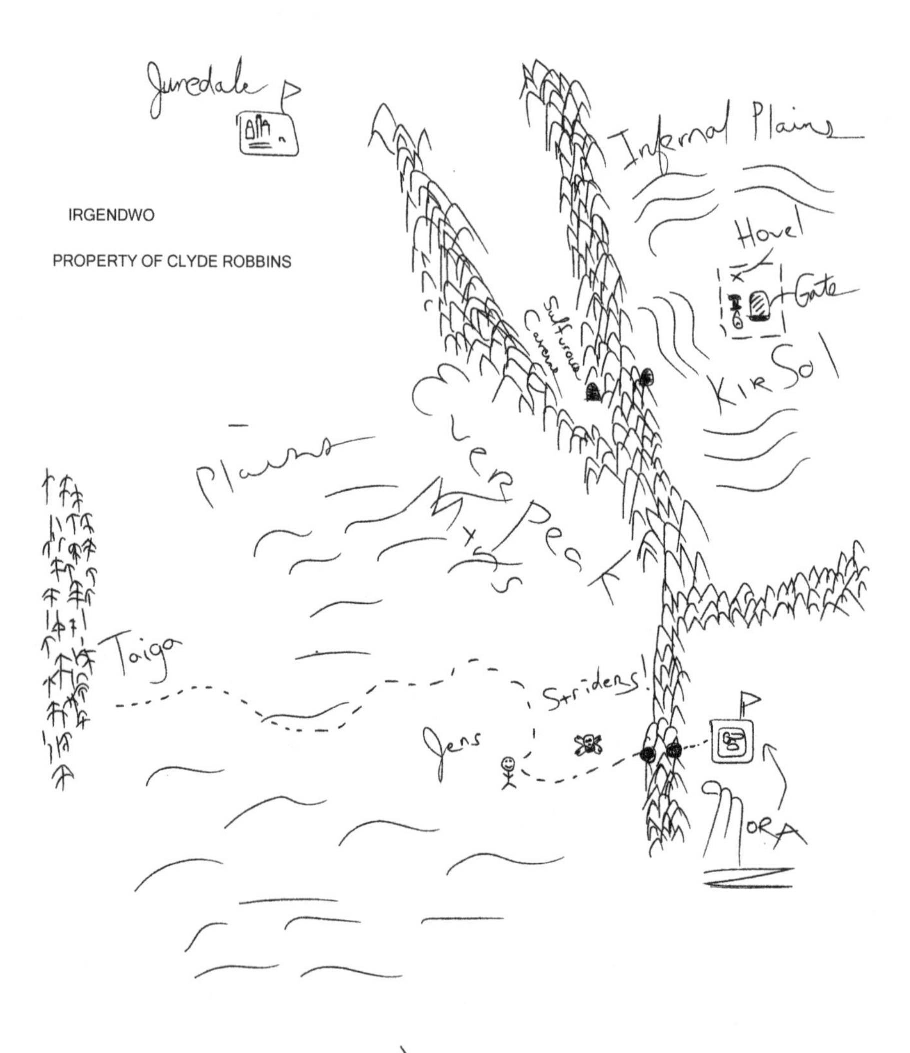

Where is my PEACE?

→ Get over it, Yank! -Keats

1 inch = who the fuck knows?

- ☑ How did I die?
- ☑ Why am I here?
- ☐ What happened to Skinner?
- ∞ Get even with God

PART I

METAL ALLUVION

And you, my father, there on the sad height,

Curse, bless, me now with your fierce tears, I pray.

Do not go gentle into that good night.

Rage, rage against the dying of the light.

—DYLAN THOMAS

CHAPTER 1

THE MAN

I believe the destiny of your generation—
and your nation—is a rendezvous with excellence.

—LYNDON B. JOHNSON,
36TH PRESIDENT OF THE UNITED STATES

"THE SOUTH VIETNAMESE ARE HUNGRY for democracy—dying for freedom from those godless commie scum." The recruiter's sharp, featureless face perfectly matched his sharp, trimmed body and tailored uniform. He sat at his perfectly organized desk with a single picture showing God's own vision of a nuclear family. Across from him sat an angst-filled young man in an oil-stained T-shirt with shaggy hair that grazed his eyeballs. That sonofabitch was yours truly.

"Yeah, yeah, yeah," I said as I counted cars through the window. "Freedom, democracy, and the American way." I had already made a decision but was playing my cards close to get the best possible deal from Uncle Sam. I spun a pen in my hand and tried to appear noncommittal. The uniformed apparatchik clenched his jaw and sighed through flaring nostrils whenever my attention drifted away, but he always managed to press a smile over those sharp teeth. His quarry was near, and I'm sure he didn't want to spook it.

"I see a strong young man in need of structure and a thousand more calories per day," he said.

I smiled and grabbed a model Sherman tank from his desk like I owned the fucking thing.

His hackles sprang up, and he pursed his lips over those pearly razors, trying to hold a smile. This bastard did not have a poker face. With all the sage he could muster, he leaned back in his chair and tapped his index fingers together. "The Sherman was the main battle tank that won us the war in Europe. I would know; I fought in one."

I spun the treads with my index finger, testing the faithfulness of the replica. "Seventy-five or seventy-six-millimeter smoothbore main gun and a Continental R975 radial engine." I spoke to the tank as if it were alive.

Irritation momentarily extinguished, the recruiter furrowed his brow and nodded. "Outstanding, son. How did you know that?"

"My mom couldn't afford presents on Christmases and birthdays, so she'd just steal library books and wrap them up in old paper bags." I ran the more memorable titles through my mind—all stamped with *PUBLIC PROPERTY* in big red letters. "Also, I don't guzzle Schlitz and fuck my sister like most of the inbred meat you shuttle through here on a regular basis."

The negotiations heated up; the recruiter pulled a corner of his lip back and snorted. "If you're so goddamn smart, why aren't you going to college?"

"Because I'm poor white trash with no way out of here and no hope otherwise, so I figured I'd try my hand at killing commies rather than my stepfather. Besides, I feel like I owe this county for all my free books." Of course, I didn't give a rat's ass about the books, but I didn't feel like explaining why my life was otherwise meaningless.

"Ah, problems at home. I hear ya," he said. "We'll give you a new family."

"One who won't call me a pussy for reading Jane Austen and writing poetry on stagnant summer days?" I fluttered my eyes like Marilyn Monroe and spun the pen faster.

"Yeah, sure, smartass. Sign the fucking papers." He grinned and shoved the pile in front of me, confident in his kill.

I snatched up the block-printed bureaucratic mess and began to read. Not bad, aside from fucking up my name. Everything we had discussed was dutifully reflected in the contract, and he had even double-underlined my signature spaces. "Robbins is spelled R-O-B-B-I-N-S, dumbass." I shook my head, corrected the errors, and struck my signatures across each block. After a final goodbye to freedom, I bunched up the papers and slid them back.

The recruiter glanced at every page then up to me, his eyes narrowing. A lupine grin spread across his face.

Game on.

* * *

I hadn't even stepped off the bus before a pile of shit fell in my lap. On our way to the reception station, some fuckhead from New York decided to get froggy, so I split his upper lip. After my first introduction to military-style punishment for misbehavior—a flurry of backhands from a motivated drill sergeant—boot camp commenced in earnest.

The old saying "the military will tear you down and rebuild you" is mostly true. However, it's more on point for some men than others. Some guys came crashing down in hunks of porcelain and candy, while others took everything in stride. In a way, I pitied the tough guys more than the pussies; I could only imagine that they ended up like junkyard dogs—obedient and vicious. I was somewhere in between. Not bright enough to just play the game and keep my head low, I often had something smartass to say. This deficit really upped my misery, but at the end of the entire eight-week ordeal, I could crush rocks with a new set of pecs.

Somewhere along the way, the powers-that-be saw something in me I didn't know existed, despite my often-shitty attitude. Whether it was motivation, hate, or a combination of the two, it didn't matter. They funneled me into an advanced leadership training course called the

Noncomissioned Officer Candidate Course in hot-as-balls Georgia. I took the extra five months of ass kicking knowing it would keep me out of Vietnam a little longer. Honestly, I kinda enjoyed the tactics, combat drills, and patrols under the watchful eyes of Rangers and crusty old infantry guys. They even had a replica gook village to make the experience as authentic as possible; we were only missing the whores in those funny triangle hats.

Graduating at the top of my class, I slammed on the rank of E6—staff sergeant. Pretty goddamn quick for a dipshit private to reach sergeant in the same year he went through basic. After pinning on our new ranks, we got a polite summons to collect our orders, which contained our unit assignments and report dates. Nearly all of us got a one-way ticket to Vietnam, except the businessman's son who got some detail at the Pentagon pouring coffee and polishing ball sacks.

Regardless, the whole process was unceremonious, and when it was time to go, it was basically get your gear, say goodbye to Mom, and get on the plane. The MAC daddies—Military Airlift Command—provided the smooth-as-corn-in-a-lump-of-dog-shit airlift to my new home away from home, which shook loose a few fillings and had me spraying my meals out of both ends. Dozens of hours later, we landed, and I *almost* prayed when the cargo bay fell open.

"This is Vietnam," I muttered as I stepped off the big ugly fat fuck of a plane happy to breathe fresh air. It was February 1969. Squealing jet engines and C130 props filled my ears just as they had when I left the US. Green men flowed out of the birds and spread across the tarmac in a torrent. The heavy duffle sank into my shoulder while I scanned the tarmac and the infinite green beyond it. Our little patch of concrete and iron couldn't hold a candle to the world enveloping it—enveloping me. We were alien specks in a hostile, primordial, *wet* land.

Let's give it a try. I looked around for HQ and walked over to check in. From that point, home in the US of A ceased to exist. And why shouldn't it? There was nothing for me back there, and, for better or worse, I had cast my lot with thousands of others just as desperate and directionless as me.

CHAPTER 2

SON OF PERDITION

Give him a chance, Clyde. Nobody in this house is without sin.

—JANE ROBBINS

LUSH HAIR, LONG LEGS, FLOWERY DRESS, bare feet—she couldn't have been more than sixteen years old, but she stood outside the base access point giggling and flirting with the boyish military police who blocked her way into Long Binh. A veritable playground for the REMF types—rear echelon motherfuckers—who "supported" the ground pounders, Long Binh was behind the lines, ahead of the times, and crawling with gonorrhea. And it was my duty to check in before heading into the shit.

"Little darlin', you know I can't let you in here without a vendor pass," said an MP in a thick Southern drawl. A sheen of pubescent grease on his face gleamed red as the girl begged and whined and twirled her dress.

"Fruit, fruit, yum," she said and shook her basket of durians. "Feed GI, help family."

"Just let her go, man. What's she gonna do—blow up the fucking PX?" The other MP winked at the girl and waved her through despite his buddy's protests. She squealed and tottered in, hugging the basket.

I stood beneath the droopy eave of a rundown bar, dragged down a Lucky Strike, and watched as her look hardened—the smile now a line—and she strode with a purpose. "Mornin'," I said when she passed.

Her eyes shifted to me for brief acknowledgment but not a speck of emotion or any words came back. She picked up the pace and gripped the basket.

A slight twist in my gut urged me forward, and I set off after her.

She must have known I was following her, because her walk became a jog. She turned down a street and homed in on a gaggle of soldiers milling outside the PX—the post exchange. She paused for a moment to root around in her basket. The twist in my gut intensified.

"Hey, stop!" I shouted.

Startled, she looked back at me then broke into a sprint toward the soldiers.

"Fucking stop!" I bolted and gripped my 1911 pistol.

The girl glanced back again, her face a canvas of fear and desperation, and she tumbled to the ground. A pained squeak left her body as she bounced and durians flew from the basket. But something else clanged against the asphalt. She charged, hand over foot in a frenzy, at the round, light yellow object and leaped upon it.

The gaggle of soldiers jogged to her, shouting obscenities at me and laughing.

She stood and turned to me, clutching something to her breast, tears streaming down her cheeks. Her tiny hands gripped a painted M67 hand grenade with an index finger twirled around the pin. She locked eyes with me and a faint smile creased her lips.

"Help family," she said.

I drew the 1911 up, staring down my arm and pistol sights. My body shook as every fiber of my humanity resisted the trigger squeeze. I had been in country two weeks and was yet to kill anyone. Was my first really going to be a sobbing teenager clutching a goddamned grenade?

She popped off the safety clip and her finger blanched white against the grenade's pin.

Electricity surged through my heart. My mind sharpened. Time stood still.

And I fired.

• • •

The act of killing wasn't natural, but it came quick and definitely wasn't what I expected. I had shot a sixteen-year-old girl with a Colt 1911. There was no glory or greatness in this. There was no pride. After she hit the ground, I ran over to her and squeezed her hand gently until her hold on the grenade—and this Earth—passed. I could only watch the life run from her body as tears ran from mine. I cried as if she were my own daughter bleeding out in my arms.

Soldiers stood around us and glared down at the spectacle in silence. Their mouths were agape, even the grizzled grunts with thousand-yard stares. An eternity passed until they stirred.

"Hard. Fucking. Core." A master sergeant gripped my shoulder.

"Buddy Holly here just saved our asses," said another younger buck—a corporal.

Apparently, I looked like the guy, and the round had struck the girl's heart. In any other circumstance, I'd be on my way to a concrete box for the rest of my life or an execution. Here, I got a nickname.

I thought of her parents: Would they wonder why she never came home? Did she have brothers and sisters? Maybe a boyfriend? I'll never know, but one thing I *did* know: I couldn't have let her pull the pin. But Christ, I shot a kid, myself barely old enough to be called an adult. Was this going to be my legacy?

No. Bloodlust didn't bring me to Vietnam, nor did any form of hatred. I was *pushed* here. I needed to come here for meaning, for something greater. And I found that meaning in a moment of horror—in those beautiful young eyes that I consigned to an early grave, a life, among countless others, snuffed for naught but the machinations of evil men thousands of miles away. I wanted so badly to save the innocent, the vulnerable, the meek while I stood watch in this nightmare. But, no, a single simpleton from Pennsylvania stood little chance against the forces at hand. Story of my life, I guess. Regardless, I was determined to try. I finally had direction.

One day can change everything.

• • •

"Give it here, fuckhead," I said, snatching the rifle away from the nameless runt who had—seconds before—been tugging at it, sloppy and unsure. *Fucking draftees.* I rolled my eyes and broke the upper and lower receivers apart in seconds and stripped off the plastic handguards like husking a stalk of corn. I arranged the pieces into neat squares on the tarp and waved my hands over them like a magician before gutting out the bolt carrier. Next came the firing pin and the retaining pin, which I pinched between my fingers.

"Don't lose this," I said with heavy emphasis on each speck of metal. "Otherwise, the whole fucking thing is as worthless as you."

Wide-eyed, maybe a bit too eager, the kid nodded and fidgeted with the toy-like parts as I watched.

I gave the bastard a full thirty seconds before heaving a disgusted sigh, snatching the parts back, and jamming the reassembled weapon into his chest. *Jesus Christ, what bucket of cum did these dipshits swim out of?*

"Don't have time for this shit," I said under my breath, but I couldn't abandon the boy to his ignorance. I looked down at him with a hard stare. "Keep it clean. Keep it neat. Keep practicing. You didn't come here to die because you can't care for your fucking weapon. You came here to kill." With a slap to the boy's shoulder, I waved him away and moved to a new area of the hooch where another group sat waiting.

"This here's the pig," I said and ran my hand over the barrel of the M60. My voice swelled with pride, and it carried the soldiers under my command—I could tell by the tight spines—and the thought made me smirk. "The pig's a high-quality killing machine well worth humping its fat fucking bulk around for the nasty sonofabitch lucky enough to kill with it."

A sea of blank faces stared back when I offered a lucky grunt the opportunity to pull it apart. Silence. Eyes darted away like frightened puppies.

OK, fuck it. I scoured the sea of ugly mugs and pointed at a private: The kid had something to him, maybe an innocence, that put a sickly unease in the pit of my stomach. His eyes were green, bright but mournful, set in a face of such youth that I wondered if he had faked his enlistment age. *Boys playing at war. . . . Gonna have to take 'em down a notch.*

"Show me how you break it down and reassemble it."

The young soldier nodded and maneuvered over the iron and wood device. Every movement was perfect. Every click and clang of its metal body had a purpose, and in less than five minutes, it was ready to kill.

"Outstanding," I said, momentarily impressed. "Private Thibodeaux, eh? What's your human name?"

"Claude, Sergeant," said the private as he stood from the weapon.

"Well, Private Claude Thibodeaux, where ya from?" As if I had to ask.

"Louisiana, Sergeant."

"Well, hot damn! We got us a bayou boy right here."

Some soldiers glared at him with envy, but the rest clearly wanted to imitate his success.

"Why the fuck they got you carrying a 60, son? You can't be more than a hundred and twenty pounds and a few potatoes."

"Fate, I guess, Sergeant." His shrug was quicker than his smile, which didn't quite come.

I laughed and rubbed my chin. There was something about him that gave me pause. He was wise beyond his years and capable. War didn't deserve him; he didn't deserve war. I could only come to one conclusion.

"You're gonna die here, boy."

My tone hadn't changed, but the kid could sense my discomfort. He looked at me, waiting for a punch line, but none came; I didn't sugarcoat my wisdom. In my mind, some bureaucrat had already stamped "KIA" in big red letters on his personnel file.

"Why's that, Sarge?" His voice was sturdy. He had heart.

"You're competent, thoughtful, and really good at your fucking job," I said. "That's just the nature of war, son. God can't make it too tough on our enemies. It's not sporting."

"Oh," said the private. The nice white ranch split-level with the perfect picket fence was probably in flames in his head.

"Also, let me guess." I sized him up further, arms across my chest and head to the side like I was solving a math problem. "You just got married to your high school sweetheart, and you got a kiddo on the way."

The private, deep in thought, nodded. "Good guess, Sergeant."

His pending nonexistence took on a fresh and palpable reality. I wondered how his bastard-to-be would throw a baseball alone. A flicker of sadness sprang from my heart, but I snuffed it, smashed it, and tried to forget it. I would not let myself get attached to these fuckers. Not here. Not now.

"Thought so." I was pleased my intuition still served me. "God's gotta fucking sick sense of humor, son. You'll see. Just keep your head down and prove me wrong for Little Jimmy's sake."

I left Bayou Boy to his thoughts and pulled a cigarette from my vest before trudging to the next group.

"So much fucking ignorance around here," I mumbled around the flame. I took a quick drag and swept over the soldiers until I found my next target.

"Hey shitbag, you're doing it wrong."

• • •

Clyde, your father and I miss you terribly. My eyes darted across Mom's cursive on the crinkled stationery as I puffed a cigar. I dipped the ass-end of the cigar in a small tin of brandy, took a heavy drag, and cursed the letter with intermittent mutterings of "bullshit," "fuck," and "liar." The others looked at me with every volley but said nothing: Papa bear being papa bear.

A large Black man turned from his duffel and shot me a disgusted look. "Man, at least you get mail regularly, motherfucker." Sergeant Collins was a fast replacement after another NCO stepped on a mine a week back. I ignored the unwelcome comment and kept reading.

Your stepfather is so proud of you—a particularly egregious lie that packed my gut with hate. "Horseshit!" That motherfucker can stick his pride in the same place he stuck his draft deferrals. I snorted and put a round in his head in my imagination. Satisfying.

The rest of the letter detailed taxes, the neighbors, war protests on television, my sick Aunt Minnie, the ex-girlfriend, corn, fishing, and our usual dire financial straits. I finished the letter, flipped it over to look for additional bullshit, crumpled it into a ball, and set it alight. It billowed another layer of smoke into the crowded hooch, mixing with all sorts of others.

"Why you so hard on your family?" said Collins, who had now fully engaged himself in my goddamn business for some reason.

"Because my mother is an idiot and my stepfather a coward, a druggy, and a liar, but that's none of your fucking concern, is it?"

Collins fell back on his cot and reread his own letters using the tip of a knife to mark each word. "That's no way to talk about the woman who brought you into this world," he said, "and my old man would beat my ass 'til I bled for things I hadn't even done yet, so I don't know what your cracker ass is complaining about."

"Things you hadn't done yet?" I blew the letter's ashes out of my hand and cocked my head at him.

His giant bloodshot eyeballs shifted to me. "Yeah, he said only God could see all the bad shit I did, so Pops would beat my ass just in case he missed anything."

A few soldiers laughed, but his words revolted me. "Sounds like Pops is a bigger scumbag than the god he follows."

Collins' jaw bulged, and he set the stack of letters on his lap. "Maybe if your real father had a little faith and stuck around, your confused momma wouldn't be fucking some needle junkie who's obviously got your number something good."

I stared hard at him, and he leveled the blade at me. Crimson crust lined the blood gutter of the weapon; it had been recently used and used hard. Neither of us blinked as the other soldiers looked on.

"Clyde Robbins, Philadelphia," I said after the tense pause. The sonofabitch had pissed me off like no other, but he spoke a cold truth I couldn't help but respect. I reached out and shook the crusted blade like it was his hand and spilled a few drops of my own blood. One good turn deserves another.

"Bernard Collins," he said, flashing a row of tobacco-stained teeth, "Biloxi, Mississippi. Call me Bernie." Fresh blood ran down the blade, and the thought of becoming blood brothers with some gook who had the supreme misfortune of meeting Bernie in the dark made me smirk.

My new acquaintance looked down at my remaining cigar. "Got an extra?" He licked his lips and pointed at the brandy. I nodded and removed a fresh cigar from my vest, dipped it in the sweet liquor, and handed it to him.

From then on, we were all right. I would have even kept him as a friend if I wasn't so goddamn sure he was gonna die. Regardless, it's mighty powerful what one cigar and some brandy can do. If only the assholes in Washington, DC, and Ho Chi Minh City knew that.

CHAPTER 3

KNOCKWURST

Holy hell, what a lightshow!

—SERGEANT MAURICE "BEAR" TURNER,
B-52D TAIL GUNNER

IN A TIME AND SPACE NOT LONG REMOVED from Clyde, the tribulations of others unfolded. A slight People's Army soldier ducked into the moist vegetation, unsure of what crawled within. He gripped a rusting AK-47 close to his chest and shuddered in the darkness. A comrade tapped his shoulder, and he forced himself forward, lead foot over lead foot. The alternative was a bayonet in the back.

The silent platoon of farm boys blended into the vegetation with such ease *they* could have been the jungle. The ubiquitous drone of an empire of insects, howling animals in the throes of death, and the pattering of gentle rain easily masked their movements. They carried simple Russian rifles like tigers wielding their claws against the dark unknowns of both man and beast, but few were destined to use them.

The young soldier paused and reviewed a map with his platoon leader, a small honor he had earned with his competence and quick wit. Vietnamese characters decorated the map, each signifying something of military or terrain significance, but the soldier only cared for the unpaved road that took him home. Oh, how far it was! Just two years ago, he had fished with his father on a nameless delta, tended to the fields with his mother, and chased city girls. A year later, he married after a brief and passionate courtship. Now, he was a single cog in the great equality machine.

The December air, cool for Vietnam, chilled him, but adrenaline was more than enough to dull the sensation, and it was a welcomed change from daylight's swelter. Their path, a torturous shadow even in a place they called home, brought them near a winding riverbank. Their target was anything white or black with green camouflage, but they knew and feared what came with the night—men who emerged from the water to kill and vanish back into it, merciless phantoms mentioned only in whispers.

But this soldier's death was not to be a quiet one.

A sudden thrill beneath his foot, an anomaly amid the soft muck, spooked him. A mine? A trap? He quieted his mind and stepped. No blast. Just another *squick* as his foot settled in the mud. But in mere moments, a second thrill shot through both heels. This time, he could not ignore it, nor could the others.

The platoon leader stopped and whispered, bringing them to a halt. A rumble rolled over the horizon, and a cone of yellow light flashed in the distance. A storm? What a strange order of succession. More cones flashed into the air, illuminating the treetops in fleeting outlines of yellow and orange. The platoon leader's radio crackled to life. A static-laden voice shouted warnings and commands, which the others scribbled down. Three rockets hissed into the sky from miles behind them and streaked overhead. The orange thrusters swept up and disappeared into a thick cloud layer.

The soldiers looked into the nether, craning their necks at the diminishing specks of light. More yellow cones flashed from beyond the shadowy tree line. The ground trembled beneath their feet. More rockets streamed upward, the second volley coming from all around them. The powerful reports of 100 mm antiaircraft artillery joined the growing tumult, hot metal slugs following the rockets.

The boys and their sturdy Russian rifles trembled; they knew this invisible terror could not be deterred. The platoon leader begged further instruction from his radio but static replied. The cones had become enveloping blazes and the tremors earthquakes. The soldiers dropped and covered their heads with their rifles as another salvo of rockets soared over them.

The young soldier focused on a single rocket that disappeared far above him and wondered for whom it was meant and where it would eventually land.

The ground erupted, and trees danced violent deaths ahead of them. Their fates were sealed. The young man stood up from his little plot of earth and squared his chest to the chaos. Picturing his wife and child for the last time, he closed his eyes and straightened his back. A final muted panoramic flash carried the young soldier out of Vietnam.

• • •

"Holy hell, what the fuck happened here?" I said, and the entire platoon stopped to survey the carnage. Through the last leg of our patrol, the unnatural and abrupt change of scenery gave us pause. The early afternoon sun cast a peaceful glow over nature's wreckage; it was as if God himself fell from heaven in a rage. Trees and vegetation were mixed in an unnatural embrace and peppered with chunks of carbon and bleached bone fragments. Long-dead men slumbered.

"B-52s," said the LT. "This was a carpet bombing . . . probably months ago." Second Lieutenant George "Georgie" Schultz, a recent arrival from West Point, hit our area of operations a short time before I did. Normally, a new dick-bag officer would last about a week before Charlie (or sometimes one of us) smoked him, but Georgie was different. The lean, tall ginger had the makings of a great leader, yes, but he also had a good heart. We protected him and he us. He was the only lieutenant I called "LT" in an unironic sense.

"Carpet bombing, eh?" I recalled reading about Curtis LeMay and his gift to the world: the practice of dropping tons of explosives in a straight line from giant flying wheelbarrows.

Sprouts peeked up from the ground—a testament to nature's resilience—but splintered assault rifles and gook gear eerily marked the moment of obliteration. It was undoubtedly pure horror for anyone present on that day, but now, it was just another monument to modern warfare.

A small flower poked up from a saucer-shaped remnant of human skull. *Helluva flowerpot.* I chuckled at the thought of becoming a minor landscaping ornament as I ambled over the shattered terrain, but a small brown satchel covered in mold snagged my attention. I kneeled and inspected it, looking for wire, string, or a pressure plate. Tales of VC booby-traps circulated as far back as basic training, and I didn't want to lose a hand to haste.

Teasing the metal clasp away with a long stick, I flipped the hood back. Bingo. I pocketed some Vietnamese money and a couple trinkets without a second thought but the pictures stopped me in my tracks. They were soggy and faded, but I could still see a happy couple in each. A few had a baby in various poses. I glanced at the skull fragment. *Was Flowerpot the dad?*

"It's best not to see them as human," said the LT over my shoulder in his thick Minnesotan accent. His voice was low and solemn. I knew he wasn't joking.

"Yeah," I said and swallowed hard. I emptied the satchel but couldn't find any identifying information whatsoever. Curiosity extinguished, I returned the pictures and stood up; it felt right to leave the dead man's family with him.

"Clyde."

I turned to the unfamiliar voice, and Corporal Jeffords stared back at me. The wolf of the platoon, Jeffords wore a predatory look that matched his fierce temper and early gray hair.

"Yeah, what?" I said, annoyed the bastard had used my first name.

"I didn't say a fucking thing, Sarge."

I side-eyed Jeffords and looked around to find who was fucking with me. Jeffords held a serious and tight gaze as he waited while I pondered my next words.

"All right, never mind."

Probably didn't get enough sleep—or enough cigarettes.

CHAPTER 4

HELL HATH NO FURY

It's funny how most people love the dead.
Once you're dead, you're made for life.

—JIMI HENDRIX

"TAKE FIVE." THE LT HALTED US, AND the boys fanned out for perimeter defense. After a headcount, I inspected our fighting positions to ensure shit was kosher. Firing lines? Check. M60s on deck? Check. Three-sixty coverage? Oh yeah, life was good.

The LT and radioman were talking in the center of the clearing.

"We gonna have some fun today?" I said as I approached.

"Something's wrong with you," said the LT, sort of grinning and shaking his head, "but we need to check the road west of the firebase before wrapping shit up." He propped open his map, exchanged words with the radioman, then said to me, "Give the boys some downtime while I get shit figured out." He picked up the mic. "And get Private Thibodeaux to join Smitty on point; he's due for some OJT."

"Roger that, sir." I shouldered my rifle and made my rounds, tossing smokes around like a Marlboro Santa Claus. It was a good time to bullshit.

“Private Thibodeaux,” I said as I slogged to his fighting position. “How’s the war treating you?” He was lying prone, eye down the barrel of the pig with his finger on the trigger guard. Next to him, Jeffords’s bristly gray head was buried in a *Hustler* magazine. He folded the girls he liked and mumbled under his breath. I was glad my lessons hadn’t been lost on the private, at least.

“Not bad, Sergeant, aside from humping this damn Volkswagen everywhere I go.” He tapped the weapon. The ammo belt snaked out of the breech over his arm and around his back, a metal serpent on a boy’s frame.

“Private,” I said, suppressing the urge to yell, “don’t wear the ammo belt like that. Shit’ll start rusting.”

“Yes, Sergeant,” he said and pulled it off.

“My fault, Sergeant,” said Jeffords as he helped tuck the rounds into the ammo can. “I wanted to make him look like a badass for his wife.”

“Oh yeah?” I said and crossed my arms. “Original Stars and Stripes material, eh?”

“No shit, Sarge. Get a load of Frenchy’s babe,” he said like a teenage boy. He rolled up the titty mag, stuffed it in his ruck, and took over the machine gun. Claude grinned, happy to be freed from the pig for a moment, and handed me her photo. He puffed up his chest with pride.

I looked over every inch of her and nodded. “God damn, son, you packing a horse’s dick or something?”

“That’s what I said!” Eyes wide, Jeffords whistled over his shoulder. “It’s always the quiet ones.”

“Come on, guys,” said Claude, now a light pink. “We’ve been going steady since grade school.”

“True love is popping each other’s zits,” said Jeffords.

“Damn. Well, you made a wise investment, Private. Good job. You ready for some point training today?” I returned the photo, and Claude tucked it away and pulled out his MCI rations.

“I am, Sergeant. I heard Smitty’s the best point man in the company.”

“He’s uglier than a boot and smells like moldy hay, but he’s good, yeah.”

"Can't smell worse than this shit." Claude displayed his bounty.

I recognized the meal immediately and grimaced. "You got fucked—beans and baby dicks again?" He looked at the can of precooked foulness, shrugged, and tore it open. Despite the fact it looked like green maggots and mystery meat, he dug in. I guess when you're hungry, taste matters less, and the cruel bastards that designed the shit knew it. I left Claude to his "meal."

All around me, spirits were high. We were near the end of our patrol, and through the canopy, I could see a crystal-clear sky; the weather was holding tight. It was temperate by Nam's standards, and sweat dribbled in disordered rows down our faces instead of in buckets. Bugs buzzed in light formations around us. Men babbled back and forth about home and broke each other's balls. For a moment, Vietnam was more like a camping trip than a meat grinder. *Something* was out of place, and electricity went down my neck.

"Hey, China White, you got any more of them fancy cigars?" Bernie lifted his shiny dome from his M60 and waved me over, pulling me from my thoughts.

"Anything for the Midnight Cowboy," I said in my best John Wayne and tossed him a baggie. He ripped it open and bit off the end of the cigar, spitting it into the jungle.

"A gentleman and a scholar," he said and twirled the treasure above his lighter. A thick ribbon of smoke drifted into the air, but his cigar ecstasy dissolved into disgust as a bloated onyx beetle scaled the M60. "Back to Hell with you," he grumbled and broiled the insect with the Zippo. What a way to go.

"Shit, Bernie, I can't tell what you hate more: Charlie or the bugs."

"One is a vile lower form of life that creeps through mud and shit for a bite to eat; the other sucks your blood."

"You'll have to be more specific," I said, which drew a wheezy guffaw from him. He slapped the weapon in approval.

"Christ, Robbins, you trying to give us away with smoke signals?" said the LT with the radio receiver clinging to his head. He glared at me and Bernie. "We're almost home but not yet. Get these dicks in line."

"Yessir," I said and nodded at Bernie, who sighed and snuffed his cigar but continued to chew the unlit remains. The other soldiers murmured and buried their cigarettes along with the chatter. Reality returned. The LT pissed on our parade for good reason, so none of us took it personally.

He finished on the radio. "Robbins, Thibodeaux: Post."

Claude gathered his equipment and scampered over to us.

"Big day, Frenchy. You ready?" The LT slapped Claude on the shoulder.

"I think so, sir." He sounded fearful but excited. My own heart raced, but I hid it better.

"All right, you're on point with Smitty until we're back. Watch everything he does. Mimic it in your mind. He's a hawk and the luckiest prick in the company, and you want some of that luck." He handed the private a small map. The LT turned to me, hoisted his arm in the air, and ran his index finger in circles. "Let's saddle up."

I glanced at Claude, feeling uneasy. Patrols can be boring, slow, muddy, wet slogs through every plant and critter imaginable. They can be long and longer, hot and hotter, unpleasant and deadly—except when they're not. Man and nature laid traps at our feet on trails, in paddies, and on the roads, and it was our job to find those traps—or at least make goddamn sure we didn't hit the lottery. I could never tell who was going to take a wooden spike through the foot, a bullet, or a snakebite, but the point man usually got first helpings.

* * *

Our footsteps were light but too quick. The tangle of men and equipment swept through the bush in a loose, expanding and contracting formation. The unusual spacing and *slinky* effect was no doubt the result of our earlier forays into undue happiness, and it bothered the fuck out of me. I had to restore discipline, and it started with the point man.

"If you keep long-legging this platoon through the shit, I'm gonna break yours," I whispered to Smitty. He threw a quick grimace and snorted without a word, but I knew I'd made my point. Claude gulped and pretended to study his map. I glanced at him hard. "Speed kills," I whispered, winked, and slithered away to the squad leaders to chew some more ass.

After paying due diligence to our formation, I returned to my position and breathed a sigh of relief. Sure, a few more guys hated my guts than earlier but that's the way it went. We were too close to home for fuckups, and I was pretty hungry. *Almost there.* I could taste the hot chow and brandy; I thought about smoking a cigar in peace. *It's the little things . . .*

"*Xung phong! Xung phong!*" The alien words split the air ahead of us, and the AK-47s opened up.

I hit the deck instinctively, got the M16 ready to reply, and fished out a cigarette. My Lucky Strikes gave me comfort and complemented, in an ironic way, my baby face, or so I'd been told. And at that moment, I sure needed some fucking comfort. The familiar reports of dozens of AKs filled the air, and the cigarette danced with me as I crawled through the elephant grass and bamboo. Vegetation sliced and stabbed my exposed flesh and ripped my uniform, but the gunfire had me numb.

Splashing into a wet depression, I lifted my rifle and sent some hate toward the Kalashnikovs. "Search and destroy, my ass!" I cupped my hand at my mouth and shouted to the south. "That's gotta be a whole fucking company! We gotta bug out!"

"Second's pinned!" a grunt cried out in the chaos. "Smitty's dead!"

"Walk 'em back, Polowski! You got this!" I bellowed, voice nearly cracking as the fate of the point man sunk in and I thought of Claude and his proximity to him.

An RPG round hissed through the air and ploughed the ground nearby. The blast knocked the wind from my chest and soaked me in mud and rotten leaves. So much for the cig. Ears ringing, I thrashed myself upright and returned fire.

Men barked orders, screamed for ammunition, and howled in pain amid gunfire and rockets—the entire jungle a symphony of war.

"First, get some cover on second!" shouted the LT. "Get the 60s rolling!" A puff of smoke and a violent hiss: Another rocket tore through the jungle in front of me. It exploded deeper in the bush, and a pained cry split the air, familiar and horrifying—one of my younger soldiers. I trained my rifle on the rocket's source, clicked the fire selector to fully automatic, and emptied a clip into the green. Seconds later, a Vietcong in bloodied black pajamas crashed out of his cover, dead. *Jesus Christ, I love instant gratification.*

"We got casualties!" Bernie sounded off and bolted to my western flank. "Second's pinned between us and Charlie!"

Vietnamese shouting rose above the calamity, and the metallic clanks of the charging handles prefixed their gunfire. They were closing in on us. Mortars screeched in from high above and exploded nearby. Bernie crashed to the ground, squealing in agony.

My head snapped toward his screams, and I subdued the urge to rush to him. "Big man, you still with us?" His screaming, though horrible, reassured me. He could still draw breath.

"Motherfuckers got me good! They got me good!" Bernie snarled as he clutched his leg.

"They're zeroing our position! We gotta bug!" I roared until my voice quit. I dashed out of the pit with lead swishing above me. Shredded leaves drifted down from the canopy, and trees lurched and weaved in protest.

"Burn these motherfuckers!" a soldier screamed. "They're everywhere!"

I sprinted back to our center and dove behind a felled tree with the LT and radioman. They hugged the earth, ready for the next round of mortars.

"Sir, second's almost cut off and at least fifty ahead of first." I pulled out a map and slammed it against the tree. "Charlie's funneling in from the valley and coming right down on us. We gotta call fire and hunker down or we're fucked." I jammed my finger into the map and traced the valley.

"First squad, start falling back!" the LT shouted, craning his neck just over the tree. Another volley of mortars smashed down through the canopy and detonated closer than the first.

Jeffords leaped from the ground and charged the LT. "Sir! Second will be completely surrounded if first pulls!"

"I fucking know, Corporal. Get back to your position!" A thumping vein arose on his forehead, and sweat poured over his brow. I could see the weight of command crushing him; there was no good option. Somebody had to die, or we all would, but I admired Jeffords in that moment. I handed the LT the coordinates. He studied them and grabbed the heavy green PRC-25 radio.

"Those are our boys! You're gonna fucking fry our boys!" Jeffords's neck swelled around his collar, and he swiped the mic from the LT's hand.

"Get the fuck back, Jeffords!" I shoved him and grasped the mic. The next round of mortars would likely be our last, and I couldn't spare a second.

His face went blank, and he lowered his rifle. "Sarge, you're gonna burn our boys alive if you do this." He locked eyes with me, mournful and desperate, begging me to change course.

But I couldn't. I wasn't about to let us get wiped—or worse: end up in a camp.

I raised the mic to my mouth and keyed it. I had to own this one. "FAC Covey, FAC Covey, this is Stag 22."

"Stag 22, this is Covey 16. Go ahead."

"Covey 16, we are pinned and about to be overrun two klicks north of the basin just west of Firebase Normandy. Request urgent fire mission at 2426 5166, danger close."

The radio crackled. "2426 5166—Covey 16 has your coordinates and birds are inbound, danger close."

A team leader from first squad bolted through the vegetation and crashed to the ground with his rifle. "Billings, Bosley, and Smith are dead!" He spun the rifle toward the enemy and unloaded another clip between his legs. "The rest are scattered to the east!"

Another two men hunched at the hips pierced the vegetation in heavy strides. I searched desperately for Claude, wishing anyone else had taken point.

"Third and fourth, fall back!" The LT peered over his rifle and searched the jungle for his men.

The radio sprang to life. "Second platoon, A7s inbound hot two mikes. Danger close. Danger close. Hit the deck."

* * *

Napalm—hell made to order. The jet jockey flashed by, and a wall of fire erupted from the ground in all mankind's manifested fury. The concussion knocked some guys on their asses, but we all felt the earth quake. The reek of gasoline and soap swept over us in wave after torrid wave, and seventy-five meters ahead, the human barbeque had kicked off.

Shrieking replaced gunfire. For a moment, I thought about praying to any god who would listen that none of our guys were in the blast zone . . . but the cynic in me knew it was pointless. The LT stood with his mouth hung open and watched the towering inferno retreat behind the smoke. Childlike wonder filled his eyes, and a smile spread across his face. *Hey, Ma! Look what we did.* But then the smile shrank. Satan had delivered his bounty, and the enemy had scattered. But now *we* had to pay.

Another burst of rifle fire—our good 'ol Mattel-plastic M16s—jerked us back to reality. A couple 60-rounds went out for good measure, but the fight was over. Only the horrible shrieking remained: the kind of primal agonized scream only fire can produce. I tapped the LT and pointed ahead. Waving the medics forward, we moved in to see what was left of second.

Slags of burning goo clung to trees and dripped to the forest floor while we weaved around the small islands of flame. We trotted through the jungle like titans: invulnerable and cruel. Arriving at first squad's main fighting position, we found two men: one dead with a hole the size of a quarter in his forehead and the other curled in the fetal position, cupping his ears and moaning. I reached down and pulled a hand away and a trickle of blood flowed down the side of his cheek. His eardrums had blown, but I couldn't feel sorry for a fucking papercut.

Looking ahead, dread filled me. The inferno's roar dwindled to a steady crackle and whoosh like any campfire. A breeze rustled the canopy, and fingers of smoke swept in the smell of broiled meat. After a few more steps into the brush, we discovered what happened to second.

My god, what have I done?

CHAPTER 5

WE ALWAYS HURT . . .

F-f-f-fucking hell, where's my Bird? Bird? Bird?

—LIEUTENANT COLONEL MARTIN P. STEINER, NEUROSURGEON

PART BIRD AND PART ROCK, THE HUEY rolled and darted over the deltas in a game of dodge the ground. Roads twisted below us among the flooded rice paddies, where civilians walked alongside their yaks. To me, a lone helicopter—my helicopter—at low altitude meant potshots galore from bored VC snipers, but the antiaircraft cannons were what made my asshole pinch. I'd heard stories of men losing their balls from ground fire, so I decided I'd rather be uncomfortable sitting on my helmet for a while. The LT didn't give a rat's ass about Charlie and was sprawled out next to me like a fucking dog in an Oldsmobile, enjoying the air with a big ol' grin.

"What condition did they say he was in?" I shouted over the noise.

"He's pretty fucked up," said the LT.

I ruminated on his words and reclined a bit on the helmet, suddenly feeling less concerned for my own skin. The chopper crashed through errant clouds, blowing them apart with rotor wash, and leaned into a dash over a small village. I admired the beautiful and thriving land below, unable to reconcile the hellish slaughters taking place every day.

The image of Bernie screaming on the ground flashed through my mind. "How about Sergeant Collins?"

"He'll live, but he's not coming back."

Charlie's lucky mortar had taken his leg below the knee—a life-changing injury. It was nonetheless his ticket out of Vietnam. I pondered the possibilities and hypotheticals until a twang of envy gnawed at me. I pictured my own bloody stump at that moment. I pictured a purple heart. A shitty prosthetic. A comfy job with the US Postal Service. I pictured myself in parades and regaling friends and family with war stories in a smelly, cheap recliner or a rocking chair on my front porch. I felt guilt. And joy. I lost myself in the fantasy until a quick jerk from the pilot snuffed it out.

His head covered in a shiny green helmet and thick aviator sunglasses, the pilot glanced back at me. "Da Nang five out."

"Da Nang five out," I repeated and tapped the LT on the shoulder.

"Oh man, how do I get this job?" He smiled wide as wind whipped his hair about.

"You have to suck a lot of dicks," I shouted and glanced at the pilot with a shit-eating grin.

His slightly downturned lips suggested he was not amused, and he yanked the cyclic to the left.

My head crashed into the window as the Huey lurched hard and then eased back to level flight. I decided against agitating the pilot any further, at least while we were in the air.

As we approached the hospital, a growing uneasiness gnawed at me. *Claude's down there.* I imagined the agony I had caused him. He was the only survivor. The strike fried two other guys, but their deaths were mercifully quick. Reaching into my jacket, I pulled out a cigarette and tried every position to light it, eventually succeeding after diving into my shirt.

The cracked helipad sat elevated from the surrounding earth and bore a large red cross. The pilot swung the Huey even with the center of the cross and put the bird down among a whirlwind of dust and loose grass.

"Don't let the door hit you on the way out, jerkoff!" He flashed me a one-finger salute, which I returned as I disembarked with the LT. I dragged the cigarette to a nub and flicked the butt back into the chopper before the sonofabitch lifted off. Small victories.

"Man, I do not want to see him all burned up," said the LT.

"Let's figure out where he's at first."

A massive complex of olive-drab tents surrounded us, but a burly major soon emerged from the tent forest and waved us down. We descended the helipad embankment and saluted him.

"Welcome to Alpha Med. I'm Major Mahor. Please follow me."

We set off down the narrow path separating the rows of tents. The dull murmur of nurses, doctors, and patients peaked and waned as we passed each open tent. A generator whirred in the distance.

"Where are we headed, sir?"

"ICU tent," said the major.

"That doesn't sound good," said the LT.

"It's not, but I wanted to get you there before Mad Marty's black mass."

"Mad Marty?"

"Lieutenant Colonel Martin Steiner, the neurosurgeon. He goes by Mad Marty 'round here."

"And his black *mass*?" The LT's voice croaked at the final word.

The major looked at him but didn't reply. We rounded a roped stake and pushed past a thin sheet of plastic into a large tent. The air was cool and refreshing but contained hints of blood and disinfectant. Dozens of injured men lay silent on simple green beds, most gawking into the air or sleeping. Jars dribbled precious fluids into their limp and bloody arms. We weaved through the tent and passed into another. Far fewer patients rested in this room, but they all had tubes running in and out of them, their chests rising and falling to the rhythm of ventilators.

"Welcome," said Dr. Steiner. Standing no more than five feet seven inches, he trotted toward us with his hand extended. He wore a jovial grin, which was remarkably out of place. Thick box-frame glasses speckled with blood sat heavy on his bulbous nose, and a scrub cap covered his head.

"Thank you for inviting us, sir," said the LT, and we both shook his hand.

"This is very unorthodox—yes, very unorthodox—but he made me promise him your presence," said Dr. Steiner. "And I am a man of my word—a man of my word." He tripped over his words, and an odd tic—a quivery bottom lip—caught my attention. He wasn't exactly from this planet.

"Claude?" I said, trying to cut our stay in this butcher pit.

"Claude Thibodeaux, Thibodeaux, Thibodeaux." The neurosurgeon rolled his shoulders, and his head twitched. "Come." He led us to a bed in the far corner of the room. In it lay a tangle of bandages and plaster shaped like a man. A plastic tube covered in drops of water snaked into his mouth.

"Burns, infection, blood loss—no good," said the doctor. He placed his hand on the smidgen of bare flesh that remained and squeezed Claude's foot. His gray eyes softened, laden with sorrow. Maybe he was at least *part* human.

I tried to peer beyond the bandages and cloth covering Claude's torched face. Beside me, the LT's breathing became ragged. When I looked back at him, I saw that his eyes were pooling with water, and he was grasping the bridge of his nose, fighting with every breath not to break down.

"Georgie, this ain't your fault," I said. "They were gonna slaughter us."

"He said the same," said the doctor with a nod.

I caught a whiff of rye whiskey on his breath but said nothing. In fact, I almost asked for a hit myself.

"Ah yes, Sergeant Robbins, he asked me to help pen a note to you as well. Quite laborious during his few moments of consciousness. Consciousness. Consciousness." He reached into his blood-streaked white coat and fished out a neat, square note. I grasped it and stuffed it in my pocket to deal with later.

A nurse and a chaplain shuffled past us and looked grimly at Steiner. "We're ready," said the nurse.

"Gentlemen, if you'll excuse us, we have souls to liberate. Liberate. Liberate." Dr. Steiner grabbed his clipboard and scribbled a few words as he peered at each patient. He set the clipboard down, removed a fifth of Wild Turkey whiskey from his lab coat, and took a long, deep, shameless swig. With a shudder and a shrug, he proceeded to unplug the ventilators, one at a time.

CHAPTER 6

CAFÉ UNCERTAIN

Mommy, why are there army men at the front door?

—NANNETTE THIBODEAUX

I STOOD AS STILL AS A STATUE AND TOOK in the moment of beauty because one never knew when—or if—another would come. Dawn crept over the horizon and painted the cumulus clouds a pleasant citrus. As the first rays of the sun bloomed and warmed our bodies, we rejoiced in the bounty of another borrowed day. To the east snaked a muddy river that had the decency to glimmer on such days; to the west, a murky jungle hungered for light, devouring the brightest rays with the same voracity as so many bright men.

I stretched toward the clouds and yawned, casting a shadow over my grunts. By the time I was twenty, I was built like a New England lighthouse. I'd always been hefty, but the army had transformed me into a heap of steel with a serpent's tongue.

Now that I was near the midpoint of my first tour, the constant slaughter had numbed me. I had seen tens of my boys shot, blown to pieces, or eviscerated by Charlie's devious traps. Fresh faces from all over the US cycled through our unit like a high school yearbook. But

Claude's death—at my hands—clawed at my soul every waking hour of every single day, sometimes while I slept too. I had sealed his handwritten note in a plastic bag and stuffed it in my pocket but couldn't bring myself to read it. Each morning, I ruminated but ultimately chose to put it off. That patrol had changed me.

"Turp me, fucker." I held out my tin mug and shook it over a bubbling pot of black liquid.

A boyish private removed the pot from its grating and strained the thick liquid into my cup. I brought it to my lips and gulped down the near-boiling turpentine and a jolt of life shot through me. *Goddamn, that's got pep.*

"Should just burn the whole fucking shebang," said Conway. He returned the pot and eyed the wall of trees with me. A kid in every sense of the word, with an awkward thin neck and a prominent Adam's apple, Private Conway had nonetheless earned my respect. He had kept his shit together in the last couple firefights and always had the coffee ready. He also reminded me of Claude in some ways, which earned him a soft spot in my heart.

"Where's your sense of sport, Conway?" I said. "God forgot about us long ago, so *we* might as well have some fun." I tapped my M16. "Can't let Air Cav and the zoomies kill all these fucking savages." After guzzling down the rest of my coffee, I popped the lid off a small tin can and shoved a lip of shredded tobacco into my cheek, one burn to replace the other.

"Amen," said another private.

I spun my head to the soldier—a young buck of no more than eighteen, whose pocked face was better suited for offering fries and a cold drink. "Just what *the fuck* do you know about wasting gooks, ya little spitfuck? Didn't you just get here?" Tobacco juice and hate dribbled around my words.

The men sniggered at the poor bastard as he struggled in my grasp. Such was the fate of every new guy who tried to talk tough.

"Well, sir. Uh . . ." The private's throat tightened, and he stuttered.

"Don't call me *sir*, private. How fucking stupid are you?"

"Yes-s-s. Sir. I mean, Sergeant." He yammered and dropped his plate of eggs.

I glanced at the eggs in disgust. "I bet the only thing you butchered in your whole life was your mama's dirty love box when she was trying to squeeze that unholy dome of yours through it," I said to the red-faced private.

The jackals howled with delight, and the private blushed further while he kneeled to pick up the eggs.

"Private, are you seriously going to eat eggs covered in yak shit?" I sneered as the dumb motherfucker started gathering them up, and I moved to stop him. Yeah, they may have been dumb as rocks, but they were still my soldiers.

"Buddy Holly Robbins—the man, the myth, the legend—have you beat your quota of crippled children this morning?" The LT emerged from his hooch smiling as he had dozens of times before, despite being in this nightmarish place. A damn good man, he was set to rotate out after six months in command, but I was glad to see him alive each day.

The flustered private threw a quick salute, and the LT returned it.

"Come on, private, don't give the gook snipers a free lunch. Never salute in the field." His thick Minnesotan accent rolled out amicably, and he patted the beleaguered but well-meaning boy on the back. If I was Papa Clyde, he was Uncle George.

"Aw, come on, LT. I don't have my own kids to discipline, so I gotta make do with these retards."

As if on cue, I pointed at another private, who had resumed collecting the fallen eggs.

The LT winced and brushed his hand against his forehead.

A whoosh of static spat from a radio—the familiar harbinger of chaos. A husky man with a rucksack and a tangle of wires walked through the breakfast area toward the command tent. The Rat Man made his rounds—a rather ignoble name for our radio-telephone operator.

"Come on, Rat. Tell us what's up," I said.

He glowered at me and sputtered gibberish into his mic, scribbling and stabbing a notepad with the nub of a yellow no. 2 pencil. The forest of wires bulging off his back and the awkward sky-high antenna always gave me a chuckle.

"Bird Dogs have spotted a platoon-size element of light artillery in tight formation about eight klicks west of here headed toward a large clearing—the shit we burned a while back," he said to the LT. "They're probably on a run-and-gun mission, but we got the fuckers."

Turning to me, he hoisted up a middle finger beside his pencil. "And don't call me a fucking rat."

He punctuated his scribbles with a hearty stab and looked back to the LT. "Thank God for Bird Dogs. Definitely not in the mood to dodge shells this morning."

"Thank God for Bird Dogs," said the LT.

"We just gotta sit back and enjoy the fireworks from afar this time, eh?" I clasped my hands and shimmied with excitement. It was nice to let someone else do the work for once.

"Yep," said the LT. "I'll put on another pot of coffee." He turned to the fire pit and caught the gaze of the weathered Corporal Jeffords, who sat sharpening his blade and glaring at the LT. The LT looked away, pretending not to notice, and walked to the fire.

I narrowed my eyes and kneeled next to the corporal. Jeffords had become a problem child since Claude's death, and my patience was wearing thin. "Let it go, Jeffords," I said quietly.

He swept his glare across the ground, no doubt tempering his reaction to me. Without a word, he thrust the knife into the dirt and stormed off to his hooch.

Normally, I'd tear a sonofabitch two new assholes for such disrespect, but I knew he was hurting. After collecting my thoughts, I pulled the knife from the ground. How many times had it been plunged into the LT in Jeffords's hateful mind?

The LT sat near the fire, slumped shoulders and tired eyes betraying a sick kind of sadness only death could rectify—but whose death, I was uncertain.

Suddenly, an A-7 Corsair II screamed overhead and vanished over the tree line. Sonorous echoes littered the air and shrank as the jet tore into the distance. Some of the men clenched their jaws and clamped their hands over their ears. A few morons tried to tough it out, and I kept mental note of who had something to prove.

"Somebody's in for a shitty day." I fanned out my fingers and lowered them one by one in anticipation. With each finger I dropped, I clicked my tongue: a countdown to wreckage.

On cue, just as my index finger dropped, a dull thud rattled the entire camp, and a massive explosion clacked and rebounded through the air. A few younger soldiers ducked and cursed as flames, smoke, and sorrow surged into the sky.

"Hooooo-weee!" I shouted. "Damn, I wish I could have seen the look on that gook commander's face when screaming death came down on him."

The soldiers cheered and whistled, some at the thought of fresh VC hamburger and shattered artillery, while others simply worshipped the power of the bomb—tribal, really.

"Check it out." Private Conway pointed high above the tree line. The faint gray jet was climbing straight up, dragging a long vapor trail behind it.

"He's going hard vertical," said the LT.

"Yeah, he's just showing off," I said. "Zoomies got tiny peckers, so they gotta live by their planes."

"Oh shit!" The LT's eyes widened.

A glowing dot burst above the trees and soared. Flares sloughed from the aircraft's body. The dot streamed toward the aircraft in an exaggerated arc, wobbling as the flares briefly confused its target profile. Seconds later, the missile and the aircraft merged. Flames and smoke spilled into the sky, and thunder followed.

"Somebody's definitely having a shitty day all right," said the LT. He raised a tin of coffee to his lips and shrugged.

The flames dwindled to a shower of sparks that streaked to earth with their own little trails of smoke. The plane's shredded husk cartwheeled and plunged into the greenery. As the radio crackled to life, breathless inaudible jargon followed, and Rat sprinted to the command tent.

I sniffed and figured the show was over so I might as well get some shit done. I turned from the spectacle and walked to the fortified living area. The stacked sandbags and berms cast cooling shadows on my approach as I sauntered to my hooch. Pulling out a simple wooden chair, I sat and collected myself for the grim task at hand. I grumbled and grabbed the nearest pen.

Dear Thibodeaux Family,

I had the pleasure of serving with Claude for two months in country, which was the entire duration of his service. During this time, Claude distinguished himself as a skilled and thoughtful soldier and something of a philosopher and scholar. We called him "Doc" around here because of his intelligence, and most of us wondered just why the hell someone with that much brain power was hanging out with a bunch of knuckle draggers like us. Regardless, he became one of us in short order, and we adopted him as our egghead brother. He performed his duties admirably and without complaint, and he never let us down.

I can still remember his first day in country. Let me tell you, that kid had a knack for anything mechanical and always impressed us with some of the crazy stuff he could invent on the fly. But it was always for others. He improved our lives in many ways.

Claude was killed on patrol at 0930 hours on April 8. Please know he was not alone when he passed. We were with him the entire time, and he did not suffer. He remained strong, thoughtful, and even witty to the end. I'm sure, knowing Claude, you will not be surprised in the least to know his last words were of Sarah and their unborn child. You will also not be surprised that his final wish was that Sarah does not marry anybody more attractive than him because he expects to see her again in the hereafter and doesn't want to worry about long-term competition while he awaits her in Heaven.

Yours,
SSG Clyde C. Robbins, USAR

I signed the letter and reread it under the sickly bulb. I couldn't bear to count how many times I lied to give the boy's family some solace, so I just sealed the fucking thing and tossed it in a pile with the others.

"Sick sense of humor," I muttered and clicked off the light. Standing from the desk, I shoved the chair in, and I trudged into the midday sun. Fewer familiar faces than the week before greeted mine, and I knew those missing were probably face up in a white sheet or face down in the brown earth. The rest of us were covered in filth—alabaster and ebony canvases smeared with blood, mud, sweat, and interwoven blots of camo paint. But even beneath the thickest layers, I could see the life was gone, the fires extinguished.

"Still love your slick LT, Sarge?" Jeffords clamped on a cigarette and half-smiled.

I stared hard at the corporal, who looked more lupine than usual, and considered sucker punching him. The venom in his voice made me clench my fist so hard my knuckles cracked. My eye twitched with rage, but I didn't want to complicate the LT's life with more paperwork.

"There's no rhyme or reason to any of it, Sarge. We're just sacrificial lambs—suckers who nobody cares about, who nobody'll miss when we're gone. It's all fucking pointless." His voice wavered a little, and so too did my anger. He pulled a dog tag from his pocket and flung it at me. Only *Thibodea* remained on the charred metal slab. Maybe I'd deliver it to the kid's family if I got out of here.

Jeffords grinned and finished his cigarette. With a long-concerted sigh, the smoke poured from his nostrils and swirled into nothingness, much like the pilot and his jet.

"Pointless." He flicked the butt away.

"Pointless," I said softly, my own heart burdened with resignation. Indeed, the body bags, metal, and endless suffering didn't make a lick of sense to me. A newly minted bastard whose father burned up like a steak on a grill didn't make sense to me. A teenage girl with a forty-five round in her chest for trying to blow up strangers didn't make sense to me. War did not make sense to me. *So why am I here? Why do I thrive? Is my sole purpose to engender pain and chaos? Can I bring nothing else to those around me besides suffering?*

"We will give you purpose, Clyde," said a soft feminine voice, the first woman who had spoken to me in months. I spun to reply, but not a single soul, let alone a woman, stood near me.

I sauntered back to my hooch and collapsed on the cot. *I'm losing my shit.*

CHAPTER 7

PUCK AND MERCUTIO

FRONT TOWARD ENEMY

—M18 CLAYMORE MINE

I KNEW HE WAS DEAD . . . EXCEPT he wasn't. Maroon circles framed unblinking opaque spheres over sunken cheekbones. His neck—gnarled bones and flesh balancing his head—curved into a pallid and emaciated chest. The vibrant youth was gone.

"I see things now for what they really are," he said. "There was never any hope."

I looked into his eyes, and a strange discomfort crept up my back. "Claude . . ." My throat tightened. Smoke swirled up from the ground and coalesced into tentacles that dragged him down. I sprang forward but grasped only the smoke, and laughter drifted in with the cold wind. "I failed you. Forgive me."

Covered in sweat, I stared into my blanket for the next three hours with tears running silently down my cheeks.

• • •

"All right, guys, take out a pen and paper, and prepare to copy." The LT kneeled and dragged a broken pool stick across the dirt. He began his strategic mud map with a simple line, which bloomed into some avant-garde aberration of war. Every cigarette butt, twig, and plastic army man had its place, and the soldiers nodded and scribbled into their notepads . . . except me.

"Sergeant Robbins?" The LT paused and tapped the ground.

"Oh, sorry sir. Just miles away in some double Ds. Your fancy West Point speak frightens and confuses me." Of course, this was a lie. I couldn't shake the nightmare; Claude's fate tormented me.

"No, Sergeant Robbins. You're right here, and I need your head in the game."

I stepped forward to the terrain map and pulled out my notepad and pen. "Roger, sir."

"You'll be leading first and second squads when we cross the line." He pointed to the pack of cigarettes. "This represents first and second on our right flanks, just west of the river." He slashed a river into the earth. "Take an extra 60 and a few claymores, and set up firing lanes and kill boxes covering both the bridge and the riverbank on either side, as well as your immediate flanks."

"Roger, sir." I whistled and clapped. "Now here's some shit I understand." I cleared my throat and flashed an ornery smirk at the LT. "Say, sir, why do I gotta be the pack of cigarettes?"

"Because I didn't take my morning shit yet."

The men hacked out their approval in howls and wheezes.

"You're lucky I like you, butter bar."

"I know," he said and brought us back to the map. Over the next twenty minutes, he gestured, scratched the dirt, and drilled every detail into our heads, platoon leadership all the way down to the dumbass privates. "All right, any questions?"

I raised my hand. "Sir, how do we know this jet jockey even survived? I didn't see a chute."

"The last contact from Captain Kao indicated he ejected. This contact was received four seconds before impact."

"Aw, shit. You're telling me we're risking our asses for some fuckhead pilot who may or may not be alive?" My anger infected the other soldiers, and they grumbled.

"That's exactly what I'm telling you, and I happen to know that *fuckhead* personally, and if there is any man on Earth who hates communists more than we do, it's him." The LT spit on the ground and glanced around at us. "Hell, he might have been the guy who saved our asses during the valley ambush."

My mind flashed to Jeffords's fury and the napalm strike. Mad Marty. The ventilators churning. *Enough! Get your fuckin' head right.*

I scribbled a few notes and ripped a cigarette from my vest. "All right, you mama's boys, rub your dicks, and grab your shit. Rehearsal's in ten." I fired up the cigarette, and the soldiers scattered.

* * *

Those shameless pieces of shit were the closest I had to family on this Earth, but I pushed them away at every opportunity. For my entire life, I'd only known the pain of loss, so I just stopped trying to connect. In my calculus, the joy of any human relationship could not overcome the suffering of its demise, and war was the ultimate taker. But every time we crossed into the bush, my asshole still jumped into my throat. I liked to think it was for the pride in my military prowess—bringing everyone home safe a testament to my skill—but, in reality, I knew I cared for them . . . if only a little bit. I'd already lost many, each a resounding personal failure, and each a lingering pain I can't describe. And therein lay the dark irony: I moved mountains to keep my boys safe only so *I* wouldn't be the one to suffer. Fancy that.

As we waited at the wire, I ruminated on how long I'd been in country and how long I'd remain. Six months had felt way longer, and this was only my first tour. Six more months to go. Shit, I'd heard stories of guys going back and forth for years 'til they got killed, got injured, or went nuts. And here I was, less than a year in country and already going off the wall.

Who would be the next LT? Georgie was a pretty good one—not a coward but not a stubborn asshole either. He listened to us and adjusted fire. It also helped that he was funny as fuck and could get down in the shit with the best—and worst—of us. His forthcoming rotation was a downer, but I took comfort in the fact he'd be making bigger decisions for all of us.

I hustled through formation and took reports from the squad leaders as they squared away their soldiers. Content with their preparations, I took position left and center and breathed deeply. Goddamn, I should have been used to it, but I shook like a fucking Chihuahua. Thankfully, because I was a big sonofabitch, nobody caught on or else morale would have tanked.

Rifles at the ready, the LT whistled and threw his hand up—time to go, weapons hot. From that point on, we expected silence as every stray noise was a gift to Charlie. Footsteps, coughs, farts, and loose gear—any mistake could draw gallons of blood, and every experienced soldier who got blown away meant a fucking new guy would replace him. Usually a draftee and fresh out of basic, these FNGs tended to get themselves and others killed because they lacked experience, and the cycle would repeat.

Conway took point. Every newbie had to take his turn as bullet sponge, but I dreaded it. The rest of us formed up single file at wide intervals just in case of mines, and in a few steps, we were in the shit.

The jungle drowned the light and assaulted our ears with sounds straight out of a madhouse. Every snap, howl, and hiss portended death. We crawled forward, backward, and vertical, eyes open for two-stepper vipers, mines, and bugs, and we cursed God in faint whispers for pushing up so many fucking mangroves. In minutes, we had soaked through our shirts, and mud clung to our uniforms and smeared our exposed flesh—a thick wool blanket dunked in a pond of leeches and duck shit.

After hours breaking the bush, the LT signaled me forward with a hand motion that transitioned to a wank followed by a middle finger. It took all I had to smash down laughter, but I managed a silent bird of my own—now *that's* situational awareness. The soldiers took a knee and brought their weapons up.

"Yeah?" I said in a guttural whisper.

He unfolded a map and pointed. "Three klicks out, I'm thinking." A large red circle marked the jet's debris field. He pointed at our location on the map, and I crunched some numbers; something wasn't right.

"I think your count is fucked up."

He pulled away from the map and looked at me. Not a look of disbelief but concern. Like I said, this guy was humble pie.

"Your pace count is fucked up. I'm putting us here." I pointed about two hundred meters from his estimate and circled it.

"I trust ya," he said and folded the map.

After a fist bump, I returned to my position, and we pressed on.

The canopy thickened as we moved deeper into the bush, and our world darkened. Time stopped, and darkness played tricks on my mind. Hell, just thinking about nightfall made me paranoid; Vietnam after sundown became a different kind of terror. I started to doubt my own wristwatch, became fixated on our pace, and was last to notice the acrid kerosene.

The industrial fragrance peaked and waned, and the LT turned and tapped his nose; we were close. With renewed vigor, we broke through the weeds and scanned what little canopy we could see.

"We all smell it. Where's the fucking fire?" he whispered. "Where's the smoke?"

I shrugged. "Pieces of him and his plane could be hanging in the trees, and we'd never see them."

The LT scowled and shook his head.

"Let's find this shithead and bring him home," I said and slapped him on the back.

The vegetation thinned, and flickering sunbeams dotted our cammies. Like rewinding the clock three hours, twilight morphed into day, and it wasn't long before the jungle relented, giving way to lighter vegetation and, finally, an open field.

The LT put us to knee at the jungle's boundary, and I moved forward again as he studied his map. I inspected the terrain with a set of binoculars and reviewed the course and pace count. Beyond the swaying reeds and grass, a rickety wooden bridge curved over a river bounding our eastern flank. We were supposed to cross that bridge.

"We're off course by two hundred meters," I said. Shame heated my collar—I *knew* we were wrong back in the bush, and we somehow still ended up wrong—on my watch.

The LT cursed under his breath. "We gotta be quick. Without any cover on the bridge, our asses are hanging out in the breeze."

"Well, not for too much longer," I said and pointed over his head. In the distance, far across the wide-open field, parachute risers wafted back and forth.

"Well, no shit."

* * *

We skirted the tree line like spooked deer. Every eyeball and nostril searched for things out of place. Even a branch bent in a funny way could mean death, so our pace slowed. The risers dangled far from us, but we could only move so fast. The afternoon waned, and I could tell the passage of time weighed on the soldiers' minds. Our little soil and concrete island—turpentine coffee, titty mags, and old letters—called to us from afar, salvation from this goddamn sea of insects and uncertainty. *Let's find what's left of this bastard and skedaddle.*

On our final trek to the wreckage, we crested a small hill and beheld our target. The empty ejector seat dangled inches above the ground in front of us like a marionette missing its puppet.

"Well, he's not in it or above it, so he may have actually made it," said the LT.

Crushed tree limbs, foliage, and blackened metal encircled the impact site.

"Or Charlie already hacked his ass down and buried him in a shallow grave," said the only voice that could make my skin crawl. I turned to Jeffords as he stared far up into the canopy.

"Always the optimist," said the LT. He rubbed his chin and nodded. "But he makes a good point. Kao could have walked—or been dragged—miles from here in any direction."

"Ya'll realize if they hadn't already captured or killed his ass, this area would be swarming with gooks, or it soon will be," said Jeffords, dead eyed and without as much as a fleck of concern in his voice. In fact, he almost seemed happy.

"I'm sure we would have been given proper warning," said the LT, and he pointed at the radioman.

"Just like we would have been given proper defense over yonder at the bridge choke point that's sitting wide open and pretty? Or proper intel before we got ambushed back in the valley?" Jeffords's tone had darkened.

His words pained me, but he was right. It was my count that put us off course, but that reckoning would have to come later.

The LT glared at Jeffords. "Check yourself, Corporal."

The others homed in on the confrontation.

"The fact we're standing here now tells me the Mongolian horde ain't coming."

Jeffords laughed out loud, and the other soldiers hissed at him. "Yeah, because we're not dead yet means bad shit ain't coming." He laughed like a maniac. "Give this fucking Marshall Scholar a medal."

The LT stepped forward and backhanded him, a vicious blow that flung Jeffords backward.

I grabbed his shoulder before he could fall. This was a whole new level of bullshit and the worst time to have it.

"Sir," I changed my tone to professional NCO, "I'll deal with Jeffords when we get back. I don't know what's come over him."

"We both know plenty well what's come over him. He's got beef with me, and he's airing it at the worst possible time." The LT shook his head and spit on the ground as he stepped away from the corporal.

"Clyde," said the distant female voice, and I whipped around to the empty field.

Jeffords's head fell backward, and he laughed, bestial grunts accompanying each choked guffaw. The man had lost his fucking mind.

He broke free from my grip and lunged at the LT but recoiled in an instant. A two-inch hole opened in his chest as a round ripped through him like papier-mâché and air hissed from the wound.

Warm blood painted my face and stung my eyes. Jeffords slipped from my grasp and collapsed like a sack of onions.

"Back in the fucking bush!" screamed the LT.

We scrambled back into the wood line and fell heavy—meat, metal, and cloth—as tracer fire zipped over us. I rolled onto my back, a blazing patchwork of orange and yellow inches above my head, daring me to stand. Snakes and bugs no longer existed; only the fight mattered.

"We gotta move before they zero us!" I shouted at the LT.

The experienced soldiers returned fire while others laid flat, unable or unwilling to move. Conway was curled in a rocky depression, his rifle slung across his back.

"Conway, get your ass in gear!"

No response. No movement. I crawled and rolled him over, but half his face was gone. Revulsion overwhelmed me, and I let go, covered the gore with his pack, and puked, not for any weakness to mangled meat—god knew I'd seen enough—but terrible grief for his mother who couldn't have an open casket. I had failed yet another family.

AK-47 and sniper fire tormented us while 23 mm cannon rounds ripped our cover apart; whole limbs rained down as the big guns unloaded.

"Fire mission! Fire mission!"

"No!" Our coordinates were fucked, and he'd smoke us all if the comms went through. I pulled out my map and waited for a gap in the gunfire.

"Danger close!"

Those terrible words fell on me heavier than the lead—time had run out. I jumped from my cover and darted toward the LT, but Charlie's sledgehammer smashed my leg and dragged me to the ground. Set on my mission, I tried to stand, but my right leg wouldn't move. When I looked down, I could only wince and hope somebody had morphine.

The fire intensified, and Charlie broke from his cover and rushed us.

Game over. Checkmate. I relaxed and pulled a cigarette from my vest, lit it with strangely steady hands, and looked around. To my left, a new and nameless private on probably his first mission clutched his rifle and shook. I whistled at him and offered up a cigarette with a smile.

He looked at me, mouth quivering and eyes red, and declined. "Nah, S-s-sarge, I d-d-don't smoke."

"Good for you, Private. You're gonna live forever."

The 1-5-5 rounds heralded their terminal descent with a decrescendo whistle, and I knew it was pretty much curtains. Suddenly, I registered the note in my remaining pocket and figured why not? I didn't want to die curious. With my last few moments, I unfolded the note and read.

PART II

COUNTRY ROADS

In the beginning, there was only Daedrina and
She dwelled in darkness.

Without time or meaning, She knew only loneliness.

Thus, She created light and said "To see there is nothing
brings me sadness," and from Her breasts, she plucked seven sons
and seven daughters and set them free.

But far away they soared, and, again, She was alone.

—FIRST SCROLL OF AI, WANDERER OF IRGENDWO

CHAPTER 8

CHTHONIC MUSINGS

It is time for Ek Maraine to make good on his promises.

—BALEDOCCUS, THIRD OF THE DAMNED

MY SON, ARISE. YOU ARE NOT SAFE HERE. The voice squeaked from my mind's deepest recesses, but it was too real to ignore. *She* was too real to ignore; she was also quite familiar. I sprang to my feet.

"Who the fuck said that?" Sweat seeped into my shirt, and pins bored into my spine. I gawked at the landscape. Something was . . . different. The world had become a phantom of its former self, but I couldn't put my finger on it. Prickled holly, birches, and a twisted undergrowth of shrubs and vines blanketed the verdant, mossy earth. *No heat.* Running my hand through the air, a slight chill pricked up the hairs on my arm. *Where the hell am I?*

The earth bulged. Shallow mounds of dirt shaped like burial plots surrounded me in the small clearing. *This must be a nightmare; you're asleep.* I sank onto a soft dirt mound convinced of my assessment and hoped to wake up. I remembered being able to snap myself out of nightmares as a kid simply by will and waited . . . but nothing changed.

Rationalize, rationalize, rationalize. I closed my eyes and breathed. Focus would be my escape. My gut expanded upward from the mound, stopped, and shrank. Air filled my lungs—cold, damp, not quite satisfying. As I drifted, a quick shot in the back winded me, and I coughed and leaped up, muscles tense and full of adrenaline.

The mound pulsed rhythmically, up and down with little streams of dirt trailing down the sides. It breathed!

"What the . . ." My whisper trailed off, and I circled the pile of dirt on a knife's edge, hoping to wake up at any second.

You're not safe here! Flee! Her voice filled my head this time, but I could not tear my eyes away from the moving patch of earth.

A muffled groan crawled from the cracks. The mound heaved farther up and shimmied. A rent appeared, and a hand clawed skyward. Its ashen skin caked with black blood and soil, the hand spread and clenched its fingers.

Having seen enough, I turned, picked the thinnest part of the forest, and sprinted.

* * *

"This is bullshit," I muttered and forced my aching body through the forest, briars, logs, and vines all intent on making my life as difficult as possible. My head on a swivel, I stopped and listened every fifty or so steps like a stalked rabbit.

"Wake up, goddammit," I said to myself and pinched my cheek. Nothing but breathless anxiety. The forest smothered my body in thick vegetation and my mind with its unnatural heavy stillness. The familiar paranoia, as if millions of eyes tracked me, tasted like Vietnam with all its shadows, but, here, something was different.

Where are the goddamn bugs? I stopped and inspected my bare arms; I could not find a single welt. The insects in Nam were a stinging, biting, buzzing torment, but their absence here brought a different kind of distress. Unable to resist my curiosity, I fell to the ground and pawed through the vegetation. Not so much as a worm. I stood and examined the bushes and then stared into the canopy. Not a single bird, not a single moth—just vegetation.

I rested in the forest's gloom, closed my eyes, and listened. Leaves rustled, and branches swayed and creaked under a gentle breeze. *Snap*. A branch cracked deep in the thicket behind me, a terrifying break in the silence, and cold blood ran through my chest and down my legs. My muscles became taut, time slowed, and my senses sharpened, ears ringing in the absolute quiet. My mind made demons of every swaying shadow. *Snap*—even closer.

As the bushes stirred, I bolted. I ran until my legs burned, not once looking back, and stumbled to a breathless tripod when the pain of flight far outweighed my fear. Again, I listened but decided against longer pauses and, after a few moments, quietly tread onward.

Maybe I'm in a coma? I contemplated the new reality and imagined my shattered frame in a bed somewhere in Bethesda, with motionless dead eyes and a river of drool running down my cheek. The irony of being stuck in my own head brought a giggle up in my chest, but I had to stifle it.

Sick sense of humor. I peeked through the canopy at specks of sky.

Look to the east. She supplanted my own thoughts again as if I had provoked her.

"What the fuck direction is east?" I whispered. Did I humor my own insanity? I folded my arms to think for a moment and felt a solid bulge against my forearm as the cloth pulled tight.

"No shit." I unbuttoned the pocket and removed a square metallic box housing a compass. The glowing radium-painted needle and direction markers wobbled. I steadied the compass and shot an east azimuth. I checked my other breast pocket for some cigarettes. Empty. "Can't win 'em all."

• • •

Hours of stomping through the woods brought only more woods and the eerie feeling I wasn't alone, but the chilly, dark asylum remained exactly as it had started. Fear of an ambush and the odd absence of any other living creature shrank to irrelevance in my mind against the urge to escape this suffocating forest.

"Any day now." The compass had wobbled east the entire time, and I had faithfully followed it for miles. My legs had fatigued over the rough terrain, and my mouth was dry.

Maybe this isn't a dream? I discarded the notion, fearing insanity as the alternative.

"I better wake up in a Thai strip club with a face full of titties," I said and hoped my mind would graciously manifest such a delight. Nope, no such luck. Just more woods.

I struggled over a particularly large log and crashed to the other side, panting. *Holy shit, I thought I was in better shape.* I *knew* I was in better shape. I sniffed and reset the east azimuth and kept moving. The foliage thinned, and I noticed the ambient light had increased a little. My heart lifted.

Blasting through a final thicket, the forest ended, and I raised my arms to the sky: *Halle-fucking-lujah.* I savored the flat ground and the fresh cool air, thankful the forest slog was over. The open expanse exhilarated me and washed away the forest's smothering embrace with every breath.

The greenery loomed on either side of me. Crisp margins reached in both directions as far as I could see. The massive wooden front abruptly halted against the dusty plains. Roots probed outward into the powdery dirt but stopped after a few meters, unable to survive the barren soil.

I squinted hard to the east. Jagged blue triangles blended into mist that obscured the heavens. The mountains gave me hope.

• • •

My lazy footfalls puffed reddish-green dust into the air that swirled and dissipated. Glancing down at the compass every few minutes, I held a steady east azimuth but thirst commanded my attention.

"A little more advice would be helpful." Desperate for water, I tried to prompt the voice but to no effect. The fine reddish powder stained my boots and caked onto my trousers, the land itself reaching up to desiccate me.

When it gets dark, you'll freeze to death out here, thirsty. My own mind offered the grim assessment seemingly out of nowhere or perhaps in recognition of what I faced. The day and night tribulations of a desert were vastly different but equally deadly . . . or so I'd read.

"Any day now," I rasped.

Wake up! Wake up! A vaguely familiar young man wearing the rank of second lieutenant flashed into my mind, grinned, and disappeared.

"What?" I said, stifling a laugh. "Have we met before?"

Met and parted and met again, the phantom said. *Just work on your pace count.* I paused and looked around. Memories flittered here and there as fireflies . . . Georgie? My lieutenant? I was a soldier. Then a blank slate. But it was better than nothing. Nope, no LT here, but I held on to the urge to reply. "Maybe if you'd got your directions straight, we wouldn't have . . ." I trailed off as the ambush drifted back. Tracer rounds flew. Wood crumbled. Conway's face was a mix of hamburger and terror.

My leg! I gasped and ripped up my trouser leg. Perfectly fine. A-OK. Hunky-dory. *Hmmm, I could have sworn a cannon round smashed me like a piñata.*

"It's all bullshit." I pushed the leg down and broke into a crisp march. "Left! Your left! Your left-right-on-left!" My voice shrank to a dry squeal, but I raised each leg and slammed it down in perfect time. Did I languish in a care home or nuthouse right there and then? What was the alternative? Hell?

"Blue curtains and a hardwood floor. I demand blue fucking curtains. How the fuck am I supposed to be a properly fed and watered vegetable if I sprout in a dump?" I laughed and tossed my hands aside and lurched to the left. Whimsical. Fun!

A gentle vibration tickled my foot. Laughter poured from me as the bizarre fantasy blossomed into conscious role play. This was it. My last vestige of sanity was drifting off with the dry red dust.

Another vibration shot through my foot—stronger—followed by a vague din that peeked through the breeze and vanished. I snapped into a primal quiet, and my senses sharpened. The fear I knew well from the forest crept back. *What's out there?* I scanned the horizon. Paranoia surged back, and I squirreled the compass into my vest. Another vibration, more intense, bit into my heel. Back to reality. The laughter had been snuffed in an instant. Perhaps insanity was a boon only for the careless.

"Get it together," I whispered and continued toward the peaks. Aches, pains, and thirst had to wait.

* * *

I had set my mind to dredging up the patchy memories that occasionally bubbled as the hours dragged on. When they finally returned, Bernie Collins with his cheek stuffed full of tobacco flashed panoramic. So too did Claude's death.

"Ah, Bernie, you crazy fuck." I remembered the hole in his knee the size of a quarter that put him face down in the muck. I had never seen a man smile so wide, let alone a man smile with such a heinous injury. "I'm out this bitch for good," I whispered, mimicking his ecstatic final words before a helicopter whisked him away for the last time. "Always the optimist."

I inspected the sky for a change—any change—but the same lifeless gray hue covered the heavens. But one thing had changed. The thirst had bloomed into an overriding torment. The meager act of swallowing was enough to spur me into coughing, and my teeth had become coarse stones against my tongue.

You're done. Just stop here. A harsh baritone joined me . . . far different from the woman's voice.

"I like the other voice better," I said, barely audible, and chuckled.

Lie down, and go to sleep.

I smiled and planted my defiant and exhausted feet into the dirt. I was sure as shit not giving into insanity again.

Lie down, and go to sleep. The voice carried an urgency—a stifled anger—as it spread in my mind.

"But I'm already asleep."

Lie down, and go to sleep.

"Fuck you." I trotted forward, rejoicing in defiance.

I had made my point. The voice did not respond. The gentle breeze picked up and swam against my uniform and exposed flesh. Perhaps a short nap was in order? I circled a small plot of desiccated grass and sprawled out. Oh, how soft and inviting it was. My joints creaked and popped until my head rested against the ground. Then nothing hurt.

• • •

"Come on, man, stop being a pussy."

"I'm not being a pussy, I'm just sighting my target. Hold your ass." I hesitated and brought the slingshot to eye level. The waning gibbous moon cast a silver veil across the night sky that blanketed the snowy landscape and drowned all but the brightest stars. White puffs steamed from our mouths and vanished. My best friend and I stood in a wooded enclave at the edge of a field that stretched a short distance to a quaint house with awkward shutters and a dilapidated shed.

"Dude, do it."

"Goddammit, I don't know how you managed to talk me into this." I snugged the stone into the cloth pouch and took aim. I drew the bands of the slingshot back until my arm shuddered and let it sail. Before the stone found its target, we were in a frantic sprint. The jangle of breaking glass clattered through the thick winter air, and we broke into maniacal laughter that hobbled our leaps and bounds over felled logs, fences, briar patches, and creeks. Each footstep crunched and lifted shards of snow into the air behind us. We fled to the limits of our lungs and halted in a small clearing.

"That'll teach that old piece of shit not to fuck with our bike ramps." I high-fived my buddy and leaned forward, choking for breath and wheezing.

"Man, you gotta quit smoking," he said and turned back to our target. He stood like a statue, scanning the darkness in the direction of Old Man Camburn's fortress. I chuckled at his paranoia and heaved out a few more chunks of mucus before turning back as well. We listened for any signs of a pursuer while I coughed violently into my sleeve.

"I could outrun that old bastard with one leg and no lungs," I said.

We laughed in between my coughing spells.

"But you'll never outthink me."

The aged alien voice froze me like a deer. I turned, blood as cold as the air, to see a shadowy figure lunge at me. The old man throttled me with a rough iron grip and landed a crushing blow on the bridge of my nose.

CHAPTER 9

A PROMISED LAND

I smell men . . . and something else. Something not of this world.

—MISHA'THIXX THE STRIDER

THE BLOW LANDED HARD AND SHOCKED me awake, but no pain followed—not in my nose anyway. I rejoined the thirst and the cool ground against my back with no desire to stand.

"If my life is going to flash before my eyes, let's start with the times I got away." I hacked a wad of mucus into the air.

You're ours now. The baritone brimmed with self-satisfaction and filled me with dread.

"Wake the fuck up," I whispered into the sky. I arched my back to force the voice from my belly. "Wake up." I clawed into the dust, ready to scream. "Wake up."

"Silence, you fool." A phantom careened into my body and rolled us prone. His callused hand fell tight across my mouth and I could little resist the grip. "Stop moving. Stop talking."

My eyes darted around, but I could only see shadows and cloth. I expected a knife in my ribs at any moment, but the *coup de grâce* never came. Strength extinguished and not giving a good goddamn what came next, I pulled breaths through crusty nostrils and waited.

"We are being hunted."

The phantom had a thick accent—perhaps German? *Hunted.* The word changed my priorities.

"They're close," he said. After moments of total stillness, he gingerly released the iron grip but kept his hand close to my face. He pointed and brushed a finger across the landscape.

Eyes narrowed and stinging, I followed his arm to the fingertip and squinted. Four or five lumps protruded from the otherwise featureless ground. They swayed to-and-fro, lazily bobbing up and down . . . *walking.*

"It's a long walk to the mountains," said the German. He pulled a canteen from his belt and handed it to me.

I ripped the cap off and guzzled the entire lukewarm contents. Water took precedence over air, and my body sprang to life as the horrible thirst vanished. The man beside me sighed and shook his head. I tossed him the canteen.

"Thank you." I choked out the words and panted.

"Don't make me regret sacrificing a day's worth of foraging." He stood us up, and we set off toward the peaks.

I plodded behind him, almost breaking into a jog, but he pointed at me.

"Don't run," he said sharply. "They can sense it."

Who are they?

• • •

"My name is Jens Grüber, but please excuse me for a moment." He homed in on his target: a spongy white patch covering the ground, intertwined with weeds and soil. After a quick glance to our rear, he clasped his gnarled hands together and struck it. With a dull *whump*, the smooth surface cracked in several directions, and he slipped his fingers deep into the substance and yanked the fragments from the ground. About two inches thick, they crumbled at the edges like crackers. He pulled the fragments up and cross-tied them with a wiry woven string before stuffing them in his pack. "And you?" He wiped sweat from his brow and exhaled.

"I'm Clyde Robbins, staff sergeant, United States Army. What the hell is that stuff you just shoved in your pack?"

"It's the finest grob in all the land." He flashed the faintest smile that lightened his weathered face. Showing the wear of uncounted scowls, his rumpled forehead sat below an angular salt-and-pepper crew cut. "And it's pretty obvious that you're an American."

"Oh, and how is that?" Another arrogant European.

"Your uniform says so." He tied the pack shut as I flushed. "How did you end up so far from the wall without any supplies or companions?"

"Supplies? Wall?"

"So, you're not from Junedale?" He approached and examined me like a goddamn sketch artist. "You're definitely not from Mora. I don't recognize you at all."

I looked at him blankly and rolled the words *Junedale*, *Mora*, *wall*, and *supplies* around in my head. Nothing.

"I woke up in a forest and wandered for hours," I said, tapping my temple in frustration. The details of even the previous day just wouldn't come.

His eyes widened. "Ah, yes, no wonder your grob question! We've had a new batch of arrivals recently, though terribly random without a properly functioning gate. Welcome to Irgendwo!"

His accent was strong, and I didn't recognize the name. "Irgendwo? This isn't Vietnam or some communist prison camp in Russia or China?"

The German shook his head and put his hand on my shoulder. "Tell me, American, who won this so-called Second World War?"

My confusion rose again, and I searched for sarcasm, snark, or irony in his voice. Nothing. His bright blue eyes and sharp cheekbones betrayed nothing but stoic curiosity.

I tapped my uniform. "We did."

"When?" He probed for details like a professor.

I shrugged and decided to humor him. "We nuked Hiroshima in August of 1945, I think."

"You're one of a number to tell me this," he said through a sigh. "I suppose it's my own damn fault for not accepting the facts."

"Germany went down earlier that same year when the Soviets and the oth—"

He waved his hand near my mouth, and I stepped back.

"Let's keep moving," he said.

"Care to tell me just what the hell is going on?"

Jens stared blankly for a moment, still thinking on our little history lesson, then snapped to a more serious appearance. "Ah yes, I flew 109s for Germany during the war."

"You didn't answer my question . . . but you're the only surviving Luftwaffe pilot I've ever met," I said. *Pilot.* Yes, the word triggered a deluge of memories. "We were actually looking for a downed pilot before coming under ambush, until I woke up here."

Jens smiled and flattened his hand, moving it in a rough approximation of a plane and spiraled it into the ground. "I didn't survive."

I tilted my head. "Are you fucking with me?"

* * *

The mountains were upon us. The once distant peaks now stood discernible, towering into the sky beyond the fine mist. I looked upward at the pure magnitude of the rock and followed the crags down to a small crack.

"We have to wait here for a Junedale trader by the name of Perry," said Jens. He slung the heavy pack holding his bounty down and reclined against it.

"What about the things hunting us?" I peered into the horizon relieved to see only dirt and dust.

"Keep your eyes peeled, as they say, and we should have more than enough time to make it to the crag if they happen to come upon us again. I am deeply in Perry's debt and cannot afford to miss this meeting."

"What the fuck?" I tapped my head. "Why don't you just meet him at the crag? And how do you know what time it is? Neither of us have a watch, and I haven't seen the sun once."

"If one of the roving patrols catches us with bootleg grob, they'll confiscate my product and throw us both in the dungeon." Jens dragged a finger across his throat. "If you survive here long enough, you'll learn relative time called *gestalt.* There is no sun."

I threw my arms down. "No sun? What kind of bullshit psychobabble is that?" I swept across the clouds in a desperate search for any point of light. Nope. No hint of the glowing sphere at all. No warmth. Not a single ray.

"Sergeant Robbins"—he put his hand on my shoulder—"you will have to forget every notion of reality you once held, or you will not do well here."

I shrugged and pawed over my compass, pondering his crazy goddamn words and the crazy goddamn fact that I hadn't seen the sun—nor would I, according to him.

Jens noticed the compass and beckoned it from me. "Very nice, very nice. What makes it glow?" He ran a finger over the glass cover and spun the box while the needle danced.

"Radium paint."

He clicked the compass shut and tossed it back. "It's said everyone's gift upon entering this world ensures their salvation, but that's just an old myth."

"Man, you're still trying to sell me the 'I'm dead' shtick?" I said. "What *gift* did you bring here then?"

"We've already discussed what I know. Now it's up to you to accept it." He stretched against his pack and yawned. "Goodness, I've been awake for at least a day trying to earn a living out here, and, instead, I find you."

"Yeah, well, you're not much to look at either." I snorted and folded my arms. "Even if you are a figment of my imagination."

"You know, there is a whole group of people here who never come to terms with their fate and exist forever in denial—a rather cursed circumstance, I would imagine. I arrived here with my Luger."

"A pistol? Man, I got ripped off with this shitty compass. What did you do with it?"

"I killed a group of bandits on my first harvest then sold it to a collector in Junedale." He grasped his chin in thought and pinched a single 9 mm round between his fingers. "Many here have no idea what a pistol is, and ammunition is almost impossible to make, but collectors are still willing to pay very well for one."

"Tits on a bull, then."

Jens slanted an eyebrow, thought for a moment, and broke into hearty laughter. "It would be better said 'a cow without milk,' but, yes, I suppose so. I'd still buy it back immediately if given the opportunity."

"You'd spend money on a gun you can't get ammo for? Smart."

He ignored my comment and huddled against his pack.

"So, figment of my imagination, how did you end up here?"

"I was a young man who wanted to fly. The Luftwaffe was my opportunity to do so."

"How was it?"

His eyes and attention faded into memories. "I can still hear the engine, growling and coughing, spinning the exquisitely designed propeller that swished through the air in a dull, monotonous whir during every second of every flight. Smashing through the clouds, my iron war machine would roll playfully, defiantly beyond the grasp of the Reich below. How sonorous the air over the canopy and through the manifolds!

"Those sounds are what I heard during most of my training in Germany . . . and I grew to hate them. I grew to hate the radial engine that flung me through the sky. I grew to hate the cannons that rattled the frame of my aircraft and my entire body. And I especially grew to hate the insipid nonsense that our commander spewed on a daily basis. A congealed slurry of nationalism, near religious in fervor, dotted with arrogant aerial jargon that seemed more like satire than instruction. But I had sealed my fate."

"We have a lot in common." I laughed in appreciation of our shared experience despite differences in era and service—or the fact that he may not even be real. The emotionless trance on his face had me doubting my own beliefs.

"But then the war came. My memories of Germany and peaceful skies rushed back the first time I saw a Spitfire. Such a cruel twist of fate, having one's own memories haunt them during a life-or-death moment. I suppose the brave young man in the Spitfire could have been having a similar experience. Then again, it's equally possible that he was just intent on killing me. I'll never know, nor will he ever be able to tell me. Our only interaction, at least any interaction of which I was aware, left him a fireball falling toward the Channel. Quite sad, but one of us had to die."

His story left my mind a panorama of air combat and blurry gray war footage I recalled from documentaries I watched as a kid. I pictured his each and every word, sometimes comparing his experiences to my own, but never interrupted. A sad ache tugged at my heart after moments of silence as I realized our common violent irrelevance. By the time I snapped out of the daydream, Jens was snoring against his pack.

"Hurry the fuck up, Perry."

* * *

"Jens, wake up," I whispered to no effect. "Wake up, asshole." I grabbed and squeezed the sleeping German's face until his eyes opened. "The bumps are back."

Jens shook off his sleep inertia, looked about, and found them. They were larger, there were more of them, and their speed was striking. He turned to the mountains and back to the creatures as he cursed under his breath and reached into the pack. Dragging out all but one of the thick white slabs, he set the rest on the ground and sealed the pack.

"We must flee now," he whispered. "Don't hold back your speed. They have our scent." Fastening his equipment, he tapped his nose and pointed directly at the crag.

I nodded, and my heart raced.

We stood, dug our heels down, and broke into a sprint. Seconds later, roars drowned the breeze and tore across the plains. The other-worldly sound, like nothing I'd ever heard or imagined hearing, withered me from the inside.

Holy shit. I looked over my shoulder.

The once lazy swaying movements had become frantic bouncing. The ground rumbled, and rabid fear spilled into my gut. My chest and throat tightened.

Jens blew by me like a wolf. "Run faster, damn you!"

The lead creature shrieked, and the rest followed.

"Wait, for fuck's sake!" My starved and tired muscles strained against the weight of my clothes.

"Don't look at them!" Jens shouted over his shoulder.

Salvation grew with each stride until the sliver of light bloomed into an entrance.

Give it up!

"Don't listen to it!" Jens shouted again and vanished into the crag.

I could hear frenetic breathing mixed with animalistic chattering as one of the beasts closed on me and lurched forward to strike. Putrid wet air poured from its maw over my neck and shoulders, and the stench twisted my stomach. Apex panic drained my last ounce of strength, and I prepared for a savage death. I bore down on my guts, and, in a final burst, I threw my arms forward and careened into the cave.

Jens seized my hand and ripped me forward, and we both collapsed to the ground.

The beast ran headlong into the rock with a meaty thud, and the entire cave trembled.

Muscles on fire, I rolled to my back, but the looming horror made drawing breath difficult.

It was a hulking monstrosity as tall as a telephone pole; its reptilian legs with knees that bent the wrong way propped up the leathery gray body. The body was spherical, bulky, and mostly maw. Its eyes were like a chameleon's, bulging on either side of its corpulent form, and the haunting, beautiful blue irises appeared almost human. A sinewy pit of razors snapped open and shut against the rock and convulsed its entire form in the frenzy.

I was momentarily grateful to God that it was unable to squeeze through the crevice. The room flooded with the essence of rotting flesh and shit, and vomit exploded from me. I crawled away, shielding my nostrils with any loose material I could grasp.

A single tooth broke from the creature and struck into the ground.

Jens gasped—the sound of opportunity meeting greed—and he moved toward it, one foot slowly in front of the other. The beast slowed its assault for a moment and snorted air, perhaps as incredulous as I was.

"What the fuck are you doing?" I spent the breath I had regained.

Jens ignored me and concentrated on his prize; I couldn't believe he attempted it. His hand shook and darted as he drew closer and buried his nose in the crook of his elbow. Mere meters from the creature, he dove, snatched the tooth from the ground, and rolled backward.

Deprived of its meal, the creature roared and writhed against the rock in pure fury.

"*Ausgezeichnet!*" Jens shouted, fist clenched tightly around the base of the tooth. He marveled at the bloodstained and serrated treasure and reached down to seize a large rock.

"Fuck you," he said and hurled the rock into the creature's mouth.

The beast shattered it into tiny fragments.

"You will pay for that, Jens Grüber," it wailed into the cavern in a faintly human voice. Its eyes narrowed, pupils spreading over its globes to pure black, and it focused on Jens.

"Not in this lifetime, you filth." Jens stepped away from the beast and over my pile of vomit to help me up.

"Come," he said.

I nodded and wiped my chin, and after a final glance at the looming nightmare, we walked into the depths.

CHAPTER 10

WANDERLUST

This lunatic—Mog, as he calls himself—prattles on about abandonment and salvation like he was the very creator of this world. Most regard him as little more than a nuisance and not to be taken seriously. But I believe we should keep a close eye on him, especially with rumors of his activities in the Taiga.

—OCTAVIUS LURIUS OF NOLA,
CYCLE 4: THE LABORS OF CREATION

"I HAVE SEEN MEN—WHOLE GROUPS OF MEN—devoured by striders," said Jens.

We moved beneath the light of a humble torch he had plucked from a communal stash. The trail twisted, ascended steep inclines, crawled through crevices, and squeezed through an endless array of craggy slits. Faint shrieks haunted the darkness behind us.

"It's still trying to get in?"

"Yes," said Jens, "their persistence is as legendary as their hunger." He paused and raised the torch to the wall until he found a small arrow chiseled in the rock.

"How did you know what I heard in my head back there?"

"I heard it too."

"That thing was somehow in both our heads?"

"They are the messengers of the Children," said Jens in his Teutonic matter-of-fact cadence, "endowed by their creators with heinous powers and voracious hunger, but some believe they've long broken free and stalk the plains of their own accord."

"Who or what are *the Children*?"

Jens shrugged. "Supposedly, the first creations of Mother Daedrina, goddess of this world. They were Her seven sons and seven daughters—according to our theologians anyway—but I am not a spiritual man myself."

I sniffed and shook my head. "Me neither."

We turned a narrow corner into a small room hewn from the stone. Fresh torches lined the dull-gray rock. Jens grabbed one, lit it, and dropped the other. As we pressed deeper into the mountain, the shrieks ceased—a small comfort—and I could at last hear my own thoughts again.

The ground smoothed to an even surface. More torches lined the walls, illuminating old mining equipment that littered our path.

As my nerves calmed, a new sensation erupted—hunger. My stomach growled loudly.

Jens stopped, reached into his pack, and snapped off a piece from his remaining square of the stuff he called *grob*. He singed it over the torch and handed it to me.

Not giving a good goddamn what it was made from, I sank my teeth into it.

"Wow, pretty good." I finished the pungent delight. "So what is this stuff?"

"It's called *manna* by the religious types, but its common name is *grob*. It's considered the first blessing of Mother Daedrina and fetches a pretty pfennig at Night Market."

The subtle floral undertones gave way to a rich, doughy-sweet palate, like fresh bread slathered in marmalade. My stomach demanded more.

"Pass the grob." I hoped I wasn't being too ornery, but hunger tended to override all manners, and I held my hands out.

The German looked at me, obviously not amused, but he cracked off another square, torch-broiled it, and handed it to me. Victory.

"I forgot what it was like to have children," said Jens, and he zipped up his pack as a not-so-subtle message that my freeloading was over.

"Tell me about your family," I said over a mouthful of grob.

He paused abruptly and stared into the flickering torch. "Perhaps later." His voice was flat and hesitant; I must have scratched a wound. He sniffed and cleared his throat. "Still think this is a dream?"

I was glad he had changed the subject. "Who cares?" I said, stomach full. "I'd stay in a coma just to keep eating this grob shit."

"If you like it, why do you call it shit?"

"I take it you learned English here."

Jens laughed. "Perhaps you're not such a lost cause after all."

• • •

The cave opened, and we marched out of the mountain. My first few steps into "civilization" granted my eyes a panoramic dreamscape that wouldn't let go. Mesmerized, overwhelmed—my notions of reality changed. Behind us towered the mountains. Ahead was a city of stone, wood, and iron buildings—some massive, some small—bathed in the light of ten thousand torches. A thick vine crawled over the buildings, embracing each torch and carrying down its length a soft radiant glow. For me, I had stepped into a lunatic's painting. For Jens, it was business as usual.

"Where's your pass?" A tall guard in leather and metal armor ambled up the hill to us.

Jens pat his hands at the air, smiling to placate the guard's concern.

"Pass. Now."

Jens shrugged. "I know Reginald Keats. We have an understanding and an agreement."

Also hoping the armed guard had an agreement with Mr. Keats, I waved like I knew the bastard.

He paused, took stock of us both, and called to Keats.

Jens turned to me and tapped his nose, and I nodded.

"Welcome to Mora," the guard said.

The featureless murmur of chatter blended with hammers, saws, and excited market bells.

"How many people live here?" I asked.

"Tens of thousands, but *live* is a poor word choice," said Jens.

"Ah yes, we're all dead." I half-raised a cheek. "Got it."

"Well, there's a bit more to it than that and again, poor word choice."

I didn't bother with a follow-up; the psychobabble annoyed me.

"Jens, my friend! Great to see you back." A stocky guard with a cyan sigil on his chest waddled up the embankment. His face was round, puffy, and dyed pink, especially his cheeks and the tip of his nose.

"And you've brought a friend?" He approached me and stopped with a nervous squint. "I don't recognize you."

He stepped back and turned to Jens. "Who the hell is this, and where is he from?"

"I don't recognize *you*," I said before Jens could answer. The sergeant in me boiled at the little prick's insolence, but the guard's jowls and sleepy eyes amused me enough to keep my anger in check.

"Want to keep your jacobs?" He squared up with me—though I stood three inches taller—and let his cloak fall open. A leather scabbard hung from his hip, revealing a sloppily sheathed blade, the ricasso visible and flecked with rust. Not a good start.

I looked at Jens and back to the guard. "Clyde Robbins, staff sergeant, 15 Charlie, US Army." I yammered out the words with minimal enthusiasm and tightened my fists.

"Yank," he quipped in a jovial high pitch with a quick smile, his previous hostility gone in an instant. "Escape from Dearth, did you?"

"Yes, he did," said Jens before I could answer.

"Strange lot, you Americans, but you gave the Jerries a run for their money, I hear," he said and nudged Jens. Judging by his accent and mannerisms, he was British and must have known Jens for quite some time.

"Twice," I said.

"This is Reginald Keats of the Grenadier Guards," said Jens, and he put Keats in a bear hug that forced out a pathetic squeak, no doubt a kind reminder from the German of what he could do.

Keats wheezed and coughed until Jens freed him.

"That's right. Lieutenant Keats of the First Battalion. Pleased to meet you—*Sergeant.*" He extended a black and pink hand, and I shook it. His wide palm and sausage digits smeared my own skin an oily black.

Keats nodded and stepped closer to Jens. "Where did you find him?"

"Wandering the plains."

"Lucky the striders didn't find him first."

"Well, they did. He's the reason I'm still alive," said Jens. "We had a very close encounter." He slid open his pack and revealed the tooth.

"Shite!" Keats shouted. "How did you get that?"

Jens raised a finger to his lips.

Keats tried to reach into the pack, but Jens swatted his hand away.

"I intend to take it to Night Market and make a fortune."

"What'll the Council think, Hun?" Keats smiled wider and giggled. He opened his palm and tapped it.

Jens sighed and zipped the pack shut. "Here's hoping the Council doesn't find out."

"What council?" I said as they bickered.

"Taxes remain a certainty, even in this place," said Jens. "Unfortunately, they are much, much higher here."

"Yeah, they certainly do take their pounds of flesh from us working types," said Keats, rubbing his thumb in circular motions against his other fingers.

"Let us discuss our little economic situation another time," said Jens. "We should show our guest around a little bit and get him registered."

Keats nodded, and we followed him down the embankment toward the city gates.

• • •

"Home sweet home." Jens jangled a crude iron key in the door and shoved it open. Warm air rushed over us as we stepped in, a welcome change from the constant chill. The single room swam thick with the aromas of grob, grain alcohol, and incense, a combination that reminded me of my grandparents' place in Lancaster—Pappy was a lush. Jens tossed his pack on the bed and crouched near a fireplace, and it wasn't long before a fire roared. He filled a kettle and grabbed three mugs from a cupboard.

"Where did you get the water?" I peered to the side but didn't see a sink or any pipes.

"It's delivered weekly," he said and slapped a bulky metal drum.

"The man lives like a king," said Keats before I could continue. He removed his sword and hefty ring of keys and sank into a puffy recliner lined with leather, pillows, and golden lace.

Other than the recliner, the place was simple. Raggedy brown curtains dangled from misshapen windows with lumpy panes of glass. A heavy iron kettle dangled over a grill spanning the fireplace.

"This is the meaning of wealth and luxury here?" I made no attempt to hide my disbelief; this place was medieval.

"Yank's got no manners." Keats shook his head, eyes closed and hands folded over his lap.

Jens ignored the comment and filled three mugs with boiling water.

"You're in a different world now, my young friend," said Jens. "And you are natural in your disbelief just as I was when I first arrived." He grabbed a handful of coins and rolled them around. "This is a year's salary for many here."

I glanced at the coins with little interest. The weird symbols on them meant nothing to me, but Keats eyed them like a vulture. "You're holding a year's worth of money, but you live in a shack?"

"Indeed. Everything comes at a substantial premium here," said Jens.

"Including silence." Keats opened his palm and tapped it.

"Including silence," said Jens. He snatched up a gold coin and flipped it to Keats.

"So, if this is the height of luxury, what it's like to be poor?" Not that I really cared, but inquiring minds and such.

"Oh, no, lad. The height of luxury is far beyond anything in this district. They all live in the Citadel District. The poorest dregs live in communes on the edges of the city or in the mountains."

"Or in the barracks, like our good guardsman here," said Jens.

Keats's eyebrows shot up, and he frowned. "Some of us weren't lucky enough to bribe their way to a deed."

Jens brushed off the comment with the slightest grin.

"Kind of sad to think poverty persists in the afterlife." I mulled the implications for a moment. "I thought the whole premise of death was resting in peace?"

"Wait a moment." Keats sat up from the recliner and looked at Jens. "Afterlife? So this bloke is a *new* arrival? Did you lie to me, Jerry?"

Jens nodded. "Yes, I didn't want to stir trouble with the other guards back there. I did find him on the plains though."

Keats seemed disinclined to press the issue, but his reaction stuck with me: *new arrival?*

"The rule of this world is conflict. Here, you'll know sickness, pain, and even death, but it's still possible to eke out an existence using one's wits." He stepped closer to Keats and tapped his head. "Regardless of one's limitations."

"What the hell do you mean 'death'? I thought we were already dead?" A flurry of questions swirled in my head.

"The body you have here is much like the one you had on Earth: It's merely a vessel."

"Christ . . ." I sniffed and gave him the same look I gave Jehovah's Witnesses when they came knocking.

"Try this." Jens retrieved the mugs and handed them to us.

I swirled the liquid, and three green rocks jangled and disintegrated, leaching green ink into the water. Steam washed over my face—mint and lavender—and pleasant tingles flowed down my neck. I blew some of the heat away and sipped, and before the warmth had reached my stomach, my muscles were jelly. Pleasant.

"Very nice, isn't it? They're called *dream shards*, and they are more valuable than grob."

"Like a king," said Keats over a yawn, and he melted into the recliner, an obese cat in uniform.

"But what about the—"

"Sergeant Robbins, I know you have many questions, but you should rest. You may stay here until we register and relocate you," said Jens. "I must make it to market to sell what little harvest I managed to keep."

At mention of the market, Keats jumped from the recliner and grabbed his pack. "We'll be back in a few hours. Don't muck around outside."

Jens pulled the strider tooth from his pack and placed it on the mantle above the fireplace. "This will require a special transaction." He admired the pulpy razor, turned, and corralled Keats to the door. Securing their packs, they left.

I yawned, relieved to be alone, and enjoyed the steady crackle of the fire. Kicking off my boots, I collapsed on the bed and stretched out. *This ain't so bad.*

As my weary body released its aches and pains, I pictured what was left of me in the other world—if there really was an "other" world . . . if there really was a "me."

Such strange circumstance, having to appear in a body—a still rather frail and vulnerable mound of meat—in a new existence that was supposed to be paradise (not that I deserved such). This flimsy shithouse of an afterlife didn't at all match what Sister Isabelle had beat into my brain during Sunday School about either final destination. I felt robbed.

And I missed my mom. The realization gave me pause. Did she know I was dead by now? A wrenching pain sprouted up from my gut and embraced my heart. I almost heard her cries.

CHAPTER 11

THE RABBLE

Lula, my treasure, you must go to Mora and find this Shadebringer. You must peer into him and learn the truths of his soul. I trust none but you with our future.

—GARRETT THE HOLLOWED

"AMEN, BROTHER! A-motherfuckin'-men!"

I awoke face down in a cot, one eye buried in a government-issue pillow and the other out of focus. So much for downtime.

"And who—I say who—is gonna pull your damned dirty asses out that boiling lake of fire?" His voice boomed and fell in a guttural decrescendo.

"Lord Jesus!" the men replied.

"Fuck," I muttered and dragged my uniform from the floor—again. No use sleeping now.

"Oh, you betta believe it!"

I stuffed my feet in my boots, laced up, and sauntered to the exit, coffee tin in hand. Several men sat on makeshift pews while others balanced on their helmets. Centered among them stood a light-skinned Black man with a shaved head and box-frame bifocals. He held a crucifix in his right hand and a cigarette in his left. Creamy Lucky Strike smoke swirled around his yellowed fingernails.

"So nice of you to join us!" The chaplain clapped carefully around his crucifix and cigarette, and the other soldiers hooted and hollered.

I flashed a false grin that turned to a frown in an instant, and I flipped them a long-hanging bird as I ambled to the coffee kettle.

"Aw, well, I guess not today," he said, prompting a chorus of boos. "I guess Brother Robbins has some super important army stuff to do and can't help us celebrate Lord Jesus's resurrection."

The early sun crept over a sand berm framing the howitzers like oil on canvas. I sat by the kettle and nursed my coffee, mind somewhere back in Pennsylvania. Man, I missed the snow. Coffee just didn't taste as good when the weather was almost as hot as your drink. I dumped another liter of the bitter, steaming black liquid into my cup and chugged it down, but the chaplain eroded my peace. He was whipping up his flock with fire, brimstone, and every variation of the word "fuck," and I couldn't drown the bullshit.

"Seems like you're doing a lot of fucking," I said.

The chaplain stopped mid-sentence and peered at me. "And what's wrong with my method of testament in your eyes, Brother Robbins?"

I shrugged. "Well, doesn't seem very godly when every other word out of your mouth is the most profane in the English language."

"Ah, yes," said the chaplain and he cleared his throat. "Profane. Profane is the very nature of man, Brother Robbins. I'm profane. You're profane. Your mother's profane. My wife's profane. Old Miss Molly, the church organist who lives with her cats back on Main Street, is fucking profane." He pantomimed scrubbing his skin. "We are all dirty shit-swimming scum in the eyes of the Lord," he said, eliciting a number of "amens" from the congregation. "Only through his son's redeeming hand can we wash this profanity from us and become clean once and for all. And if I need to wade deep into the pool of shit myself to reach these humble grunts," he said and extended his arms outward, "I will."

"Well, the Lord better bring a fire hose, because you are some filthy motherfuckers."

Half the congregation chuckled while the other half scowled at me.

The chaplain smiled from ear to ear. "Tell me, Brother Robbins, why do you think we were chosen to come to this strange country, fight this nameless enemy, and oppose their vile ideology?"

"Because some of us were dumb enough to volunteer, and the rest got volun-told."

"Not in the least," said the chaplain. "We're here because the Lord so graciously chose us to be his implements of cleansing. We are his fire. We are his blades, each and every. And our duty is to purge this land of the heathen."

"I'm sure their witchdoctors are telling them the same silly shit in their little underground tunnels right now." I turned from him and enjoyed the orange sky. There was only so much bullshit a man could take.

"We are doing the Lord's work. We are on the Lord's side," said the chaplain in a frenzy. "We will not waver in our righteous service. Don't you see? We cannot lose."

"Yeah, but apparently we can't win either." I washed down the grinds and walked back to my hooch. "You know, chaplain, if god exists, he probably doesn't like ass kissers."

I zipped the entrance shut and fell to my cot, hoping for peace. Within moments, I heard the zipper slide down, and I opened my eyes, ready to tear into a sonofabitch.

A skeletal hand reached in and ripped the flap open, and the wind froze in my throat. The chaplain and the congregation had vanished. A meaty green leg bent before the entrance, and Bernie's mutilated face peeked in. He smiled.

I tried to scream, but nothing moved.

"Always room for one more," he said and sank his fingers into my neck.

• • •

I shrieked and crashed from bed, tangled in sheets. Dull pains shot through my ankles and legs, but I was too relieved to care. My breathing slowed, and I wiped a line of sweat from my brow. *Holy shit, what a dream.* Oddly enough, I was glad to still be dead.

A small flame now moped below the kettle, a mere shadow of its former glory, unable to resist the encroaching chill, which quickly set my bones and muscles to aching. Miserable. For a moment, I imagined home or maybe some military hospital minus a limb if that's what the Fates demanded to get me out of here.

Gathering the sheets, I crawled back into bed and balled up. As my eyes drifted to the mantle, I noticed the strider tooth, blackened dried blood and capillaries at the root tapering to a tip finer than a sewing needle. *I wonder how much he'll get for that.* Of course, the thought launched my own ruminations on money. How would I survive? What kind of work could I do here?

Keats's grating voice and jangling keys heralded their return, and the door swung open, breaking my worry streak.

"Rise and shine," said Jens and he shook the bed. "It seems you had some rather vivid dreams!"

Still exhausted and smarting from my fall, I pulled the sheets over me again and nodded. "Side effect of the tea?"

"Hence the name *dream shards*."

"We need to go to the Citadel District and get you registered," said Keats. "They're going to ask you about your life, death, and origins. They'll also give you an aptitude test for job placement."

"I woke up in some f—"

Jens raised his hand. "You awoke on the plains, and I found you wandering there." He glanced at me and then at Keats.

"Yeah, I have definitely never been here before."

"Well, alright then. Let's go," said Keats, and we walked out.

• • •

The streets were a mishmash of cobblestone, chiseled granite, and knobby clay, and the lumpy-bumpy pressure against my feet reminded me of childhood jaunts through Old Town Philadelphia. Men and women strolled or limped along storefronts and homes, backs burdened with bulky packs or work equipment. Small groups loitered beneath the torches and glowvine and huddled for warmth. They bantered back and forth in hushed whispers and eyed us nervously as we passed. A few donned their original uniforms, mostly unrecognizable to me, though most wore dyed twill. To the very last person, their faces and hands bore a grayish-black hue, like coal, with tired eyes floating in deep pits. *Does anybody sleep here?*

Humble cottages grew into large townhouses and then mansions as we drew closer to the city center. The denizens took fuller forms, and the ubiquitous black stains tapered to normal flesh. The scent of broiled grob drifted through the air, spilling from colorful windows with the sound of cordial chatter and clattering pots. Keats flashed crisp salutes to every guard we passed, and many knew him on a first-name basis. They exchanged words in the strange pidgin speak, and more than once I caught an errant look, grin, or befuddled furrow that let me know they were talking about me.

"Fooda? Grob?" A voice squeaked from the shadows.

I paused, and an emaciated child skittered to me and tugged on my uniform. Her clothes were ragged, and a cloth hood covered most of her face. Without a second thought, I reached into my pockets and removed a few remaining flecks of grob. Kneeling with the treat cupped in my hands, I smiled.

"Do you need us to broil this for—" I peered into her hood and recoiled.

Her eyes were Protean—undulating and colorless—puddles in a storm with pinpoint pupils that bobbed like driftwood. Fire burrowed into my chest.

Keats gasped, vaulted between us, and booted the girl in the belly. "Piss off, you bloody Hollow!"

She keeled forward with a grunt and a whimper. Shouts of "halt" and "Hollow" went up among the people as they screamed and bolted.

"What the fuck is wrong with you?" I seized Keats by the throat and smashed his bulbous nose, sending him to the ground in a bloody fountain.

I kneeled beside the young girl, gently grasped her hand, and helped her up. I handed her the grob as she sobbed and lifted her head. She locked eyes with me, and I froze—a formless void flooding my head. The pain returned and fast became agony. Every heartbreak in life coalesced in the moment and concentrated in my chest, but I could not look away.

A powerful force held my eyes open, and the burning spread across my face and down my back. Dread flowed through me, and my heart pounded like a steam hammer.

"Don't look! Don't look," said Jens, and he shielded my eyes.

With the gaze broken, I tightened my muscles, turned my head, and wheezed.

The child pocketed her bounty and fled into an alley with two guards in pursuit.

"You . . ." Keats ejected a slab of semisolid goo from his nose and swiped at trickles of blood flowing from his nostrils and down his chin. "Fucking . . ."

"You had it coming, Keats," said Jens, staring down at the bloody pile of Briton.

"Wha . . . wha—" I pointed. "What was that?"

"They're Hollows," said Jens. "Soulless children born to this world who can kill you with a single gaze. The Council offers a hefty bounty on every one of them."

Keats crawled to a nearby post and righted himself. "I'll kill you myself or have you hanged for assaulting a Council guard!"

"Oh, shut it, Keats," said Jens. "How else should a man respond to assault on a child?"

"It's not a bloody child; it's a monster. I should have just run her through and collected the bounty."

"He's been here a day; do you think he knows what a Hollow is?" Jens pulled a handkerchief from his pocket and offered it to Keats.

"What kind of society hunts children for bounty?" I glanced at Keats while he patted blood from his nose.

"The Council fears them, for one reason or another," said Jens. "The Silver Serpents hunt them mercilessly, and all pregnancies are terminated along with their mothers. A dreadful circumstance, but such is the nature of this world. Not even the cursed striders will touch them."

"I really doubt *that* assessment." The hunger and tenacity of the damn things lingered with me; a kid would make an easy snack.

Keats stumbled at me and grabbed my hand. He squeezed and shook it surprisingly hard for a little fella, which I guessed was his retribution.

"Come on then, let's get this bleeding-heart idiot to the registrants." He strode ahead and gingerly petted his bloody and crooked nose.

• • •

Jens slowed, allowed Keats to gain some distance, and pulled up beside me. "What came over you back there?"

I gazed forward beyond Keats and saw multitudes of people milling about some makeshift shacks but shifted my attention to Jens. "What do you mean?"

"With the child . . . You bashed Keats in an instant."

I thought for a moment. "I remember being that kid."

Jens nodded but didn't press for details, thankfully. We closed the distance to Keats, but he abruptly stopped.

"Let's stop for a moment," he said with a nasal twang. "I have a friend I must see."

I chuckled lightly and looked away when he glanced at me.

A broad, open-air shanty stood at the center of a clearing flanked by others forming a tortuous network of displays. Cracked wooden shingles were strewn about the dilapidated roof network with eaves that drooped like wet cardboard. Support beams rose at random intervals connected to a series of planks and flat boards enclosing the display tables. Men and women clothed in rags and light blue armbands ambled about the interior of the market with their baked goods and produce, bartering and ringing bells. I recalled the grungy farmers markets my mother took me to as a kid as I examined the neat rows of fruits and vegetables on display here—at least what I thought were fruits and vegetables; I'd never seen some of the things.

"This is Mother Hen's Grocery," said Keats, who scurried over to his "friend." He blew a kiss to a frumpy woman who stood, arms crossed, behind the table.

She scoffed at him and stuck her nose in the air without further acknowledgment. Eagle-eyed and serious, she watched the fingers and handbags of every customer and barked orders at her staff.

"That's Frau Gilda," said Jens. "She burned to death in Dresden."

People stalked about the tables and pawed the produce, some stopping to haggle with the old woman or her associates. The mundane scene lightened my mood—a moment's peace in a bizarre world.

"There's something about grocery shopping I've always liked. You're just another goddamn bird scratching around for dinner on a termite mound."

"One of five sanctioned food markets in the district," said Keats. He waved again at the old frau and puffed up his chest, but it could not compete with his belly. The scene was rather pathetic, but I couldn't fault him for trying; this place must be worse alone. "Her twin runs a market in Dearth, though they haven't spoken since she fled." He crept into her line of sight and nudged the handle of his blade. The polished metal glinted a speck of light to her eyes, but she only offered Keats an unimpressed glare. Ouch. He blushed, retreated from the table, and ushered us forward.

"Where does the food come from?" The parched plains offered a scant patch of grob (admittedly delicious) but, otherwise, only weeds and dust, and nothing edible appeared to have been growing in the forest. "There was lots of weird shit back th—"

Jens looked at me with a start and raised a finger to his lips. "Almost there," he said.

His answer irked me a little, but I didn't press the issue.

He ogled the homes and whistled at those that struck his fancy.

I could see gears turning in his head.

He said, "Would need to move a lot of dream shard to buy in this neighborhood . . . if gathering the stuff was still possible."

"Why isn't it?" I figured a conversation would speed things along, and if I was to exist in this world, I might as well learn a way to make money.

"The stuff grows high in the Everpeaks. Too dangerous now."

"Then how are you paying your bills?"

Jens shrugged like a man who just bet it all at a horse track and lost. "Grob and credit."

We turned onto a smooth granite street enshrouded by and ending in a wall of the glowing vine. Walking through a humble arch, we emerged at the periphery of a sprawling mall many magnitudes larger than the open-air grocery market. Thousands milled about dilapidated shops, dancing street performers, and mobile vendors. In the center, a marble fortress climbed triumphantly into the sky. Stairs encircled it and ascended to a plateau lined with hundreds of guards in neat order: a well-guarded island in a sea of peasants.

"Jens, Reginald, welcome back to the Citadel District," said a guard, and she grasped Keats's hand. "Who is this?"

"I am not bound to please you with my answer," I said in my best Bard.

The guard sneered and shook her spear at me.

"Clyde Robbins," said Keats over an impatient sigh. "Clyde Arsehole Robbins, if you'd like."

"I found him wandering the plains. He's an escapee from Junedale, and he saved my life," said Jens.

"Junedale? Don't you mean Dearth? Do you vouch for this outsider, Reginald?" The guard glanced twice at Keats; his round face had become lumpy since our "disagreement."

Keats nodded and handed the guard his sigil, which she inspected and handed back. "New registrant to the southern face." She stepped aside.

I approached the southern face with my two escorts: one an obviously successful merchant (and perhaps mercenary) and the other a fat dumbass who somehow eked out an existence despite himself. The thought of ending up like either of them or like some of the poor bastards I had seen along the way here haunted me. So too did the thought of struggling every day for a bite to eat. Maybe I'd mouth off and end up hanged instead. Then what? What's after the afterlife? Goddammit, I didn't deserve this. Why the f—

"Hey, wanker, move it," said Keats and he beckoned me to follow.

CHAPTER 12

ABANDON ALL HOPE

Anastasia Nemsov, you have on three occasions failed to meet quota during your mandated grob harvests. Consequently, you leave me no choice but to sentence you to death for the crime of High Sloth.

—INQUISITOR THADDEUS SYKES,
DUKE OF ADMONITIONS

WE WALKED TO THE BASE OF THE FORTRESS, and I paused, mouth agape as my eyes crawled skyward with the towers. *There must be some talented sons of bitches in this world.*

"This is the Ziggurat of Baledoccus," said Keats, "the seat of power of the Council and home of the Kir Endra waygate, the only safe way out of Irgendwo."

"Well, no shit. Take me to the waygate then!" I said excitedly, ready to bolt up the steps and get on with eternity.

Keats laughed and patted me on the back. "Yank, if it was that easy, nobody would be here."

"What's the holdup then?"

"The Council determines who goes and who stays, and getting a ticket out of here is a very, *very* special endeavor."

"Their rites of passage are highly secretive but largely predicated upon service, longevity, and circumstance," said Jens.

"Sounds like slavery," I said and sniffed.

Jens blinked rapidly and glanced around. He put a finger to his lips and shook his head.

Strange symbols connected in artisan stonework adorned each step. We ascended under the watchful eyes of statuesque guards who tracked every movement. My legs burned over the final step, and I wheezed like a wheelchair-bound vet with a tank of oxygen on my ass. I guess there was something to be said for metaphysical fitness too.

"Why the fuck am I sucking wind?" I said. "I was a goddamn gazelle before getting here."

"New body, new start," said Jens and he flexed his bicep. "Physical fitness matters in this life too."

"Better shape up, Yank, or they'll have you cleaning the sewers." Keats laughed and walked us to the main entrance.

With great effort, I bit my tongue. Keats's corpulence made him an easy target, and I'd already broken his nose.

A gong reverberated through the air, and we froze. Another strike followed, and Keats scampered to the eastern precipice and waved us behind him. In unison, the guards lining the stairs quarter-stepped left and looked down to the plaza below. Sooty throngs poured from the four corners of the mall and gathered at the base of an expansive elevated stage. A third gong hushed them.

I squinted hard at the stage, a toy diorama from our elevation, until the sight of swaying nooses took my breath. "What the fu—"

Keats spun to me and hissed over his finger, his usual impatient response, but there was neither anger nor irritation in his eyes this time—only fear. Something told me I best shut up.

A fourth gong brought everyone to attention, and a procession of guards and shackled prisoners shambled from the building. Naked aside from chains draped over their bodies, they ascended the gallows, up the stairs, and turned to face the crowd.

A man in ornate black robes emerged from the ziggurat with a large scroll tucked beneath his arm. He traipsed up the gallows, stopped mid-stage, and opened it. "For crimes against the people of Mora and the Council—"

"Praise them! Praise them!" the crowd cheered, and a chill ran up my back. "These nine criminals are sentenced to die, here and now, by decree of Lord Ek Maraine for crimes to include theft, blasphemy, sedition, fostering Hollows, and sloth."

"So, it is said, and so shall it be!" thundered the crowd.

The gong struck a fifth time, and the guards led the prisoners over the trapdoors, fitted the nooses on them, and stepped away. A dull ache spread across my belly as the executioner approached the lever. Rolling up the scroll, he raised his hand into the air, the crowd roaring in approval, and he triggered the trapdoors. The bodies dropped. The gong sounded for the sixth time, and it was over. As quickly as they had arrived, the people dispersed from the gallows, leaving nine fresh corpses swinging in the breeze. Bells and spirited haggling continued like nothing had happened.

Keats pulled me away from the steps. "Two gongs mean you stop what you're doing and watch, else you too may end up swinging."

"People are executed here for being lazy?" I said and looked again at the nine unfortunates. *If we're already dead, what happened to those folks?* The thought almost reached my lips.

"And for a lot less," he whispered. "But it's better than being out there." We looked to the plains and, from our elevation, the barren expanse took on a new and overwhelming grandeur. Jens had truly saved me.

Keats scurried off to the south-face entrance at the apex of the ziggurat and exchanged words with a couple guards.

"Hurry up," he said and waved us through.

We passed beneath a small portcullis into a room littered with books, scrolls, and ledgers. Torches and candles lit every nook and cranny, and sages in drab green robes shuffled back and forth. Paper swished, heavy books *whumped* shut and *cricked* open, and pens whirred across rough paper. The place smelled like a dank public library.

"Bureaucracy is more eternal than God," I said half-disgusted and half-amazed.

Jens smiled, but Keats again told me to shut up.

"Welcome to Mora," said a slight figure with a quill in his hand. He beamed, and his aged face wrinkled. "And how can bureaucracy be more eternal than She who is the Alpha and the Omega?" The sage tapped his temple.

"Somebody will have to stamp Omega's death certificate." I tapped my own temple and scrunched my nose at him.

"Daedrina snipped this one from the snarky corner of the Yah'w."

The sage and his colleagues giggled, and I forced out my own guffaw, though I had no idea what they were talking about. *Score two for the home team.*

Keats also pretended to laugh but glared at me the entire time.

The sage heaved a tome from beneath his desk and clunked it on the counter. "I'm assuming you are a new registrant?" His voice was feeble and coarse, and he waved me forward.

"How old are you?" I said, curious about the discrepancy between the man's face and his voice.

Keats groaned.

"I perished in the Channel in 1588, but I've long since stopped counting my time here. Now, what is your complete name, and what was your date and cause of death, young man?" The words were surreal.

"Staff Sergeant Clyde Chesty Robbins. I died in combat . . . but I can't remember the date." A dull fog hung over my memories. Bits and pieces.

"What date?" Keats snapped his fingers, and I turned to him slowly in full-hate mode. Maybe another bloody nose *was* in the cards?

"Knowledge will come in time. I'm more than satisfied at this point," said the clerk. He thumbed through the tome to a blank page and scribbled what little information I provided as another sage shaded a rough sketch of my face. Her lacy fingers breezed over the paper like a goddamn hummingbird, and my face took form in charcoal.

"This conflict has such nebulous origins," said the sage, pawing through his book. "Though I suppose if war can rage over the death of a single man, it can be ignited by much less."

"Yeah, standard twentieth-century bullshit," I said.

"If I remember correctly, we had a large African fellow in the same conflict, surname Collins, come through recently."

I started and clamored for the book. "Let me see."

He seized the book and scanned through it. "Let's see here." He squinted through his glasses at every neatly written era and name with its adjoining sketch. "Barrows, Berkley, Cathcart—oops, wrong war—Calhoun, Colgate . . ." He paused and cross-checked the name. "Ah yes, Collins." He flipped the book around and pushed it in front of me.

"Holy shit, Bernie?" My mouth fell open. "When did he get here?"

"Souls tend to arrive in batches, so not too long before you," he said. "He was quite descriptive about the heated jungle environs and the creeping terrors that lived therein."

I laughed and smacked the countertop. "Yeah, that's Bernie alright. He fuckin' hated all the bugs. Kind of weird there are none in the jungles here."

Jens's face dimmed and, in an instant, I knew I had fucked up.

The sages paused and focused on me. Jens wrinkled his nose and sighed. No covering for my dumb ass this time.

"What were you doing in the Taiga?" His tone mixed intrigue and accusation as he went from DMV to FBI in a second. "What were you doing so far from Dearth?"

The other sage pushed her spectacles up the bridge of her nose.

"I found him on the plains," said Jens. "He was coming from the direction of Jun—I mean, Dearth—and in quite a hurry. Perhaps he was just lost in the Taiga."

"Young man, please expound upon your origins a little further."

Jens tried to answer for me, but they waved him back. I was the center of attention, and when two others fled from the room, I knew we were in some shit.

"Let him speak for himself. Now, young man, what were you doing in the Taiga?"

"Well," I said, confused, "I woke up in a thick forest, disoriented."

"Go on." He scratched out some words and scribbled new details as fast as he could.

Keats wrung his hands and sweat dripped down his forehead. "Oh fuck, I knew this one was trouble. Why didn't I listen to my gut?" He dabbed away the sweat and flushed.

The sage snapped his fingers at Keats. "Sergeant Robbins, did you awaken in the forest among fresh graves?"

"Yeah, I did—how did you know that?"

"Did any stir as if they were alive?"

"Yeah, one moved, made noise, and scared the shit out of me. I thought I was having a bad dream or something."

"The bad dream is just beginning," said Jens.

"Absolutely remarkable," said the sage, and he stamped my dossier with a strange symbol. Guards poured through the entrance and surrounded us, swords drawn.

"What the fuck is going on?" I said.

"Bloody trouble. I knew it," said Keats.

The soldiers seized us and guided us toward the exit.

CHAPTER 13

HOME IS WHERE THE HEART IS

If only his culinary prowess was as sharp as his tongue.

—ISABELLA BATISTE

"IN. GET IN, NOW." THE GUARDS SHOVED us into Jens's cottage and secured the door. Jens fixed his disheveled collar and set off for his bookshelf while Keats and I moved away from the windows.

"We're fortunate we weren't thrown in the dungeon," said Keats, and he paced back and forth patting sweat away. If we survived this, I would have to teach him to play poker . . . to pad my own pockets.

"Mora's dungeon is in the ziggurat," said Jens.

"No shit," said Keats, "and what does that have to do with anything?"

"They wouldn't dare allow a shadebringer near the Kir Endra way-gate," said Jens, and he grabbed a hulking tome of a book from his shelf. "Assuming there's any truth in the lore."

He flipped through the old hidebound book and squinted. "The shade, an entity of prodigious power, shall bind its purified and selected vessel, and, together—these souls unified—they will cleanse this world of evil men and their evil magics." He closed the book and stared at me. "The shade can only access this realm through a waygate."

"I'm just some fucking grunt that got unlucky in a Southeast Asian jungle. They got the wrong guy."

Jens shrugged. "Regardless of whether that's true or not, they see you as a threat. They fear their vulnerabilities."

"If it's only *his* head that matters, then *why* are we here with him?" Keats looked out the window at a group of guards. Probably former colleagues of his, they stood motionless with weapons drawn.

"It's not just his head that matters," said Jens. "They're going to do all they can to prevent this information from reaching Junedale. I fear the poor bureaucrats back in the Citadel District are already dead."

"Well, that certainly doesn't bode well for us!" said Keats.

A guard spun to peer through the window, and Keats quickly composed himself and waved. The guard narrowed his eyes in obvious disgust and turned away.

"Aw, come on, Batiste! It's Keats!" he pleaded through the window. "I cooked for you and your wife just three weeks ago!"

The guard didn't bother responding.

"What exactly is going on?" I could barely get my words out as Keats's sycophancy turned my stomach.

"They think *you* are the one who can break their hold on Kir Endra," said Keats.

The bastard might as well have been speaking Latin. "So, what does that mean?"

Keats growled and shook his head. He flung his arms out and turned from his former colleague.

"Reginald, calm yourself. He didn't choose to bear a shade."

Keats puffed up his chest. "Are you daft, Jens? Does that matter to us at all? Do you think we're making it out of here?"

He did have a point. I recalled the unfortunates swinging from their necks in the middle of town.

Keats plopped down in a chair and twirled his sigil. "Maybe they'll have mercy on me for my fine service."

"Keats, you're as corrupt and lazy as any of them and easily replaced. Don't delude yourself; you can't ev—" Jens shut his mouth and growled over sealed lips before more words slipped out and he returned to his book.

The room fell silent aside from Jens pawing through the pages.

Rapid thumps and muffled voices at the door startled us. Keats jumped from the chair as the door flung open and guards flooded in. At the rear, a lean figure entered last. A simple purple robe with black trim covered the figure from head to toe, face indiscernible in a heavy hood. I stared into the formless black and felt slight discomfort, unsure what peered back at me.

"To what do we owe this honor, Lord Ek Maraine?" Keats kneeled but a guard booted him back.

The guard captain stepped forward, a massive double-edged axe just a toy on his back. "Who is this alleged shadebringer?"

"I suppose that's me," I said.

Ek Maraine whispered to the guard captain, and both approached me.

"You told our sages you awoke in a forest surrounded by burial mounds. Is this true?"

I nodded.

"Before you left your mound, did it say anything to you?"

"No words," I said and remembered the strange noises.

"Did you wake with anyone else?"

"No."

Ek Maraine stood as still as a statue. I was certain he—it, whatever it was—stared through me. A pale, disfigured hand emerged from the capacious sleeve and twisted a thumb downward. *Oh, shit.*

"His Holiness thanks you for your honesty," said the captain.

More whispers. The captain winced, a momentary flash of emotion. Keats stepped back, and Jens set his book down. Ek Maraine shuffled from the cottage, and a guard closed the door and locked it. Others hung black sheets over the windows. Keats stuttered and hawed. He couldn't quite get his pathetic words out as he fumbled his sigil.

The guard captain brooded and lowered his head. "I'm sorry."

Keats turned and shook the sigil before him, from guard to guard, but each ignored it.

"Seize the shadebringer, and kill the other two. Do not let them suffer."

The guards drew their onyx blades and tightened the circle around us.

"You're going to kill your own?" said Jens. His matter-of-fact tone confounded me. The man feared nothing.

"We have orders."

"You'll eventually have to leave Irgendwo, Parnel," said Keats. "There will be a reckoning for this." A momentary speck of defiance from Keats, though meek and shaky, renewed a bit of the man's pride—and my respect for him.

But it did no good. The captain turned to his lieutenant and nodded.

* * *

I stepped in front of the guards as they advanced. Some hesitated, and their weapons trembled in their hands; they didn't want to kill us, but orders were orders, I guess. Funny, the similarities of this world and the previous one, but I wasn't going to make it easy.

I grinned and tightened my muscles. Almost giddy, I eyed the guards one by one, trying to find the one most deserving . . . the most *profane.* The junior officer, possibly some goof in the Prussian Army ages ago, judging by his uniform, inched forward and focused on Jens, a sadistic grin on his face and blade as still as a pond. A serpentine scar crawled down his arm to his blade. The placidity with which he approached his task revolted me. I had my target.

Leaping to a nearby bookcase, I snatched a glass orb anchored to a hefty iron slab—perhaps a paperweight or maybe an old gift—and launched it at him. The metal and glass connected above his right eye, and he went down like the goddamn Hindenburg. I clenched my fists and threw them upward. "And Bunning throws a perfect game!"

The captain charged and heaved an elbow into my gut that keeled me over, and at that moment, I prepared for death.

Then all hell broke loose.

The door crashed down in a shower of splinters and metal strips. Black-tipped spears swarmed into the room and impaled three guards before the last splinters hit the floor. Keats cowered at the sudden calamity and dove to the ground. The guard captain turned his back to us to face the chaos, and with speed I would have never thought possible, Jens seized the strider's tooth and thrust its imperceptible tip through the captain's armor. It tore through him like straw until Jens's knuckles slammed into the captain's back. Body rigid, the captain exhaled in a stuttered cough, and blood sprayed from his mouth. Jens gripped the weapon and held fast until the captain fell forward. The tooth glowed blue, and a rush of light sank into the very substance of it.

"I'll liberate your soul at the waygate," Jens said. "I promise."

More spears surged into the room and butchered the guards without question or mercy. A thin man in a dark tunic covered in ornamental metal leaned through the doorway. "We must flee! Ek Maraine returns!"

Keats clamored from the floor, stepped over the bodies of his former colleagues, including Batiste, and bolted. So much for dinner.

We tore down the streets as citizens screamed and ducked into their homes and people shouted from every corner. The man in the dark tunic led us and showed neither fatigue nor fear as he killed guards mid-stride. The luxurious homes and rich merchants near the city center waned to shanties and beggars with every step toward the mountains. My lungs burned, and vivid memories of the striders electrified me.

"Through here!" the thin man shouted and paused at the cave entrance to ignite a torch.

A distant rumble, like thunder, drew my eyes back to an opaque black cloud that rolled over the ground. "What the fuck is that?" I gasped and turned to our leader.

"He's near! We must flee now!"

We ducked the craggy ceiling and weaved recklessly through the darkness—until the voice returned. I stopped, straining to hear it over my own breath.

"Do not let them escape." As sure as air flooded my burning lungs, the deep and disconcerting baritone voice had returned.

The thin man yanked hard at my arm, but I resisted. "Come, you fool!"

"Back to those giant spheres of teeth?" I said. "I'll take my chances with the cultist assholes first."

The man growled and dragged me eye to eye. "The striders are distracted, I promise you, but if the Council seizes you again, your fate will be infinitely worse than a monster's belly."

I had little time to ponder the meaning but did not resist again.

We bolted through the dim maze of rock until the small crevice leading to the plains appeared. I crushed the fear down in my gut and sprinted out, half-expecting to meet the vengeful beasts again. Every muscle in my body burned, and my heart raced. Furious voices and the burgeoning rumble bellowed out from the crag, the pursuing guards—and whatever that rolling black cloud was—close behind.

"Blow it!" The leader shouted back into the cave. A powerful explosion shook loose rocks and dust from the face of the mountain, and flames lapped from the darkness. The collapsing rock silenced the screams and metal in an instant.

"Your men were still in there!" I shouted. And I froze. A wall of flames roared into my mind. The screams, by God, the screams . . . the reek of gasoline and oil. All by my hand. Could I do nothing right? Did I only exist to cause suffering? The world slipped away as the vision assembled like a demonic puzzle in my diseased brain. Then it fell away as quickly as it had come.

He turned to me and nodded, eyes like ice cubes and brow straight. "I knew the risks," he said, "and so did they."

I looked back, small trails of dust and smoke snaking out from tiny crevices but no sign of the black cloud and definitely no guards.

"Why?" The act so repulsed me I could scarcely acknowledge him as a leader.

"If Ek Maraine had made it through, he could have recalled the striders."

Another glimpse of the smoldering rock silenced me. Sacrifice was all well and good unless you were the one making it.

We paused to catch our breath, and I noticed Keats sprawled out on the ground, his fat ass smack in the middle of a strider's triple-claw print, one of many that circled the former crevice. I smiled faintly and nodded at him, impressed he had been able to keep up. The tracks appeared to converge and accelerate south. I followed the claw prints with my eyes until they were specks in the distance. *I wonder what they were chasing?*

• • •

"Oh, we're in a world of shit now," said Keats.

"We were doomed before these Junedalians intervened, so I would venture we're probably doing quite well," said Jens.

"Amen to that," I said.

Our escorts trotted along in silence as we hurried along the base of the mountain. Scouts broke away and ran large swathes at regular intervals.

"Their athleticism is legendary," said Jens. He pointed at one whose long, loping strides reminded me more of an ostrich than a man.

"Few city dwellers know our proper demonym," said the man in the dark tunic. "You must be a regular with us."

Jens nodded. "The Council of Mora has slandered you as barbaric savages, but my interactions with your kind on the plains have been quite to the contrary."

"It's humorous how demagogues and tyrants never change, even in death." He sniffed and wiped specks of blood from his hands. "My name is Jacques. I am first advisor to Lord Octavius and commander of the Roux."

Jens extended his hand. "I am Jens Grüber. This is Clyde, a new American arrival. And my frantic British friend here is Reginald Keats."

Keats peeped sideways at the mention of his name and nodded.

"So, this neophyte is a shadebringer," said Jacques. The tone in his voice was a mix of astonishment and condescension, as if he'd just seen a fat kid do a backflip.

"Apparently," said Jens. "But he did bring down a Silver Serpent before you intervened."

Jacques nodded. "Impressive."

"That dead-eyed asshole with the scar?" I smirked a little. I beaned that fucker good.

"The cursed few who have bound themselves in blood and spirit to Ek Maraine—they are vile even by the Council's standards. Ruthless murderers and hunters."

"Don't think I supported them but for a second!" said Keats with some alarm.

"Does your conscience haunt you, fat man?" Jacques looked Keats up and down.

"I can assure you that I would not keep the company of anyone who hunted children," said Jens, much to Keats's relief.

"You seem to be a man of honor, but our judge advocate will know if any of you participated in Morite crimes or associated with the Silver Serpents."

"I would expect nothing less," said Jens, and we continued on our way.

A Junedalian darted out to our far-left flank and lowered his ear to the ground in a fixed push-up position. I gawked at the spindly man and his motionless embrace of the ground. The entire party froze.

"Listening for striders," Jacques whispered, awaiting the scout's verdict. After minutes of stillness and absolute silence, the scout nodded at Jacques, and we continued.

"Where are we going?" I said.

"Junedale," said Jacques.

"You would not be shocked to discover the new name the Morites have given it," said Jens.

Jacques smiled. "What are they calling it now? Aditus ad Antrum? The Pit?"

"Dearth," said Keats, his first words in a while.

Jacques raised an eyebrow. "That's a new one."

"The Council's official line is you've all turned to cannibalism and your society is on the verge of collapse."

"That's been the Council's official line for the past dozen cycles," said Jacques. "But the new name is creative."

"Well, the war rhetoric has been on the upswing recently, and I don't know why," said Jens.

"War?" I rubbed my eyes and stopped. "Wait, wait, wait." A guard nudged me onward but Jacques raised his hand. "We all died at different points in time only to show up here for more war?"

"This place is neither Heaven nor Hell," said Jacques. "It just *is*."

"Then why us? Why are we here? Of the billions of people who have ever existed and died—why us?"

Jacques nodded and pointed to a soldier, who snapped to attention. "William, when did you transition?"

"Brandywine, 1777," he said without hesitation.

Jacques pointed at soldiers down the line.

"Kashmir, 1947."

"Stalingrad, 1943."

Jens's expression told me he had taken note of that last answer, but he remained quiet.

"All soldiers?" I said.

Jacques nodded again. "This world is full of dead warriors . . . mostly."

"I might be some nameless idiot from Pennsylvania, but I sure as shit know there are way more war dead than this. Where are the rest?"

"A question for the ages," said Jens. "We simply don't know such details."

"The universe's most shite lottery," mumbled Keats.

Jacques uncapped a leather canteen and offered it to us. "Jens is correct: Precious little is known about this world . . ." He trailed off and winced, seemingly pained by the recollection. "But Daedrina will deliver us."

"Who or what is Daedrina?" I said, recalling the name from previous discussions.

"Daedrina is mother to Irgendwo, the creator, and She who blesses all its inhabitants."

"She's doing a shit job," I said with a scoff.

Jacques furrowed his brow at my apparent blasphemy and leveled a finger at me. "It's Her children and corrupted mortal men who have turned Irgendwo into a nightmare, yet She still provides."

I pulled back a corner of my lips but couldn't bring myself to argue further.

"Been fighting for Junedale this whole time?" said Keats.

"Indeed, I have," said Jacques. He turned his attention from me, dark brown eyes lost in a surge of memories. "The Morites have cast their lot with the Children, and I cannot fathom a world molded by their evil hands."

"I've heard the war has been going particularly well for Junedale as of late," said Jens.

"We've delivered to the Morites a number of stinging defeats," said Jacques.

"Bunk, hearsay, and bullshit," said Keats. His voice slipped a little, not the proud Morite guardsman he was just a few hours ago, but he still held remnants of his delusional identity.

"You truly doubt my words after having been moments from sacrifice at the hands of your own men?" Jacques laughed and exhaled. "I don't know if you're incredibly loyal, stupid, or both."

"We all must have something in common besides war," I said and pushed my way between Jacques and Keats.

"Yes," said Jens with a smirk, "we're all the butts of a great cosmic joke or the playthings of a greater power of unimaginable cruelty."

One of the soldiers snorted at Jens. "Mother Daedrina will deliver us."

"Directly to Azurocus himself, no doubt," Jens snapped back, and the two started arguing.

I decided to sit this one out and ignored them. I refocused on my fractured memories, step by step, and tried to pull together a complete picture. A part of me still believed I lay dying in a Vietnamese jungle. A small part.

"What the fuck is that?" Keats recoiled and covered his nose. The revulsion in his voice dragged me out of my own head. Swearing in multiple languages erupted as the air wafted over us. *Holy shit, that is foul.*

Jacques brought a cloth to his nose. "Strider shit." He stepped forward and thrust his spear into the mound. The tip clanked against something, and he ejected it skyward. Kneeling with his nose still covered, he poured water over the mess until metal gleamed in the torchlight.

"Perry disappeared six days ago," said Jacques. He rolled the defiled blade over. The strider's gut had dissolved the leather handle but the engraved initials "PKG" along the silver blade survived. A wave of nausea pushed up half-digested grob in my belly, and the realization that I had narrowly avoided a similar fate made me weak.

"Poor bastard," said Jens. "If his weapon wasn't silver, his fate would have been forever a mystery."

I looked on and wondered if they were the same striders we had encountered. The smell was familiar, but the fact this pile was once a man revolted me far more than the odor itself.

"I'll tell Octavius when we return," said Jacques. "Ensure the blade is spotless." He tossed the dead man's weapon to a soldier, who retched and scrubbed away the rest of the filth.

"Who was Perry?" I said. Jens had already risked both our lives for this guy.

"A wealthy trader, judging by the personalized silver dagger," said Keats, his eyes fixed greedily on the befouled blade.

"A trader, expert archaeologist, historian, artist, arcanist—you name it. The closest thing to a da Vinci here. He loved and served Junedale," said Jens. I could see the loss hurt him.

We marched onward, silent and heads hung low; a soldier cradled the blade to his chest and prayed. The act saddened me. Prayers meant nothing on Earth, and I assumed they fell on deaf ears here too. *What exactly happens after death in a place after death?* Maybe beaming that Silver Serpent lieutenant back in the cottage condemned him to Hell, but I still felt good about it.

A familiar distant roar reverberated across the plains, and the soldiers faltered. They looked around nervously, and our formation fractured amid nervous chatter.

"Back in line," said Jacques, and he banged his shield and ordered additional scouts to scour our flanks. Slowly, the soldiers closed ranks; the formation tightened, and our vigilance tripled. Had I not already seen a strider, I would have thought these soldiers undisciplined. But now, even with fifty of us, I knew *we* were the hunted.

CHAPTER 14

A HOUSE OF TWIGS

What I do, I do for Junedale.

—OCTAVIUS LURIUS OF NOLA

DAYS OF MARCHING—AT LEAST, WHAT I thought were days—brought us sore feet, parched throats, and empty heads but, thankfully, no further surprises. The mountains loomed eternal on our right flank and the plains to our left, until the faint silhouette of a wall brushed up from the horizon. The silhouette grew into a mammoth structure that challenged the mountains themselves in its majesty, and it wasn't until we were much closer that I could make out the wisps of smoke and tangles of glowvine that encircled the city.

"Junedale's grandeur is remarkable, given its humble origins," said Jacques.

The downturned eyes and beaten faces brightened at the sight of the stone gates, and chatter picked up as we drew closer. It's amazing what home—and high walls—can do for the heart.

"A refugee camp, I believe?" said Jens and he grasped his chin.

"Yes, and unlike Mora, Junedale did not have the natural protection of the Everpeaks from the horrors out here."

"Quite remarkable it lasted," said Keats.

"A beacon of resistance to the uncivilized, the barbaric, and the evil," said Jacques, "and a sign of hope." He signaled the lead scout, who unfurled a parchment, studied it for a moment, and blew a horn in musical sequence. Within moments the gate struggled free from the ground and climbed.

"You'll be the guests of honor tonight, and our food is untainted."

"I had hoped for good food and security in Mora too, but look where that got me," I said sharply. "What do you mean *untainted*?"

Jacques laughed. "Ask your colleague Jens how Mora feeds its people."

I turned to Jens, confused, and recalled the produce on the old woman's pallets . . . and the question he had dodged.

"Aside from grob and the rare plains beast, food is summoned and centrally distributed," said Jens. "The Council carefully guards its secrets, but some say they slaughter their own citizens as offerings to the Children for a good bounty."

"First of all, what the hell do you mean *summoned*?" I said.

Jens put his finger to his nose. "Maybe *conjured* is a better word?"

"Yeah, OK."

Jacques stepped closer to me. "You'd be wise to trust the knowledge of your friend. The rules here are vastly different, and if you fail to adapt, well, you know . . ."

"No, man, I *don't* know."

"We saved your souls once, but such luck is the exception to the rule."

"Souls?" I snorted and shook my head. "You mean you saved our asses—whatever definition that holds here."

"Quite the contrary—your eternal, sentient, and cursed souls. If you perish here, your essence is set to wander this world like an oak leaf in a storm, unless you perish near a waygate and you're pulled in without first being purified."

"The waygates," said Jens, "long ago had a benevolent function in Irgendwo while in proper and caring hands."

"Like getting people the fuck out of here?" I said, half-serious and half-dismissive.

Jacques acknowledged Jens with a nod. "This man knows his history;

you may want to keep him around. And yes, these gates served as both *entry* and *exit* points for all souls."

He pointed back toward Mora. "Ek Maraine corrupted Kir Endra for his vile ends, sparking the war. When the Morites discovered they couldn't win or maintain their possession of the second gate—Kir Sol—Mog shattered it, long ago now, in a final act of malevolence."

"I can't imagine any more ends so vile than hunting children and executing people for being lazy," I said, shuddering at the fresh memory of the public executions.

Jacques paused and locked eyes with me. "Ek Maraine is the conduit through which an unfathomable evil probes this world. He used the gate for experiments in reanimation, communing with the Children, and dimensional rifting. But time is not on our side. Let's not dwell on small details."

I snorted and disengaged from Jacques. Obviously, a man who considered the murder of children a *small detail* had seen everything or cared for nothing.

But, Clyde, you killed a girl. The voice stabbed into my mind and weakened my knees. She looked up and smiled at me then vanished. *I'm so sorry.* I inhaled deeply and pressed a few thin tears from my eyes, hoping the others didn't notice.

The gate inched higher as giant iron cogs turned and ground on their axles. As the metal and stone pillars cleared the height of a man, the bustling city edged into view: glowvine, torches, candles—like Mora but bearing its own unique architecture and statues. The buildings were mostly wood, with the occasional stone and concrete reinforcements, the architecture coarser and more angular. I could only surmise the artisans and architects of this city had to scrounge for precision equipment. The statues appeared to reflect gods and goddesses of various Earth societies and were flawless.

Jacques approached Keats, cut the guardsman's crest from his uniform, and held out his hand. "Hand over your sigil."

Keats stepped back and grasped it like a child. "This has at least two ounces of gold in it!"

"You are all now de facto citizens of Junedale, and if anyone here catches you with the Council's sigil, they'll probably kill you."

"As to be expected," said Jens, and he pointed at the sigil then pointed at Jacques's hand.

"Poor in the last life, poor in this one." Keats sighed and placed the sigil in Jacques's hand with no further argument.

"Welcome to Junedale." Jacques brought us to the head of the formation, and we passed under the gate as it creaked and dribbled pebbles and dust on us.

Before the last rank had crossed the boundary, a soldier blew the horn again, and the gate crept smoothly downward as a clockwork contraption of gears spun, some whirring like circular saws while others ticked slowly and methodically like a clock. The engineering was masterful.

"Looks even sturdier than the damn mountains," I said, unsure how an army could move these stones.

"Fall in!" shouted Jacques and the soldiers fell neatly into a square before him with the utmost discipline, but their eyes betrayed a hunger for home. Jens, Keats, and I followed suit with no particular assignment in the formation. "Excellent mission. Rank and file, fall out to your homes for seven days of rest. I'll ensure the dead are honored properly and their loved ones notified. Shadebringer, fat man, and Jens, follow me. We're needed at the Hall of Antiquity."

The men and women excitedly scattered to their homes . . . the ones who had survived anyway. A subtle but familiar twang of sorrow tugged at my heart for those who had perished in the cave and their loved ones, who would be dining alone tonight.

I brushed a few layers of dust from my uniform and set off after Jacques.

• • •

"The sages of our Arcane Academy have really come through this time." The aged man's weak, raspy voice matched his decrepit physical appearance. A few singular white gossamer strands erupted from his leathery scalp, which flowed into a high forehead. His eyebrows were thick, wild, and unkempt like patches of crabgrass. I thought him more an eccentric librarian than the ruler of a city. He leaned in and squinted, studying me so closely I could see individual nose hairs. I remained still as he circled me but tracked him with my eyes.

"But forgive my rudeness, my friends. We welcome you to Junedale. I am Octavius of Nola, and you now stand within the Hall of Antiquity—a testament to our history, resolve, and prowess."

The expansive stone chamber was lined with statues of every metal and material that could be dug up or chopped down. War machines resembling catapults sat proudly in each corner. The skeleton of a strider stood as the centerpiece of the entire hall, fastened together with iron brackets and pins.

Jens glared at the skeletal beast with obvious uneasiness, as if it could spring to life at any moment. "How did you conquer this monstrosity?"

"At the cost of fifty men and nineteen women," said Octavius, "but its insight has proven invaluable, as have its teeth."

"I am familiar with the legends, Lord Octavius, and recently had the good fortune to come across a tooth myself. Will I be getting it back?"

Octavius nodded. "Yes, yes. There is something to be said for the legend, and your treasure will be returned in due time. My soldiers tell me you dispatched a Morite guard captain with the tooth and, thereafter, it glowed. Our necromancers will wish to commune with the guard captain's soul for information."

"Yes," said Jens. He looked at his hand while opening and clenching it. "I remember the burn."

"His soul is now anchored to the weapon, which could be a blessing or a curse to him, depending on how cooperative he is with our spiritual interrogators."

"Being stuck in this shithole would be a terrible fate," I said. "No offense."

"Well, there's no alternative. The Kir Sol waygate was destroyed, and there's no way to safely pass through the remaining waygate in Mora while it's in their possession."

Jens stepped into the shadow of the skeletal maw. The beast could have swallowed all of us in a single bite, but I couldn't understand how such narrow legs supported the giant bodies. "These things can savage your mind," he said.

"Even now, it sometimes speaks to us but only in dreams and whispers, its soul weakened through the ages," said Octavius. "But let us talk of more immediate and pressing matters."

He clapped his hands and turned to me. "So, you're the shadebringer in our sages' visions."

"Whatever that means, but yeah, I suppose so. Jens here saved my ass." I pointed to the surly German, hoping to deflect some attention.

"We honored the prophecy well," said Jacques.

"Indeed you did, Commander Pariseau, and with your victory we have a unique opportunity to strike a fatal blow to the Council of Mora."

"So, what does this have to do with me?" A rising heat in my collar—a notion of unease I'd had since I was a child—pressed my attention, my suspicion, to the men.

"A spirit of special power, the *shade* as we call it, chooses to bless this world when a chosen vessel arrives—something that happens with incredible rarity."

Octavius directed my attention to a grandiose painting, a cracked fresco that adorned the wall behind the strider. Lush and vibrant colors intermingled to depict a woman in full plate armor slashing a multi-headed serpent. Her hands of flesh and metal melded with that of an apparition, and, together, they clutched a massive sword—a *Zweihander* as the Germans called it.

"This is Uta the Great, the first shadebringer of Irgendwo, vanquishing Baledoccus to reclaim the world."

"With the shade, she was unstoppable," said Jacques. "Or so they say. This conflict predates even Mog."

My intuition served me well. The heat rising in my neck turned to white-hot rage, and I shook. "So, I'm denied a normal death, dragged into this nightmarish, barren, cold pit of a world, and expected to act as a secret weapon because some mysterious spirit *chose* me?"

"That's the short of it," said Keats, and he chuckled, no doubt enjoying every second of this.

Prick.

"Fuck that," I said. "I'm done fighting for other people over things I couldn't care less about. I tried to be a hero once already but only ended up killing a young girl and the guys around me. I'm a fucking nobody. This shade thing has clearly made a mistake."

Jacques's mouth fell open.

Octavius raised his hand. "You don't understand the nature of this life—this conflict—young man," he said, voice waxing ominous.

He walked to a strategic battle map of extraordinary artisan design and detail. Stone and metal figurines dotted the large sand and stone map.

"Ever since the madman Mog and his cursed Council took control of Mora and transformed it into a malignant death cult bent on extending the domain of the Children to our world, war has raged between our cities."

He removed a handful of metallic figurines that looked like Junedalians, I think Jens had called them, from the map and dropped his head.

"Though long dead, Mog charged his most trusted—and most evil—lieutenant, Ek Maraine, with subjugating us, but we have fought them to a bloody draw in every corner of this world."

He cleared his throat and tossed the figurines away from the map. " . . .Until recently."

Jacques's jaw bulged, and his eyes darkened as if he had taken a personal insult. "My lord, we have fought them away at every engagement! Junedale cannot be harmed with the Roux at the ready!"

"True, Commander Pariseau. As long as the blood of the Roux flows through Junedale, we shall not want for security, but our losses have been great and the Morites ceaseless. It's only a matter of time before our veins run dry."

"Well, that sounds like your fucking problem, not mine," I said before Jacques could respond.

A collective gasp went up among the guests.

"I see in you a good man with a radiant heart," said Octavius, "and I understand your misgivings, but much more than you can now comprehend is incumbent on our success."

"What's this *our* shit?" I said to the old man and shook my head. "This is a war between two cities I couldn't care less about."

"You don't underst—"

I threw my arms up before Octavius could finish. "I damn well got it. Check. Roger. Ten-four, good buddy. I'm the fabled *shadebringer.* I can help you win this war. But I didn't ask for this, and this sure as hell isn't my war." I coughed and cleared my throat. I had a point to make, and I was only going to make it once. "I just want to live out whatever time I have here and move on or disappear or whatever."

"*Live* is a poor word choice," said Jens, "because we simply exist here at best."

"Save the metaphysical bullshit for someone else, Kraut. I'm out of here."

Jacques stepped in front of me. "Insolent fool," he said through pursed lips, and he cocked a hand at me. The old man motioned to him and, slowly, he lowered it. Lucky man.

"You're free to do as you wish," said Octavius.

I looked at him with rising suspicion.

Jacques stood in the doorway, shoulders and back tight, ready to fight. "Lord Octavius, certainly you don't mean to—"

"Yes, I do," he said and bowed his head again. "If I were to mock the free will of this young soul, then our own ideals would be moot. We would be no better than the Morites."

"My lord, the needs of so many rest on this one individual. He cannot be per—"

"And if need be, we will wait on the coming of another shadebringer. We will persevere no matter how long it takes."

Lord Octavius sealed his decision with a wave. Jacques stood still as the guards opened the chamber doors and parted from the exit. I hastily walked toward it, glancing around with my head on a swivel. Something didn't feel right.

"Get the fuck outta my way, Frenchie," I said, squaring up with him. He glared at me with the most hateful eyes I'd seen since boot camp, but he stepped aside.

"Please see Sergeant Robbins to his new quarters, Commander Pariseau."

"Quarters?" Jacques's voice pitched higher.

"Yes. Quarters," said Lord Octavius over his shoulder as he strolled toward the other exit. "Our blessed Perry won't be needing them anymore. And speaking of Perry, see to it his blade is entombed in the Crypt of the Lion; he's earned the honor."

The other guests looked on in confusion. Jacques glanced down at Perry's partially digested weapon and then up to me. I couldn't tell which disgusted him more.

CHAPTER 15

NOT QUITE LIMBO

Oh, these earthen creatures are so unworthy of Mother's regard: foolish, conniving, cruel, selfish, all under the guise of favored creations. We, at least, do not wear a righteous façade. Come, we have much to discuss.

—AZUROCUS, FIRST OF THE DAMNED, MOG'S GREAT VISION

JACQUES BOOTED THE DOOR OPEN, and it crashed against something sturdy behind it. I followed him into the cottage, shouldering my pack. Simple wooden furniture filled most of the quarters, and a small bed with a single pillow fit neatly in the corner. Ashes sat beneath a kettle in the fireplace.

"Your new quarters, as deemed fit by Lord Octavius," said Jacques. He struck the keys down on a chest of drawers.

"Very kind of him. I am grateful." I wasn't in the mood to fight, and besides, this was a pretty sweet deal, and I didn't want to blow it.

Without warning, Jacques seized my collar and slammed me against the door. The entire cottage shook, and the thick pane of glass rattled on the sill.

I coughed as the wind flew out of me—the sonofabitch had some strength.

"He sees something in you I do not," said Jacques as his jaw bulged and knuckles whitened. "Every day here is hell—our hell—and you, you petty foolish man, are, in some sick twist of fate, our way out."

He gripped my jaw and twisted my head toward the dead light beaming through the window. "Two hundred years, Shadebringer. Two hundred years of that. Look at it. Away from all I held dear in the times I knew."

His eyes spilled more rage with every word, and I thought he would kill me if he kept speaking. My heart raced and muscles drew taught ready to fight.

"And I will see to it your duty is fulfilled." He released my collar and stepped away to Perry's desk.

"What about my companions?" I adjusted my clothing and tried to change the subject. I gave the man a pass for saving our lives earlier, but if he put his hands on me again, I'd break his jaw.

"What of them?" Jacques shot back. "They'll be given refugee status, temporary quarters, and, eventually, permanent quarters if they outlive the other conscripts. Our victorious military campaigns do come at a cost."

"Conscripts?" I didn't like the sound of that.

"Ah, well, you didn't think you gentlemen were going to stay here for free, did you? As Octavius said, our numbers run thin, and times, indeed, are desperate. Perhaps you now see the inevitability of your fate? Whether you like it or not, Irgendwo has you."

"And I have Irgendwo." I sniffed at him, a flint of my disdain.

"Indeed, such is the nature of living under the Council's yoke." Jacques made his way to the door. "You will report with the conscripts to the central barracks in five days. If you fail to do so, I'll kill you myself—shadebringer or not."

"See you in five days," I said.

He slammed the door and strode off.

"Fuckin' prick." I spat at the door.

After my nerves settled, I found some flint to relight the fire and sat at the dead man's desk, which was still covered in papers, books, and stationery. The new accommodations were Spartan, like Jens's place, but still comfortable.

A coil of glowvine cast warped light and shadows over Perry's desk as Junedalians outside strolled past. Among the stacks of paper, notes, and lists, I noticed a small journal covered in odd symbols. Sliding the papers away, I cracked the journal open; it smelled of old paper and grob. French handwriting in various hues of ink stretched across the crinkled pages, interspersed with runic symbols and characters from languages I didn't recognize.

There's something to this. I pulled the drawer open to store away the journal. Coins of every size and color slid forward. "Huh," I muttered and scooped up a handful. Strange things. I couldn't make sense of their value, aside from the familiar Arabic numerals. *Oh well, I hope they spend.*

"This one's on you, Perry," I said and walked out of the cottage, pockets jangling.

* * *

NOT QUITE LIMBO.

The letters were painted bold on thick wooden blocks and framed with glowvine. Two detailed mug carvings sat on either side of the letters—my kind of dive. I stopped and peered through the window. A thick crowd of drunken Junedalians shuffled by, whistling and hooting, strangely mirthful, given the circumstances.

"Aw, best bar in the Six Points!" said a tall African man.

"Olga's Mughouse is better, I think," said his companion as she wheedled him forward.

"Stout or bust." An Asian man pointed into the bar with authority. "Superb stuff."

"I'm convinced!" I said.

The crowd cheered my decision, and I pushed open the saloon-style doors and, oh baby, home sweet home. Colorful bottles stood before a large mirror and cast prismatic sheens on the polished countertop. Wooden stools, some cracked and broken and others without defect, surrounded the bar. I grasped a handful of the dead man's coins and brought them to the counter with a clang.

The bartender, a youthful man wearing his best attempt at formal attire, looked at the coins then up at me. He cocked his head a little and then nodded like he had solved a riddle. "You must be the shadebringer everyone's talking about."

I let out an obnoxious sigh. I really didn't want to engage in this horseshit again but a bartender was a bartender. "That popular already?"

He grabbed a mug from under the bar and ran a cloth around it. "Well, no, but anybody who would come in here and plop that much cash down is either new around here or completely insane. And I know who the crazies are."

"Smartass," I said but I already liked the guy. He took a single coin, dropped ten smaller ones in its place, and then took two of those.

"Honesty is the best policy. For the amount I took, you can get the best of anything I have."

"Well, in that case, get me one and get him one." I pointed at an elderly man sitting at the end of the bar. His glassy eyes reflected an empty mug as he sat motionless and unblinking.

The bartender leaned over his arm. "Henry's one of the *touched* ones," he whispered, trying not to look at the old man. "He refuses to accept his death. Says he's waiting for the missus to return from Atlanta."

I thought for a moment and shrugged. *What difference does it make? Man needs a drink.* "Then get him your best, too." I pushed some smaller coins across the bar.

He sighed and nodded and poured us mugs of a grimy brown liquid that looked like unfiltered percolated coffee. When the heads settled on our drinks, he slid them to us, but the old man sparsely acknowledged the gift. Eyes still vacant, he grabbed the mug and took to nursing it.

"Told ya," the bartender said and returned to his dishes.

Maybe a bit too curious for my own good, I strode to the other side of the bar and plopped down next to the old man. "Clyde Robbins." I gulped down a mouthful of the drink and extended my hand.

Immediately, the flavor hit me: *Bitter with hints of something unknowable. De-fucking-lightful.*

"Henry David Rollins III," he muttered and ignored my handshake.

I pulled my hand away slowly. "What are you doing around these parts, Henry?"

"Waiting for my wife, Belinda. She's the delicate type and prone to fits of cough in this cold weather, so I need to be ready to leave as soon as she arrives."

"How long have you been waiting, Henry?"

The old man's eyes edged down to his lifeless wristwatch. Curly gray wires of hair sprouted from his wrist and tugged against the watch's band as he rotated his arm.

"Oh, about three hours, I reckon," he said.

I patted him on the back and returned to my seat.

The bartender returned and leaned in. "Ninety-five years," he said and withdrew again to the sink.

I shuddered at the thought of being stuck here for a week, let alone a hundred fucking years, and buried my nose in the mug.

"Pretty good." I tilted the brew back and guzzled the liquid. Ghost booze went down extra smooth. I tossed a few more coins on the bar, and the second drink arrived with a smile. Then the third. Fourth. Fifth. Sixth. Ninth. Tenth. Subtle guilt tugged at me, building in my stomach with every mug, but I was determined to drown it. What good was money if it wasn't getting spent?

"What's your story?" I slurred the words in the general direction of the bartender, who moved in fuzzy circles.

"Oh, just a humble bartender trying to make it in the afterlife. Thankfully, the Junedalians let me pursue my passion here." He swished a rag around a dirty mug with a thoughtful glint in his eye. "I was in the second group eschewed from the Kir Endra waygate by Mog's legions after he seized power, so I figured I was going to be here a while."

"How did you die?" I leaned over my drink. "Lemme guess . . . landmine?"

He cocked an eyebrow and narrowed his eyes at me like I'd just made a pass at his wife. "*An arrow*, like many of the older souls here, but it's quite rude to ask someone about their demise when you've only known them for—what—three hours now?"

"Fuck, don't be so sensitive," I shot back. "I'm your best fucking customer." I pointed out that his only other customer was a mute bum, and I was spotting his tab anyway.

"Sheesh, nobody ever said anything about the shadebringer being a foul-mouthed drunk," said the bartender.

"Jesus liked his wine, didn't he?" I laughed and knocked my drink over. "Fuck, gimme another one."

"You're cut off." He folded his arms and puffed up his chest.

What the fuck was this? High school?

"Prophecy nothing—I ain't doin' shit until I'm good and drunk." Coughs and laughter mixed with drool.

"Well, for some reason"—the bartender frowned and crept back, no doubt an expert at reading drunken body language—"somebody chose you to bear the shade, and there's no escaping that."

I attempted to respond, but the words were blocked somewhere between my brain and my throat. The room accelerated, and I crashed from the stool onto the lumpy floor. The bartender lurched over the bar top, and all three copies of him sneered at my sad, helpless ass.

"They can't handle it like they used to," said the bartender.

"No sir-ee," said Henry.

CHAPTER 16

REFLECTIONS

Shhhh! Curse you. Don't speak so loud. But yes, indeed, yes . . . The interrogators believe they have uncovered the whereabouts of Mog's rectory. Can you imagine what artifacts it holds?

—PERCIVAL PLUMM, CHIEF OF CUSTODIAL DUTIES, MORA INQUISITION CHAMBERS

CRUSHING HEADACHES WERE NOT unique to the first life. I awoke nauseated, my skull in a vise, with fractured memories of the previous night trickling back.

"Oh, shit." I sat up, and a blanket slid off my face.

"It drinks like a light pilsner but hits like a barley wine," said Keats. He tapped his gut and lifted a canteen to his lips. "Your mincers were bigger than your belly, but practice makes perfect."

"I guess you got me home somehow?" My voice ran an octave lower, and my mouth was parched, full of cinnamon and sand.

"Well, not exactly *home* by our standards but to your place of domicile for the moment—yes." He finished the canteen and dragged a sleeve across his mouth. "Please forgive the abrasions on your back and head.

I had to drag you. Also, try not to gain any more notoriety. It does tend to stick."

"Gee, thanks. People already hate me because I won't jump into another war. What's a little drunken mischief gonna do?"

Keats shook his head. "I don't claim to know what's at stake here. I was just some nameless Tommy in the Council's service. But for some reason, Lord Octavius has faith in you. That says a lot."

"If the Council of Mora is so goddamn evil, why did you serve them?"

"A roof over my head and three meals a day . . . and maybe the opportunity to move onto the next life if I was patient enough," he said and opened a small red book. "I've never been part or party to their alleged evil though, and I'd never believed any of the cultist nonsense."

"Now you do?"

Keats shrugged. "Doesn't matter what I believe. I'm nobody. Don't have a job, a home, or a future anymore. Lots of people here are in the same boat. Maybe the prophecy is all we have left."

"Prophecies are bullshit," I said. "They don't account for free will."

Keats scratched his head and ignored my comment. "So, how exactly did you perish, Sergeant Robbins?"

"I'd like to say an ambush." I tried to recall the battle, and my memories stirred, fuzzy, distant, and strange.

"But?" He looked up from the book.

Then suddenly it hit me. "But it was probably our own artillery. Our LT called a fire mission in the heat of battle. He screwed the coordinates. Well, I screwed the coordinates. I got us killed." Short reels of the battle returned: Lead whistling through the air and wood falling . . . the young private mauled beyond recognition by an antiaircraft round.

"Ah, yes—artillery," said Keats, and he brought a hand to his chest, a graceful thespian on the Globe's stage. "*Ultima ratio regum.*" The final argument of kings.

I squinted at him as the glowvine worsened my headache. "It's farm boys and miners who do the arguing."

"Indeed. You're not the jackass I took you for."

"Do you Brits think you've cornered the market on brains?"

"No, but you Yanks haven't even a business plan."

We shared a quick laugh, but I retreated from the painful jolts. I rubbed my forehead. *Maybe this guy isn't so bad after all?* "So, Keats—how did you die?" I took notice of the red book, and he pocketed it.

"Oh, well, y-y-you know. Nothing special. A bullet or shell or something. Been a while, you know?"

His stutter piqued my curiosity, but I recalled the bartender's warning and decided not to press the issue.

"So," he continued, "we'll be seeing you again at the barracks, I hope?"

"Barracks? Oh, yes. I'll be there. Not much choice otherwise." I sank into bed as he walked to the door.

"Oh wait," I said with a start and another jolt to the head. "Do you speak French or know anyone who does?"

"Oui," he said, and I climbed from the bed and removed Perry's journal from the drawer. Keats examined it and shrugged. "Should we really be reading his personal journal?"

"The man was an explorer and whatnot. Maybe there's valuable information in there."

"Market cornered," he said and swept across Perry's writing.

CYCLE 400 AND 11 DAYS

Rumors of the cave network appear to be true. The flapping gums of some Morite bureaucrat have proven more valuable than ten battlefield victories. Oh, what horrors that poor Hollow must have endured with the Morite interrogators. The depravity of the human heart, if the Morites remain any bit human, never ceases to amaze me. Regardless, Junedale must capitalize on this information, and we must act with haste. The Morites may be a grim and bloodied lot, but they take their artifacts seriously. If this is truly Mog's rectory, the knowledge therein could turn the tide of the war.

CYCLE 400 AND 13 DAYS

The Everpeaks are deep and mysterious and have been home to countless mystics, recluses, and beasts throughout the ages. Of the human dwellers, some find the squabbles of Junedale and Mora to be tiresome, and they extricate themselves to obscurity, while others are forced there as exiles or criminals. I had occasion to spend six days among the rocks on a prior expedition, and the conditions were treacherous, and how anyone can survive there is beyond my understanding . . . Well, of those who do survive. Further, how a low-level bureaucrat came across such information stretches my credulity, but I believe this lead must be explored to the very end.

CYCLE 400 AND 17 DAYS

Octavius finds my expeditions to be superfluous as of late, and convincing him to fund them has become more difficult. Naturally, I find his lack of faith troublesome, given the history of my labors. Who excavated the Stone of Zeal? Who translated Azurocus's final words to Mog? Who discovered the formula for sapfire? Oh, but I stroke my own ego. In all honesty, my recent undertakings have yielded little and cost much. But ripe harvests come with patience, and God help us if the Morites seize the initiative.

CYCLE 400 AND 19 DAYS

Excellent! I can barely put pen to page in my excitement! Lord Octavius has agreed to fund this expedition, despite significant objection from his advisors. Therefore, it must be fruitful; I must be successful.

I have been assigned a scout named Pewter to assist me, but truthfully, I'd rather be alone. Others tend to become liabilities in such dangerous environs, and word of Morite infiltrators has engendered a strong paranoia in me. Oh, such woe to Junedale if I were to make a fantastic discovery only to have an aide slit my throat and slink off to Mora. Peh! Now my mind just wanders. Regardless, we leave in the morrow, and I must be ready. The physical demands of the Everpeaks are extreme, and I am not young.

CYCLE 400 AND 23 DAYS

The entrance to the caverns was exactly as the rumors described, but someone long ago had gone out of their way to conceal it. Thankfully, a sharp ear for wind tone differentials saved the day. Indeed, one must simply listen to reveal life's (death's) mysteries.

Pewter and I spent a good hour carefully unpacking the stones that blocked the entrance. When we walked in, I knew immediately that we were the first in ages to enter. I was somewhat tempted to rebuild the stack, at least partially, in the event that another expedition came upon our discovery. But no, with what time we have, we must begin exploring.

CYCLE 400 AND 25 DAYS

This labyrinth is maddening. Its depth goes far beyond any archaeological site I have ever explored. The corridors twist and turn back on themselves as if the whole point was to mislead the occupants. Thankfully, we brought a burgeoning supply of torches to see us through, especially since I have a terrible habit of stopping to copy every new symbol I see etched into the stone. And there are many. They're really quite beautiful, but the etymology is completely abstruse.

Another confounding situation arose today. Pewter, whose disposition was quite agreeable at the outset of our journey, has become quite unpleasant. Curt, irritable, and sarcastic, basic conversation with the man is a chore. Further, his own idiosyncrasies have slowed our pace, for he insists there are traps everywhere and oft falls to his hands and knees to examine each fissure in the rock.

CYCLE 400 AND 26 DAYS

Today, we rested—or at least tried to. Having found a small patch of soft sand, we settled down and torched some grob. All seemed right again until Pewter began talking to himself. What has thrust him into the halls of madness, I know not, but his gibbering has my eyes open at all times. I am tempted to seize his blade if he ever falls asleep, but the consequences of failure are too high.—not just for me but for all of Junedale.

CYCLE 400 AND ???

Pewter went mad. I huddle in the darkness after barely escaping his blade. I am loath to even scratch these few words out for fear of alerting him. Now I wait.

CYCLE 400 AND ???

I forced my body and dwindling supplies into a crevasse and pulled in all my loose clothing. For what seemed like a day, the madman stalked these cramped rocky halls, screaming and speaking in tongues. I could only cower in the darkness and hope he not take notice of me, as he could carve me to bits in my hiding place with little recourse.

After extinguishing his voice, he moved through the halls silently, and there were moments he stood mere feet from me—close enough to smell the acrid grob sweat pouring from him. He made these circuits many times until he abruptly vanished, and it is only now, after many hours of silence, that I have the nerve to strike up a torch. Should I fall victim to this lunatic for such a trite act, let it be known I died a brave fool rather than a slinking coward . . . if I am ever found.

CYCLE 400 AND ???

Poor Pewter. I found him slunk against a wall with terrible wounds that appeared to be self-inflicted. Worse, he was still alive when I found him, recalling nothing of his preceding madness. I could only wait by his side until his hour arrived, and for this, he was grateful.

Alas, I suspect the Children are responsible. I remember tales from long ago of their power within these mountains. How they can simply seize a man's mind and twist it in such a manner is beyond my wisdom, but, thankfully, I was spared.

CYCLE 400 AND ???

I have been in near complete darkness for about a week, assuming my gestalt has remained intact, and I have nothing to show for it. These warrens must have something to bear. Why else would their creators have gone through the trouble of sealing them? By all accounts, we were the first to see them since their creators stacked the last rock centuries ago. Now, nothing but decorative stone walls and low ceilings. This endeavor is maddening. How can I dare return to Octavius with naught but tales of a dead scout and pretty drawings?

I fear my days of exploration are at an end.

CYCLE 400 AND ???

A moment of weakness, I admit. But mere hours after my last entry, I stumbled upon the answer. Rather, it hissed at me. Stopping to rest for a moment, my torch set an arrow painted in blood above me to a foul sizzle, which drew my attention to a nondescript stone. Pressing it, the wall receded into the ground, revealing a hidden mausoleum. Indeed, Pewter had scrawled the answer in his own blood! Thus, the question arises: How did he discover this trigger in the pitch black? I surmise the answer is diabolical and confirms my suspicion. The Children are behind this.

Such a realization set me to greater vigilance, as nothing good comes from their intercession. Thence my survey of the stale room proceeded slowly as I tapped here and there for traps until I felt safe.

Glyphs adorn the walls in tight patchwork, beautiful and detailed. They show no signs of decay, despite their presumed age, and they appear to tell a story of creation and early Irgendwo. New arrivals would arrive through the Kir Sol waygate into the ready arms of the Elated—the covenant of women and men who settled new souls. When they had achieved Daedrina's absolution, they would rejoin eternity through Kir Endra. Oh, what a time! Such beauty. Such mercy for the unnatural dead. Until he arrived.

From what I can tell, these glyphs long predate the rise of Mog. How the fiend procured this beautiful venue for his evil undertakings is beyond my understanding. Alas, I doubt the answer is here, but it matters not.

The last item to examine is an ornate sarcophagus. When I finish copying the glyphs, I'll attempt to open it.

CYCLE 400 AND ???

Mog's very words. The words of commune. A scroll of purification—in his own hand. Incredible. I must get this discovery to Octavius.

"That's it?" I said.

Keats nodded and flicked through the journal. "After the last entry, he tore out the pages."

"That's odd. What was he trying to hide?"

"Obviously, whatever Mog had recorded. They called him Mog the Mad for a reason."

"The namesake for the council that governs Mora?"

"Indeed, the first thaumaturgist of Irgendwo and the one who promised to transform this world into a paradise greater than Heaven itself. Lofty promises, if I do say so myself, and of course, not without sacrifice."

"Sure, buddy, three hots and a cot."

"A man has to do what he has to do." Keats scoffed and looked away. "The meals were never hot, and sleep was never sound, but it was better than scrabbling for subsistence in the mountains or that deathtrap Taiga."

"Deathtrap? I didn't see a single living thing."

"Because everything alive is killed and eaten by everything dead. Can't really explain how you made it out."

Nor could I. The stirring mound and rotting hand still haunted me. Maybe fleeing into the woods was the best possible decision at the time. In fact, I knew it was. I had learned to trust my intuition and the guiding voice, whoever it may have been.

Keats cleared his throat, drawing me from my thoughts, and he squinted into Perry's journal. "Thus, it is written: *Ille qui nos omnes servabit.*" He snapped the journal shut. "Looks like Latin—definitely not his handwriting either."

The words struck me, and I missed a breath. My mind returned to Vietnam beneath the waning light of late afternoon. I remembered the distinct rough feel of the folded note in my pocket. I remembered opening it as the 1-5-5 rounds whistled down. And I remembered the words—the exact words—Keats had just spoken.

"Sounds like Latin," I said in a daze. "Thus it is written . . . what?"

"Afterlife's mysteries," said Keats with a chuckle. "Perry was an eccentric genius and guarded his work carefully. I'm not sure who else could have written this." He yawned and stretched his corpulent frame upward and out. "I should be getting back to my quarters."

"Yeah, I guess. And thank you, Reginald."

Keats smiled and handed me the journal, and I placed it back in the drawer. "Stick to the pilsner," he said and left.

Oozing back under the covers, I replayed the words in my mind. How did they link Claude and Perry?

My mind raced, and ol' Henry's wrinkled face faded in. "Train'll be here anytime now."

CHAPTER 17

A LOST CAUSE

The common Hollow had little interest in the conflict between Junedale and Mora until Ek Maraine himself decreed they all be purged from their society. For what reason, you may ask? We simply don't know. But it is our duty to shelter these strange refugees even if they do pose a threat to our own wellbeing.

—GENERAL (RET.) TAIWO ADAMOLEKUN,
THIRD COMMANDER OF THE ROUX

I HAD ABSOLUTELY NO INTENTION of reporting to the barracks. I hated to let these people down, but as far as I was concerned, this was not my battle. I'd done enough fighting and dying for ten lifetimes, and I wasn't about to relive it. Kind of fucked up how the human soul strove for conflict long after it should have known better, but I couldn't say I was surprised.

It seemed I'd managed to alienate myself from two cities already, though in my defense, the circumstances of the first had been beyond my control and understanding. What would I have been doing if my transition to this world had been more . . . *normal*? Perhaps slinging shit in the sewers, as Keats said, but it was probably still better than being an outlaw. Anyway, these were my circumstances now, and I had only a day left before everyone figured me out. Fuck 'em. Jacques wanted my head on a pike anyway.

I needed to buy up enough supplies to survive on the plains and make it somewhere less populated. I'd probably need a weapon too, and I had not seen anything even resembling a rifle, so it looked like it would be a sword or some shit. Also, aside from grob, I wasn't exactly sure what folks ate here to survive; plants and animals were nowhere to be seen, aside from weeds and trees. I might as well have been on another planet, one without a fucking sun—just the same old pale gray nastiness.

It was sad it had come to this. I thought I'd have been at least deserving of proper judgment after my death. Instead, I was stuck in some in-between reality with two medieval cities to choose from. Shit luck. I'd miss these quarters though, because it was only downhill from here.

From what I could tell, Perry was a good dude who met a bad fate. Oh well—that was the common theme to life and the afterlife, it seemed.

I was going to miss my new bar too, even though the bartender was kind of a dick.

* * *

I threw on Perry's spare clothing and set out early with my remaining coins. Shop after shop, I browsed, haggled, and collected items I imagined essential for survival. My coin reserves dwindled as I filled my pack with food and water rations, rope, a sleeping bag, climbing equipment, an archaic magnifying glass, and what passed for medicines in this weird place. The final stop was the blacksmith.

I walked into the open-air shop with a glowing forge set in the center. Armaments of every variety drooped from the racks, walls, and stands dotting the room. A bulky olive-skinned man drenched in sweat sat at the edge of the forge and hammered away. I approached him and waved.

"What can I get for this?"

He gawked at the coins and back up at me with a confused look on his face. "Marg," he said.

"What's a Marg?" I tilted my head slightly—an old habit my mom said made me look like a beagle.

"Marg," he said again and returned to his work. I stood for a few moments, unsure what to say, but to him I no longer existed.

Another man hurried from the indoor section of the shop and waved. "Oh, don't let Marg put you off."

"Marg," said Marg.

"My name is Till, proprietor of Junedale Iron Works, and this fine young Norseman is Marg, my apprentice, although I may lose him to the legions if there aren't enough recruits this season. He has a *different* way of doing things, but his skills will rival mine soon enough."

"Marg," said Marg and he smiled a little. At least he understood us.

Relieved, I flashed my remaining coins at Till. "What can I get for this?"

"Eh." Till scratched his chin. "Let's see." He moved about the stall and pawed through the racks. Swords, maces, hammers, halberds, spears, and other weapons clanked as he moved them about, occasionally pausing to size me up. "Here we go." He grasped a short sword and handed it to me. The hard leather grip sat cool and snug in my grip, and the blade sliced through the air with ease. "Marg's finest work," said Till with a smile.

"Marg." He bowed slightly.

"How much?" I presented the coins in my open palm and hoped for the best.

Till thought for a moment and plucked all but a few away. "Fair?"

"I suppose." I feigned disappointment but didn't know one way or the other if he had ripped me off.

"Special deal for the shadebringer," said Till. He winked and walked back into the shop.

I secured the weapon and hoisted my pack, wondering how my reputation had already spread so far. "Have a fine day, Marg."

"Marg."

• • •

I set out on the main drag toward the city gates long after the citizens had retired to their homes. Glowvine lit the empty streets and houses with a strange beauty I could not ignore, and I often found myself pausing to trace the lights. A simple candle imbued many feet of it, but the torches put it to such radiance that even the alleys glowed. I pulled the collar up on my coat and adjusted a cap so it sat low on my brow. My backpack jangled with every step.

Stone buildings flanked me during my lonesome escape; no doubt they would stare down on me in disgust if they possessed any sentience. Some cast dancing shadows onto the streets as their occupants milled about the windows, while others remained dark. As I plodded down a slight decline, I noticed one had no windows. It stood taller than the others, with marble steps that climbed from the street to a spacious landing, and I stopped. As I scrutinized the unique building, I noticed colorful chalk racing across the base and down the steps—children's artwork. Odd forms, some monstrous, in pastel pink and green hues breathlessly depicting a battle scene. Or perhaps a hunt? I found this interesting since I hadn't seen a single animal aside from the striders. I had to see more.

I ascended the stairs to the landing, also covered in chalk, paintings, and a few scattered toys. Large wooden doors reinforced with iron bars stood as the only entrance. Someone had designed it with as much interest in keeping something inside as keeping others out. A stone slit next to the door shined. *Donations Appreciated!* etched in about twelve languages adorned the stone beside the slit. Reaching into my pockets, I gathered my remaining coins and stuffed them in.

"My word!" said a woman from inside the building. Little footsteps pattered to the doors, which were cracked open to the farthest extent the bars would allow. "Thank you for such generosity." She pressed her face to the narrow crack. A red blindfold covered her eyes, but she beamed and tittered.

"No problem." I admired her youthful beauty, somewhat glad she couldn't see me smile or flush. Or could she? "Is this a school or something?"

"It's a Hollows' orphanage," she said. "The only one in existence."

"You have some serious dedication."

"This, you mean?" She ran her finger over the blindfold cinched tightly across her eyes and brow. "This is nothing. Our matriarch removed her own eyes, and soon I will make the sacrifice."

I shuddered. "Why the hell would you do that?"

"To better see, of course." She blew me a kiss, waved, and yanked the doors shut.

I stood in silence, wishing I had a few more coins just to chat a little longer. The woman intrigued me, and I was more than curious as to how she found meaning in this place . . . and how she got here. She didn't seem the warrior type, but then again, neither did I.

Officially penniless, I proceeded down the steps and back onto the main drag.

You can't escape your fate. A feeble voice invaded my thoughts, similar to the strider on the plains but much weaker.

"Maybe, but there's no harm in trying," I said aloud as the gates drew closer. I widened my steps, exhilarated and fearful. It was winter again, and I was about to hurl a sinker at another old man's house.

I know you evaded my brothers and sisters before, but such good fortune is not guaranteed twice.

I looked over my shoulder to the Hall of Antiquity. Shadows of the skeletal strider danced against brilliant stained-glass windows, bathed in the light of the torches within. A tickling sensation rose in the back of my throat, and, drawing a deep breath, I coughed into the crook of my arm, but a hoarse bark escaped easily. Man, what a rattle. I nervously looked about to see if anyone had heard me.

Nor is poor fortune. I thought the retort clearly, as clearly as psychic gymnastics go, and deep laughter filled my mind—an unusual sensation.

A stubborn fool by any standard, but a good, strong soul nonetheless. The Council has quite a force to contend with. The beast's eloquence surprised me; it was a far throw from the horrors I had met on the plains. But I didn't have time for conversation. I turned to continue my journey but felt a gentle tug on my pack.

"That damned strider has mellowed in his old age."

Startled, I reached for my blade and drew it slightly. Octavius, dressed in a simple gray robe, stared up at me.

"You see, in my younger years, I would have carved you in two for desertion, but living here for so long has taught me a thing or two about the value of life."

"You mean the value of a weapon. I've lived and died by the sword once, and I'm not repeating the mistake." I wavered—not from fear but guilt.

"Most here share your sorrow." He folded his hands behind him and sighed. "This was once a place of second chances, a place to edify the soul before greater things." He peered beyond the gates into blackened clouds that gathered far away, the first sign of rain I'd seen. "Now, Irgendwo is a battlefield, one or two victories from becoming another hell."

"Your hell or someone else's?"

Octavius smirked a little and looked down. "Tell me, Shadebringer Robbins, what do you want?"

I tried to answer but had nothing. The question caught me off guard, but I doubted the old man truly cared about what I had to say. Hell, what *did* I want? Having spent my life as a drifter with a penchant for violence, where did that leave me now?

"I haven't seen my family in fifteen hundred years," he said. Lightning forked across the sky, and, seconds later, thunder grumbled. "Nor has anyone else since the time they arrived."

My mind wrapped itself in knots trying to fathom such a measure of time, let alone suffering through every second of it. And Octavius was just one man. What of the countless others here, those who would end up here—what of *me*? I looked from the storm to him, a proud, dignified, and wise man whose haggard eyes retained a dim light. He too was tired of fighting. Yet he persisted and, given enough time and enough battles, would simply perish, as was the fate of all warriors. Then what?

"What do you want from me?" I finally said.

"Become hope." He placed a hand on my shoulder. "Become even the smallest candle in this darkness, and you will have our eternal gratitude."

I gazed beyond the gates and imagined what awaited me. The endless dust, the striders, the solitude—there was nothing for me out there. And

I was tired of drifting, of being alone. I had sought meaning in every aspect of my own narrow existence; perhaps now was the time to seek it for the good of others?

As the winds picked up and the clouds rolled toward us, I turned from the storm and walked with Octavius toward my quarters.

"Training begins tomorrow, bright and early," he said.

"Bright and early."

CHAPTER 18

OLD HABITS

Heute kannst du nicht weglaufen.

—UNTEROFFIZIER HELMUT STOSS,
SCHARFSCHÜTZE

"I TOLD YOU THE COWARD WOULD flee at the first opportunity."

I opened my eyes, body cold and weary from restless sleep. I recognized the French accent outside my quarters and jumped from the sheets. "I'm up!" The icy air tormented me as I scrambled for my equipment and Jacques pounded on the door.

"Get your ass out here!" A second unfamiliar man sounded off among the murmurs of others. Charging to the door half-naked, I flung it open and pleaded for more time.

Jacques stood in full armor at the head of the formation. "Well, you've failed your first task, but at least you didn't flee." He stared at me, single upturned lip and slanted eyebrow like every French caricature I'd ever seen. "Put on your uniform, and get out here. Training begins today."

I nodded, retreated into my quarters, threw on the rest of my uniform, and grabbed my sword. After kicking the escape provisions beneath the bed, I ran outside.

"Why do you have a sword? Is that one of Perry's?"

"It's mine."

"The shadebringer isn't a coward," said one of the trainees. "He's even bought his own sword!" The group chattered excitedly while I stood there like a fool.

Jacques wasn't convinced. He held out his hand. "I promise you'll have it returned if your aptitude tests show you excel with single-handed blade weapons. Until then, you get a wooden training sword. The rest of you shut up, and speak only when spoken to."

I handed him the sword and took the flimsy wooden trainer in return. What a shit deal.

"Fall in!" Jacques shouted. We scrambled to and fro until we formed a perfect rectangle. Jacques moved center-left of the formation and marched us toward the central barracks. People stopped in the streets while others leaned out their windows to wave and whistle. Some threw malted grob treats and others random trinkets at us—out of sympathy, admiration, or pride, I'd never know.

The grimy conscripts wore a mishmash of clothing and uniforms from various eras and cultures, some fantastically unique from times I had only read about. A samurai marched in front of me with a rigidness that far exceeded any sergeant major of my time. African warriors lined up to my right and spoke back and forth in Swahili. Jens marched a few ranks back to my left in his Luftwaffe flight uniform—not exactly prime material for medieval combat. Keats followed just behind him in a generic twill trainee uniform dyed light blue. I snickered at his appearance until I realized his former colleagues probably burned every vestige of his identity back in Mora, where every guard seemed to proudly don their distinct uniform.

After our triumphant (or pathetic) march through Junedale, we passed through the gates of the central barracks onto a sandy parade field and halted. Jacques stepped away from the main formation and blew a whistle. Armored soldiers flooded from the surrounding stone buildings and set upon us, screaming into our faces in pidgin or whatever language they preferred. Some conscripts fumbled over themselves in confusion amid the chaos, while others just stared forward. The brave ones returned the attitude and earned swift jabs to the gut. I stood at attention and hoped none of the instructors would recognize me. And none did, except Jacques.

"Welcome to Junedale, Shadebringer!" He shouted in my face, and the others turned to us at the mention of the word. The sonofabitch glowed in the attention. "Let's see what you've got." He grabbed my arm and pulled me from the formation. Removing a wooden sword from his hip, he pointed the tip at me. "*En garde!*"

I raised the wooden shit-stick (god damn him) and swung it hard, joyous at the opportunity to beat the arrogant Frenchman to a pulp, but he easily dodged it. The momentum carried me to his right, and he snapped his sword against my back. A crescendo of *oooooos* went up from the formation with a few claps. The jolt of pain shrank to a dull burn across my flesh, but the embarrassment remained fresh.

"You have all the grace of a cannonball, Shadebringer."

He lunged forward, I lost my footing with a clumsy defensive swing, and the sword sailed from my hand. I sprinted and dove into the sand for the weapon, but before I could turn, Jacques stood over me with his sword at my back.

"You've been killed three times in the last minute, Shadebringer. Now get back in formation."

I dusted off and sauntered back, face warm and red, and tried to ignore the others as they stared at me.

* * *

"You've got a long way to go, Yank," said Keats. He waddled about the room with a broom in his hands and rags dangling from his belt.

Our first day as conscripts passed much like my experience on Earth, where menial tasks took on the greatest importance. I dragged a rag along a dusty windowsill, engrossed in the work, partly to give my bruised ego time to heal. Keats had been sniping me since Jacques kicked my ass and wouldn't let up. "Fuck off."

"This is going to be a long indoctrination if you two keep at it," said Jens.

Exhausted, we scoured our cramped quarters for grime and filth as instructors barged in at random intervals, inspected the room, and demanded more work.

"You didn't exactly wow anybody out there either." I grit my teeth and flicked a burgundy gash on Keats's forehead—a wound his big fucking mouth had earned him from an instructor. A small trickle of blood seeped out.

"Cheers, wanker." Keats growled and palmed the wound.

"Cease the nonsense," said Jens a little louder. He buffed a rag across his boots until they mirrored his reflection and set them at the base of the bed. His sheets were flawless and crisp, with neat square corners—not so much as a wrinkle.

I gathered my sheets and pulled them across the bunk, but after minutes of tugging and tucking, they remained a ruffled mess. "Leave it to the Nazi to have everything in perfect order."

"I was not a member of the Party and, judging by your performance as an American soldier, I'm not sure how we lost." Jens sighed and fixed my sheets like a magician; he understood as well as I that punishment would be shared if our room looked like shit.

"You lost because you fucked with the Russians."

"Probably for the best, from what I've heard."

Keats snorted and shook his head as he tried to imitate the perfect sheen on his boots. "You belligerent sods tried twice in thirty years to conquer the world and ended up destroying half of it. Maybe you need a different hobby?"

"Ironically, I was dodging Russian bullets when I checked out." My voice evaporated into a murmur, and a tickle in my throat set me to hacking.

"You were dodging Russian bullets fired by Asian soldiers in a French colony over a clash between a German's and a Briton's concept of government?" Jens climbed onto his bed and sprawled out.

"That's the crux of it." The tickle returned, and I coughed harder.

A guard barged into the room, clattered two swords together, and we snapped to attention. "Site inspection, report!"

"Madame at arms: three bunks ready, room scrubbed, uniforms

prepped, weapons polished, ready for the morrow." Jens threw a crisp salute.

The guard returned it and eyed every corner and crevice of the room like a hawk. "To bed!" she shouted, and we clamored into the sheets. She stood in the doorway until we were neatly tucked away and then snuffed the candles.

"It's blunt weapons training tomorrow, I think," said Keats.

"I didn't buy a fucking mace; I bought a sword," I said.

"Judging by your performance earlier, maybe it's not the weapon for you."

"A mace is a fine weapon," said Jens. "It has certain advantages against reanimates."

"I don't like the sound of whatever a *reanimate* is," I said.

Keats sighed. "Oh, give it a rest, Kraut. Reanimates haven't attacked in ages."

"Ask our friend Clyde here about his experience with them." Jens pointed at me.

"What do you mean?" I said.

"Did you ever wonder what stirred in the shallow grave you awoke upon?"

Memories of the rotten gray hand flooded back, its desiccated fingertips probing the air as the shallow mound of loose dirt undulated. "I thought it was a nightmare."

"Reanimates tend to rise when a rift opens between this world and one or more of the other hellish ones known to exist. This affords those tortured souls a chance to flee into a fresh corpse here, and the Morites took your ill-timed recollection as proof of this."

I heaved up another round of coughs and stuffed my face in a pillow. The other two waited.

"I've heard that cough before," said Jens. "You should see a—"

A heavy boot kicked open the door and startled us. "Shut up and sleep!" The guard slammed the door again and stormed off.

I buried my face deeper in the pillows and brought my lungs up, straining my abs with each episode. The fits didn't seem to bother Keats;

he was soon snoring hard enough to shake the windows. Forcing my eyes closed, I stifled the painful coughs and breathed in carefully through my nose and out my mouth. The fits eased over time, but the effort exhausted me, and I started to shake. I dozed off to Jens swearing quietly in German.

• • •

"He has the hush. Don't go near him."

"Shadebringer, can you open your eyes?"

The words registered, but agony overwhelmed me, and their meaning faded. The muscles in my head and scalp spasmed and sent electrical lances into my brain. Each breath came through a straw, and I strained every fiber in my chest to get it. I drowned in slow motion.

"Send for the arcanists." It sounded like Keats, but I couldn't be sure. "Right away."

Spit pooled in my mouth, and I tried to swallow. Instead, my throat clamped down and sent the liquid into my lungs. Arching my back, my chest squeezed, and a column of liquid oozed out of my half-closed mouth.

"Roll him on his side. Side. Side." Cool hands on my back and chest rolled me as the final drops left my mouth and I pulled for breath with my last ounce of strength.

"On his back now. Now. Now." The voice was familiar and frantic. Still no breath.

"Knife," said the voice, and seconds later, pain flowed through my neck, followed by a *pop*. I contracted my diaphragm and cool air flooded my lungs.

"Good work, doctor." Jacques's distinct French-nasal din, no doubt. "Now quarantine his bunkmates, and seal this room." The voices and footsteps faded out as the pain in my neck receded to a warm tickle.

• • •

"Open up."

I awoke to a hand forcing my jaw open. A glass bottle perched at the tip of my lips and a stream of cool liquid sank into my mouth and spilled down my throat. My eyes shot open as the liquid burned like sulfuric acid. I tried to scream but could only grunt and wiggle my toes.

"You'll be glad you don't remember each serving," said a woman. Her tattooed face slowly came into focus, and she snickered.

"Three servings a day, and he might live," she said and passed the bottle to Keats. She grinned at me and left the room, robes swishing with each step.

The burning intensified then disappeared. My throat slackened, and air rushed in—a relief like none other.

"She's an animated one, she is," said Keats. "Kind of a freak though." He pulled up a chair and sat next to my bed.

My eyes shot around the room and landed on Keats's ugly mug; not much of the rest of my body would move.

"Hrmmphh," I mumbled despite my best effort to form words.

Keats sighed and scooted forward. "It's called the hush for a reason. You're lucky we had a doctor here to open your airway. Said he knows you too."

"Mrrrrrrr." My best attempt at "Steiner." What was he doing here?

"*Mrrrr* right back at you." He crossed his arms and leaned back in the chair. "You'll be able to speak again in a few days, if you survive the night."

Asshole, I shouted in my head and blinked at him rapidly. Even Steiner had better bedside manner.

"*Stop being difficult.* I'm here because I must take care of you. Few others have survived the disease. Miriam is risking her life simply entering this room."

I hope Jens is OK. I had coughed a few times near him but figured the pillow had taken most of whatever I'd hacked out. Hell, I was even a little worried about Jacques. Nobody deserved this kind of pain.

Keats stood and scratched a line down a chalkboard and returned to my side. Sliding his fingers beneath the sheets, he lifted hard and rolled me up. Every muscle in my back and shoulders clenched, and my vision faded. He released the sheets, and I rolled back with equal agony. I could only stare at him with hateful eyes.

Keats sat again and shrugged. "Sorry, lad. I know it hurts, but it's better than a pressure sore. Be glad that tube's out of your neck too." With a yawn, he reclined in the chair and hummed off key. Maybe this *was* Hell.

CHAPTER 19

SHAME IS FOREVER

You will come home before the leaves have fallen from the trees.

—KAISER WILHELM II, AUGUST 1914

MY MIND FED ON ITSELF FOR DAYS, locked in a body that could do little more than breathe and blink. Time dragged on, and I eventually regained the ability to sit up and grasp things. I needed to find a way to kill the boredom. The bare room didn't contain much to look at besides the medical equipment, sheets, and a single chair, and none of my caretakers had any desire to chat.

Sensing a burn in my lower back, I knew it was time to roll. The job remained a slow exercise in torture, but at least I could do it myself now. With a groan, I turned onto my left side and waited for pins and needles to rush down my back as fresh blood spread into my skin and muscles.

Keats's little red book sat at the base of the chair, the only new thing in the room for days, and curiosity got the best of me. *Why not?* I plopped my arm down, nudged the book to its side, and opened to page 1:

REGINALD CHARLES KEATS—PRIVATE! MY MEMORIES OF FRANCE, APRIL 1916

I remember that night well—one of few that comes back to me completely. A night of distant suffering, and with every dull thud or whump, a shell lamented the state of mankind. And there were many, though the Big Bertha rounds had us twitching even at such great distance. The annoying specks of dirt that danced off my own brow seemed trite.

"Better the French than us," was the slogan. We all agreed, but the unspoken sorrow and pity in each of our hearts lurked behind the bravado, for we knew what it was like to be on the receiving end. We also knew our turn could come at any moment.

I had finished that night's watch list in a hurry and triple-checked it for fear of the company commander's wrath. The boys selected for watch lost a night's sleep protecting us from infiltrators and other terrors in the dark, but so it goes. Everyone got a turn at some point, but, thankfully, it wasn't mine that night.

When I reclined on my pack, I looked up to God's great canvas. The stars were beautiful away from the city and shined brighter than any city night. I had connected each of my favourites with a cherished memory, so I needed to only glance up to pull myself from the conflict. Sadly, there is no such blessing in Irgendwo, and for these memories, I am eternally grateful. Oh, the irony.

The brightest star in the sky—Sirius, I think they call it—served my best memory: my first Christmas. Well, the first one I remembered, anyway. My eyes jumped through the heavens. Another star was Mum in Cornwall, and its neighbour was our first dog, Lawrence, God rest him. I could almost hear Lawrence's bark in the distant artillery. Not bad for a terrier.

The screech of a phonograph needle against cellulose took me away from the skies above to our plot below. Oh, I did love it; music mixed into the night, trickling down the trenches, rising and falling as the lads bickered over their preferred volume. A crooning, ghostly but familiar voice drifted gently from the Amberol record padded with static.

They were summoned from the hillside,
They were called in from the glen,
And the country found them ready,
At the rallying call for men.

I can sing it now. And sometimes do, especially if I meet another doughboy, though such occurrences are rare here. I'm uncertain why, given the mass death in our war.

RATS AND MEN

"Fame, fortune, adventure, women." I lit a ragged cigarette and cherished the brief warmth against my cheeks. I inhaled hard to bring the tobacco to life and exhaled the weight of England in a large cloud.

"Fuckers got us good, didn't they?"

My head sat a foot and a half below the crest of the trench, but, somehow, I could picture the scarred brown earth that stretched for miles around us.

"I would've signed up just for the women," said another soldier, who beckoned a cigarette from me.

"Get your own, Lemley," I told him.

The soldier, a stocky farm boy of sixteen years on this belligerent rock, swore under his breath and leaned against the trench wall. He eyed my cigarette like a vulture. Oh, Lemley, I remember you well and am thankful you didn't end up here.

A large rat sprung from the shadows and skittered along the duckboards and piles of mud, triggering a flurry of stomping and swearing. The sight had me doubled over in stitches as the rat jumped and dodged for its life. The memory brings me mirth whenever it surfaces. Indeed, my colleagues in the guard give the oddest looks whenever I break into spontaneous laughter.

"How are we supposed to hold off the Hun if you Suzies can't kill a fucking rat?" I said.

The rodent dodged a final frantic rifle butt and disappeared into a crevice.

I locked the cigarette in my lips and clapped. "Come on, lads. Let's invite all the bints to the front and show them how real Englishmen fight!"

"I think the Jerries snagged all the cut from here to Langemarck," said Hess.

"Cut?" I looked at Hess. "Don't you mean cunt?"

"No, I mean cut," he said. "It's the cut that never heals." His voice rose to a whimsical pitch like he was about to sing. The others chuckled and slapped their knees. Some mouthed the word in the most obscene manner, repeating it with exaggerated Ts and sensual Us.

"What are you perverts on about?" said Hess, holding his curious and jolly octave.

"That sounds like German talk to me. What do you think, boys?" I narrowed my eyes and stared at Hess but couldn't suppress the ornery smile. Hess was always an easy target. Sensitive lad.

"Aye," said another soldier. "I think Hess here is a spy."

"Oh, fuck off now," said a rather dour Hess. "Are you itching to see me hanged?"

The soldiers laughed, sniping him with "Kaiser," "Herr," and "Fritz" comments.

"Calm down, Hess. It takes more than a few snarky comments and a German surname to hang." I offered the nub of the cigarette to him.

Hess pounced on the treat, but, after a single drag, a raindrop snuffed it.

"Ah, fuck it all!" He cursed at the sky and flicked the butt away. Thick ashen clouds rolled in, bringing the reek of rotting flesh and

sulphur—Lucifer's own petrichor. They say the sulphurous caverns here have a similar reek to them, but they'd be hard pressed to send me there for any reason.

"Looks like our rat's going to a watery grave." The sky unbuttoned, and I stepped to slightly higher ground in the trench. The water assailed us in sheets and clattered against every pot, pan, and helmet with such vigour that we had become the rats scrambling for shelter. A soldier trotted over to the rent in the duckboard and slammed his foot down victoriously, blocking the rat's escape.

"Not very sporting of you, Francis." I shooed him, but he didn't move. The rat squeaked frantically.

"I hope he drowns, slowly, with his rotten little claws scratching helplessly at my boot," said Francis, glancing between me and the rising water. Rivers of mud careened down the trench walls. Had Francis ended up here instead, I believe he would have been a shoo-in for the Silver Serpents.

"Aw, come on, Francis. Give him a chance." Hess took the tone of a child begging his older, meaner brother for mercy. He licked his lips and looked down at the motionless boot.

"Move your foot," I said.

Francis shrugged, a sadistic smile spreading over his dampened white flesh, and he stared at Hess. "Give the squeaky little fucker a proper eulogy; it won't be long now."

"Move your fucking boot." I drew my gun, pulled the hammer back, and levelled the barrel at him. "That's an order, Private."

Francis looked back and froze, staring into the bore of my Webley. All movement ceased, and the men pleaded for restraint. I had no bloody sympathy for the rodent, but I would not be disobeyed.

Francis's mouth contorted. "All for a fucking rat," he said and lifted his boot.

Hess's face brightened as the rat blitzed from the murk and raced down the trench, out of sight. I eased the hammer forward and slipped the revolver back into my belt.

EXIT STAGE LEFT

My end haunts me. It's so vivid and complete that I fear I may never feel peace again. I can't help but conjure these memories without much prompt, like I'm destined to punish myself forever. I probably deserve it.

"Keats, be a good lad and check on second platoon."

As usual, the captain had something for me to do he didn't want to do himself. Rank has its privileges, I suppose. I sighed and stood from my comfortable moulded mound as the early morning sun arrived to dry us up.

I jogged through our trenches, dodging puddles and streams that had formed the day before, but the muggy air had me drenched worse than if I'd gone headlong into the muck. Some of the boys slapped me on the back with cordial hellos, while others simply glared at me. I'll be the first to admit I'd had more than one run-in. Comparatively, I'm well liked among my Morite colleagues.

A few twists and turns brought me into second platoon's trenches, and I didn't waste a moment pouring a canteen over my head and shaking off like a hound.

"Keats, what do you want?" said a young officer, a Canadian, obviously not thrilled to see me. He crossed his arms. Not sure why everyone from that continent is so pernickety, but I wasn't having any of it.

"Just a sitrep for the captain. Shit, why the attitude?" I could only shake my head at the lieutenant and wonder who had pissed in his porridge.

"Nothing on this side, nothing from third platoon, and nothing from the scouts," he said and unfolded a map. He stretched it taut and pointed to our position.

"Any news on what's going on up north? Word is the Jerries broke the French lines."

"Do I look like a fucking soothsayer?"

"I wish command would tell us more about what's going on."

"Not me," said the lieutenant, "because loose lips invite spies and more fucking shelling."

"Gas!" A voice boomed down the trench line, and the blood in my balls went icy.

That single word had engendered a fear in me I've not felt again to this very day. Even Irgendwo, with all its horrors and uncertainty, cannot hold a candle to the terror of weaponised gas.

Soldiers flooded from the bunkers with their rifles ready and perched toward the German lines. Brave fools, all of them. Especially the lieutenant who climbed to the edge of the parapet and combed No Man's Land through a set of binoculars. I scuttled up the ladder for a moment to sate my own curiosity. Not far beyond a mass of interweaving barbed wire and splintered stumps, a wall of green rolled across the desolation. I was swift to leap back into the trench like a coward.

"To the ready!" shouted the lieutenant, who momentarily glanced back at me in disgust, and the men hugged their rifles. "Fire!"

They emptied their weapons into the opaque wall. Gunfire roared for minutes until the order to cease-fire spread down the line. The last reports echoed into No Man's Land, and we waited in stillness: no silhouettes, no screams, no counterfire repaid. The soldiers glanced at one another and then to their NCOs, murmuring as the gas crept along. The lieutenant looked down at me, no doubt a pathetic sight shaking and barely keeping my knickers dry.

"How's the weather down there, you chickenshit?" He grabbed a clump of mud and plopped it down on my helmet.

My cheeks flushed, and a new layer of sweat rolled down my back.

"Gas, fifty meters!" an NCO shouted. "Shallow breaths!"

"Piss in place!" said the lieutenant. "Cover your mate!" We threw handkerchiefs to the ground and urinated on them. Picking up the yellow-soaked rags, we tied them over our noses and mouths. I retched with the damp acrid rag against my face, certain life could not get any worse. Boy, was I wrong.

"What is it?" A panicked soldier squealed, and others coughed.

"Chlorine!" shouted another as the cloud swept toward the trenches.

I climbed the ladder to the opposite crest and gawked back over my shoulder at the encroaching cloud. Swirling silently, it filled every crack and depression like oil. Oh, how that image is forever burned into my mind. A gale blew a slab of it over the trenches farther to the north, and the coughs turned to shrieks. The noise weakened my knees.

"Hold the fucking line!" shouted the lieutenant.

Most held fast, staring green death in the face, while others shook, jostling and uneasy, no doubt looking for their opportunity to bolt. The officers took note of this and drew their service pistols. Face the gas or the pistol.

"Dig in, you bloody cowards!" the lieutenant howled and held his revolver in the air.

German machinegun fire erupted far behind the cloud and ripped into our fortifications. I crouched on the ladder, a rising terror taking hold of me as the gas loomed. Men coughed, cried, and hacked through their piss-soaked masks, some swiping layers of mucus away with their nails. I watched in horror as a young Algerian clawed his own eyes to bloody streaks, unable to relieve the agony, before turning his rifle on himself.

The rags did nothing, I realized. My nose burned, and I ripped the mask away.

The lieutenant, eyes swollen and red, glanced rapidly between the gas and me. "We defend in place."

The man had gone mad, and I stood again on the ladder ready to flee. He brought the revolver down and aimed it at me. "Not this from an officer! Not now!"

I froze, one leg perched on the parapet, weighing the gas versus the lunatic willing to kill us both. "We don't stand a chance against it, for Christ's sake," I pleaded, but he stood firm. My revolver tugged desperately at my hip and grew heavier every second. It was now or never.

"Don't you run, or I'll fucking shoot you," said the lieutenant. He peeked back at the cloud and cinched the handkerchief to his face.

Oh, that dumb glorious bastard; I'll never forget him. I ripped the pistol from my belt and shot him in the back. With a grunt, the lieutenant spasmed and collapsed into the trench, and I scurried over the crest. I caught a glimpse of the poor fool staring up at me and froze.

"Help," he said, mouth open. Pain wracked his face.

"Too late, lad," I said and the cloud spilled over him. I rolled away hard and righted myself, stumbling away from the green death. Gunfire poured into our broken line, and I sprinted from the gas and flying metal.

"Gott mitt uns! Geradeaus!" German battle cries heralded their assault.

I fled with several others, bullets whistling by and ploughing up the earth around us. Some took rounds to the back, mere metres from me, and fell dead. Others met the cursed fate of a leg wound that bound them to the advancing gas. But none of it mattered except survival. My course was singular. I ran and ducked and hugged the ground until the gunfire dimmed and the cloud vanished and only remote sounds of battle remained.

When my legs burned worse than my lungs, I slunk to my knees. "Bastards," I said, a heaving wreck, and wiped snot from my nose. "Barbaric, evil monsters." I coughed out each word. Loosening the grip on my revolver, waves of guilt crashed against me. Oh, what had I done?

"I'm the monster." Every detail of the lieutenant's agonized face burned bright in the void that was my brain. There I trembled, trying to imagine his wretched death beneath the gas. A death I had brought him. I, an officer in His Majesty's Service, Reginald Keats!

A single bird chirped and fluttered overhead, oddly out of place. I looked up at the rare sight and, for a moment, forgot about the war. I shuddered on my flimsy knee, unable to stand, and dropped the pistol. My mutilated knuckles remained blanched, and my hand shook. "Steady, steady, it's not your fault. Nobody saw it. It was either you or him."

I breathed deeply and exhaled, and the guilt subsided. I had lived! A smirk crossed my face. My cunning had saved me. I saved myself! I had never smiled so wide. Joy surged up in my belly, and I howled in delight.

Then everything went black. And cold. My heartbeat slowed and vanished, but I had heard the gunshot. I still hear it.

"Friede auf Erde."

I peered down at the sniper still prowling No Man's Land through a scope. Smoke danced from his rifle. How had he seen me?

Everything soared far and away into a grey haze. Now, here . . . I suffer.

My left side ached, and my arm lay numb beneath me as I read the last of his words. Small black dots pocked the remaining pages to the very last, in some places running to the edge of the binding, though I was unsure what he tracked with each mark.

Poor tortured bastard. Tapping the book to its original position, I rolled onto my back and pondered Keats's experiences. The recollections were vivid—much more vivid than any of mine—but why? Maybe it was some karmic justice for fragging his own? Maybe more details came with time? I didn't know, and part of me didn't want to know, considering some of the wicked shit I had done. Regardless, I pitied him. And if I'd had more strength, I would have destroyed the book.

"Ah, there you are," said Keats as he trudged into the room, secured the door, and snatched up his book. Moments of silence passed with only his guarded respiration audible. He no doubt eyed me suspiciously as I pretended to sleep but relented, and I heard the clink of glass as he pulled out the medicine bottle. "Wakey-wakey," he said and pinched my shoulder.

I opened my eyes and glared at the bottle, dreading the medicine, but it was better than suffocating. He tipped the bottle at my lips, and I gulped down more acid liquid. I recoiled as usual at the taste, but my breathing eased.

"Try to survive the night, Yank. I need a new pub mate, and Jens isn't the drinking type." He pulled the covers over me and left. Relieved at the benign mention of Jens, I settled into another painful slumber . . . but at least I was in good hands.

CHAPTER 20

ASPIRATIONS

A warrior's mettle comes not from size—a village girl with a sling ended my time on Earth—but rather the fire in their belly.

—GOR THE SAXON

BY THE TIME I FINISHED THE LAST dose of the burning piss water, I was able to sit up, speak, and hobble to the shitter when I needed to. Prior to that, well, I felt very much indebted to Keats. After a physician—or whatever the hell he was—gave the all-clear, guards removed the curtains from the windows, and visitors piled in, mostly politicians and their military toadies. Of course, I couldn't get a word in amid their schmoozing and plotting, but I was able to understand some of the frenzied pidgin. Much to my relief, nobody else had contracted the crud from me. There was some talk about Perry's death and a little gossip about a Morite commander. But really none of it mattered to me, aside from the fact nobody else had fallen ill. I disengaged from the bullshit and waited until the room cleared out. *Peace and quiet ret—*

"Good morning, Shadebringer." Jacques, in full battle uniform, threw the door open and smiled at me. It was not a nice smile by any stretch of the imagination but, rather, the smile a demented kid with a magnifying glass would give an ant mound.

"Good morning." I stretched and leaned forward, hamstrings snapping like icy branches. Just a week of downtime had reduced me to a fragile waif, but I felt my strength returning with every step.

"Welcome to the one percent," said Jacques.

"One percent?"

"Yes, only one in one hundred survive the hush. Your survival will no doubt fuel the prophecy furor you've created."

"I didn't create a damn thing, and prophecies are horseshit," I said and stretched down a little farther.

"I tend to think so too." He stepped near me, boots clopping on the wooden floor. "I see nothing but a feckless coward who simply gets lucky over and over again."

I straightened and looked the bastard in the eye. "Are you here for a reason?"

"Indeed, yes." He smirked and pointed to the parade field. "You're due out there in two hours for blunt weapons training."

"Are you fucking kidding me?" I struggled to lift my backpack, arms shuddering like jelly. "I'm weaker than a goddamn kitten."

"Well, no time like the present to fix that." He kicked the pack, and my belongings showered the floor. With a tip of his ornate black bicorne hat, he pointed again to the parade field and stepped out.

My face flushed red, but I didn't have time to rage.

"What a bloody mess!" said Keats as he pushed the door open against the scattered gear. "You're due out on the par—"

"Yeah, two hours. Got it," I said and fell to a knee to collect my stuff.

* * *

"There we go, Little Thor, brute force and hate your way through my shield." The instructor, Gor, sidestepped my feeble attack and kicked the back of my knee. It buckled, sending me to the ground with the war hammer's help. Grabbing the scruff of my neck, Gor helped me back up for perhaps the twentieth time. Getting my ass kicked felt unpleasant and unnatural, but if it wasn't Jacques doing the kicking, I didn't mind.

"Perhaps this weapon is not for you." He lifted the massive iron and wood hammer from my hand and twirled it like a twig. I looked on in amazement until I realized his forearms were thicker than my legs.

"I'm fine. Just getting over an illness," I said and beckoned the weapon back. I wasn't exactly small and figured I could master it if he gave me a chance. Gor laughed and dropped the war hammer. I scrambled for the weapon mid-fall but it dragged me down once more.

He rolled his eyes and slapped his forehead. "When you stop letting your ego fight your battles, big man, training will become a delight." With the snap of a finger, an assistant rolled a cart bristling with weapons to us. Gor sized me up, grabbed a mace from the heap of metal, and handed it to me.

"The weapon is an extension of you, and it must move with you as if it were your own flesh." He shoved me backward with little effort, and I buckled.

Steadying myself, I gripped the weapon, eager to try it.

"You see," he said, "a mouse with a horse's phallus is a useless mouse."

I leaped at him and brought the mace down on his shield with a *thud*. The weapon dragged me forward, and he smashed my ribs. A faint *crack*, like stepping on a twig under fresh snow, escaped my bruised chest. Christ, that was gonna hurt for a bit.

"Better," said Gor, smiling, "but you're still dead."

"Don't we have any goddamn guns here?" I sputtered the question with what breath remained.

He looked at me for a moment, confused, and his eyes lit up. "Ah, yes, the sticks that spew metal! I've heard of their wonders." He pretended to cradle a rifle.

"Yeah, that's right—guns, rifles, bullets. All that shit," I said.

"Cannon and catapult exist—I've seen the destruction they can bring—but the strange tools described by the men of war who have arrived in the recent past have no match here."

"Recent past?"

"Ah, yes, well, I know I don't show it, but I'm quite old. *Battle-axe vintage*, as the young'uns call us." He smiled and tugged his graying groin-length beard.

"It is a pleasure to meet you, Shadebringer," he said and extended his hand. I reached out and shook it.

"Clyde R—"

Before I could finish my last name, Gor strangled the blood from my hand, pulled me forward, and punched me in the face. I reeled backward and collapsed on the sand. A symphony of *oooooh*s went up from everyone around us. Gor strode over to my sad heap of ass and shook his head.

"*Gibrokan!*" he shouted and lifted me to my feet. "Never let your guard down!"

Half expecting another haymaker, I closed my eyes and hoped it would be quick. Instead, he dusted me off and placed the mace back in my hands. With a wave and a bow, he excused himself from the field and strode away.

Another instructor approached while I wobbled and patted some dust from my shoulders.

"He said he broke you."

"I gathered that." I sniffed and spit out a gob of blood.

* * *

Days turned to weeks and weeks to months, yet the world never changed. The only essence of time I understood was waking up and going back to sleep and marking each day with a nick on my bedpost. My body swelled under constant strain, much as it had during my Earthly enlistment. I noticed a similar change in my buddies but less so in Keats, who had become an expert at shamming out of his duties.

Each morning, we scrambled out of bed for invasion drills, but when the gates ascended, the promised legion of Morites and their siege engines never materialized. Only once, we caught a strider in the near distance, which sent us into a panicked frenzy. The instructors overlooked the mass cowardice as the creature's psionic scream rattled the most hardened recruits even after the gates fell.

The dull souls who couldn't hack it were reclassified into shit jobs around the city. Those who demonstrated exceptional aptitude in mathematics, science, or the skilled trades were sent to the academies. The rest of us would go on to specialize in various forms of combat, based on our physique, aptitude, or abilities. Day by day, the trainees dropped by one or two at a time. Sometimes, newcomers replaced the losses, if they were skilled enough to start their training at our level.

I wore the title of shadebringer with dubious honor, but as training progressed, the other soldiers began using my real name. Only Keats reminded me of my alleged importance, though this was nonetheless lost on me . . . until graduation came.

Much to my surprise, my combat talent lay with the mace—a weapon I considered ugly and imprecise but grew to love in its pure savagery. Jens excelled with daggers and other clandestine weapons to such an extent that many instructors questioned whether he was a Morite assassin. Keats's physical abilities were lacking, and so too were his classroom skills. These shortcomings drew lots of attention from the instructors, who were very interested in "motivating" him. But somehow, the pudgy Brit avoided expulsion, no doubt in part because he had saved my ass, but it also turned out he excelled in anatomy and medicine. Who would have known?

"To the training field!" A runner bolted past the barracks, shouting and banging on his shield. We scrambled out of our beds and into our uniforms and posted. Hundreds of guards in their most ornate uniforms lined the four edges of the field. Politicians and military leaders sat in the center of the field. The graduates assembled into perfect formations before the dignitaries.

The commandant of the central barracks marched front and center and halted. His plated armor gleamed in the torchlight and lit his scarred face. He executed an about face to address the group.

"Those before you have yet again, in this life as in the last, risen to the call of duty to their homeland. They have selflessly offered themselves as resistance to the evils of the Council as countless others have since Junedale rose from the ashes of the Cataclysm. In this sacred duty, we see the honor and humanity that brought them to this world, and we see the eventual triumph of good over evil. It is with profound honor that I induce these young soldiers into the Junedalian Army, with their branches as follows."

On this cue, a line of instructors marched from the barracks, each bearing a distinctive crest on their breastplates. They centered on the commandant. The pomp and circumstance was similar to my Earthly enlistment graduations, except much more . . . medieval. Some of those bastards bore weapons larger than their torsos. The commandant greeted each by name and removed a scroll from his belt.

"Reginald Keats!" he shouted after glancing at the scroll. The irony was not lost on me—the lowest performing individual was first to be called.

Keats scampered forward to the post and stood at attention.

"Forward medic, first class."

Applause erupted from around the field, at least from those who didn't know Keats personally. One of the instructors stepped forward, executed a right-angle turn, and approached Keats. He removed a pin from his pocket and attached the distinctive sword and snake crest to Keats's lapel. The instructor then removed his own medic satchel and handed it to him.

Disappointment was clearly written on Keats's face, and he wasn't trying to hide it. "A bloody medic?" he said incredulously. He dropped the bulky satchel and crossed his arms.

The dignitaries murmured, and groans rose from our formation. The flummoxed instructor glared at Keats and retrieved the satchel.

"Get over yourself, Keats. Medics are the most valuable people on the battlefield!" someone called. The anonymous protest had some of the dignitaries clapping.

"I'm being classed as a flipping nurse. Give me a weapon, not a bunch of bandages."

The instructor, a hefty man bearing a Staff of Asclepius tattoo over his mangled right cheekbone, stepped closer to Keats. "I've killed just as many as I've saved, you insolent fool." He bumped Keats back with his chest. "If the honor of this assignment is too much for you to handle, then by all means, drop your satchel again." He shoved the satchel into

Keats's chest and released it. Keats clasped it for dear life and said nothing. "Wise decision, little Saxon."

Keats saluted the instructor, who begrudgingly returned the gesture, and returned to the formation. I sighed heavily, half expecting Keats to be dragged away screaming for his behavior.

"Marg, no last name!" The official's voice rose as he belted out the name and looked toward the formation, but Marg had already jaunted to the front.

"Heavy bladed weapons, third class!" Marg grinned with the ensuing applause. The Master of Blades approached, heaved a double-bladed battle axe from his back, and passed it to him. Marg grasped the giant weapon and smiled even wider.

"Marg!" he roared into the air and heaved the weapon up and down. He returned to the formation, braining a few other recruits with the weapon's handle in the process.

"Good job, Marg," I whispered as he strode past.

"Why, thank you," he said in a thick Scandinavian accent.

I shrugged.

"Clyde Robbins—the shadebringer."

The crowd drew silent again. I stepped from the formation and up to the line of instructors.

"Thaumaturgy, first class." The official's voice inflected again, and he tilted his head at the scroll to ensure he had read it correctly. The word meant nothing to me, but I immediately recognized Octavius when he stepped forward from the others. He removed an onyx and silver crest—an index finger bearing a small flame at the tip—and pinned it to my lapel.

"That doesn't look like a mace," I whispered to Octavius.

He smiled. "Your training has only just begun," he said. "Junedale needs your gifts." He shook my hand and returned to the line.

I looked to Gor, whose disappointed, sallow eyes were on the verge of tears. He cradled a mace, and I detoured to him on my way back to the formation.

"Congratulations are in order regardless," said Gor. He handed the mace to me and extended his hand. I grasped it and dodged a swift left hook. I snuck a quick strike to his ribs with the mace's handle, and he coughed.

"Ah, well, I did teach you something after all!" He hugged me and sent me back to the formation amid applause.

I tapped on the crest and repeated the strange term in my head. *Thaw-muh-tur-jee. Thaw-matter-jee.* Fuck it, I got a mace anyway.

Soldier after soldier, the process continued until everyone had received a branch and its token. Jens received honors and an ornate blade forged from his strider tooth, though the process had reduced the once-massive incisor into an incomprehensibly keen blade. Following the branch assignments, the dignitaries clapped and exited the field.

Next came the unit assignments. With far less pomp and circumstance, the officers barked out names, and new formations emerged among the gaggle. I watched soldiers trickle to their new assignments, and I secretly hoped Keats, Jens, and I would end up in the same unit. I listened intently, ready to move, but my name never came up.

A sagely figure tapped me on the shoulder. "Congratulations on your selection to the Academy of Thaumaturgy. I am Li," he said and extended a gnarled hand to me.

I looked the thin Asian man up and down, rather unimpressed by his droopy cloth attire and flowing blue robes. I reached out and shook his hand, repressing the urge to crush it. "Thanks, but what the hell is thaumaturgy?"

"You will learn to manipulate the forces of this world with thought and subtlety."

"Sounds like voodoo bullshit to me," I said.

Li nodded excitedly. "Yes, I was told to expect a bit of a rough character, and I know Octavius is never one to disappoint." He flicked out his right index finger and a small flame sprung from the tip. It corkscrewed clockwise then counterclockwise.

"Pretty sweet parlor trick," I said. I wasn't even bullshitting. I was impressed.

"This is called a cantrip, and it's the most basic of the magics you will learn."

"Almost rhymes with bullshit."

Li rolled his eyes and sighed. He formed his hand into a gun, his index finger the barrel, and squeezed the imaginary trigger with his middle finger. A small fireball spit to the ground and exploded, kicking dust and embers into the air. Soldiers jumped away from the impact while others cursed and muttered "witch." A circle quickly cleared around us.

"Just like in the past life, the masses fear and ridicule what they cannot comprehend." Li reloaded with another flame, but I shook my hands before he fired it, having seen enough. "There are precious few with the mind and the attunement to manipulate these forces, but it's a gift given to every shadebringer . . . even the least deserving of such power."

"All right, I'm a believer."

Li nodded and beckoned me to follow him. He extinguished the flame by pointing his finger into his mouth and spewed a fountain of smoke that took the form of an eye that winked and vanished. "That's the parlor trick."

CHAPTER 21

FUNNY BUSINESS

The waygates, Kir Sol and Kir Endra, were once symbols of rebirth and hope. Now, they are obelisks of terror—festering wounds that torment this land and lay bare the immutable truth that Mother Daedrina has abandoned us.

—ACADEMICIAN FYODOR ZHUKOV,
THE LIGHT EXTINGUISHED

"I SUPPOSE YOU'VE PROVEN ME WRONG," said Jacques. He shook my hand and invited me into the tower.

My hackles shot up as the rough flesh of his hand grazed against mine, and I considered sucker punching him. We walked in, and Li followed close behind and latched the heavy iron door behind us.

I was immediately struck by the turbid air through which we almost *swam*. The moisture carried well the unmistakable must of rotting wood, and a chill easily set into my bones. We proceeded down a circular flight of stairs into the depths, gingerly treading over crumbled steps and empty boxes. Flickering torches spiraled into the abyss and occasionally sizzled as errant water droplets fell from far above.

A distant sound caught my ear—a faint lamentation like a young girl crying in the dark. I stopped and craned my head to see if I could better locate the origin, but it was impossible; it seemed to come from everywhere. I tried putting my hands over my ears. Still, I could hear it.

"You can hear Azurocus?" Li said, and he stopped to observe me.

"I hear something, but I'm not sure what it is."

"That's a good sign," said Li.

I stuck my fingers in my ears, but the noise persisted. "So, what is it?" I said, unplugging my ears to better hear Li's response.

"The Great Ai wrote that Azurocus, eldest son of Daedrina, was banished to Kull at this very spot. His wails are eternal, and those who know his true voice are less apt to be fooled by the Lord of Deception."

"Sweet yarn," I said.

Li rolled his eyes. "There you go. That's the spirit."

The last step brought us to a dank landing littered with barrels and scraps of paper. I followed Jacques and Li down a single corridor lined with torches that stretched far into the darkness; the distinct trickle of water battled the sputtering flames. The air sat heavy in my lungs. Heavy beams straddled the ceiling, and featureless doors adorned both walls. How the masters of this cryptic shithole kept track of what was behind all those doors stumped me.

"This is where your mind will be attuned," said Jacques, stopping outside one of the indistinct doors.

"It can be a rather unpleasant experience," said Li. He pulled a set of spectacles from his robe, gingerly placed them on his face, and inspected the door. "Yes, indeed, this is the right one."

"I guess this is mandatory then, huh?"

They nodded. Jacques clicked the handle, and the door swung into pure darkness. I grabbed a torch and pushed it through the doorway, but it was instantly snuffed. Not what I had expected—or wanted—to see.

"You just have to walk in," said Li, "but whatever happens, don't follow *any* manifestations you see in there, or you will be taken."

"Christ," I said. *What the fuck does that even mean?* I inhaled deeply and approached the doorway. Raising a leg and planting it forward, my foot found emptiness, and I tumbled into the blackness.

* * *

I found myself staring up at a simple wooden ceiling, memories of the plunge omnipresent and timeless. I could not gauge any passage of time aside from my own heartbeat. I inhaled deeply, dry stale air now filling my lungs, and stood.

The room was ornate—the kind of ornate one would see in an old Southern plantation, minus the sweet tea, of course. Four decorative oak doors with shimmering gold handles stood as *ostensible* routes of egress, as the Brit would say. A Persian rug sprawled across part of the room, leaving only a bare rim of wood on the periphery. A mahogany dining table sat heavy on the rug, with a single candelabra adorning its spacious surface.

I looked over every inch of the room before taking a step. Muffled creaking of the wooden floor snuck from beneath the carpet. *Kek, kek, kek.*

"Hello?" My voice pierced the uncomfortable silence, and, oddly enough, I expected a response. But the crackling of the candles and my own ringing ears were all I heard. I approached one of the doors and squeezed the handle. Locked tight. I tried all the other doors with the same result. *Shit.*

"Fall through eternity and end up in grandma's dining room. Seems about right."

I pulled out a chair and sat at the table in complete silence. The rhythmic sound of my own breathing bothered me; I became too aware of it. Goddammit, I needed to get my mind on something else. I folded my hands on the table and took inventory of every minute detail. When my mind ran out of objects to organize, I started from scratch, poring over every nook and cranny.

"This place sucks. The décor is shit, and it smells like old man in here. Two stars at most," I said aloud, hoping to piss *something* off. Silence. More awareness—this time of my own heartbeat. My leg beat against the undersurface of the table, and I picked at my fingers.

"OK now, I'm ready for whatever horrific epiphany you have for me." With those words, *thunking* footsteps rattled the door across the table—not hurried but not relaxed either. Something was making its way toward me with purpose.

I stared at the door and gulped. "Should just keep my mouth shut." I stood and leaned on the table, muscles tight. The steps ceased just behind the door, and the handle creaked. The door swung open.

"Bernie Collins?" I tilted my head. There was that goddamn beagle again. Still wearing his field-green uniform with the sleeves neatly rolled up his giant black biceps, he stepped into the room. I looked past him into the darkness, but he shoved the door shut with a swift kick.

"Clyde Robbins, you crazy motherfucker. How's death treating you?" Bernie ambled to the table and pulled a cigar from his sleeve. He twisted the aromatic delight over a candle and sat with a satisfied yawn. I was glad to see he was in one piece again.

"I gotta say, Bernie, not terribly well." I shook my head slowly from side to side. Perhaps a little bit of an understatement, but I wasn't too keen on making small talk.

Bernie nodded and pulled the cigar from his lips. "Well, my friend, turn that frown upside down, because I've got a deal for you." He blew a thick, undulating ring of smoke into the air that dissipated on the ceiling.

"Oh, you know I'm always eager to make a deal, Bernie."

"Glad to hear it, Clyde. You know, you've always been a favorite person of mine. Not afraid to speak your mind. Not afraid to test the unknown. Not afraid to take chances. I'm so *very* glad I got to know you back in Nam."

I forced an uneasy smile. "You're a favorite person of mine too, Bernie. I was sorry to see you go but glad you were able to get out of country and . . ." I thought for a moment. "What happened when you got back to the States? I saw your name come up in Mora."

"I never made it back to the States, sad to say. Everything was looking good until the gangrene set in. Came out of nowhere. One day I was flirting with some Thai honeys and sipping hooch, and the next, I literally felt my balls and ass rotting off in bed."

"Oh man, Bernie. That's awful. But what are you doing here?"

He laughed and puffed the cigar. "The Morites cut my heart out and threw me into the waygate as a sacrifice for their goddamn overlords."

I stared at my old friend, unsure what to say. "Bernie . . . shit, I'm sorry."

"Don't be." He leaned back in the chair and looked to the ceiling. "*They* have shown me things."

"They?" The hairs on my neck straightened.

"I have seen reality for the first time, Clyde. They have shown me what I am, what I can be—what *you* can be." He leaned over the table with the cigar pinched between his fingers. "Just walk back through the door with me, and all this nonsense, all this uncertainty, all this confusion over your destiny will be over." He pointed to the door, snapped his fingers, and it flew open.

I remembered what Jacques said about *manifestations*. "Well, you know, Bernie, as Momma always used to say, I can't be following phantom spirits through dimensional gateways without knowing exactly where they're going."

Bernie smiled and shrugged. He folded his hands over his shiny shaved head and took another voluminous hit on the cigar held between his teeth.

"*We* know what happens when you go and defy Momma." He stood and chewed on the cigar from the corner of his mouth. Slowly traipsing around the corner of the table, he brushed the smooth surface and hummed. "You sure you don't want to come take a li'l peep?"

"I'm sure, Bern."

"I guess there's no convincing you." He frowned and gestured. "It was nice seeing you, anyway." He extended his hand and stared me square in the eye, and without thinking, I moved to shake his hand.

Never let your guard down. Gor's voice sprang frantically into my head, and I whipped my hand away as Bernie pounced with an inhuman shriek. He fell through me as if *he* were made of cigar smoke and dropped to the floor. A deep resonant warble groaned through the door and shook the candelabra on the table.

"I'll never go back!" Bernie screamed. "Give me another chance!" He crawled along the rug and sank his fingernails into the thin cracks of the wooden floor.

A rush of living darkness splashed through the door and flowed under the table and across the room, knocking aside the chairs. Whipping tendrils sprang from the horrific black mass and impaled Bernie through the back. The tendrils curled violently, a monstrous sea creature embracing a doomed ship, and dragged him toward the door.

"I'll never go back!" he screamed again, clawing against the force, his once masculine and smooth voice now that of a man being skinned alive.

The flesh on his face bubbled as a tendril speared through the back of his head and burst from his mouth. It coiled tight around his jaw and snapped his neck into an unnatural pose, and the strength drained from my knees. With a final heave, the darkness lifted him into the air, cleaved him in half, and dragged the screaming fragments through the doorway.

The door slammed shut, and again the room was silent.

"What. The. Fuck." I shuddered, barely able to support my own weight while I inspected the floor, but not a drop of the darkness—or Bernie, for that matter—remained. I righted one of the hefty oak chairs and sat down, wishing Bernie had dropped the cigar.

"It can get a lot worse," I said. "It can get a lot worse. It can get a lot worse." I gnawed on my lip.

Knock. Knock. Knock. Another door rattled, and I tumbled from the chair. "Fuck, not again."

I stared over the table at the golden handle. Rising slowly, my heart pounded as I edged toward the door, but in moments, something slammed it again, and I jumped back. Whatever it was had become impatient.

"Hold your goddamn horses," I said. I forced my jittery hand to the handle and pushed it down. As soon as the latch disengaged, a strong cool breeze blew the door open and filled the chamber, a welcome respite from the stale air. The candles flickered, and I shielded my eyes against a cloud of dust. When the dust cleared, a familiar sight loomed beyond the doorway: Empty plains rolled into the blue and gray horizon.

"Huh." I kept my distance from the door and inspected the segment of horizon I could see. "Hello?" Unsure who had knocked, I approached the verge of the doorway on full alert and popped my head out to the left. Nothing.

"Bonjour," a ghostly voice groaned from my right, and I spun my head to it.

I catapulted back into the room and scrambled to the opposite side, crouching like a dog behind the table. The gnarled and muscular legs of a strider swept past the doorway and planted themselves in the ground outside the door, rattling the table and candelabra. The creature turned and faced me, most of its massive frame beyond view, and dug its arm-length claws into the ground. I braced for an attack, but seconds turned to minutes, and the creature only stood there. Its bestial snorts and breath conjured memories of my first encounter, but this one seemed . . . content.

"What the hell do you want?" I shouted through the door, but it ignored me. Forcing myself up, I crept again toward the door, and the strider's familiar stench worsened. I passed the threshold of the doorway and looked up. Every fiber of my being screamed *flee*, but my shoes were filled with concrete. The eyeless, rumpled gray-green head angled down on its sinewy legs as if it were looking at me. A layer of slime oozed from the corner of its jaws and splattered on the ground, littered with flecks of meat and metal.

A gift. The familiar baritone spoke into my mind, and the leathery corners of its maw pulled back—a smile. Its mandibles unhinged with a click, and the lower jaw fell open and thumped against its body like a massive wooden trunk, revealing a cavern of razors. The strider heaved a sonorous breath, as if it prepared to strike, and twisted down to me and screamed.

Tepid air rolled over me as the screech ebbed. Vomit rose in my throat, and I bore down and clenched my jaw to contain it. *Steady like the mountain*, I thought.

When I had collected myself, I beheld carnal horror: A man, or what used to be a man, writhed on the razors. He struggled to free an arm impaled on one of the creature's teeth. The arm slid from the tip of the tooth and the man plunged his skeletal fingers beneath the tongue, pulling free a small metallic object. He limply tossed the object toward me, and it clattered to the ground near my feet. I picked it up and wiped off the muck, revealing a metallic snake with tiny red jewels as eyes.

"What the hell is this?"

When I looked up, the beast and its victim had vanished; only the putrid stink remained. I stepped back into the room, shoved the figurine in my pocket, and closed the door.

"OK, two left." I returned to the table and tried to decide which door to try next. The candles continued to flicker and dance, but the wax never receded. I blew on the flames, and they swayed in protest but did not extinguish, no matter how much force I used.

"Hmm, it may take a while, but I'm pretty sure I'm going to run out of oxygen if these goddamn candles never die," I said aloud, certain *something* was watching me. "Not a single book to keep an idle mind in purgatory occupied. How cruel a world." I cradled my head in my hands as notions of reality slipped away.

Trial by fire. The soft feminine voice returned, and my brief relaxation evaporated.

"Oh, knock it the fuck off with the innuendo and metaphors," I whined and waited for another door to spring open.

Pitter-pattering escaped the dark beneath one of the remaining doors, and I craned my head. Soft but rapid, the noise waxed and waned then vanished. I narrowed my eyes and frowned. The skittering resumed in uncertain staccato bursts. I fell to a push-up position and pressed my ear to the ground like a cat. The noise strengthened: someone drumming their fingers against a wet tabletop. I squinted beneath the door. *Perhaps I should have grabbed a cand—*

A set of chitinous needles attached to an oval head lunged from the dark. I whipped my head back just in time to hear the needles snap together. The rest of my assailant skittered out of the darkness.

"OK, that was stupid." I thumped my forehead and looked down at the insect. It reared up on its back legs, antennae tasting the air, and raced along the floor toward me.

"Vile thing." I jumped onto the table as the centipede disappeared beneath it. More skittering. Another flowed out of the darkness. And another. And another. They raced out, one behind the other, and then side by side until they poured out in a brown and yellow wave.

The lead centipede sprang to the edge of the table, dragged its disgusting mass onto the tabletop, and squared up with me.

"Holy shit!" I charged forward and punted the bastard, splattering it against the wall. But before my foot could even drop, a slight pressure nagged my heel: Another had clamped down on my boot but couldn't pierce the leather. Venom spewed from its head and down the side of the boot, and I squealed and smashed it. Its body tore from its head, but the oozing curved razors remained embedded in the leather. Another flung itself at me and soared over the edge. I stumbled and jumped across the table as the assault intensified. The floor writhed. The hard, chitinous bodies of the bugs clattered against the wood, drowning out the ruckus of my clumsy tabletop gymnastics.

The insects surrounded the table and began scaling the legs. I snatched up the candelabra and swept some away, but the horde simply reformed and pressed on. In desperation, I leaped to the ground, still carrying the candelabra—my only weapon—and ran to the final door. I pounded desperately against the door with my shoulder, slamming the handle with my free hand, but it didn't move. With no other option, I turned to confront the encroaching mass.

Burn them, said the familiar voice.

The image of Master Li's brilliant pyromancy surged into my mind, front and center, and I knew my course.

Overcome with revulsion and fear, I raised the candelabra in front of me, arm stiff and fist clenched white on the base, and opened the palm of my left hand. Flames spiraled upward from the wicks of each candle and coalesced into a ball of liquid energy that rolled in my palm. *Groovy*.

A fountain of fire erupted from my hand, and I thrust it forward with every ounce of revulsion in my gut at the charging insects, immolating their segmented bodies and blasting them across the room. Flames lapped across the table and chairs and devoured the walls, floor, and bookcases.

"Fuckin' A right!" I shouted.

The table heaved up an inferno, and the flames climbed the walls and blackened the ceiling. Satisfied the bugs were no longer a threat, I reached down, plucked the centipede head from my boot, and flicked it into the fire. I turned to the last door and shoved the handle, but it still wouldn't budge.

"Ah, yes." I reached into my pocket and grasped the figurine. The eyes glowed red in the light of the encroaching flames, and it seemed to wink at me as I pondered what to do. I pressed my fingers into each bejeweled globe and, with a sharp click, a key flung from its mouth. The key fit perfectly in the lock, and the handle easily gave way as I threw open the door.

Wispy forms of Li and Jacques stared back at me from the void. With a single step, I disappeared into the darkness and awoke in the inner sanctum.

CHAPTER 22

SIMULACRUM

Once so proud, so righteous, so moral, and now you approach us—
on your bloodied knees no less—as our supplicant? Very well.
We will provide. But you will pay dearly.

—BALEDOCCUS, THIRD OF THE DAMNED

"LAST GUY DIDN'T PICK UP THE KEY," said Jacques, and he clapped.

"How'd it go?" said Li.

I stood, smoke rising from my clothes, and inspected my hands. "Not bad, but . . ." The words wouldn't come. I thought of Bernie and what he had said.

"But what?" said Li.

"My friend, another soldier I knew, said the Morites cut his heart out. Said he wanted to make a deal with me."

Li's eyes hardened, and he nodded. "The Morites are in league with the Children, the banished sons and daughters of Mother Daedrina—beings of immense evil, conniving, and hunger. The Morites routinely sacrifice souls to them, especially those they consider *undesirables*. The deal, no doubt, was to relieve his own suffering, which is understandable if one believes the tales of Kull."

Sacrificed. I shuddered and could only think of the poor bastard's face when the darkness ripped him in two and dragged him through the door into . . . "Kull?" I remembered Li mentioning the word earlier too, though I hadn't been in the mood to ask more questions then.

"Their world—their torment—their fate for betraying Daedrina." He bore no emotion aside from a solemnity that I could imagine came with knowledge. "The Council of Mora—indeed, the entire city of Mora—thrives on terror, blood, and sacrifice."

"We have learned nothing." I boiled with anger. How could Keats have served such evil? Why the hell would Jens do business with them? What kind of god would allow that place to exist? *I shot a child dead and went to lunch an hour later.* The reminder snuffed my righteous anger. Perhaps I deserved to be there with Bernie.

"You see what's at stake now, I hope." Li placed a hand on my shoulder, snapping me from my thoughts. "Now we must continue your training. Divination comes next."

"Seeing the future and shit?" I scratched my head.

"Precisely. And Giuseppe is a master of the art. We will go see him." Li locked the door and we proceeded down the corridor. The occasional torch lit our path, but I still had no idea how Li would know which door to select in this darkness. Everything looked the same.

"Here we are," said Li, and we paused in front of yet another featureless wooden door. He rapped three times and folded his hands.

"Go away!" shouted a raspy, weak voice from the other side. "I'm busy!"

Li sighed. "Giuseppe is quite eccentric and not very personable, so please don't mind him," he whispered to me. "Giuseppe, it's Li. We have a guest!"

"Oh-oh," he stuttered, "one moment." Clattering and clacking rattled from the other side of the door before it was flung open. Giuseppe looked us up and down through his single functioning eye then stepped aside. "Come in."

Even in the meek orange light, I couldn't look away from his hideous face. A moist globe drifted around a baggy eye socket, and if his nose had been any more crooked, I feared it would have impaled the remaining eye at any moment. He was an ugly sonofabitch.

"I was just telling the shadebringer you're the master diviner."

"And?" said Giuseppe, making no attempt to mask his annoyance.

"And you're going to introduce him to divination." Li's voice sharpened as he raised his brow.

Giuseppe looked away and nodded quickly.

The room was musty, dank, and lined with laden bookshelves. Candles dotted the few bare spaces on the shelves and cast just enough light for us to be able to avoid crashing into things. We walked to the center of the room, where colored dust formed some arcane symbol in the middle of a polished stone floor. Spooky shit.

"Observe," said Giuseppe. He turned to the center of the circle and made a gesture, and a speck of light appeared and hovered above the floor. It bloomed into a sphere of light and bathed the entire room in its soft glow.

"Fucking neat!" I shouted.

"Silence!" Giuseppe snapped. "Quickly, come here." He pointed next to him.

I walked forward and stood where he demanded.

"Now look."

I stared directly into the sphere of light, which had begun to expand.

"Don't say anything. Don't do anything. Just watch."

Giuseppe uttered a few words I couldn't quite make out, and the sphere enveloped us. Suddenly, I was back on the plains, watching a group of villagers.

* * *

"Father, this patch is too thick. I need a hammer." The child clawed and struck at the patch of grob to no avail. The man rose from his harvest site and walked to the child. He shielded his eyes and dropped a stone hammer at the boy's side before turning away.

"Thank you, father." The boy snatched up the tool and started pounding the grob.

"Not so quickly," snapped the father from his patch. "You'll attract the striders."

The single mention of the word made the others nervous, and they continued to pick and chisel at their individual harvest sites while looking over their shoulders. The work pace slowed.

"Come on, people, we don't want to be out here a second longer than we need to," said the father.

"Make up your mind. Do you want fast work with striders or slower work with our company?" An old woman tossed a small piece of grob at the father, which bounced off his head. The boy giggled at the spectacle, and his father murmured.

"I'd rather take my chances with the striders than with this damned soul-eater," said a young man.

"We don't use that word here," said the old woman. She walked to the Hollow, who was obviously hurt by the words, and hugged him in front of the others. "You see? Perfectly fine as long as you don't look into their eyes," she said.

"At least the striders won't eat me," said the Hollow. He fidgeted with his hammer and kept his wavering eyes cast upon the grob patch.

"No, but then you'd have to live the rest of your miserable life with no parents, which I guess is better than a stupid father," said the young man. The old woman clipped the man's ears and placed her index finger over her own lips.

"Ugh, what's that horrific smell?" a woman sneered, casting her forearm across her nose.

The others sniffed the air and immediately frowned as the odor rolled into their group.

"Just the sulfurous caverns," said the father. "Better get used to it, because future harvests are planned even closer to them."

"Just so the rich can have their precious luxuries," said the old woman.

"Would you rather be toiling for the Morites and their crooked Council?" said a younger woman as she lifted a hefty slab of grob from the ground and snapped it over her knee.

"At least the Morites don't tolerate Hollows in their midst," said the young man. The old woman slapped him across the face, sending his head sideways and a wad of spit loose from his lips, and pointed at him. He clenched his jaw and stared at her with the blank eyes of burgeoning rage.

"That's not the sulfurous caverns," said the Hollow quietly. The others ignored him, fixated on the showdown.

"Stand down, Peter," said a man, placing himself between the two.

"This gormless bastard needs a lesson in humility and mercy." The old woman spit on the ground. "I've got another lesson for him ready to go." She cocked her other hand above her head.

"Do it again, you old coot! I dare you," said Peter. He stepped into the man standing between them, and the man quickly shoved him back and away from the old woman.

"It's more than just the caverns!" screamed the Hollow.

The entire group turned to him.

"Garrett, what is it?" said his father. The boy kept his deathly gaze to the ground, face flushed from the scrutiny. His father walked to him and kneeled, placing a hand on his shoulder. "Go on, dear boy, what's wrong? Do you sense striders?"

The rest focused on them. Garrett's red hue brightened, and a bead of sweat ran down his neck. He hammered meekly at his grob patch.

"Reanimates," Garrett said to the ground.

"He's just trying to scare us," said Peter. He kicked a cloud of sand at him. Garrett absorbed the sprinkle of dirt and cracked a faint smile. "What's so funny, you soul-eater freak?" He started toward the younger boy, but one of the men grabbed his collar.

"He could destroy you with a single gaze, you foolish whelp, yet you insist on tormenting him?" He threw Peter back.

Garrett stood from his patch, gaze still cast to the ground, and walked toward Peter. The others watched his every movement, ready to block their eyes in an instant. Peter, struggling against the old man's iron grasp, glared at Garrett as he approached.

Garrett folded his hands in front of him and tilted his head to look at Peter's right foot. He smiled broadly, eliciting a fierce scowl from Peter, who clenched his fist. Garrett's eyes sat mournful and still in his head, his pinpoint black pupils darting back and forth with each thought.

"They're almost here, and when they arrive, they're not going to show you the mercy of a quick death." He pointed at Peter. "And when they're done with you, I'll pluck your soul from what's left." Garrett looked into Peter's eyes, and the purge took hold. Peter's body stiffened to a plank of wood, and his fingers flared. He grunted and shook helplessly, unable to break the gaze. The Hollow's father dashed in between the two and swept his hand over the boy's eyes and cursed.

* * *

The glowing sphere receded, and the room faded back into existence. I immediately stretched and yawned, sore and a bit tuckered from my time in the void. "What happened?" I looked over to Giuseppe.

"I must speak to Octavius at once," said Giuseppe, and he sprinted out.

Jacques and Li glanced at each other and then to me.

"The Hollow's warning about reanimates must be investigated," said Li.

"And it will be," said Jacques.

The vision had spooked me. I had been caught in a Hollow's gaze before, and it hurt like hell, but that little antagonistic shit no doubt deserved it. No, it wasn't that. It was the mention of reanimates. Just the word put a chill to my spine, and I feared for those people. "Who were they?"

"We beheld a sanctioned forager team in that vision," said Li. "It's every citizen's duty to forage for grob if they're called randomly to the task."

"Looking for food requires a draft?" I said in a somewhat amused timbre.

"Everyone—even those unfit for military service—serves in some capacity in Junedale," said Jacques. "Many groups simply disappear and are never heard from again."

"Fuck that noise," I said. His dismissive tone irked me, though I knew it shouldn't; this was a merciless place.

"In the meantime, let's continue to conjurations." Li cut our discussion short and stepped through another door that led us into a twisting hallway.

As we approached a grand set of double doors, muffled voices and excited squeals crept from beneath its massive frame. Finally some goddamn happiness (or at least life) in this place.

Li nudged open the doors, and we walked into a large, well-lit lyceum burgeoning with instructors, students, and equipment straight out of the Middle Ages. Glass vials scorched over tiny candles, bubbling their contents into the air; a large cauldron wafted green mist over its congregants; and students toiled over yellowing books. Li scoured the room for a moment and walked to a rectangular pit of sand, in the middle of which stood a wood-and-hay training dummy.

"The manifestation of every spell springs forth from the creeping void only on the conscious power of will," said Li. He grabbed my right hand, forced my palm flat, and aimed it at the dummy.

"Yeah, yeah, yeah," I said, exhausted after the previous experiences, "save the Lovecraft for someone else." I tightened my arm and stared at the dummy. Nope, no fireball.

"No, no, no." Li smacked my forearm, bent my elbow slightly, and adjusted each individual fingertip. "Relax, demonstrate proper form, and stop questioning your master, *trainee*."

I rolled my eyes and permitted the ragdoll manipulation.

"There we go. Now focus."

I tried my best to hold the molded position and focused on the dummy. My palm warmed. *Hm, maybe the old bastard is on to something.* A single spark jumped from my hand and plopped to the ground. I looked at the tiny scintillation and frowned. What a limp-dicked showing.

"How is it I went all goddamn Oppenheimer on those bugs back there in Dimension X but can only manage a spark here?"

"Oppen-what?" Li waved a hand dismissively and continued, "Well, your focus came from fear in that instance, and you were also in a manifest realm, where one's magical ability is markedly more attuned." Li wrinkled his brow and rubbed his chin. "Ah, yes! I have an idea."

He looked about the room. Spotting someone, he called, "Miriam, come here please."

"Right away, Master Li." The familiar young woman scampered to us, twisted wand in hand, and greeted Li.

"Oh, I know you. Big fan of my elixirs," she said and winked. Her thin robes matched her coal-black hair, flowing together thick and graceful about her shoulders and back. Strange tattoos covered her angular temples and high cheekbones, some coursing below the margin of her robes . . . Man, how they made my mind—and eyes—wander.

"Up here, snipe," she said and snapped her fingers inches from my face. Blushing slightly, my eyes shot up to hers, which were blue and brilliant. They reflected a fixed and dreary melancholy that spoke of two lifetimes of torment, but they radiated a genius that was not of this world—or the last one. This both excited and unnerved me, and I looked away.

Li smiled at her and pointed at the dummy. "If you would please, summon a reanimate just behind the dummy."

Miriam bowed and walked to the figure. She removed a stone kris from her belt, pricked her scarred palm, and spilled a few drops of blood onto the sand. With some unintelligible words, she tossed a handful of white dust onto the bloodied ground and stepped away.

"Weird bitch," I said under my breath. The little smirk she wore while cutting her palm had made me shiver, and my throat tightened when she glanced at me and smiled.

The blood glowed faintly at first then intensified and coalesced into a black pool that bubbled and smoked. The white dust spread across the pool and flowed upward into a humanoid figure like a candle melting in reverse. Miriam cooed and clapped as the mutilated entity took form, but the sight had the rest of us inching backward.

The creature looked about, its white orbs twinkling and bending light with every movement. It stared at its palms, seeming to take stock of its new existence. The desiccated flesh of its fingertips clung to spidery digits. With a snarl, it pounced on the dummy and sank rows of disorganized teeth deep into the hay.

"That-a boy," said Miriam, clasping her hands together. The ashen tattoos flowing over her countenance turned upward as she smiled. Her revelry disgusted me, but I couldn't help but admire her power.

After a fierce rip, the creature spat cloth and hay to the ground and leaped back. It turned to us and smiled—*fucking smiled!*—at Miriam, revealing crooked rotten gums and a tangle of black and yellow teeth worn to the nubs. Shifting its attention to me, it trotted forward.

I inched a little farther back, and my heart thumped in my chest.

"They can leap up to six feet and are surprisingly agile," said Li. "Dispense with it quickly."

I held up my right palm and attempted to replicate Li's earlier teachings.

The reanimate broke into a shambling sprint, puffs of sand flying up behind it. Li readied his right hand as he observed my amateur flail. A small fiery sphere readily formed at his fingertips.

I pumped my hand, hoping for something—*anything*—to happen.

"Come on, shit! Fire!" I retreated a few steps. The reanimate opened its mouth wide, hunched its back, and pounced. I reeled back and screamed, throwing my other hand up. A translucent wave blasted from my left hand and slammed into the beast, flinging it backward into the dummy.

Miriam put her hand to her mouth and looked away. The reanimate attempted to stand, but its fractured femur buckled and pushed through its thigh. A slight nausea rose in my gut as the maimed creature gurgled and crawled toward me; I almost pitied it. Despite the horrible injury, it didn't show an ounce of distress. I, on the other hand, felt like a truck had hit me; I was sore and completely exhausted.

"How is that thing even moving?" I said.

"The pain the reanimate feels on this plane is a tiny fraction of the suffering it experiences in its own realm," said Li.

"Hell?" I said.

"Some come from there, yes," said Li. "Most are from Kull, where the Children dwell. I often wonder which would be a worse fate, but our summoning of these poor souls offers them a merciful interlude regardless of the violence we visit upon them." Li centered his sphere of flame on the reanimate and obliterated it in an instant.

Miriam shielded her eyes and turned to Li. "Will you be needing anything else, Master Li?" she said, holding back tears.

"No, Miriam, and thank you for your time."

She bowed and returned to her research area as she rubbed her tumid eyes.

Li observed the smoking meat and hay in the test area and grinned. "Seems you're a lefty." He pointed to my left hand, which glowed faintly.

I looked down at it and then at my right hand.

"Damn, well, I did use my left hand to burn the bugs up, but what was that shockwave thing that just happened?"

"You had the motivation to get the reanimate away from you and the energy to accomplish the task, so you generated a shockwave. Instinct can save your life, but it wasn't the cone of flame I was looking for. You need to practice on your focus."

"Gee, thanks," I said, still marveling at my handiwork. "I would have felt more confident if I'd had my mace with me." I thought of Gor and the awesome graduation present.

"Mind and body combat forms are not mutually exclusive," said Li. He unsheathed a narrow dagger with a sparkling gemstone embedded in the hilt. "But I find that neophytes need to devote more time to learning the arcane arts."

"Why is that?" I peered into the crimson gemstone.

"Unless the secrets of the arcane existed during your time on Earth, I can safely assume those new to this world have never been exposed to their intricacies."

"Didn't seem so intricate to me." I grinned, formed my hand into a pistol, and shot it at the dummy.

Li shook his head. "Don't get too cocky. The reanimate Miriam summoned was of the weakest variety and more often used to train children and cripples." The other arcanists erupted into laughter, but Li turned to the stairwell. "Housekeeping! Cleanup in the sanctum range!"

A young Hollow girl charged down the stairs and posted in front of us.

"Well, girl, where is your custodial gear and bin?" Li patted the girl on the head, carefully averting her gaze.

"Sir, I'm not a custodian, I'm a runner with an urgent message from the central barracks."

"Well, out with it," said Li.

"An order to muster has been issued for first and second battalions with request for support from the Arcane Academy, including Shadebringer Robbins." She placed a scroll in Li's hands and saluted.

"Ah, an excellent training opportunity for us, but somewhat curious that they'd request the shadebringer by name," said Li as he pored over the order. "Return to the central barracks, and report that we will be ready within the hour."

The girl bowed and bolted back through the stairwell.

The others looked on with excitement.

"A most fortuitous occurrence for the academy," said Li. "Whenever we have the opportunity to offer our services and prove our worth, we must take it with the utmost haste." He strode to what I assumed was his own desk and thumbed through the registry.

"Miriam Urdegaard, Giuseppe di Medici," he said and turned to me, "and Clyde Robbins. Prepare your gear and report to the parade field in one hour. I'll send word for a dozen other thaumaturgists." Li checked off twelve additional names on his scroll and ordered an apprentice to summon them.

The room broke into chaos on Li's final gesture. Miriam and a few of her assistants scrambled from their project and disappeared into the stairwell.

"I have no idea what's going on or what I'm supposed to do," I said.

Without looking up from his own preparations, Li said, "Put on your gear, grab your mace, and report to the parade field. I'll find you when I arrive."

CHAPTER 23

RESERVATIONS

We can only surmise the forces at play when the dead are reanimated.
We can only hope those suffering such a fate are far from either waygate.

— AI, WANDERER OF IRGENDWO,
CAUGHT BETWIXT REALMS: A TREATISE ON REANIMATES

THE FIRST AND SECOND BATTALIONS stood in perfect formation on the parade field, their banners rising proudly into the air. Guards and runners inspected every corner of the field while commanders barked orders and exchanged tactical maps. Robed men and women stood far off from the armored battalions, calling out strange names as they picked through various spell reagents and potions. I stood quietly and adjusted my armor, twirled the mace, and occasionally glanced at Miriam.

"Aye, this greenhorn wants his first taste of blood, does he?" Miriam shambled to me, left armpit burdened with books and her pockets overflowing with equipment. She smiled and emptied the blood of a decapitated rat into a small flask.

"As long as it's not my own," I said. "Where did you find that, anyway? I haven't seen a single animal since arriving here."

She laughed and tossed the corpse aside after shaking out the last drop. "Oh, you just need to know where to look. No shortage of rats or politicians in Junedale." She sidled up to me with an ornery grin and ran a sharp fingernail across my cheek. "I could summon some mighty souls with some of this young buck's juice," she said, biting down on the fingernail.

I gulped and sidestepped away to the others, trying not to look her in the eye. My face grew warm and flushed, and I stifled a smile.

Li approached, clapped, and we turned crisply to him and saluted.

"A Junedale forager group last reported in the vicinity of the sulfurous caverns is now three hours over its expected return time since our planar vision." Li etched the relative locations in the sand and marked the caverns with an X.

"Wait, what?" I said. "Is this the same group we saw during the divining lesson?" I remembered the ragtag group of villagers complaining about the reek of sulfur.

"Yes," said Li. "So, whatever happened must have happened very fast and immediately after the vision ended."

"Striders?" said Miriam excitedly.

"The stink of the caverns generally masks the scent of their prey, but an unfortunate errant encounter is possible," said Li.

A battalion commander howled a call to attention that the other officers parroted to the platoon level. Thousands of boots slammed together at once in a crisp *thump*.

"We saw there was a Hollow in the group," said Giuseppe. The ugly bastard looked even worse in better lighting.

Miriam beamed and folded her hands together. "Oh, they're magnificent and fascinating creatures—such beautiful and dreamy eyes."

"Yes, for soul-sucking aberrations of fate, they do have nice eyes," said Giuseppe.

"Hollows are invaluable for searching out and rerouting striders," said Li. "Another reason an encounter is less likely."

Giuseppe removed a handful of dried leaves from his satchel and sprinkled them in the air. The leaves tumbled and swayed erratically at first then assembled themselves on the sand. "It says nothing of the fate of the foragers," said Giuseppe, nudging the leaves for additional clues.

"What is the exact message?" said Li.

The leaves tumbled and twisted on the sand as if alive and, although I had no idea the message, I could not look away. Giuseppe tilted his head and pawed through them.

"I think it means *dishonor*," said Miriam, and she scratched her head. "But I could be wrong."

Giuseppe shrugged and covered the leaves with sand. "The whims of magic make its messages rather nonspecific, and such vagueness is useless."

"No shit," I said. "How many were in the forager group?"

"One hundred, plus a small detachment of volunteer blades," said Li. He held his chin, eyes still fixed on the ground. "Usually if there is trouble, a runner is dispatched back to Junedale, or a smoke signal is sent. Again, we can only assume that whatever happened must have been quick and overwhelming."

"That alone can't be the reason for taking two thousand soldiers out on the drop of a dime," I said.

The others nodded and looked to Li.

"You're a lot smarter than your words betray, Sergeant Robbins," said Li as he tapped his nose. "Foul things are afoot that cannot be openly discussed for fear of causing mass panic. Besides, it's not your place to question the leadership."

"Just when the hell *can* we question the leadership?" I snorted and swirled my index finger around my temple.

"Well, if our fears come to fruition, your curiosities will be more than sated."

"Arcane! Post!" shouted a battalion commander at our group.

Li turned to the commander, saluted, and marched us abeam of the armored battalions. Some of the soldiers stared at us from the corners of their eyes as we stood at attention.

Their gazes bothered me, but I tried not to show it. I wasn't really sure why, either. I only cared about a few in the group, Reginald and Jens, maybe Marg too, and could barely recall their names otherwise. I guess being *the other* kind of sucked in any situation.

* * *

Each battalion separated into twin companies and shuffled their heavy weapons to the front. Rhythmic footfalls erupted dust dervishes that carried off in the breeze. Metal clanged and jangled amid hushed chatter, and gracile scouts sprinted out in multiple directions from the formation, swinging wide and scrutinizing the horizon with their spyglasses. The arcanists and I remained near the command group.

"Are you ready to be tested, Shadebringer?" said a short Scotsman covered in heavy plate armor. I looked over the layered plates, ornate helmet, and bulky bracers and marveled at how such a small frame supported so much steel.

"Sir, I'll do my best but I—"

"That's the spirit," said the short man. "Yours is not to question why." He grabbed a mace from his hip and held it in the air. In an instant, one of the beanpole scouts trotted next to him.

"Take a partner and triple your distance to the east toward the sulfurous caverns. If you encounter striders, have your partner bait them downwind of the caverns and report back to me." They exchanged salutes, and the scout sprinted off.

"I am Colonel Hop of the second heavy weapons battalion," he said.

"Pleased to meet you. I'm Clyde Robbins."

The long strides of the scouts carried them fast away from the formation, and I looked to Hop. "But if you're heavy weapons, why are you moving scouts around?"

"Because I'm the commander of this expedition as a whole, and I need information." He paused for a moment, face waning grim. "Even if it means sending them to their deaths."

"To their deaths?" I turned to see the two swift men disappear on the horizon.

"One will likely not return," said the colonel. "The weight of command, my young friend, is heavier than any metal."

I looked away in disgust at the colonel's trite platitude; I knew it would be purchased with another man's blood. I stepped away from him and closer to the arcanists as they pored over scrolls and maps on rolling platforms. I continued to visualize the scout's death in any number of savage fashions in this savage world and wondered what awaited the rest of us. *Anything but fucking striders*, I almost said as my mind manufactured fear.

"Colonel Hop is a good soldier but arrogant and brash," whispered Li from behind me.

I slowed my march and walked next to him. "Were you eavesdropping?" I said with a wry grin.

"No, of course not, but you project your internal strife quite readily."

"Yeah, I get it that every sad soul here is expendable, just like we were in the past life, but it doesn't make it any easier."

"Something far worse than a pack of striders may be out there," said Li. "And what is the death of two men if many more can be saved?"

The marching mass was a blend of metal, wood, and flesh that reminded me of a single living being from afar. Regardless, one only needs to seek the eyes of its constituents to behold different faces, each a life with individual pains, concerns, and memories. "Seems like apathy toward sacrifice is what brought us here in the first place."

• • •

We moved across the plains until the gates of Junedale vanished. Scattered flecks of grob dotted the dead ground where previous harvests had long passed, but other soldiers picked the ground clean before I could grab any. I marched close to the arcanists but scanned up and down the formations for Jens and Keats.

The command group, an ornate flock of officers and bureaucrats, marched abeam of our formation, their gleaming armor and colorful flags contrasting against our simple metal, leather, and cloth. Colonel Hop strode outside the command group and weaved between us and the soldiers. Laughter erupted on occasion as he chatted and gestured wildly among his troops, even getting a hearty guffaw from Li during a brief exchange.

"There's something on the horizon!" A shout echoed from the lead formation.

Pulling out his spyglass, Colonel Hop perched himself on one of our mobile platforms and scanned the landscape. An abrupt jolt told me he'd spotted something and his lips turned downward. "Battalions, halt!" he shouted.

A loud metallic clang followed, and every soldier stopped.

"Good god," he said, pulling his eye from the spyglass. "Medics and a litter, now!"

Two medics heaved a stretcher and bolted from the formation toward two small dots in the distance. We waited as the dots took the form of men on their return, one leaning hard and limping as the other pulled and dragged him forward. The medics arrived and heaved the injured man onto the stretcher and sprinted toward us. As they drew closer, I could discern wails among the litter team and droplets of blood sprinkled down from the injured scout's body.

The medics stumbled into the formation, sweating and breathless, and lowered the stretcher to the ground. On it, a lanky man writhed—one of the scouts the colonel had dispatched earlier.

"Son, what happened out there?" Colonel Hop kneeled next to the stretcher and placed his hand on the scout's forehead.

Half the scout's face had been shredded beyond recognition. His left leg ended in a jagged drapery of flesh just above the knee. Slashes crisscrossing his abdomen extruded internal fat and loops of bowel below his navel.

"Kir Sol," he said on a brittle exhale, "is open." He closed his eyes for the last time.

"What terrors await us," said Li, emotionless, as he stared a mile into the distance. "This is but a small taste."

The four simple monosyllabic words spread quickly outward from the extinguished scout, and the soldiers chattered and murmured. To me, it meant little; my eyes were fixated on the mutilated scout.

Miriam sauntered to the dead scout and sank her fingers into one of his wounds, and the profane *squish* of her digits penetrating his flesh made me gag. The soldiers looked away and cursed, apparently equally disgusted, as she stirred her fingers in his belly. Pulling them free, she focused on the sullied digits, rolling the meat and filth between her thumb and forefinger. She raised her hand to the other arcanists and Colonel Hop. Blackened grime crept across her hand and plunged beneath her fingernails.

"It's the living rot of the reanimates," she said with ghoulish delight. She removed a rag from an oily reagent pouch and cleansed the rot from her hands.

"What happened?" Colonel Hop turned to the surviving scout.

"He was on his back, covered in the things—the reanimates—fighting and panicking when I found him." The scout shook and cradled his head in his hands. "Another fresh skeleton lay a short distance away, also covered. Most of the creatures stopped their feasting when they saw me and came for me. I ran a wide circle back to Po, killed the few remaining on him, and helped him back here."

"A valiant act deserving of high honor," said Colonel Hop. "Were you followed?"

The scout shook his head.

"Sir, my circuit brought me close to the entrance of the sulfurous caverns. Thousands of the beasts were milling about the mouth, and the unholy lamentations of hundreds more were issuing forth from within."

Colonel Hop looked toward the caverns and back at the dead scout. The creeping black rot had spread over his body.

"He must be dealt with soon, or he'll turn and attack us," said Miriam. She placed the back of her hand on the corpse's forehead and nodded. "The rot gathers inside."

Colonel Hop looked again at the corpse and waved. Two soldiers dragged it downwind of the formation and set it alight. Before they returned, the immolated body reanimated, stood to its feet, and then collapsed in a burning heap.

Flames and an explosion surged into my memory. The jet bolted by again. I heard Charlie screaming. I smelled the napalm. I saw Claude wrapped head to toe in bandages. The Vietnamese girl pointed to the hole I'd put in her chest and smiled. I shook my head hard, panting, and the visions vanished.

"We must assume that this was the fate of the foraging party," said Colonel Hop as the burning corpse billowed smoke into the air and crackled. "Colonels Adams and Partridge."

The two officers posted with crisp salutes.

"Arrange each of your battalions into assault formations, heavies to the front and support elements on each flank, wheeled midline."

The officers saluted and bolted off amid shouts and jangling metal.

Li hurried to the colonel and pulled him aside. "Colonel, do you intend to attack the gate?"

Colonel Hop smiled and patted Li on the shoulder. "Indeed I do, Master Li. We must seal it again, or else every forager party will be at risk."

"Wait a second," I said to Li, which simultaneously raised Colonel Hop's interest. "If the gate is open now, can't we all get the fuck out of here?"

The colonel snickered and glanced at Li.

"Mog shattered Kir Sol at the height of the conflict between our cities as a final act of spite. This broke the link between Irgendwo and the blessed hereafter and left an open rift through which legions of horrors invaded and almost destroyed us all. Walking through that gate would lead you straight to Kull."

"Seems like an asshole thing to do," I said.

"He was losing the war and wanted all of us to share his fate—and we may well have if we hadn't sealed the gate when we did. It seems now someone has deliberately reopened it. And we neither know the count nor the composition of the creatures that stir from the gate, beyond the estimate of *thousands*."

"Nor will we until we've finished counting their bodies," said the colonel, polishing the handle of his mace. "Our scouts cannot penetrate through the legion of the things, and your diviners have said nothing of any significant value. Our only course of action is to strike early."

"Sir, we should wait and—"

The colonel raised his hand and waggled his finger. "We are going to strike at Hell's heart and seal that damned gate, and that's all there is to it." He pulled down a set of spectacles from his ornate metal helmet and walked off with his advisors.

The soldiers melded into their assault formations amid shouts and shuffling equipment. Another gong from the command detachment set them to a brisk march. I trod next to our mobile platforms, excitement building in my belly.

CHAPTER 24

GREATER EXPECTATIONS

I miss the taste of figs most, though ruminating on such things is pointless. I am no longer who I was. I am now merely a servant. Maraine will light my path to salvation. And should I fail, I will live on in the memories of my children, wherever they may be.

—DIARY OF EK MARAINE

I RAN UP AND DOWN THE TWO MAIN formations in search of Jens and Keats. Men and women marched in excited lockstep as rumor of the confrontation spread.

"Jens." I recognized the German, though he had augmented his flight uniform with a heavy black leather doublet. His face appeared more wrinkled than usual.

"So, it appears we are marching on the waygate," he said.

"Yes, I was there when Hop made the decision. Li was very much against it, but Hop didn't give him the time of day."

"Hop has a reputation for being impulsive, but he's always come out on top. I do have my reservations, though."

"Why?"

"Mog destroyed Kir Sol at the apex of the conflict to engender chaos and entangle Junedalian forces with the horrors that spilled out.

However, these creatures don't care whether they feast on Junedalian or Morite flesh, and both cities are vulnerable to attack."

"If we don't attack the gate, we're in a world of shit. And if we do attack the gate, we're in a world of shit."

"Yes, that's the crux of the situation," he said. The man was completely humorless.

"A catch-22 if I've ever heard one."

"What?" He cocked his head.

"Never mind. Where's Keats?"

"The medics are mixed with the fighting units," he said, shaking his head. "He got his wish."

"Everyone wants to be a fucking hero until the shooting starts—or should I say *slashing*?" I said.

Jens cocked an eyebrow. "You do realize most of us, including Reginald, have taken fire in one or both lives?"

I inhaled to respond but had nothing. Indeed, Reginald had probably endured a level of gunfire and artillery shelling that would have broken most, but Keats's hunger for the front lines still eluded me. "Then why would . . ." I trailed off as his diary entries trickled back.

"We all have our demons. Some in this life, some in the last, some in both," said Jens in a tone that almost suggested he had long come to terms with his own. The Vietnamese girl barged into my mind again, blood smearing her beautiful dress and countenance, and she waved. My heart burned.

With every step, the mountains drew closer and the reek of sulfur stronger; the otherwise ashen mist in the sky began to stain a rich crimson. Scouts ran wide missions to our flanks and rear, but only the bravest and fastest dared approach the caverns.

"Where are the bodies?" said Colonel Hop. "The scouts are saying they've seen no bodies." The stout Scotsman tapped his armor with his mace and locked eyes with Li.

"Giuseppe," said Li, "what do you see?"

The unsightly diviner poured water into a small snuffbox pinched between his gnarled fingers and brought it just below his lonely eyeball.

He gazed into the reflection the placid water provided then shook his head in a dissatisfied huff. "The future is muddled and opaque, even the immediate future," he said. "Something is blocking my visions."

"What good are your magic tricks?" Colonel Hop scoffed and tapped his mace. "Steel and muscle will settle this, not witchery."

"Sir, we must be vigilant. Our vision has never been blocked like this," said Li. "We do not know who reopened the Kir Sol waygate or why."

Hop chuckled and wiped a layer of sweat from his brow. "It doesn't matter if it was a lone group of cultists or the goddamn Morites themselves who reopened the gate. The problem now is reanimates. Reanimates don't organize ambushes. They kill, and they eat. That's all they do."

"Reanimates are the least of my fears, sir. Somebody or something had to reopen the waygate, and we *must* glean their purpose."

Colonel Hop rolled his eyes.

Miriam sprinted to Li and tapped him on the shoulder.

"What is this?" he said and investigated her cupped hands.

"Lots of bone dust mixed in with the soil," she said, smiling. "Lots of necromancy going on here, Master Li." She scattered the dust to the ground and giggled. "This isn't Morite work."

"Caverns in sight!" the herald at the front of the formation bellowed through a large horn.

The yawning entrance belched gray and black plumes that rushed over the rust-colored rocks surrounding it. Just the sight of it conjured memories of the foulest midsummer industrial odors the Port of Philadelphia had provided me as a kid. The smoke rolled out in industrial clockwork, but not a single reanimate appeared.

Again, the gong sounded, and the formation stopped. Soldiers stood at the foot of the caverns as the rocks breathed. My calves, thighs, and shoulders ached under blotches of sweat that soaked my uniform, but the balmy air blasting forth from the caverns kept me sweating.

"Foolish beasts must have pursued something into the caverns and fallen into the chasm," said Colonel Hop with a laugh. "So much for the looming menace of the reanimates."

Excusing himself from the command group, Li consulted with

Giuseppe and his leaves to little effect. Miriam examined the dirt, grain by grain. I considered asking her what she was doing, but she seemed completely absorbed in the task.

"Sealing the gate will be a child's task," said Colonel Hop. He looked to Li and waved him forward. "Perhaps even our costumed compatriots could lead the heavy battalion's charge?"

Li's mouth turned downward at Hop's patronizing bullshit, but, otherwise, he maintained his composure.

"Kind of like your logic of bringing your only super weapon on a grunt mission," I said under my breath. Apparently, it was not far enough under my breath; Miriam broke into a shrill cackle, and the colonel glared at me.

"Boy, did you have something to say?"

I averted my attention to Miriam and feigned conversation. "Oh, nothing sir, just shooting the shit with the death witch here." My face burned.

He glanced at me a final time and returned to plotting. Miriam looked up from her pile of dirt and dragged her tongue across her upper lip.

My skin crawled, and I stepped back and away from her.

"How are we going to get two battalions of soldiers into that cavern if it's an inferno?" I asked Li.

Li stared at Colonel Hop, who was colluding with his advisors. "That was a major problem the last time we had to seal the waygate," said Li. He pawed his chin and timed the billowing cycle with his other fingers. "The chasm fills with smoke at certain intervals, which can be managed in small groups, but that is the least of the perils in there."

"Of course," I said and awaited further gloom. "And we haven't even accounted for the reanimates that supposedly massacred the foraging party and killed two of our scouts."

"Correct."

"So, what do we do?"

"Whatever Colonel Hop says."

"But *we're* supposedly the experts on weird shit, aren't we?"

"Supposedly."

I sighed and thought about how things weren't too much different between this life and the last. The experts would no doubt expound on their warnings in some dull tome that only they and future experts would ever read.

* * *

The soldiers stood in silent trepidation while the officers bullshitted and laughed, cut maps into the sand, and sharpened their weapons. Colonel Hop scribbled into a small notebook, occasionally pointing and barking orders while others darted around him. I marveled at how one-sided the entire undertaking appeared to be: He delivered his performance, and the others clapped.

Jacques stepped from outside the circle and shook Colonel Hop's hand, and they exchanged words. Turning an occasional ear to them, I observed Jacques altering the map at his pleasure, with Hop nodding.

Li appeared just as amazed at the Frenchman's audacity as I. "Having such a close connection to Octavius must be emboldening," he whispered. "Just about anyone else would have earned a backhand for fuddling with Hop's map."

"I have a plan," announced the colonel as the command circle broke. Jacques retreated to his own formation, and other subordinates rushed to fill his place. A hush fell over the formations, and Hop raised his mace. "First battalion will enter the caverns first, in company-size elements, en route to the waygate. Second battalion will guard the cavern entrance should any errant striders catch our scent or any reanimates return. Once first battalion is posted on the opposite side of the caverns, we will send a scout through to signal second battalion to join us. Then, together, we will march on the gate and seal it. Any questions?" Colonel Hop observed the eager soldiers as they stood at attention.

"Let's get it done!" he shouted. A spirited "hurrah!" resounded from both battalions, and the officers set to organizing their troops.

I pulled Li aside. "Why the hell are we splitting our forces and going through a cave?" I whispered.

"The caverns are far too narrow for our full contingent to safely traverse, and the mountains stretch south for hundreds of miles."

"And over them?"

Li shook his head. "One of Hannibal's own lieutenants wrote a treatise on mountain warfare before he departed Irgendwo long ago. Needless to say, scaling the Everpeaks would be more costly in soldiers and time than even a southern march."

"It can never be easy." I shook my head and kicked up some dirt that rose and swirled away in the wind.

* * *

Our two battalions stood before the maw of the caverns. Waves of smoke, each preceded by a cacophonous whistling wind, rolled out and onto the plains, showering us with soot. A bloody glow flickered from deep within, dying the rocks a dark red. The younger soldiers reminisced on the reek of cordite and black powder, while those of more distant eras ruminated on mines, volcanoes, and other geologic phenomena.

I followed the endless rocks skyward until they vanished into the ubiquitous mist. The first two hundred or so feet appeared scalable to an athletic soldier with little equipment. The ascent from there on looked impossible: a smooth vertical face rose with so little as a rent or jut in the rock for a bird to comfortably perch on. The sight made me appreciate Li's words and gave me a fleeting desire to read the book he'd mentioned.

"On the other side of this cave are the Infernal Plains," said Li. "The corruption and chaos that spread from the gate after Mog sundered it have rendered an entire geography of this world a hellscape."

"Ek Maraine and his lackeys . . . You'd figure that the evilest souls would have already been sent to Hell—instead of ending up here."

"They weren't evil to begin with," said Li. "Their doings here corrupted them both spiritually and physically. Ek Maraine and the other high councilors of Mora are rumored to be hideous beneath their opulent robes. The Silver Serpents brand and slice themselves in honorarium of their overlords' twisted forms."

I paused and remembered the hooded figure back in Mora and the clown I'd smashed with a paperweight. "These poor stupid fucks, opting for more conflict after being snuffed out by it on the first go around. It's a profound madness this place even exists."

"*She* deems it fit," said Li.

"Sounds like whoever is running things doesn't know what the fuck they're doing." I made no attempt to hide my casual heresy. The thought of a higher being toying with the eternal fates of thousands of war dead enraged me—motivated me—to such iconoclastic heights that I was ready to confront any believers who took issue with my words. But none seemed to hear or care. The caverns held their attention.

A gong crashed and broke my attention.

"First battalion, split and double file to your assigned location!"

The four companies of soldiers and their support units, about twelve hundred souls, separated and assembled; the arcanists and I followed to the left detachment.

The caverns dwarfed us as we marched forward, shrinking us to insignificant mounds of flesh as nature—or what passes for nature in this weird fucking world—tended to do. The ceiling hung jagged and dark far above our heads, with thousands of stalactites needling down on us. With every deluge of smoke, we hacked and wheezed as embers and soot washed over the rocks and rained down. And it was a short time before the dim light of the plains gave way to the crimson hue of the awaiting fire pit.

"The scouts certainly have their work cut out for them," said Li. He clumsily negotiated the rocky surface and poured out sweat.

"It can't be easy," I said, though I reconsidered my words as Miriam darted by. She maneuvered over the terrain on all fours, ignoring the filth and grime, and pawed through the rocks and bone fragments that littered the cave floor. Her glee fascinated and, in a way, invigorated me. But dragging my big ass over the rocks still proved painful. *Man, this has gotta suck for Keats.* I chuckled at the thought.

As we reached the chasm, the faint red glow bathed us in a terrible pall and a worse heat. Two narrow stone bridges spanned the inferno and appeared to be the only routes across, and I saw fear spread quickly across the ranks when we realized we'd be using those bridges. Stacked heavy with armor and supplies, sweat and soot combined to form black rivers that ran down our faces, stung our eyes, and soiled our clothes. And with every eruption cycle, more ash caked in our nostrils and clung to our faces.

"Crossing!" The gravelly voice of a sergeant bounded about the cavern.

Li sidestepped and peered around the line of soldiers that snaked in front of him. "This is where it gets interesting." He pulled his robes taut and tightened his sandals. The rest of us followed suit, except Miriam, of course.

Our momentum slowed at the crossing points to an unpleasant crawl. We languished behind dozens in front of us at the bridges as the sergeants shouted in between the surges and staggered the first waves across. Nervous energy sent my feet a-tappin' and my arms twitched; I fucking hated heights. The sentiment seemed widespread; many others had plenty of their own energy, and every discrete and labored step brought us closer to the source of our agitation.

"Surge!" The familiar shout sent us ducking just before the ground shook and the smoke rolled over us. A tumult of shouts perked my ears, and the line stopped. The soldiers whispered and gasped. The whispers grew to a rigorous murmur of surprise, fear, and incredulity.

"What happened?" I said to anyone who would listen.

A very tall African warrior turned to me and covered his heart with his hand. "A soldier was struck by surge debris and fell into the pit."

Jesus tap-dancing Christ. My nervousness bloomed into hand tremors and more sweat. Minutes passed, and a name—Bertram—of the heavy weapons company made its way back to us. He had apparently been struck by a molten rock and lost his footing. After the stir subsided, the line advanced. I pictured one last time a screaming descent into roiling lava and how a man, only forty feet in front of me, had just experienced it. *Good God, I hope it was quick.*

"Next!" the sergeant shouted, and I heaved myself over a rocky terrace. Miriam waved, and, together, we approached the platform leading to the bridge. The heat was unbearable, and every breath scorched my throat. A dull ache swirled in my stomach as we approached our stone bridge, which was about the width of a park bench—a goddamn bench! I wondered if the other bridge that ran parallel to ours was any less terrifying, but it was too late to check. Translucent heat waves blurred the paths across the searing abyss, and the group on the opposite platform looked like a smeared mural. I envied them as I looked again at the impossibly long stretch of the narrow bridge, and, suddenly, I understood poor Bertram's fate.

"Surge!" I beheld the ubiquitous sergeant covered in ash and small burns duck and shield his face. And for the first time, the pit came alive before my very eyes and blasted across the ceiling. It was like the cartoon oil geysers I'd seen on TV as a kid—a flowing column of black that exploded out of the abyss.

"This is gonna suck."

"Oh, what's a little bonfire to us?" Miriam giggled and wiped a layer of soot from her brow and smeared it on my nose.

"You know you're fucking nuts, right?"

She tilted her head and shrugged, part affirmation and part apathy. Kind of cute in a way.

The two companies opposite ours filed across their bridge in similar fashion, calling surges while sergeants sent them out in staggered intervals. From our platform, they looked like pewter toys, but my heart thumped heavily in my chest as every soldier shuffled across.

"Surge!" belted the voice again. The ground trembled, and a cloud of smoke and embers enveloped us, and I held my breath in fearful anticipation until it cleared. Counting every figure on the bridge, I made certain the number was the same, and I did so with every cycle. Torture.

"Our turn soon," said Miriam. She poked me in the ribs and winked.

Our short line advanced with every cycle, the anticipation driving me mad. Arriving at the edge, I peered as far down as my eyeballs would let me before the heat shut them. Waves of molten rock roiled below.

"You'll go blind doing that, you silly sod," said Miriam, but I ignored her, too focused on steadying my nerves.

"Next two," said the sergeant, and he waved us across.

Miriam started her trot over the chasm and turned to me, walking backward, her long robes dangling over her toes and brushing both edges of the narrow bridge. My head spun, and my stomach ached at the reckless sight as she motioned me to join her. Trembling, I forced myself onto the bridge after stomping a couple of times to test its steadiness. Eyes focused straight ahead, I pretended the fall was only a few feet—to little effect—and walked. I crouched to drop my center of gravity and took one careful step after another.

"Surge!"

"Oh, fuck." I squat on all four limbs and clenched everything as the ground trembled and Miriam howled with delight. Embers and smoke blitzed past and drowned out all other sounds, and when I opened my eyes, Miriam had doubled her distance and pranced onward. "Crazy bitch."

I arrived at the ledge to slow claps and whistles: quite the ball busting. Miriam pinched my cheeks and congratulated me in some demonic tongue, and all I could do was take it on the chin. But at least I wasn't Bertram.

Looking back to the other side, I saw more soldiers flowing across the bridges. A sentry was posted ahead of us to protect the advance as the remainder crossed. A bit embarrassed but no worse for the experience, I leaned against a rock and waited.

"I hope the terrain evens out a little bit," I said to nobody in particular, feeling the need to mix up my embarrassment and stress with a little chat.

"It levels out just before it opens onto the Infernal Plains," said a soldier I didn't know.

I glanced at him, a bulky olive-skinned warrior with a shaved head. "Sounds like a real fun place to be."

"It was a paradise before the gateway flooded it with unspeakable filth."

"Sounds like New Jersey."

"New Jersey?"

"Never mind. Where are you from?" I kicked a small pebble into the chasm.

"Venice." He leaned against his halberd and looked up. "The city states are now united in one Italy, I hear."

"Ah, you must be *battle-axe vintage.*" I remembered Gor's terminology for "old" and hoped he didn't take insult.

"Indeed, I am." He smiled and reached out to shake my hand, and I warily returned the gesture, recalling my previous lessons. "Dante."

"Clyde."

As the smoke rushed past, we peered over the chasm to inventory the troops.

"And you were present during the first waygate battle?"

He ruminated on the question for a few moments, glassy-eyed, and nodded. "Si, I was."

"How was it?"

"First time I ever saw a strider—paralyzed me right where I stood. I was one of eight in my platoon to survive. I sometimes recognize reanimates of our fallen from that day. Makes cutting their heads off a little more difficult."

"Man, you got some balls coming back for more."

"The tides of batt—"

A crooked arrow ripped through his throat and lodged in the ground with an audible shudder. Dante stared straight ahead and crumpled; the shock was frozen on his face.

I kneeled beside him and inspected the heinous wound. Medics ran to him amid shouts that spread wide across the chasm. I craned my neck to the distant ceiling: Bones and wood swarmed in the ash like maggots and coalesced into reanimated skeletons; their gracile, ash-stained hands gripped simple wooden bows.

"Ambush! Reanimates!"

The shouts grew panicked. Thousands of bow strings creaked as the skeletons pulled them taut.

"Oh shit." I dove. "I thought these fucking things weren't supposed to be organized?"

Whistling splinters fell thick on the soldiers and smashed into their bodies as they scurried over the bridges. Those killed instantly fell limp into the inferno, while others buckled and wheeled under a deluge of arrows. Some panicked and ran into others, and I could only watch in horror as they plunged to their fiery deaths or clung to the rock.

"To the defense." Li pulled me to my feet and turned defiantly to the enemy as they again aimed their bows.

With a synchronous *snap*, wooden death rained down.

Li threw his hands up and a cone of energy blasted from his fingertips and shattered droves of arrows midflight and blew the rest harmlessly into the walls.

"OK, you bastards." I opened my left hand and aimed at the ceiling. A small ball of flame formed in my palm, and I fired it upward. It soared and connected with the arm of a random reanimate and blasted the bow from its hand.

But the overall effect was limited, and pure exhaustion followed. "Holy shit, what happened to me?" I fell to a knee.

Li winked at me. "Not a bad start."

The reanimates nocked their arrows and took aim at me and the other arcanists. Nearby soldiers threw a wall of shields up as we cowered from the barrage. Shouts of agony rang out amid heavy *clanks* of arrows on metal. A soldier ripped an arrow from his chest, snapped it in half, and fell dead at my feet.

Li chanted and sent a triad of fireballs hurtling into the ceiling to devastating effect. The explosions blasted bones and bows into the pit with a slurry of ash and pebbles and stalactites. He gasped and held his breath as detritus plunged downward on the fleeing troops, but none were struck.

The remaining soldiers continued their hurried retreats or advances to either of the two ledges. A final wave of arrows ricocheted off the rocks or embedded in shields, and the skeletal mass sunk into the ceiling and disappeared.

"Anybody struck is going to turn," said Miriam. She picked up an arrow and rubbed a layer of living rot from the tip.

The commander cursed and stomped the ground.

One of the soldiers threw off her bulky armor and darted toward a wounded comrade.

"Xi, get back here!"

Soldiers shouted and waved their arms. The skeletal mass began to reform as she crossed the threshold of the bridge. She darted and dashed over the bodies and rocks that littered the path until she reached her target. She swept an arm beneath the man and lifted him to his feet, but he craned forward, weak and bleeding, arrows nestled in his back. The two started back toward us.

"Covering fire!" said the commander to Li, and he nodded and conjured another triad of fireballs as the skeletons reformed and took aim at the two. Li loosed the fireballs skyward and, in a trio of thunderous blasts, the enemy fell as fragments of wood and bone into the pit. But in mere seconds, the survivors reformed and nocked their arrows.

"I can't loft another volley," said Li. "I'm exhausted."

The two soldiers hobbled back to the ledge and a wall of shields surrounded them as more arrows fell. The arrows clinked and shattered on the hard stone and metal but struck no flesh. The group retreated deeper into the cave, out of sight of the reanimates, and set the wounded soldier down.

Miriam examined the spreading rot that coalesced around the embedded arrows and shook her head. "The rot's inside him. This one's a goner," she said and stood from his side.

"How much time?" said the commander.

"Any moment," said Miriam.

"Do we . . ." I paused and swallowed hard, "kill him?"

The soldier's eyes darted frantically about as we discussed his fate. Xi kneeled at his head and covered her eyes with a hand. The man grasped her other hand and pulled her close as tears streamed down both their faces. "My cherished rose, my warrior, you have made Irgendwo my Heaven, and you have saved me from Hell. *Wo zhi shu yu ni.*"

The moment weakened me, but the beauty was immutable, terrible. I beheld at once suffering and love in each of their eyes, these two warriors from different eras of existence. They had found each other in this terrible place—brought together by arcane circumstance—and thrived. And now they would be torn apart. My heart ached.

"Touching," said Miriam, and she sighed, "but unless you want to join him in undeath, you should back away."

Xi slowly pulled her hand from his and left her stricken lover to his fate.

"He may prove useful when he turns." Miriam cleansed more rot from her fingers and pawed through her scrolls.

The commander shook his head and scowled at Miriam. "You vile witch! He's earned the right to a proper death, and your sick experiments will not take that from him."

She snickered and put her hands on her hips.

"Not while I draw breath," said Xi, and she drew her sword.

The wounded soldier raised a finger and coughed up a mouthful of blood. "Let her speak."

Miriam curtsied and pointed her dagger-shaped index finger at the dying man. "They run in packs, and their senses are acute, especially the recently turned." She tapped her head. "Hood him and bind his hands, and let me guide him at the head of the main formation. If there are more of them ahead, hidden or not, he'll attempt to move toward them, and, by extension, we'll know where they are."

The arcanists nodded, as did a couple of the foot soldiers. I thought the entire idea pretty disgusting, but the pragmatist in me—and my fear of Miriam—kept me silent.

The soldier coughed another fountain of black blood forth and wheezed. He looked up at Miriam and grinned. "Death witch, you may use me if it will save the others."

Xi gasped. "Diokles, my love, is this your will?"

"It is my will."

* * *

"God damn Hop, that arrogant fool," said the commander through clenched teeth. Dozens of soldiers lay riddled with arrows and motionless over the chasm, while others moaned and cried out for help. "We need to help them," he said and waved his hand over the carnage. "We need to get word of the ambush to second battalion. There must be something lying in wait ahead. We cannot proceed without second battalion."

"I suspect that second battalion is already gone," said Giuseppe. Everyone in earshot turned to him.

"On what madness do you base this assessment?" Panicked, the commander swallowed hard, sweat trickling down his forehead.

Giuseppe uncovered a glass sphere. Inside it, hundreds screamed. Metal struck metal. Reanimates. Blood. Strider. The commander stared into the glass dull-eyed as the scene unfolded. A familiar roar blasted through the caverns and over the chasm until it was drowned by a surge. The soldiers chattered and begged their commander to make a decision. My heart sank at the thought of Jens and Keats meeting such terrible ends. The tragedy of warfare tasted as bitter here as it did in life.

"Whatever attacked second battalion is coming for us," said Li.

The commander looked over the scene of carnage but waved the artifact away and fell to a knee and grunted. "We're all doomed," he whispered into his forearm. "We've followed that fool blindly to our doom."

"Commander, with all due respect, this is not over yet, and you are here to lead—not brood," said Li.

The commander had the thousand-yard stare; Li's words meant nothing.

I looked down at him and shook my head in disgust.

He glanced up for a moment at me. His eyes rolled unnaturally away from one another, far beyond the margins of his sockets, and I recoiled from the amphibian spectacle. *What the fu—?* But a sudden burst of coughs drew my attention again to the dying soldier.

"We need a decision soon, or else it'll be right hard to control 'im," said Miriam. She grasped the afflicted man's blackening hand and squeezed it.

The commander said nothing. Li waved over two soldiers, and they looked to Miriam.

"Hood him, bind his hands, and fix a pike to him firm." Miriam pointed at the soldier.

The soldiers looked at each other, waiting anxiously for the other to act, and then down at their stricken comrade.

Diokles turned his head and coughed a plug of black slime onto the ground. His once vivid blue eyes had drifted to an opaque gray. "You heard the woman," he said with bestial notes emerging in his voice. "Get on with it."

The soldiers emptied a bag of rations and placed it over his head. They tied the bag loosely around his neck with thin rope and then bound his hands behind his back. Lifting him to his feet, they stripped off the head of a pike, affixed the wooden shaft to his hands, and walked him to Miriam.

The man known as Diokles shuffled off the last vestiges of his humanity. The creature now gurgled and groaned and followed Miriam's pike. With a heavy heart, I looked to Xi, who gazed blankly upon her former lover—a look of loss.

"Commander, assemble your troops. We must go forward." Li, still preoccupied with the commander, kneeled and grasped his shoulder. Head buried in his forearm, the commander continued to mumble and swear in various tongues.

"Hey, asshole, fucking think," I said and smacked the back of his head. The soldiers gasped, but the commander ignored the strike. "Fucking great. This catatonic asshole is no good to us."

Li nodded and called aloud for the next in command. Commander Jacques Pariseau trotted forward.

"I guess that's me," said Jacques, and he immediately called formation.

What was left of our decimated group centered on him. I stifled my disdain and settled on the rear of the formation to avoid trouble.

"We are proceeding toward the Infernal Plains to complete the mission," said Jacques. "We will fight our way through if necessary, but we cannot turn back. I need thirty souls to defend the bridges across the chasm while the rest of us proceed."

Hands began to rise, but Jacques picked most of them himself. Some dumbfounded, others stoic and resolved, they parted from the main formation and took up defensive positions near the bridge chokepoints.

Xi donned her armor and joined the vanguard. Whether she actively sought death, I did not know, but I well understood her reasons.

"Miriam, lead your canary into the cavern," said Jacques. He sneered at the former commander like he was a crushed insect.

Miriam smiled, took hold of the wooden pike, and began walking the fresh reanimate. The creature hobbled with little resistance and moaned in protest.

"Let's go," said Jacques, and our dwindling detachment trod toward the Infernal Plains. The former commander whimpered and twitched in the grip of madness.

CHAPTER 25

DULCE ET DECORUM EST

Pro patria mori

—WILFRED OWEN

THE GROUND CAME ALIVE BENEATH the soldiers of second battalion.

"Oh, god!" A soldier screamed, kicked, and flailed against a rotten hand that held him fast. A second hand sprang from the ground and wrenched his leg below the knee, snapping it backward and tearing it from his body.

The soldiers panicked and leaped like frightened rabbits as hands, bones, and rusting tools burst from the ground, some of the fresh living corpses still carrying grob on their backs.

"More of them! Alphas, assemble! Double intervals now!" a young captain shouted to no avail as his soldiers scattered from the writhing earth, trapped as molasses by their bulky armor. Bravo Company rushed to save their comrades, but the sea of hands tore many to pieces where they fell or eviscerated them through their armor.

"Hack this filth where it forms!" The Bravo Company commander raised her halberd high and pruned the reanimates with a savage swipe.

She sounded a command horn, and her heavy weapons company charged into the mass; reanimate arms, torsos, and heads filled the air. A second patch began to claw themselves to the surface, followed by a third and a fourth.

"Bravo and Charlie companies to the right flank. Alpha can handle the first patch," said Colonel Hop to his lieutenant.

Horns sounded, and the commanders howled for vengeance, wheeling to meet the living dead. Reanimates parried and struck with their tools, their inhuman strength shattering bone and weapon alike. Clanging metal and shouting reverberated through the mouth of the cavern.

"Oh, shit," said Keats, and he crept back.

A skeletal reanimate crashed headlong from the melee and leaped back to its feet. Its head swiveled on its narrow, bleached spinal column, and it swung its scythe wildly, impaling a bearded sergeant. The wooden handle shattered in its bony grip, and, grasping the blade, it snapped off the remaining metal in the soldier's back. Pleased with its kill, it paused in ghoulish and detached calculation, head spinning until the empty black orbits fell on Keats.

He scuttled backward and screamed for help, falling as the creature pounced on him and snapped its jaws inches from his face, its fingers digging into his armor.

A hefty, armored leg booted the skeleton at the waist and broke it in half.

"Marg," said Marg, and he pulled Keats from the melee.

Blubbering incoherently, Keats fled to the rear.

Soldiers hacked and smashed the corpses as they rose, pushing the army of dead to the mouth of the cave and finishing them against the rocks.

"Give it to this scum right hard, lads!" Colonel Hop shouted with delight. He seized his mace and sped from the command group. Advisors hung from his sides and begged him back, but he shoved them and charged. "Scottish ham for you, you filth!" He launched a stone at a reanimate and patted his bulging armored belly, and it attacked. After destroying it with a single blow, he reached down and plucked a gold tooth from the jawbone.

"Oh, come on now." He arched his back and shouted into the sky, "Is *this* the best Daedrina's bastards have got for us puny mortals?"

As if the gods themselves had heard him, the ground quaked. As it fractured and shook, Hop struggled to keep his footing.

A roar exploded from the depths, and a geyser of soil, rocks, and Scotsman surged into the air with the heaving gray corpulence of a gargantuan monstrosity. Its jaw opened and crashed shut, snuffing out the colonel's existence in an instant. Smashing into the ground and righting itself, the strider dug its triplex claws into the soil and charged into the nearest formation of soldiers, crushing and impaling some and devouring others. It warbled and shrieked, blood and bones dripping from its maw, in ecstasy of its feast.

"Pikes up!" the Bravo Company commander shouted and blew a horn to raise a wall of iron spikes.

Futility! the strider screamed into their minds, freezing many in icy paralysis; the pike wall buckled as some of the soldiers dropped their weapons and fled. The strider sprinted and crashed fearlessly into another group of soldiers, obliterating a squad. Claws soaked in blood, it righted itself and charged down two fleeing soldiers and shattered their bodies like crystal with a single kick.

"Keep it together!" screamed the Bravo commander. She stormed to the front of the formation and raised her halberd defiantly. "Give us your worst, you foul abomination!"

The strider spun, gulping down hunks of metal and meat, and warbled at the commander, baring its teeth to mock her. The soldiers enveloped her in a wall of pikes as it broke into a sprint. Bracing her halberd against the ground, she kneeled and faced the monstrosity. It bounded and pounced, maw hanging open, and crashed down as she rolled away. The halberd and a dozen pikes sank deep into its head, and it screeched. The soldiers held fast while it thrashed and stomped, their bodies flailing like toys in a child's hands. Some slipped and were heaved into the air, but most held strong. A second group of pikes charged into the creature's leg, hobbling it. The mass of bodies, metal, and pikes dragged it down, and the soldiers poured their rage and fear into it.

"Aye, men! Another exhibit for the Hall!" The Bravo commander pulled a gladius from her belt and sank it deep, and her soldiers roared with approval.

With a meek and waning cry, the strider's lower jaw dropped open like a massive trunk, and a spiral of bilious effluent exploded from its mouth. Bone fragments, metal, wood, rocks, and chunks of undigested fat rained down in incomprehensibly vile liquefaction. Those soaked screamed for moments before disintegrating into amorphous pools of humanity and metal. Exposed flesh melted with the slightest spatter, while metal and cloth armor hissed and smoked. Soldiers scattered from the toxic pool, frantically disrobing anything the bile touched.

"You're already dead," said the strider, muddy words escaping from its throat. "Soon, we will all be one." It capsized on its hulking maw, legs and claws twitching.

Soldiers swarmed the fallen creature and hacked every inch of exposed flesh until all motion ceased. The Bravo commander bounded up the creature's body using every impaled pike as a step. She stepped onto the apex of its rounded maw and planted Junedale's banner. Cheers exploded from every corner of the battlefield, but screams of the wounded soon replaced them.

"Keats, are you OK?" Jens approached his shaken friend, who was cowering on his heels and cradling his head.

Keats nodded.

"Were you bitten or slashed?" Jens helped him to his feet and brushed away the dust.

"Yes, but it didn't get through my armor." He inspected his shredded leather tunic. "How many were infected?"

"More than we have salve to treat the rot. They'll have to be put down before they turn unless the source can be amputated."

Keats shook his head and shirked from the carnage, but the cries for help forced him to act. He swung his satchel forward and took inventory, and with a shaking hand, he removed a flawless steel bone saw and inspected the blade. It undulated gracefully toward the blackened leather handle—firm, sharp, and ready. Grasping it with whitened knuckles, he turned to a young soldier squeezing his savaged and blackening forearm.

"I am Reginald Keats, and I—" He froze and gulped. "And I need to take this off." He gripped the soldier's forearm above the rot and inhaled deeply as he aligned the bone saw. But his arm wouldn't move the blade. He dropped it, squeezed his hand, and reached into a pocket. Fumbling through his little red book, he flipped to the final pages and squinted: *I will love you forever.*

Smoke and ash poured from the mouth of the caverns and sprinkled down on them, the smell acrid, industrial, and choking. The Western Front breathed upon him once again, and every soldier looked exactly like the young officer at the bottom of the trench.

* * *

"Apply the tourniquet above the joint. Above the joint. Above the joint." Steiner grabbed Keats's hands and guided them along the sickly white flesh just above the soldier's elbow. Below the joint crept a dusky layer of rot that moved with such vigor that Steiner's usual methodical technique was discarded for haste.

"Allow me," he said, and his lips twitched. He removed the cloth from Keats's hands and cinched it down on the soldier's arm. The steady ooze of blood slowed to a drip from the jagged injury. He then pulled a scalpel from his belt and sliced circumferentially around the soldier's scant remaining normal flesh. The soldier clenched his teeth and growled through them in agony, but Keats held him fast.

"Bone saw," he said and reached out for Keats's instrument, but Keats was too busy restraining the soldier to respond. Steiner shrugged and seized the saw from the ground himself, and after forceful back-and-forth heaves, the arm flopped into the dirt. Blood wept from the fresh stump, which Steiner and Keats slathered with a green poultice and covered in thick bandages.

Keats leaped from his seated position when the limb twitched and dug its fingers into the ground.

"Unnatural, unnatural, unnatural," said Steiner. He peered over his thick glasses and inspected the limb while it pulled itself toward his foot.

He grasped the reanimated arm and examined the wiggling fingers just out of reach of his face. With a shrug, he tossed the arm into a writhing mound of limbs and snapped his fingers. Two soldiers scurried over to the mound, doused it in pitch, and set it alight.

"We have too many casualties to move," said Keats to a hulking and irritated Spaniard.

The Spaniard looked to Steiner, who nodded and handed him a tally of the casualties. The Spaniard's gaze darkened, and he crumpled the tally and tossed it into the flames.

"Movement is compromised, mobility limited. We're vulnerable and ripe for slaughter," he said, addressing the remaining troops and his aides. "But we must press on." Murmurs erupted among the soldiers, but he raised his hand and the chatter ceased. "Hop is dead, and I must assume command of this expedition."

"We can't leave our wounded," said Keats. "More than half are immobile or unable to defend themselves."

The Spaniard quickened to anger but held his tongue. Keats was right. He surveyed the carnage and then gazed at the dead strider. Medics rushed back and forth between the wounded and the dwindling supply caches.

"OK," he finally said, "Jens Grüber, post."

Jens trotted over to the new commander and saluted.

"You were a famed trader on these plains before coming to Junedale."

"Yes, sir."

"Have you been through these caverns?"

"I have."

"Then you are to proceed through the caverns and find out what happened to the shadebringer." The Spaniard removed a dagger from his belt and pointed it toward the bellowing crag. "And if he has been compromised, you know what you must do."

"Not without me," said Keats. He stepped near the two and slung his medical kit over his shoulder.

"You'll just slow me down, Reginald," said Jens.

"No," said Keats before Jens could continue, "I can help the injured in the caverns, and if the shadebringer is hurt, I could attend to him."

"What of the injured here?" said the Spaniard.

"I'll manage fine, fine, fine," said Steiner. His nose twitched, and his lower lip quivered.

"Keats, accompany Grüber on his scouting mission," said the Spaniard.

Keats grinned and slapped Jens on the back.

"Very well," said Jens. His lips turned down slightly, and he narrowed his eyes at the jubilant medic as he tightened his equipment and stuffed his pack with more bandages.

CHAPTER 26

THE INFERNAL PLAINS

The dreadful loneliness of this place
makes me think I may indeed be in Hell.

—REGINALD KEATS,
CYCLE 401 AND 51 DAYS

I HEAVED MY ACHING BODY OVER A sharp and sooty overhang and pulled Li up with me. He brushed himself off and glanced back into the darkness. "The injured are beginning to turn," he said, voice solemn. "They'll fall into the chasm if the fates are merciful."

Jacques took note of our slow pace and slammed his hammer against his shield. "Move your goddamned asses! Are we here to fight or natter away in this endless gloom?"

I side-eyed Jacques and crept closer to Li, who was struggling to keep his footing as we picked up the pace. "How are we going to get this done with half our force either dead or on the other side of the chasm?" I whispered.

He placed a finger over his lips and guided me away from the others. "As far as I am concerned, this mission is over. Our priority is getting you safely back to Junedale." I took a deep breath, exhaled, and hoped nobody else heard the remark. If Li's sedition met Jacques's resolve, there would be blood.

I leaned in closer. "Then what was the point of this entire venture?" The insanity of it all weighed on me, and I longed for a mug of dream shard tea.

Li looked to me and then away. A sorrowful expression took hold of his face as he pondered my words. "This venture was not *just* to find the foraging party."

"Yeah?" I narrowed my eyes. The words carried implications beyond my immediate understanding, but betrayal nipped at me, like when a parent tells their kids Fido had to be *put to sleep*. I braced myself. "What else?"

"You and the shade must be joined," he said, "and in order for that to happen, *you* must enter a waygate after being purified. Octavius wanted us to send you through the Kir Sol waygate. Now that it has been reopened prematurely, though, I am concerned we will not make it there."

I looked at him blankly. "But . . . you told me the gate leads only to Kull. You'd essentially be sending me into Hell?"

Li grimaced. "We are running out of time to win this war. With your reluctance, we thought it best not to discuss these . . . details with you. Our hope was that the shade would find you in the void between realms."

"Your *hope*?" I cried, incredulously. Li's words were molten lead. I wobbled for a moment and guided myself to a rock. Ruffling my hair, I groaned and glared up at him. "The whole point of this expedition was to push me into some dimensional gateway and *hope* I came back your goddamned weapon?"

"Shadebringer Robbins, you are the risk we must take to win this war, and we *must* win it at any cost. The consequences of defeat are unspeakable."

"Same shit all over again," I muttered. I wasn't the fucking chosen one. I was no hero; I was a pawn, same as always. I should have killed that old man on the streets of Junedale and fled into the mountains. Disgust welled in me. For a moment, I contemplated a jaunt back into the darkness and over the ledge into the chasm—not out of hopelessness but out of spite. I was tired of being a plaything, a nonentity subject to the whims of others. But no, being incinerated didn't sit well with me either, and quite honestly, I was curious in much the same way a death row inmate ponders his electric chair. "Assuming I don't end up in Hell or wherever after I enter the gate, what happens when the shade joins me?"

"You and it merge, and you become the conduit to pass judgment. The judgment of the shade is the *only* way to rid this world of Ek Maraine and his overlords."

"What's left of me afterward?"

"We don't know." Li hesitated for a moment. "The history is unclear."

I exhaled as another deluge of smoke and ash passed overhead and subsided. The moans of the dead had doubled in intensity; there was no going back alone—between Scylla and Charybdis. I came to this calamity by forces outside my control, but I could still swing a mace. It would be my hand—and mine alone—that sealed my fate. At least I could act of my own free will now. "Fuck it, let's do it."

A flicker of pride crossed Li's face. "Your stoicism is remarkable, but our force is too weak to confront the terrors of the Infernal Plains now."

"That's obviously not what our current commander thinks."

Li and I rejoined the main formation. Jacques cursed and shoved his officers forward, and they, in turn, marshaled their soldiers. The pure, bland, ubiquitous *drive* that kept each warrior marching forward, even toward certain death, enraptured my imagination. I didn't know where this force came from, nor did I care; I could only marvel at its futility.

Li drew his lips over his teeth, and his eyes darted about. "We need a plan and fast."

The urgency in his voice alarmed me. I had sensed little emotion from the man otherwise; I could only imagine what awaited us.

"We sure as shit can't go back," I said. The distant adagio of the dead underscored my point. I expected crashing steel at any moment when they finally met our vanguard.

Li grimaced. "Then we have no choice but to go forward."

* * *

"That's a good boy. You're such a very good boy," said Miriam. She prodded the reanimate along the treacherous terrain. Each time it stumbled or collided with the rock, the creature groaned, but it never fought against her; Miriam's control over it was complete.

"How will you know when it senses danger? It makes too much noise as it is," said Jacques.

"Because I'm the necromancer witch, and reanimates are my thing, of course," she said, not bothering to face him. She patted the reanimate's head and shushed it, and the groans diminished.

The other soldiers watched their former comrade sway like a drunkard, and one trotted up beside Miriam and gawked at him. "Hey, witch, is he still in there?"

"Dear grunt, of course not. He's with his family and their favorite hound, running free in the Fields of Elysium." The soldier's eyes lit up until Miriam burst into a shrill cackle, and he fled from her.

I smirked and chuckled a little under my breath. This bitch was sharp.

"Aye, you like that one, Shadebringer? I've got plenty of juicy ones just for you." She turned and winked at me and spit an ochre ball of phlegm onto the rock.

The obscene sensory overload made me queasy, and I fell back to Li.

"I don't think they like us too much, my dear," she said to her pet and cackled again.

"Glad she's on our side," said Li. He poked me and clicked from one side of his mouth. "I think she likes you."

I shuddered, still picturing her ball of spit. "I don't think I'm her type."

"You mean living?"

I laughed hard. Miriam was beautiful and intelligent but hid both behind layers of coarse eccentricity. Regardless, I *did* like it.

Gentle moans wafted in from behind us, and nervous soldiers peered over their shoulders into the shadows.

"Infernal Plains ahead!" a scout shouted in the dark. A faint red dot marked our exit. An irrepressible gloom gnawed at my heart. Reputation and experience didn't matter; the pure hatred that seeped from the open rift polluted even the smothering air of the caverns.

The faint red dot bloomed into crimson sky as we passed through the cave mouth, and the uneven ground rolled into a flat sandy hellscape. Soldiers joked, but their voices emerged scratchy and uncertain, their throats constricted with angst. Their pace suffered, but Jacques drove them forward and cursed. The dry heat, near equal to that over the bridge, oppressed us, and soldiers quickly shed their hulking plates and chains.

"Fools!" shouted Jacques. "Do you offer yourselves as meals for the beasts of this hell?" He pounded on his plate. "Get it back on!" Slowly, the sullen soldiers retrieved their gear.

Sudden commotion burst from behind them, and Jacques silenced the soldiers with a single hand. We listened as the cacophony peaked and waned then emerged again as bestial growling and the occasional scream.

"Their sacrifice will not be in vain," Jacques said with all the concern of a stranger reading a newspaper's obituary. With a casual snap of the fingers and a whistle, he turned to Li. "Magician, lead us to the gate."

Li stammered, and rivers of sweat rushed down his head and neck.

"Sir, we are only a fraction strong!" said a soldier. He was right: Only about fifty of us remained after the ambush.

Jacques froze, did an about face from Li, and approached the soldier with an amiable smile. Without warning and while still wearing that noxious smile, he smashed a hulking iron gauntlet across the soldier's face, and the man collapsed in his heavy metal armor like a stack of cans. The other soldiers gasped and murmured, but none had the nerve to confront Jacques over it. I grit my teeth and started toward the Frenchman, but Li restrained me.

"Does anyone else have a problem with our numbers?" said Jacques. His face betrayed a madness that shocked many of the other soldiers—but not me. I had seen this before. He glanced at the downturned heads, looking for anyone to challenge his authority, and back to Li. "Lead us to the gate. Now."

"Very well," said Li. He peered across the smoldering sands until he appeared to recognize the faint ruins that scalloped the horizon. Li nodded and pointed our course. "Follow me."

"Pikes to the sides and route step," said Jacques. "Leave the coward where he lies. If his bones haven't been picked clean by the time we return, we can collect him then."

The officers sounded off, and we scrambled into a ragged formation and began our trot.

Miriam guided her domesticated corpse astride the main formation. Jacques frowned and leveled a finger at her. "Get back in formation; we don't need that cursed thing anymore."

"Oh, we don't?" said Miriam. "How would a muck snipe like you know that?"

Jacques ripped his blade free and leaned into her.

My heart raced, and I reached for my mace.

"Wait, wait, wait!" Li shouted and rushed between the two. "She's right. The creature is useful for more than detecting reanimates."

Jacques looked at Li and then to Miriam. Slowly, he sheathed the weapon and moved to the front of the formation without a word.

Li turned to Miriam and swallowed hard. "No more," he said.

"He'll regret such behavior." Her face darkened, and she nudged the corpse forward.

"What now?" I said.

"We hope for an opportunity among the ruins," whispered Li. "We must preserve you at all costs, and I suspect this fool would kill any of us if we attempted to turn back."

"No shit."

* * *

Our plans are finally coming to fruition. Neither god nor demon can deny us this bounty. The madness—it eats at them!

Indeed, the delicious essence of their souls is almost too much to bear with this hunger. Soon they will filet one another, and the shade will deliver.

My brethren, it has been a long time coming. Soon, we feast.

You're all damned!

The voices broke into our heads with all their malignant glee, whispering horrors familiar with our darkest secrets. Soldiers plugged their ears to no avail. "What is this madness? The striders know we're here!"

"These voices come from beyond the gate!" Li shouted. "The closer we get, the stronger they will become. Steel yourselves!"

We crested a final dune with much effort against the wind and shifting sands, and the ruins of a long dead city rose before us. Shattered homes long abandoned and wilted spires sprung from the sand like desiccated stumps in a marsh.

Fear spread through the ranks like a plague, but Jacques's expression changed only to mild exertion as we slogged through the sand to the remnants of a wall at the city's periphery. Our ragtag formation fought against the final barrages of wind and sand to reach a bleached wall fragment looming before us. Jacques waved, and we broke formation and huddled at the base of the wall, allowing us just enough time to guzzle from our lukewarm canteens.

"Welcome to Kir Sol," said Li. Wonder spread across his face as he studied the ruins. Pulling a map from his robes, he pored over the geography, mesmerized.

Jacques strode to him and leaned in close. "Where is the gate?"

"City center," said Li, barely acknowledging his presence, "but we must not risk the shadebringer on this assault with so few men or—"

"The Morites are expecting the shadebringer at the gate, and I am not one to disappoint," said Jacques, and his eyes narrowed like a predator's at first sight of its prey.

I stepped back from him. Jacques was a cruel stalwart, but I never took him for a traitor.

Li's mouth fell open, and he shot up from his map. "You can't do this. There's more at stake than you can comprehend."

"I've existed in this world for two hundred years and never have our *glorious leaders* given us hope of redemption." He ripped Junedale's sigil from his breast and tossed it to the ground. "But those ancient beings—Daedrina's Children—supposedly our enemies, have shown me the way. They have promised me paradise for my service, and I intend to take it."

"Jacques," said Li, aghast, "*they* will show you neither favoritism nor mercy."

Jacques smiled. "Well, if that is the case, then I'll be in good company. Giuseppe," he said and waved the arcanist over.

Li glared at him. “You too, Giuseppe?”

“We’re going to live like kings when this war is finally over,” said Giuseppe, keeping his one good eye fixed on the ground. “I’m tired of fighting, tired of living like a servant, tired of that fool Octavius and his worthless visions.”

“If the Morites win, no soul in this world will ever know peace,” said Li.

Giuseppe blinked a few times and crept away without a word.

“Enough of this charade,” said Jacques. “Out with it!” He drew his sword and circled it twice in the air. Twenty soldiers fell in behind him and drew their swords. The rest of us looked on in shock and confusion. “Don’t hurt the shadebringer!” Jacques whistled, and the traitors attacked, hacking down the others with brutal precision; the ambush had been planned long in advance.

“You two-timing pieces of shit!” I shouted.

A soldier charged Miriam. I leaped and threw her to the ground as his blade swished by her head. He lurched to the side under the weight of his weapon, and I punched him in the mouth and shoved him into the reanimate. Frenzied by the commotion, the creature snapped free from its bindings, seized him, and sank its teeth through the hood into his shoulder.

“Don’t fucking hurt the shadebringer!” Jacques roared and stormed over to us. “Take them alive. Hood the arcanists like the cursed corpse.” He sliced the reanimate’s head off and kneeled before his wounded soldier.

“The damn thing got me good,” the soldier said, gripping the jagged wound.

“Indeed, he did,” said Jacques, and he beheaded the man without a second look.

Li ran to Miriam and helped her up, and we shrank from the encroaching traitors, everyone else left dead by their treachery. Swords hovered around us from every angle; there was no escape. Hoping to spare my friends execution, I put my hands in the air.

• • •

The hood closed, and my tepid breath swirled around my nostrils. Specks of red light pierced the stitched fiber, but I could see nothing else. A hand gripped my arm tightly and forced me forward.

"I knew the prophecy was nonsense the second I laid eyes on you, Shadebringer." I recognized Jacques's arrogant voice through the whistling winds and clanking armor. "You know, nine men died at the hands of the Morites during that raid to rescue you. Nine men among thousands who died for a few words on some ancient parchment—a sick joke, don't you think?"

"Seems to be a common theme," I said.

"Well, it's soon to come to a conclusion," said Jacques. "And I'll be the one to light the fuse."

"You sure like hearing your own voice, asshole. Are you sure your own men didn't buy your ticket here?" A fierce blow landed in my ribs, tipping me slightly. I coughed and forced out a laugh through the pain. "Did you hit me, Frenchie, or is your fucking grandmother trying to tickle me?" Jacques snarled and smashed me in the ribs again, and I keeled forward. The satisfying defiance almost made the intense pain worthwhile. Almost. I swallowed a mouthful of warm metallic blood and gasped for breath.

"Ay—got any of that to go around, you stinking traitor?" Miriam giggled in her distinct and ornery voice, and I was both glad and fearful to hear it.

"The Morites can have the shadebringer, but this one's mine," said Jacques. He growled and ripped our hoods off as his men held us fast. "You can give my regards to Azurocus or Lucifer or whomever when I'm done with you, bitch."

He cocked his hand back and swiped it across Miriam's face, his knuckles popping as they rebounded off her jaw. Her head recoiled, but her smiling face snapped back.

"Commander Pariseau, I beg you, do not hurt h—" said Li.

"One more, please, for the Queen, you sad little man," Miriam interrupted Li. With a snort, she curled her upper lip and spat in Jacques's face.

In a fit of rage, Jacques wound his arm back and stepped into a savage strike. His hand smashed across her face, and a shower of blood rained onto the sand, but it was Jacques's screams that echoed through the forgotten city.

Miriam grinned and spit out his curled and twitching fingers and licked blood from her teeth.

He cupped his bleeding stumps to his chest and screeched as the entire party glared at the scene in mixed horror and fascination.

"Holy shit," I said, gawking at the fingers.

Miriam winked at me and whispered a guttural incantation at the bloody digits, which began to smoke and hiss. Strange blue light sprang from them, and they burrowed into the sand like worms.

"Kill her!" screamed Jacques. A large red stain spread across his leather doublet, and the soldiers raised their weapons.

"What in hell?" a soldier squeaked as the sand puffed up in small eruptions around his feet.

Skittering insects poured from the wounded earth—a creeping plague that swirled and attacked. The traitors scattered, some clawing their eyes while others slashed their own flesh to dislodge the ravenous arthropods. One soldier darted down the main street, flailing and choking, spitting gobs of crushed and writhing insects from his laden mouth. A sonorous hiss split the air, and a set of barbed claws snatched him from the street and dragged him into an abandoned stone building. Seconds later, the creature's giant bloody head emerged from the doorway, its independently moving eyes observing the carnage as it chewed. After a few moments, it slowly withdrew into the building.

The remaining soldiers fled, some to their doom with random horrified yelps from nearby alleys. Miriam's plague dissipated into the sand, and quiet returned, except for the whimpering from Jacques, who sat meek and covered in welts, grasping his bloody stumps.

"The beasts of Kir Sol will be well fed tonight," said Miriam. She stroked a single insect perched on her finger.

"What should we do with him?" I said.

"I'd have already crushed his skull with that fancy mace of yours, but I can't have all the fun," said Miriam.

"For the greater good of Junedale, he must face proper justice as a traitor," said Li.

Miriam rolled her eyes and gently blew the giant tick from her finger. "Yes, sir," she said like a disappointed child.

"Where did that chickenshit Giuseppe go?" I thought of the spindly traitor's beady eye as I peered down the streets and scanned the nearby buildings.

"Probably in some creature's belly as we speak," said Miriam. "Hopefully still alive." She looked down at Jacques and crinkled her nose in glee. "You need more flesh in your diet, traitor. Your blood tastes thin and weak."

Jacques looked up at her wide-eyed and fearful.

A horn sounded in the distance.

"He may have already made it to the Morites," said Li. "They'll be here soon."

"We gotta haul ass then," I said and looked over at Jacques. "What about this asshole?"

"We'll need to bring him with us; he must face justice," said Li as he gathered his belongings.

"Aw, he'll give our position away with his painful squealing if he doesn't call them over to us," said Miriam.

"We have no other choice," said Li.

Jacques's eyes darted back and forth as we spoke.

"Respectfully, Master Li, we can't risk him turning us over to the Morites, or else they'll get the shadebringer."

"Miriam!" said Li, his patience extinguished. "We will not compromise our—"

"No!" screamed Jacques.

I brought the mace down on his skull and ended the argument. His body collapsed into the sand and went limp. Li covered his mouth, and Miriam glanced down at the wound and up to me with a satisfied smile.

"Shit's solved," I said, unable to recognize my own voice. I kneeled over the corpse and rifled through his belongings. "Motherfucker has it here somewhere." After a few moments, I ripped a scabbard from his body and fastened it to my belt. "This belongs to me."

"Didn't know you had it in you, Shadebringer," said Miriam.

"Neither did I."

"Let's go," said Li. He threw his pack over his shoulder and shuffled toward the main drag.

I sighed and looked down at Jacques. The bastard's eyes were still wide open, and he was wearing the same look of shock he'd had right before his death. A twang of guilt bit into me as I swept my palm over the dead Frenchman's eyes to close them.

"You did the right thing," said Miriam, desert winds drowning her voice.

I stood, scraped bloody sand from my clothes, and grasped Miriam's hand before setting off after Li.

CHAPTER 27

THE ENCLAVE

We offer no mercy. We plead no forgiveness. We feel no regret.

—INDUCTION MANTRA OF THE SILVER SERPENTS

"LOOTERS AND ADVENTURERS PILLAGED what valuables were left in these ruins," whispered Li. His eyes darted about, searching every inch of the doorway into the nondescript stone hut. "Though many met the same end as their pilfered treasures in the guts of these creatures." He crept around the corner of the stone entrance, the wooden door long ripped from its hinges, and waved us in.

Miriam and I crept into the hut and sat down. Aside from the splinters of a shattered table and loose rocks, the room was empty. Fine yellow sand filled most of the room and lay along the ledge of a boarded window, but the walls offered respite from the battering winds. I stretched and gulped down a few mouthfuls of water as I rested against my pack. "What now? Are the others coming for us?"

"I suspect they believe we have been annihilated," said Li. He removed a satchel of papers from his pack and picked through them. "Just as we thought they were."

"They were; we saw it in Giuseppe's orb . . ." My voice trailed off. "Sneaky bastard."

"He's a master of deception, and unless someone made it back across the chasm, the others are none the wiser. They too were left with one of his orbs." Li plucked a map from the satchel and opened it.

I sat up and looked over the map. "Damn, this place is big." The scrawled ruins covered a large plot of land that represented the Infernal Plains. A tiny red X marked the waygate in the center of the ruins.

"There are catacombs beneath the chapel," said Miriam.

"Chapel?" I was perplexed. "Who is worshipping what here?"

"Not sure," she replied. "I don't blame them though. This place is like Hell with better weather."

"We have been forsaken," muttered Li beneath his fogged spectacles, eyes low and fixed in study. "But that's unimportant now. Miriam is right. We must move onward if we hope to escape."

A dull groan startled us. The throaty depth of the noise made grains of sand dance on the floor. A malformed claw planted outside the entrance and dug into the sand. Li looked to Miriam and me, brought his index finger to his lips, and raised the palm of his hand in front of his face, covering his eyes. The claw shimmied in the sand as an elongated burgundy neck stretched into the room from above the doorway. A single unblinking globe bulged at the center of the creature's serpentine head, while arm-length fangs quivered in the air. I sat still, fearful of even moving my eyes, as Miriam marveled at the beast with much less concern. A sudden high-pitched and distant shriek pierced the silence. The creature finally blinked and tore off in a frenzied sprint.

I exhaled with a shiver and gulped. "So, what in God's name was that?"

"That was a dreadican," said Li just above a whisper. "They're an evolutionary variant of striders that have adapted to this infernal desert." Li rolled up the map and stuffed it in his pack and placed his hand on my shoulder. "Our next move is purely your decision, Shadebringer, because it is truly eternity you risk."

"I've got a date with a gate," I said and grinned.

Miriam inhaled and gently placed a hand on my elbow. With a soft squeeze, she looked into my eyes and betrayed a look I'd never seen on her before: fear.

Li nodded and gingerly removed the scroll of purification from his belt. "The only known purification scroll left in Irgendwo." The awe in his eyes was unmistakable. "Our final hope." He swallowed hard and unfurled the scroll, holding the ancient brown parchment as one would hold a newborn.

"Are you ready to meet your destiny?" said Li with a faint smile.

"Enough with the bromides, old man. Just do your fucking magic."

He blinked a few times, and the smile grew.

I had no idea what to expect, but there was no going back now. The moment had come, it seemed, and I nodded.

"*Molkah Daedrina, pershe die nonye kloon topre fooscatta,*" Li chanted. "*Par zhenk datta, Molkah, die nonye kloon topre semparzi.*"

The scroll radiated heat and a weak orange glow as Li spoke. A strange sensation sprouted in my chest.

"*Enye die bach hazza schkwoon.*"

The radiation deepened to a searing heat, and Li's voice climbed, rough and bestial, and he raised his palm to me. The sensation bloomed into a maelstrom of heat, fear, and excitement. It burned. It spread across my limbs and climbed up my neck. I opened my mouth to scream, but nothing emerged. Li had become a Hollow, his palm the gaze.

"*Molka Daedrina—*" His head fell backward and the room shook. "*—ille qui nos omnes servabit.*"

The scroll disintegrated to dust and swished away in the wind. The fire in my chest was snuffed in an instant. Li fell to a knee and wheezed.

"No worse for the wear," said Miriam as she glanced around the room. "You, I meant—not the scroll." She cackled.

Li shuddered and pushed his spectacles back up his nose. "I hope that worked."

I scanned my hands, arms, and body. Nothing had changed, and the pain had gone. "Let's see what happens." I reached down to Li and stood him up.

"Thank you," he said. He shouldered his pack and glanced out the doorway. "We had better get going. Follow me."

Miriam and I darted across an arid gravel path after him, but, soon, another scream pierced the air.

“The beasts must be feasting on Morite scouts,” said Miriam with a snicker.

Li halted at the verge of a main street. He ducked and peered in both directions then signaled us. We slinked across the street and disappeared into another cramped alley. A growl and a whimper startled us in mid-sprint. I stumbled to a halt and backtracked to the intersecting alley. Our earlier visitor now clawed and gnashed at a small crevice in the side of an adjoining building. A bloody leg kicked and pushed against the beast’s maw.

“Hah! I was right!” Miriam giggled and shook her head.

I looked on as the desperate scout cried for help and beat against the predator.

“You there! Please help!” screamed the Morite. He thrashed against the creature’s grip and pulled himself back into the crevice.

I bit my lip and sized up the beast, which stood nearly triple my height. A gnawing weakness—pity—filled my heart.

“Don’t do it, Shade—”

I drew my sword and sprinted at the creature. I heaved the blade back and struck into its leg with all my strength, and the sword jumped from my hands as momentum carried me to the ground. The creature’s neck shot skyward, and it roared in pain.

“Paradise!” The bloody Morite scout exploded from the crevice and slashed at me.

I kicked backward and dodged his vicious plunging slash, which landed square in the beast’s foot. With a whoosh of air, the beast swept down on the scout, pinned him against the earth, and tore into his chest.

Adrenaline flooded my legs, and I leaped to my feet and fled back to the others. So much for mercy.

“See what sympathy gets you?” Miriam slapped me across the face, pulled me forward, and we took off down the cluttered alley. I glanced back as the beast crashed into the alley and broke into pursuit, its long legs swishing through the air. One man-sandwich just wasn’t enough.

“This way,” said Li breathlessly, and we juked down another alley.

The beast careened past the entrance and backpedaled; dust and rocks sailed into the air as it clawed the stone and dragged itself after us.

My sword, still embedded in its leg, raked against the narrow walls with every bound, and bloodied cloth flapped from its jaws.

"Here!" An open palm jutted out from inside a building, and Li veered left to grasp it. We flew into the building and hurried into a dank cellar.

"Shit!" Li shouted as he lost his footing, and we all tumbled down the cold steps and crashed to the floor. Still flush with adrenaline, I dragged the others to their feet and rushed through the darkness. The scraping metal drew closer, and the creature roared.

"This way!" said a boy, and we poured through an opening in the stone. "Is that everyone?"

"Yes," I said.

With a tug of a chain, a heavy iron portcullis fell into its iron slats. The creature hissed and slammed into the metal with a *clang*.

Goddamn, that musta hurt.

The beast's single giant eye peered through the crisscrossing barrier, and it nipped the metal, probing for weaknesses.

"Not in a good mood today, are you, Norris?" said the boy. A ratty brown robe drooped from his diminutive frame, and an oversized hood shrouded his face. He walked to the portcullis and petted the rough scaly skin around the creature's eye.

My breathing slowed, and my mouth hung open as the creature cooed and leaned into the boy's gentle scratches. After a few moments, it turned to ascend the stairs.

"Gimme back my fucking sword," I said at the realization that my hard-earned weapon was walking away. The sword clanked slowly against the stone wall with each hobbled step the beast took.

"It's Norris's sword now," said the boy with authority. "You're lucky he didn't catch you, because he likes to toy with his prey before eating it alive." He grasped his chin and nodded. "Yes, that Morite scout has a long and painful road ahead of him. Maybe he got lucky and a hopper finished him off while Norris was chasing you."

"We are citizens of June—"

"Junedale, yes," the boy interrupted Li with a wave. "We know. We've been watching you and the shadebringer very closely."

"We?" said Li.

"You call us 'Hollows,'" said the boy. He kicked a rock across the floor. "You say we're evil and take the souls of the living."

"Your gaze causes death. It's a known fact."

"What is death?" The boy raised his hands, palms upward, and shrugged. "If you mean cessation of your shell here, then yes, that is a common byproduct of purification."

Li looked at me, and I shrugged.

"But let's talk about details later. By the way, you can call me Garrett." He walked to the opposite side of the room and pushed a stone block into the wall. A rectangular segment of wall sank into the floor amid mechanical clanks and grating stone. He waved us in.

* * *

"We don't often have visitors, so please excuse the lighting," said Garrett. "We snuffed many torches so you don't catch one of our gazes. They're really hard to break."

"I know." The deep searing pain was hard to forget.

"Amazing," said Li. He scoured every detail and scribbled into his notebook with such fervor that he tripped over his own robe.

Stone and wood huts pocked the voluminous cavern. Tendrils of glowvine snaked about the buildings and up the sides of the great dome that formed a sky within the dwelling. "I have never heard of such a place. Not even in legend."

"It's a place of our own, away from the suffering above and the constant torment of others."

"You're protected by law in Junedale," said Li.

"And we're protected by beasts here," said Garrett. "Teeth versus paper. Which would you choose?"

A little girl darted out from a hut and latched onto my leg. "Thank you for saving me from the fat man in Mora," she squealed.

I couldn't see her eyes (thankfully), but I recognized the frazzled white-blonde hair in an instant.

"Yes, Shadebringer, I thank you for defending Lula, my sister, from that vile Morite guardsman," said Garrett, and he pried his little sister from my leg. "This world would be unbearable without her, especially since I just lost my father."

"I'm glad I could be of service, and I'm sorry about your pop."

The little pixie darted to her friends, and, together, they whispered and giggled and scampered astride our group as we walked.

"Who were your parents?" said Miriam.

"Our parents here are of different flesh, but our souls come from the same well—the same cut of the Yah'w," said Garrett, and his sister skittered back to us. He gripped her hand and swung it back and forth as she skipped along. "We come from the same soul line, but war took our parents long before they ever met."

"So, it's true!" said Miriam.

"Yes, we never had a chance to be born on Earth, so we ended up here." Sorrow shaded his words, and his little sister looked up at him. "But I'm glad we found each other," he said and ruffled her hair. "Many will never find their *other* and are cursed to exist in this place alone." He waved to a few random Hollows that peeked out from their homes.

"Here we are."

A stone and wood building rose from the ground. Glowvine ensnared its face, and small stovepipes sprang from the roof and puffed smoke into the air. Inviting orange and red light flickered from within, and shadows danced through every window. We climbed two dusty steps onto the porch, and Garrett rapped on the door.

"Enter," said a serious voice. Garrett pushed the door open and walked in first. The scent of grob made my stomach grumble, but Li darted to the bookshelf.

"Welcome to Hovel," said a young Asian man with a strong accent. He scribbled at his desk and tossed papers about.

"Thank you for having us," I said.

He looked up, and I quickly moved to shield my eyes, but his gaze triggered nothing. His face, smooth with thin lips, blended with the lights and shadows of the hearth fire and candles. Lean and serious, he shined wisdom far beyond his youth.

"That's a strange name for your city," I said, fascinated, "and where are you from?"

"*Our* city," said the young man, "and I'm from the same place you are."

"Philadelphia?" I said.

"No, fool. Vietnam."

I looked him over and nodded; there was something strangely familiar about him. "I'm Clyde Ro—"

"Robbins, yes, I know you well."

"How?" I scrutinized his face and form but could not place a name.

He smiled. "Call me Do."

Miriam smirked at the boy. "You're no Hollow."

"You're right. I'm not."

"Not a Hollow?" said Li, and he turned from the bookcase and looked into his eyes. "Then why are you here?"

"Fate? Punishment? Chance?" Do leaned against his desk and dangled a wispy silver locket from his fingers. He stared at the dancing trinket as it twirled and glimmered in the firelight. With a sigh, he set it on his desk and pulled up his sleeve. A leathery pink scar in the shape of a serpent crawled up his arm.

Miriam gasped, and a look of disgust crossed her face.

"You are a Silver Serpent?" Li covered his mouth.

"Ek Maraine himself inducted me."

"There is no salvation for you," said Li, his tone dark.

Do looked down and folded his hands. "I thought so too . . . until I found Nora." He paused at the mention of her name and palmed the locket. "I found her cowering in a sewage pipe one night during a raid, and I didn't have the heart to kill her when she stared up at me clutching this to her breast." He raised the locket and let it twirl on the chain.

"None of this changes the fact that you're a mass murderer." Li's rage crested but stopped at simple words.

I could feel the hatred radiating from him and Miriam, but they didn't have the nerve to confront Do in his own domain.

"She reminded me so much of my daughter back on Earth. Despite everything I had been taught—everything I had done—I took her back to my home and hid her away. And then, I grew to love her." He rubbed his flickering eyes and looked away from us, too proud to show us tears.

"Inevitably, someone found out and forced their way into my home to collect the bounty. He hurt her before I was able to take his head. So, as she lay bleeding out on my living room floor, I decided to leave this world on my own terms. I removed the twill cap she would wear to protect my eyes, and I looked directly into hers. The physical pain was unimaginable, but it was nothing compared to watching her die. Just as I began to slip away, I felt peace. But you can only imagine the horror I experienced when I woke up, still alive, still here and covered in her blood."

"You survived her gaze?" said Miriam.

"Indeed, I did. She purged me, and I lived. And ever since that time, I've searched for a way to restore her—or, failing that, join her."

"If what you say is true, you have been purified and can leave this world. Quite hard to believe, given your sins." Li eyed the young man suspiciously.

"Remember, old man, I have no shade to pluck me from the void should I attempt to step through Kir Sol, unlike our shadebringer here, and would surely be devoured." Do recoiled at the thought. "The Morites control the only functional waygate, and even if I could sneak through the Ziggurat to use it, I would choose to rot here for all eternity if I couldn't take Nora with me." Do rapped his hand on the desk.

"How do you know she's still in this world? You know as well as I that she could have been taken b—" Li stopped abruptly.

"I *don't* know," said Do. He looked up at me. "Yet."

I stared at him, and an inkling of familiarity grew in my mind.

He smiled at me. He knew. "Your intuition is right, Shadebringer. Follow it."

"You were the one in the photos I found." I grasped my chin and nodded. "The voice I kept hearing." Anger surged beside every epiphany. "You're the fucker who dragged me into this world."

"The voice was—is—Mother Daedrina." He smiled faintly, tears flowing over his cheeks and massaged the tiny locket. "*We* brought you here, Shadebringer, with Perry's help."

CHAPTER 28

WE WALK TOGETHER

Never, never, never give up.

—SIR WINSTON CHURCHILL

JENS STRAINED AND GROANED AS HE dragged his hulking body over the rocks, but Keats's exertions were threefold. The stout Briton stood nearly four inches shorter than his German companion and had a physique better suited to a bakery.

"Help me up, Kraut. This is a team effort," said Keats as he struggled to pull himself onto an overhang.

Jens sighed and pulled the corpulent mass and baggy equipment of his companion upward.

Shambling forward under the awkward weight of medical equipment and his single short sword, Keats gasped for breath and coughed.

"You're slowing me down," said Jens without looking over his shoulder. He stretched his strides across the level ground and forced his body up sharp inclines and around boulders.

Keats continued to hack and cough but kept pace.

"You're trying to ditch me just hoping I'll turn around. I know it," said Keats. "I'm not leaving you." He trotted up to Jens's side and glanced at him with a widened grin and a heaving chest. Sweat poured over his brow.

Jens paused for a moment and thought on Keats's words, allowing both a momentary rest in the sweltering air. "You're right," he finally said, "but we're too far in to split up safely, so just try to be quiet."

Keats nodded with glee over his nugget of victory.

Jens set off again, and Keats sprang forward, but almost as abruptly as they had begun, they both halted and crouched.

Ahead stirred a soldier, face down in full plate armor that scraped against the ground.

"He's one of ours," whispered Keats. He slung his medic bag in front of him and stepped forward, but Jens seized his shoulder and held him fast.

"No," whispered Jens, "not anymore," and he pointed at the arrow seated deep in the soldier's neck.

Keats sized up the mass of metal and flesh and shivered.

Jens beckoned Keats forward and stepped softly into the dark like a cat.

A raging tide of smoke, ash, and embers rushed along the ceiling with a tempestuous grumble. Thousands of dancing red scintillations wafted downward, casting every nook of the cavern in a red pall.

Keats set off after Jens, but a sudden glimmer caught his eye. He froze and focused on a prismatic sheen that bloomed from something on the fallen soldier's belt. Greed surged in his rotund belly, and he glanced around for Jens. After moments of stillness, he crept forward with silent, slow, and deliberate footfalls. His singular obsession grew in sheen and sparkle, and he licked his lips.

A gentle moan crawled up from the soldier, and Keats craned his neck. Listening intently, the sounds were more than simple moans. It was muttering, throaty growling, perhaps even words. Keats gingerly approached the downed man and reached for his prize. He grasped it and pulled a leather-handled dagger free of its scabbard.

The soldier spun to his back with a clatter of metal on stone and gripped Keats's throat. Lurching to his knees and then to his feet, he raised Keats into the air with a single gloved hand.

The soldier's face framed two pale white orbs that stared emotionlessly at Keats, oblivious to the arrow protruding from his shredded Adam's apple as if it were a piece of jewelry. Keats flailed silently against the reanimate's vise grip while the world began to dim around him, and his own grip on the creature's forearm weakened.

Guess this is it, he thought as the world faded to gray. *Can't say I don't deserve it.*

"Foolish, greedy *Huerensohn*," Jens hissed and cleaved the creature's head in half.

The reanimate dropped Keats and fell to the ground, twitching.

Keats drew a high-pitched breath and held his throat. As his airway gradually reopened, he hacked into the crook of his arm. A trickle of blood oozed out of his nose and stained his sleeve red.

Jens ripped him from the ground and glared at him, rage spread across his otherwise peaceful brow. "If the beast had been able to make any noise, we'd *both* be dead," he said through clenched teeth. "And for what? A few fucking pieces of glass?" He raised Keats's treasure to his face and twirled it. Simple glass baubles decorated the otherwise rotten leather hilt of the dagger.

Keats glanced at the cheap misshapen glass and looked away, on the verge of tears.

Jens snorted in a final spasm of anger and contemplated hurling Keats to the ground. But no . . . his fingers loosened, and he placed Keats gently back on his feet. He thrust Keats's treasure into his chest.

Keats folded his arms around it.

"You earned it. You keep it," Jens said and stalked off into the dark.

• • •

They crept deeper in silence. Keats plastered his eyes to the ground and clutched the worthless dagger close to his chest. Jens forged ahead with ruthless zeal over the terrain, caring little for Keats's discomfort. After a while, Jens paused and scanned the craggy ceiling.

"This is familiar," he said. He pulled a canteen from his belt and drank deeply before offering it to Keats.

With a sheepish glance, Keats grabbed the canteen and drew a few sips, thanking Jens in murmurs.

"The chasm isn't far off," said Jens.

"Chasm?" said Keats, his voice barely audible.

"Two stone bridges cross a volcanic pit," said Jens, "and lore has it that one of Daedrina's Children, Maloccus, was chained in the molten stone after the Cataclysm with his screams casting up this cursed smoke and ash."

"Sounds like a bad lot," said Keats with a shrug. "How do we get over it?"

"We don't," said Jens. He gripped Keats's hand and hoisted him up onto a high ledge.

Dozens of shadowy figures shuffled in the dim red light on the near side of the chasm. Some dragged swords behind them. Others limped about aimlessly, just sentient enough to avoid stumbling into the pit.

"There's another way, I take it," said Keats.

Jens smiled and tapped his temple. "Smugglers carved a hidden path through the rock ages ago. There's barely enough room for one man at a time, but it's better than running from reanimates."

"All right then," said Keats. "Let's go."

"There's only one problem." Jens cleared his throat and shrugged.

"What's that?" Keats eyed the German nervously.

"This place is alive, and to be so closely embraced by the rock allows permeation."

"Permeation?" Keats's voice pitched higher, and he furrowed his brow. "What do you mean permeation?"

"There's an ancient evil buried deep in the magma that infests every inch of this place," said Jens, "and it will surround us in there."

"Bunk," said Keats. "Let's press on," he added in a wavering voice.

It didn't take long for Jens to lead them to the passage. The narrow cave whistled as both men approached the pitch-black entrance. Keats grabbed a pebble and skipped it into the darkness.

"There's a bit of decline all the way to the exit, so tread carefully," said Jens, and he secured his pack and weapons. "Try not to get stuck or loot corpses." With a wave, he bent forward and stepped in.

"All right then. In, lad," Keats whispered to himself and sidestepped into the narrow crevice. His bulky equipment and gut dragged along the rock with each awkward step.

The men squeezed through the contorted and tight passage, each step a labor.

Keats coughed and grunted, stopping often to adjust his equipment or drag it free from a snag. "Hey, hold your horses," he said and shuffled forward to catch up. Planting his foot into an unsteady rock, he tumbled forward and slammed into the ground. The glass baubles on the dagger shattered in a clamor and rang through the depths. "Fucking hell," he whispered. "Slow it down, Jerry."

"You hopeless runt! Shut your cursed mouth!" Jens spit into the dark over his shoulder, part whisper and part growl.

The shuffling stopped. Keats licked his lips and inhaled deeply as he fought to catch his breath and collect his gear. A cold fear washed over his body, weakening his knees.

"Jens Grüber, your rage couldn't save Elise either."

Jens paused and turned to Keats. "What did you say?"

"I didn't say a word," said Keats, stuttering and sheepish.

"Poor Reginald, even your friends hate you. Such a terrible fate to be neither loved nor appreciated—in either world."

The words stung him little, as he knew they weren't from Jens. The hairs stood stiff on his arms. "Jens," he whispered, "there's something in here." The wind groaned painfully and rescinded.

"Jens, there's something in here," he repeated. He stepped forward and pawed the darkness in front of him. "Jens, where are you?"

"Elise, forgive me," Jens whimpered.

A gentle sobbing cut the dark, and Keats advanced to it.

"Jens, it's in your head. Fight it," said Keats, kneeling and grasping the German's shoulder. "Fight it."

"Elise, forgive me."

* * *

The night sky was pure ink. A swirl of blinding clouds lurked beneath the hidden moon. Jens Grüber and his Bf 109 fighter plane slid through the sky like a shark in the ocean depths.

"Butcherbird 5, we have radar contact one hundred kilometers west–northwest of Dusseldorf." Jens released the mic.

"Affirmative, Gunter 26. Climb to seven six hundred meters on heading three zero zero," replied the wing commander.

"Seven six hundred at three hundred, understood."

He tapped the stick back and to the right. The fighter drifted upward through the unending clouds, its engine protesting the strain and thinning atmosphere. Jens glanced deftly over his instruments, completely blind outside of his cramped cockpit but trusting completely the creeping needles and bobbing altitude indicator in front of him. Grasping a knob, he leaned the fuel mixture, placating the oxygen-starved engine as the plane clawed higher.

Circles of light swept in huge arcs through the sky, occasionally engulfing their fighters in a fleeting glow. Jens glanced out his window, half-expecting the trigger-happy Flak gunners to pour death upon them from their 88s. But as they climbed, the dense clouds swallowed the beams.

The fighters broke through the ceiling just before their target altitude and settled above the clouds. Jens scanned the empty void, a million specks of starlight masquerading as potential targets. His eyes jumped about the constellations he had memorized as a boy and, for a moment, the war ceased to exist.

"Gunter 26," chirped the radio, and he snapped back to the cockpit.

"Go ahead, Butcherbird," Jens replied.

"We have positive identification of the radar contact. They're Lancasters."

"Understood," said Jens.

"Bombers are in stream formation on heading zero nine zero."

Jens jerked the stick with a start and exhaled through his mouth. "So, either Dusseldorf or Essen," he said, trying to steady his voice.

"We'll get them. Elise will be fine," said the wing commander.

"Visual contact at 315!" said another pilot.

The fighters swung their noses to 315 degrees and began their descent. As if God had ripped away a tablecloth, the clouds vanished beneath them, revealing a featureless black landscape aside from searchlights and the occasional blast furnace.

"Descend to five two hundred meters," said the wing commander. "It's time to drop the hammer."

Jens looked on and said nothing. He had been "dropping the hammer" for years in a conflict that seemed increasingly unwinnable. Sending teenage boys to their fiery deaths had lost its thrill, and now with every kill, he could only think of a mother back in England receiving a telegram.

A quick flash in the distance grabbed his attention. Dozens followed in rapid succession. The accompanying *thuds* after the brilliant orange and white explosions reminded him of fireworks.

"Tenderizing the meat," said the wing commander. The searchlights coalesced on the stream of bombers, and the snapping, flashing meat grinder picked up pace.

"Oh my God, there are so many of them!"

The stream of fork-tailed Lancasters stretched deep into the night sky like an endless trail of ants.

"Call off the Flak," said Jens. "It's time to get our hands dirty." He lifted the trigger guard on the stick and, as if on cue, the explosions ceased. The trademark silhouettes of the bombers bobbed lazily in the sky. The fighters nosed downward on their quarry head-on.

"Slaughter," said the wing commander, and the formation broke.

The ballet of death had begun. Jens picked a random Lancaster and pushed his 109 toward it. The plane screamed downward, and he eased the reticle onto the target's shadowy form. His thumb dropped, and his plane spewed glowing metal. The bomber immediately replied with a stream of machinegun fire, and Jens rolled hard and away. Like hail on a tin roof, the Lancaster's .303 rounds peppered his fighter but to little effect. Systems nominal and controls free, he pulled the plane into a steep climb and prepared for another hammer fall.

The sky twinkled with machinegun and cannon fire, burning aircraft, and explosions. The radio burst to life with shouts of terror, target, and pain.

"Vogel down," said one of the pilots, the first friendly loss of the night.

Jens glanced a 109 aflame at the cowling and coasting toward the ground, but he remained focused on his prey. He loomed high over his victim and rolled into a hard dive, targeting the top of the wing where it met the fuselage. He fired again, and a shower of sparks fell from the stricken plane. The fuel line ignited, flames racing along the wing before bursting into the tanks. Jens pulled away as the beast exploded like a dying star, briefly framing every aircraft in the sky in orange and yellow.

"Brothers, please forgive me," whispered Jens, his eyes fixated on the fractured and flaming bomber plunging toward earth.

"Nice shooting!" said the wing commander amid cheers and yowls over the radio. The celebration was short-lived.

"Herz is down," said another pilot and the cheers vanished.

"They should have dropped by now," said Jens.

No response. The bombers filled the night sky, many more than what the searchlights could slather with light.

"The target is Essen," said the wing commander.

Jens clenched his jaw. He imagined Elise working the graveyard shift in the factory and their children fast asleep in bed with his own mother dutifully knitting downstairs. He ripped his fighter back into the fray. Bloodlust he had not known for years crept back into his heart. He looked down to the sparkling Rhine.

"We have ten minutes to target," said Jens. He picked another bomber and shredded its wings and body with shells until his cannons ran dry. The plane lurched hard to the left then broke into a terminal dive. The belly of the beast laid wide open but not by his doing. The bomb bay doors of the Lancasters had opened; they had started their run.

The formation leaned north to follow the river. Stricken goliaths belched smoke and fire from their engines and wobbled with torn wings and bodies, but onward they pressed with single-minded intention.

Rage filled Jens's heart, and, again, he pulled his battered fighter into a dive.

"Gunter 26," said his wing commander, "we're peeling away—the Flak is about to resume."

"No!" shouted Jens into the radio. "Give me more time!" He fired into the engine of another bomber, but the smaller machinegun rounds had little effect. A fierce reply of tracer fire smashed into his aircraft. Blinding pain ripped into his arm, and his hand fell limp.

"Son of a bitch!" he screamed and grasped the controls with his other hand.

"Jens, get out of there!" shouted the wing commander.

Jens clicked off his radio and pulled his fighter around for another pass. Warm blood spread across his chest and underarm, and his vision dimmed, but the hunt would continue.

The fireworks resumed, and he chased the bombers into the maelstrom of explosions and black smoke. "From Hell's heart," he whispered and peppered a trailing bomber with his final rounds. His vision dimmed further, and his eyelids drew heavy. An 88 shell burst at the nose of his fighter and cracked the canopy open like a hard-boiled egg. Freezing air rushed into the cockpit and seized his breathing.

"Forgive me, Elise," he whispered as the bombers loosed their deadly cargo.

The cockpit faded into nothingness. The enshrouding night sky overtook his eyes, and the freezing air drifted away. Here, there was naught.

Such delicious terror from such a pitiful man. The voice broke into laughter that trailed into a satisfied groan. *Alas, my meal is being cut short. But soon our feast will be . . . unending.* The laughter resumed, horrible and inescapable, thundering through Jens's mind.

The Ziggurat of Kir Endra appeared, its steps bathed in blood and severed limbs. Screams rebounded from the four corners of the mall, and piles of human skulls rose from the granite.

"Jens, wake up, lad. Wake up," said Keats. His voice echoed in the dark. "Wake up!"

Jens reached into the sky, and the Ziggurat and its enshrouding horrors began to fade.

* * *

"Heavy bastard," said Keats through a groan. He clutched Jens's massive boot, leaned backward, and kicked off the rock. The German slid forward a couple feet, and Keats staggered on one foot and crashed to the ground. Air rushed from his lungs, and he swore before righting himself and repeating the process.

"Essen," said Jens. "Bombers . . . Elise! No!" He twitched, spasmed, and whimpered.

"Come on, lad," said Keats. He grasped and heaved yet again. A few curt hops on one foot, and the ground gave way behind him, and he rolled backward. Keats clutched in every direction as he slid down the rock, finally coming to a stop with two jagged handfuls. He looked about and recognized the main chasm, with its familiar red glow. Springing to his feet, he scurried back to Jens and dragged him from the mouth of the narrow tunnel.

Jens sprang up, eyes darting around and body shaking. The dead god had lost its grip on his mind, but the terror lingered. His brow beaded with sweat, and tears seeped from his eyes.

Keats kneeled and embraced him, slapping him on the back. "There, there, buddy. You're out."

Jens blinked a few times, his hands steadying, and focused on Keats's goofy, grinning face. The flames and gunfire receded. He pulled his exhausted friend in for a crushing hug.

"I'm sorry," he said into Keats's shoulder.

Keats sputtered a friendly, awkward laugh. "Eh, well, no worries," he said. "I owed ya for almost getting us eaten back there, I guess." He cleared his throat and rested his chin between thumb and forefinger, looking perplexed. "Why didn't it invade my mind?"

Jens swallowed hard. "The Children feed on fear. I was the one most afraid." He looked up at Keats and then away. "I have seen their plans."

"Well," said Keats with a thoughtful pause, "I don't—"

"Who goes there?" a voice erupted from the dark below.

Keats recognized it immediately as Darius Klug, a light arms officer in his platoon. He peered down at the faint shadows.

"Hey!" shouted Keats. "It's Reginald the medic and my colleague, Jens!"

Two soldiers stepped out of the shadows and looked up at them.

"Keats, what are *you* doing up there?" said Klug. He turned and whispered to the other soldier, and they both laughed.

"We've been sent on a mission to determine the fate of the shade-bringer," said Keats. "We were ambushed and took heavy casualties."

"Come on down. We need to talk," said Klug.

Keats helped Jens to his feet and crawled to a sharp overhang. Sliding his legs over the ledge, he plopped down onto an embankment and tottered clumsily downward. Jens leaped from the overhang, landing heavy on his feet.

The two men drew their swords. Keats stepped forward, smiling, and a blade pressed into his chest.

Jens stepped back and squared his shoulders.

"I don't understand," said Keats, still smiling. "Are you joking?"

"I'm afraid not," said Klug, removing his helmet.

Keats recoiled at the misshapen and mangled face once that of Darius Klug but now monstrous, mutilated, and sharing the same pale glistening orbs of the reanimates.

"What the fuck is this?" said Keats, raising his hands.

Klug seized Keats's sword and shoved him.

"Hands up, and keep them up," said the other soldier as he closed in on Jens, sidestepping him and grabbing his weapons. "Ah, a famed strider blade," said the soldier, marveling at the weapon, "forged from the fang of one of those abominations."

"Indeed," said Jens.

"It'll make a nice addition to my mantel."

"We'll see," said Jens, staring forward, face blank.

"All right, move it," he said, eyeing the German, and he shoved them onward.

They trudged down a chiseled stone pathway toward the far-side ledge of the chasm. The dull red glow waxed to a bright and balmy radiance that bathed them. With a final turn, they stepped down to the massive platform connecting the twin bridges.

"What in god's name is this?" said Keats.

They stopped. A small detachment of soldiers lingered among a sea of shambling reanimates, chatting and laughing as if the creatures weren't even there.

Jens looked on in amazement. "How is this possible?" The fresh corpses, some he recognized, groaned and swayed peacefully among the living. A reanimate brushed Keats and snarled briefly before ambling forward.

"When you pick the winning side, all things are possible," said Klug. He clapped and a dozen others snapped to attention. "Unfortunately, you will never make it back to your comrades. Your accident is really quite tragic." With another wave, six pikemen closed ranks and surrounded them.

"Move it!" they shouted and jabbed. "Toward the bridge!"

The two men shuffled backward against the encroaching steel, the pikemen prodding and edging forward.

Jens looked back as they neared the pit, the heat roasting his back.

"Halt!" shouted Klug, and the pikemen froze. The bubbling waves of liquid stone rumbled far below, roiling against the gargantuan foundations of the bridge.

"You're going to throw us in?" said Jens. His eyes were calm and his voice controlled, almost resigned.

Klug glared at him. "That would be unsporting," he said. "You and your fat friend here are free to walk back across the bridge."

The pikemen laughed.

Jens looked over the distant expanse of stone. Armor fragments, broken arrows, and corpses littered its entire length. He stepped, boot crossing the threshold between the platform and the bridge. Clattering erupted above him as the ceiling came alive, white and writhing, bones stacked upon bones that formed misshapen skeletal bodies. He pulled his foot back, and the creatures sank into the soot and rocks, falling back into oblivion. He turned slowly to face Klug, who wore a sadistic grin, with placid dead eyes that cast a faint green glow at the anticipation of death.

"Looks like this is the end of the line," said Keats. He looked at the pikemen and then to Jens, trying to bury his fear. He reached into his tunic and pulled out an angular black pistol with a shiny brown grip. He slipped the weapon into Jens's hand and quickly covered it with the other. "I thought you'd want this."

"How did . . ." Jens trailed off, his eyes fixated on the Luger. "I sold . . ."

"It cost a pretty penny when I found the collector," said Keats, smiling, "but I figured I'd already taken enough from you."

Jens gripped the pistol and ran his index finger over the trigger. His hands moved in pure wonderment over the weapon, as unchanged in this world as it was in the last. He blinked rapidly, heart filling with fury and resolve, and looked to Klug.

"Start walking!" shouted Klug. A bestial growl blended with the voice of a man.

The pikemen shuffled forward and prodded.

Jens squared his chest to Klug, defiant, and lifted his chin. He reached into a breast pocket, removed his remaining 9 mm Parabellum round, opened the breech, and slid it into the receiver. He leveled the pistol at Klug's head and fired. The round burst through his eye and exploded out the back of his head, sending his limp body to the floor with a dull thud as the report rang deep through the caverns.

The curse holding the reanimates broke as the last ounces of life spilled from Klug's head, and they tore into the soldiers, a flurry of claws and teeth, tackling many to the ground. The pikemen scattered as the creatures slammed into their formation. Jens and Keats stood still, backs to the raging inferno, and watched the dead tear the living to pieces.

"Run," whispered Jens, and the two men sprinted. Jens searched the chaos as they ran a wide arc around the slaughter until he spotted his target. "Stay close to the wall, and keep moving toward the Infernal Plains. I'll rejoin you," he said. Sprinting headlong into the melee, he dove to the ground amid a flurry of claws and screams. Spotting the mortally wounded soldier, he crawled to him and took his weapon back.

"Please, help," said the soldier through a mouthful of blood. He grasped Jens's arm with his remaining strength, a reanimate's head buried in his open belly.

"You don't deserve this," said Jens. He removed the blade from its sheath and put the man out of his misery with a quick thrust. The weapon glowed momentarily, as it had when it claimed the guard captain in Mora. Jens sheathed it and sprinted to Keats.

"Shit, man, what now?" Keats sprinted after Jens into the cavern, a group of reanimates in pursuit.

"Up here!" a voice hissed from above. The two men slid to a halt and looked up. An armored hand grasped Jens and hoisted him to a high ledge. Together, they grasped Keats and dragged him up. The reanimates shambled to a halt below them and glared upward but made no attempt to ascend.

"You're from second battalion? You escaped the massacre?" Xi wiped a layer of sweat and soot from her brow.

"Massacre?" said Jens. "We lost many but vanquished the reanimates and the strider."

"We thought *you* had been destroyed in these caverns," said Keats.

"Many were," said Xi and she glanced down, "but Commander Pariseau marshaled the survivors and continued onward to the Infernal Plains. A group was left behind, including me, to guard their egress, but Klug and other traitors among us attacked and enslaved the reanimates. I'm the only survivor."

"Something is rotten in Irgendwo," said Jens. "You must cross back and tell the others what is happening."

"How will I bypass the dead?" said Xi.

"Leave that to us," said Jens, and he looked to Keats with a smile. "We're going to be bait."

"Oh, bloody hell, man. Can't we come up with a better plan?"

CHAPTER 29

CLOSE BUT NO CIGAR

I'll be back! I swear on your crooked crosses that I'll be back, and you will remember every second of my vengeance.

—MIRIAM URDEGAARD, DENMARK, 1537

WE RESTED WELL IN THE SMALL HUT. Deep underground and fortified beneath the creeping hellscape above, I felt secure among hundreds of these soul-eating Hollows. Li thumbed through books on the crooked shelf while Do sat at his desk writing. As my body and mind began to wind down from the earlier shitstorm, I noticed Miriam reclining on the floor with her chin in her hand. Pale, lithe, and bedecked in a thin cloak, her curves were quite noticeable.

"Miriam," I said.

She sighed and rolled onto her stomach to face me. "Yes, Shadebringer?" She elevated her head on both hands and blinked. Her sharp teeth flashed through full lips that seemed remarkably healthy given her cadaveric complexion. Her attention made me nervous, but I had asked for it.

"Were you a soldier?"

"No," she said. Her legs bent at the knee, feet kicking up and down, a movement I could not understand aside from nervous energy or excitement.

"Then how did you end up here?"

She paused, twirling locks of her hair with a finger. "Well, have you perchance heard of King Christian IV? Right prick that one was." Excitement rose in her voice, and she kicked faster.

"Never heard of him," I said, not quite placing that particular monarch.

"Well, some of us he burned were actual witches!" She broke into shrill laughter and stroked her neck. "Oh, I haven't felt such delicious pain since."

She licked her lips and winked at me. Miriam had the distinct ability to both horrify and arouse me at the same time. "If you weren't a soldier, how did you end up here?"

"I communed with Daedrina's Eldest, silly. It seems to be the only other way to get here besides dying in war." Her eye twinkled like a child's first gander at a shooting star. "Vile backstabber Azurocus took the form of a rabbit and led me deep into the woods. There, I built a fire, and up from the flames, I saw his face—his true face . . ."

"Then what?" I couldn't turn from her.

She shrugged. "He taught me the incantations, the ancient words of conjuring. I experienced his pure power and couldn't stop. He told me I could have it all if I joined him . . . and . . ." She trailed off as the glimmer died. Her eyes sank downward.

"Then you lost the world's most important game of chess to an ancient evil being," said Li, closing his book and shaking his head.

She sneered at him and turned back to me. "He again took the form of a rabbit and led a group of hunters to the copse with my little campfire. They found me. They heard my words. And after a short trial, they burned me at the stake with three other girls who simply liked to dance naked in the woods."

"Why would he bring you here?" I said.

"He wanted me for himself, the greedy bastard, and the Children can only harvest souls through the waygate," she said. "Lucky thing too, or else they'd be eating them by the handful from Earth."

"The Children seek a means to take all of our souls," said Li quietly to himself, "and the Council of Mora works toward that very end."

"Irgendwo somewhat suits you," I said and smiled. "Kind of an odd name though."

"Yes, Uta herself is said to have named it when she reigned. I kind of like it here."

"Irgendwo is a waystation—a timeless place," said Li. "The word captures its essence beautifully."

"*Was* a waystation," said Do, dropping his quill on the desk. He read over a scroll, snatched it up, and slammed his other hand down. "The Morites have turned it into a prison."

He stood from the desk and walked to me, scroll in hand. "I have made a mistake." His voice quivered.

"Mistake?" I looked up at him. I could see guilt in his eyes and braced myself.

"Yes," he said. "You are not the one I intended to bring here."

My heart sank. I had only just come to terms with my role, and now I was finding out I really wasn't anyone special after all. I fucking knew it.

Li's ears perked up. "What do you mean?"

"A man named *Claude* was meant to bear the shade, not Clyde." He tossed the scroll to Li. "I misread Perry's handwriting."

Li read the scroll, pausing and mumbling as his thumbs raced down the margins. His brow shot up, and he stared over the edge at Do. "Dear gods, you selfish fool . . ." he gasped and reread it. "Where did you get this?"

Do hunched slightly and crossed his arms, shamed but too proud to look at any of us. "Your very own Perry Gavrel."

"This is planar magic, a forbidden and ancient craft far beyond the abilities of even our brightest arcanists, let alone a reclusive neophyte!" Li spat his words out with rage and a hail of saliva. I was taken aback by the emotional display. But with a mere groan, he sat on the floor and drew his knees to his chest. "Why . . . why would Perry keep this from me . . . from Junedale?" He shuddered and rested his head in his hands. "I used the last scroll of purification on him; I used our last hope on the wrong man."

"Oh dear," said Miriam, and she raised a hand to her mouth. It was the first expression of concern I'd heard from her, and it was authentic. Such a litmus for dread.

Li stared ahead, unblinking, lost in his own mind. "In mere weeks, the Morites will break our last lines of defense and sack Junedale and . . . and . . ." He trailed off as his brilliant mind no doubt manifested scenarios of catastrophe—scenarios of doom. All because some amateur fucked up a name.

"Stop it," said Miriam. Her eyebrows sat high, perched in all seriousness with just a glint of fear in her eyes.

"So much for the fucking prophecy," I said with a nervous laugh and clasped my hands behind my head. The weight of my fate—of our fates—slithered into my heart: I would either be trapped in Irgendwo forever or ritualistically sacrificed and sent to a veritable Hell.

"Please," said Do, "you must help me find Nora." The boy seemed to have no concern or care for the weight of his error. A great tempest rose in my belly.

"Your little magic SNAFU got me and my buddy Bernie dragged into this shithole and doomed everyone else here, and you expect us to help you?" I said. "Get the fuck outta here." I scooted next to Miriam and wished for a cigar, unsure if I wanted to beat the shit out of Do or feel sorry for myself.

• • •

Mistake. The people of Irgendwo had—again—become the butts of a giant cosmic joke and I, Clyde Robbins, was the goddamn punch line. Just another page in the book of their eternal misery, and I was only beginning the first chapter.

The great irony of the situation was that, as I pondered Do's actions, my irritation waned. True, he had deprived me and a few around me of a natural death, but I couldn't hold the young man's passion against him. What he did, he did for love to the best of his ability and at great personal risk. And in a way, I respected it. History was littered with such examples . . . good intentions and all. But I suppose *that* road led here.

"If Giuseppe survived, this place is at dire risk. The Council will certainly bring everything to bear to capture you, Shadebringer," said Li. He stood before the window and gazed out among the Hollows as they played. His voice, once emotional, had returned to an erudite monotone: not quite resigned but not hopeful either.

"They'll slaughter everyone here if they find us," I said.

He nodded. "We can't stay for long."

"And if we leave, the Morites capture us, or we get eaten by something out there."

Li looked on without saying a word as Do sat with his hands folded and his head hung low.

"Well," I said, lifting my mace and slinging my pack over my shoulder, "looks like we only got one option then." The others looked up at me. "Grab your shit." I moved toward the door. "Time to find out if this shade and I can still be buddies, even if I'm not the one it wanted."

Do's eyes lit up, and he sprang to his feet.

"If you step through that gate and the shade doesn't come for you, you will end up in Kull," said Li.

"And if we keep moping like a bunch of nuns in a whorehouse, we'll still end up in Kull, one way or another. Let's move." Miriam shot to her feet, grinned wide, and winked at me.

"I'll show you the way," said Do.

Li and Miriam collected their belongings, and, together, we left.

We made our way back through Hovel, Hollows scampering about and giggling. Garrett trotted up beside us and led us to the secret entrance. Tapping at the rock, he activated the hidden mechanism, and the entrance rumbled open. We stepped into the barren rotunda, and the Hollow walked us to the heavy iron gate.

I peered through the bars, shoulders and neck tight, gripping my mace. "Norris isn't gonna be waiting for us up there, is he?"

"He's probably napping now," said Garrett. "That scout was pretty fat."

I cracked a slight smile.

"But I wouldn't try to take your sword back if I were you."

"Good advice, Garrett, and thank you for your hospitality." He unlocked the gate, and I pushed it open as it squealed on its rusty hinges. We walked through and climbed the stairs back toward the ruins.

Creeping to the edge of the doorway, I held the others fast and listened. Soldiers marshaled in the distance. Clanging metal rebounded down the alleyway, mixed with screams, as the Morite heavies came face-to-face with Kir Sol's beasts.

"Come," I said, and we skittered down the alley. Ducking into another shanty, we hid, and I tried to get my bearings. I pulled my compass out, and the needle spun like a propeller. "Which way to the gate?" I whispered.

"I can get us there," said Do.

I looked to Li, and he nodded. "Lead on," I said, and Do peeked out the door and snuck to the left.

"Move along the sides of the buildings," he said and patted the stone wall. "Some of the creatures hunt by shadows."

We lined up behind him and slinked along, stepping over debris like cats on our own hunt and peeking in every door and window.

Feeling a light tap on my shoulder, I turned, and Miriam stared up at me with a grin.

"You're no mistake," she said and planted a kiss on my lips.

I flushed slightly, my heart fluttered, and I kissed her forehead.

"Shadebringer!" A deep voice exploded into the air with a column of white light. Dust and pebbles shook from the sills and eaves of every stone building as the voice boomed and rebounded across the city.

"This ends here and now!"

The column intensified and pierced the mist, casting a faded glow across every corner of the city. "Show yourself! Come to the gate, or your companions will meet the Children themselves!"

"They've primed the gate," whispered Li. "They're preparing for sacrifice."

"Why in hell would they want a purified shadebringer at the gate?" said Miriam.

Li opened his mouth to reply but hesitated. "The Kir Sol gate only leads to Kull. They must believe there is no risk of Clyde joining with the shade. Perhaps they communed with the Children and learned of the mistake."

He turned to me. "In any case, you cannot go through the gate, or you'll meet a fate far worse than anything you can imagine."

"They've got Jens and Keats," I said. "I can feel it."

"Then who knows what evil they've planned for you?" Li stepped in front of me.

"You're right." I brushed past him. "But I know exactly what kind of evil they have planned for my friends." Caring little for what creatures lurked in the shadows, I broke into a jog toward the column of light.

"You damn fool," said Li.

CHAPTER 30

OMEGA SLEEPS

You are cut from the tapestry that I hath woven;
from here to eternity, your spark unspoken.
Not nameless, not forgotten, and will unbroken;
your fate, Shadebringer, was long ago chosen.

—MOTHER DAEDRINA,
CREATOR OF ALL THINGS

WE FOLLOWED THE TOWERING column through the maze of stone. As we neared the gate, our shadows grew, and our eyes narrowed. Its luminosity, the closest thing this world had to a sun, reminded me of the tunnel of light reported in near-death experience stories, and I couldn't help but chuckle at the irony.

We rounded the corner of a fallen church, and the ruins of the Kir Sol waygate shined before us. Arcs of pure energy danced between two giant stone pillars that sat perched upon a pocked marble dais. A phalanx of Morite soldiers drew their swords as wind whipped their capes.

"Wise decision." The voice arose from behind the phalanx, and the soldiers parted. Ek Maraine stood at the base of the gate, his hood flapping about in the wind. Turning to us, he drew back the hood, revealing yellow eyes and scales that glistened in the light.

"That is one ugly motherfucker," I said.

"One of the original souls of Irgendwo—once a man," said Li.

Ek Maraine raised his arm, and two soldiers dragged Jens and Keats forward and threw them to the dirt. "Come forward, Clyde Robbins—shadebringer . . . or perhaps not—and meet your fate."

"Game on," I said and walked toward the gate.

Trudging through the heavy sand and shielding my eyes, two guards seized my mace and escorted me to their master. The slight figure looked more serpent than man, scales spreading out from the corners of his yellow eyes and fangs peeking out from his lips.

"Good to see you, Yank," said Keats, looking up from the sand, his face purple and swollen.

I expected more from you. The baritone voice that had stalked me on the plains spoke into my mind as Ek Maraine stared at me, his triangular pupils waxing and waning in the light.

"Sorry to disappoint," I said and sneered. "What do you want?"

Ek Maraine pointed at the waygate.

I looked into the blinding light and back to Ek Maraine. Li's warnings about Kull returned to me in force, and I hesitated.

"Go," he said aloud, then gestured at Jens. The German's body levitated from the ground like a ragdoll. "Or he goes for you."

"You drive a hard bargain, snake man."

As he brought Jens back to the earth, I ascended the stairs, and cold air jolted me about. Squinting hard and mouth pinched tight, I took a deep breath. One way or another, I was stepping into that gate. "Here goes nothin'!"

• • •

I was weightless. I was nothing. My reality became panoramic darkness; I was a rat in a tin shed during a snowstorm. Echoes sputtered across my sentience and vanished. Some were familiar; some were foreign.

"Join us," whispered a voice. "You've come so far, and now it is time to rest." A cloud of black smoke coalesced before me and formed into a hand, and I recoiled. "Don't be afraid, Clyde Robbins, your time has come . . . finally." The hand beckoned gently, playfully, and light giggling emerged above it.

"I'm a man on a mission, shithead. What do you want?"

The hand ceased its beckoning for a moment and clenched into a fist.

"You!"

The fingers flew open and grabbed my arm; an unseen force dragged me forward.

"Piss off," I screamed and jerked back hard.

The hand redoubled its assault, and a sonorous growl emerged from above me. Suddenly, my forearm glowed bright orange, and the hand ripped away with a howl. The energy flowed out as a torrent, coalesced into a human-like form, and assailed the hand with jabs and strikes. The smoke, formless now, flowed back into the abyss, and I steadied my arm.

The glowing entity paused then turned. The face of a woman smiled and faded into the abyss around me.

• • •

The bulky limbs of an oak tree in full bloom spread over me, beams of sunlight peeping through the leaves. Warm air brushed my face, and I heard the faint din of a busy lawnmower somewhere over the ticky-tacky. A worn asphalt street with crooked yellow lines weaved behind me, and ahead a white picket fence sprouted from the lawn. The gate was open.

I walked through and approached the front door of a quaint suburban rancher. After ringing the doorbell, I waited with my hands folded behind my back. The door of the home across the street opened, and a vaguely familiar man in a robe stepped out, gripping his coffee, and grabbed the newspaper. He waved and stepped back into the home. I rang the doorbell again.

"Come around back!" A screen door squeaked on its hinges and banged.

I made my way to the back. Squeezing by some hedges, I stepped onto a manicured terrace.

"Hi, Sergeant." Claude smiled at me as he nudged beef patties on a charcoal grill. His frame, much wider than I remembered it, stretched an apron over his belly. He looked older.

"Bayou Boy, holy shit." The war came roaring back. "You're dead."

He cocked his eyebrows and flipped the burgers. "No shit. So are you."

He was right, of course, but somehow the truth kept eluding me, or I it.

He cracked a cold can of beer and handed it to me.

"Damn, it's been a while." I sipped the fizzy brew and took in the rich scents of charcoal and meat. My body felt light and clean; there was not a fleck of ash or blood on me. I wore airy slacks and a short-sleeve button-up that ruffled in the breeze. Glancing around, I shrugged. "Where are we?"

"We are Nowhere," he said and flipped a burger onto a bun before passing it to me.

"Uh huh." I bit into the burger. Top notch. "This sure tastes real."

"It *is* real. I never said it wasn't."

"Then where are we?"

He sighed and tapped on the window. "Sarah!" he called. "We have a guest!"

A young woman carrying a chubby baby stepped out of the home and waved. The baby squirmed and cooed in the crook of her arm. "You must be Clyde Robbins. I've heard a lot about you."

"Yes, ma'am, ninety percent of it is bullshit, and the other ten percent is maybe."

She laughed and lifted the kid's arm to wave at me. "Say hi, Max."

I waved, and both stepped back into the home. "Are they dead too?" I said when I was sure both were gone.

"Sure are," he said. "Everyone here is."

I sipped my beer, unsure what to say next. "So, uh, how did your kid die?"

"He died in his sixties in a car crash."

I stared at him blankly. "OK."

"Let me explain."

In an instant, the world changed. Leaves vanished. Snow covered everything. The shrubs were gone. The neighbor's house became an open lot.

My breath flowed out in clouds, and I shivered. "Where are we now?"

"*When* are we is the better question. Twenty years forward."

Claude scraped his shoes against the welcome mat and stepped into his home. I followed.

"Hey, Dad," said a young man sitting forward on the couch. He clutched a plastic rectangle connected to a gray box in front of the TV.

"Max, this is Clyde, an old army buddy of mine."

The boy took cursory note of me and returned his attention to the TV. He was the spitting image of his father, almost identical to the young man I had known back in Vietnam. I couldn't decide whether a person aging twenty years in front of me or the gray box—*Nintendo* written in red on its front—that controlled the TV was more impressive.

"Time has no meaning here," I muttered as I watched a small red and brown man hop across the screen.

"Bingo," said Claude. Looking to him, it took extra effort to see the gray hairs.

And what of his wife and kid? If he could zip around in time, did they have any say in the matter? "I have so many questions."

"I know, but *your* time is limited here. Come." He twisted open an old door and descended into the basement. I looked again at the moving screen, grabbed one last beer from the fridge, and trudged down after him.

The basement air felt stale and cool and quite unwelcoming. As I took my final step onto the concrete floor, the door behind me slammed shut and vanished. *Fuck. Guess I should have grabbed two beers.* Cracking the can and chugging it while I could, I walked over to Claude, who stood in front of three strangely out-of-place doors.

"If you take the door on the left, you go back to Irgendwo. The center door takes you back to Earth for a new birth. And the right door will allow you to move on, like I have."

"What about the shade?"

Claude laughed. "Free will reigns, Sergeant. *You* are with the shade; the shade is with you. Daedrina chose *you* and *you* accepted." He grinned.

"I thought I was a mistake."

"Daedrina doesn't make mistakes. *I* would have never stepped through that gate. She knew this."

I raised my hand to interject, but the ground rumbled a little, and the light flickered. Claude looked at me with urgency. "Please pick, Sergeant. Your presence here is unnatural and causing quite a stir."

"Yeah, yeah, yeah—as fucking usual." I stepped forward and looked at each door.

Definitely not going back to that shithole Earth. Another tremor shook dust from the rafters. A sudden and interesting statistics conundrum crossed my mind, but I didn't have the time to entertain it.

Turning the handle, I walked through.

* * *

I arrived on the stone platform and immediately felt the soot, sweat, blood, and metal again. The aches, fear, thirst, and hunger returned as well, but my hatred of Ek Maraine swelled as I peered down on the abomination from the shifting light. Minutes had become twenty years in a simple exercise of free will, but here, now, time flowed ahead, and I had a job to do.

"How did you return?" Ek Maraine's confusion turned to shock then rage. "That gate leads only to Kull! What lies did Giuseppe feed me?"

A red glint leaked from the gate, and the brilliant light dimmed.

"No matter," he said. "I will dispatch you myself, and these sacrifices will do just fine." He whispered to a hulking man in coal-black armor—his bodyguard, who smiled and gestured to the soldiers.

Soldiers dragged Miriam, Li, and Do to Keats and Jens and made them all kneel. Robed acolytes shuffled in through the formation, each clutching a twisted onyx dagger, and positioned themselves behind the prisoners. Jens, stoic, stared straight ahead, eyes half shut. Keats shook like a leaf. Miriam smiled.

"Positions!" Ek Maraine roared, and the acolytes readied their daggers. The gate turned redder and groaned. "Clyde Robbins, false shadebringer, you get to watch." He raised his arm.

Not thinking, not feeling, not *caring*, I leaped from the platform onto the sand, fists clenched, and charged at Ek Maraine.

His pupils shrank, and he flinched—a hint of fear—but his bodyguard brought me down with a heavy mail fist.

Careening to the ground, lungs locked and gut screaming in pain, I wheezed and spit out a mouthful of dust. A plated boot fell onto my back and drove me further into the dirt.

Ek Maraine and his guards laughed, and the gate darkened further.

Should have picked the door on the right. I blew blood from my nose amid the pain, shame, and embarrassment. *Prophecies are bullshit.* Lifting my head from the ground, I looked to Miriam, and she locked eyes with me and winked. Not an ounce of fear. Almost . . . wonderment? God damn, she was the real deal.

Become hope, Clyde. You are not alone. You are no mistake. The soft voice whispered into my mind, blocking the tempest around me and snuffing out the pain. Peering beyond Ek Maraine and his guards, I saw dozens of twinkling eyes peering back. The Hollows had come, shoulder to shoulder, Garrett standing in front of them.

Sensing the disturbance, Ek Maraine turned to them and then back to me, and the speck of fear I had seen in his eyes grew to terror.

"It is dinner time, my pet!" shouted Garrett, and he gestured at the gate.

The very stones shrieked and rumbled; light swirled and pulsed as if it were alive (perhaps it was alive?), and the rumble became a quake. Steps. Monstrous steps from beyond, and then I was certain. I knew what was coming but did not fear.

The strider tore into our reality with a mighty heave and crashed down on the Morite guards and roared into the heavens. Ek Maraine screamed orders that fell on deaf ears. Acolytes and guards bolted in every direction. Part in horror and part in grim satisfaction, I smiled as merciless butchery found the Morites.

Pulling an ornate staff from beneath his robes, Ek Maraine trained it on the strider and chanted.

The beast seized in place and warbled—such a strange noise—and turned its bloody mass toward the Hollows, its shadow stretching long over them.

The boot on my back yielded as the bodyguard wavered. Bracing my hands on the ground, I shoved up with all my strength and sent the bastard tumbling to his back. Jumping to my feet, I felt them cool as black ooze spilled from the gate and washed down the steps. The guard stood, covered in the muck, and ripped a sword from his belt. With a grunt, he lunged and slashed at me, and I dodged and braced for combat. "True believer, huh, motherfucker?"

"*Hostibus nocendum est!*" A bolt of energy flew from Ek Maraine's staff, and the strider trembled and stammered forward, twitching, bent under the wills of two masters.

"No, you bastard!" Keats clamored to his feet and jumped through Ek Maraine like he had tackled a shadow.

Concentration broken, Ek Maraine hissed, baring his fangs, and swooped down on Keats.

Keats howled in pain as the serpent pierced his flesh. "Fucking hell!" He spasmed, clutched his shoulder, and curled into a ball as Jens rushed to his side.

Smiling with what capacity he had left and ignoring the ichor smeared across his mouth, Ek Maraine focused again on the strider and continued the spell.

"You must break his hold on the strider!" shouted Li as I dodged another slash from the bodyguard.

I threw an uppercut into the man's gut, and the guard reeled back. Miriam thrust a spear through his neck and brought him to the ground.

You must act. The alarm in her voice made me tremor.

Turning to Ek Maraine, muscles taut like violin strings, I clenched my fists and charged. He sidestepped, but I found my mark and brought him down, ribs crunching against my shoulder. He hissed as we rolled, revulsion filling me as my face bore down on the smooth scales. With my weight pinning him to the ground, I reared back and smashed his face over and over until greenish slime poured from his nose and eyes.

"Such a misplaced fighting spirit!" Ek Maraine cast me off and tore through his robes. Before our eyes, he grew twice in length and height into a serpentine horror as I scrambled to my feet. He lunged and snapped up a mouthful of dust as I parried. With a sweep of his tail, my legs flew forward, and I crashed to my back.

"Clyde, your mace!" Do lobbed the weapon to my side, and I snatched it up as Ek Maraine struck down on me.

I braced the weapon across the corners of his mouth, struggling under his immense weight, his fangs inches from my neck.

Clyde Robbins, killer of children, you struggle against your own, he screamed into my head. The face of the young girl I shot filled my mind, and I trembled . . .

The Vietnamese girl—healthy, beautiful, smiling in her flowery dress—flashed panoramic and brilliant before me. A white light flowed out from her form as she reached down and gently touched my forehead. *I forgive you*, she said and vanished. My heart filled with joy, electricity, power, and my arms tightened.

Ek Maraine hissed and prepared to strike. *A fitting meal for the O—*

Jens booted at him with vicious fury, but his strike sailed through Ek Maraine's substance, which became a dense mist. I rolled to the side and jumped to my feet before the monstrous body reformed, and he turned his head to hiss at Jens.

Gripping the mace with both hands, I swept down hard and smashed Ek Maraine's lower jaw loose from its hinges. The creature shrieked, and I rejoined with another blow that spattered the ground and my face. Pure joy: I loosed righteous fury on the serpent, pummeling his head and face to puree.

Laughter reverberated from the gate, and the ooze twisted around Ek Maraine's scaled neck. "Now we feast."

"No!" Jens rushed to Keats and latched onto his boot, but the ink had wrapped around Keats's body and dragged him over the sand.

"Find the tooth!" I shouted, still wrestling the squirming serpentine body of Ek Maraine. *How is this thing still alive?*

Miriam and Jens scrambled about the battlefield for Jens's weapon while Li and Do seized Keats and held fast. But the oozing tentacles were too strong; they squeezed and heaved the bodies the strider had crushed like wet cordwood.

"Got it!" Jens grabbed the weapon and dashed to the stairs, where Keats was being pulled closer and closer to the gate. Jens sliced across the tentacles with a *clang*, but they only swirled and reformed and latched on again.

Ek Maraine's eyes shot open, and he lunged at Jens, unhinged jaw dangling, and I threw us both to the ground. His body twisted tighter around mine.

"You have to do it," I said and coughed and fought against the constriction. Jens embraced Keats and cried, clutching the strider's tooth between them. The gate neared. The Children whispered into our heads as maniacal laughter split the air. The feeding had begun.

"Do it, Kraut—don't let me end up with them," said Keats. He stared into eternity, eyes glassed over and face white.

"I love you, my brother," said Jens and he thrust the tooth into Keats's chest.

Keats winced and closed his eyes. The weapon glowed, brilliant and powerful, dissolving the writhing black mass around him.

I struggled against Ek Maraine mere inches from the screaming nether. He squeezed me with his remaining strength, unable to bite, intent on dragging me to his masters—a final act of vengeance. The others ran to the platform and grasped my outstretched arms and wrenched me, but Ek Maraine held tight.

Twisting my head toward the portal, I saw a familiar face staring back at me. Bernie Collins, half his face a menagerie of flesh and bone, struck through the light and seized Ek Maraine between his massive bicep and chest.

"You owe me a cigar," he said with a wink, and he crushed the serpent's head and dragged him through the portal as the coils loosened and I tumbled away.

Anguished cries echoed from beyond the gate, and faded, black ooze flowed back from where it came. Peace returned. The desert winds whistled again and blew a thin layer of dust over the carnage. The strider, under firm control of the Hollows, swayed in the breeze.

I stood and walked to Jens, a man in the throes of bereavement, and touched his shoulder. He glanced back and shook a single tear from his cheek. Reginald Keats lay dead. His final selfless act, one I hadn't thought possible from the man, had probably saved us all from the strider's savagery. Ashen white and motionless, he appeared at peace, no doubt his final moments a great relief as his soul settled in the charge of his best friend. I reached down and pulled his little red book from a pocket sleeve.

Jens released Keats's body gently to the ground and stood. "His homecoming gift. He wrote in it religiously . . . except on the last few pages."

Unable to contain my curiosity, I flipped to the final pages. Graceful French cursive stretched across the last few wilted sheets of paper. I couldn't understand any of it except the final words:

I will love you forever.
—Sally

"He didn't write those words," said Jens.

"When I first got here, you told me how these gifts ensure salvation."

He nodded. And suddenly I understood. I closed the journal and tucked it back into Keats's sleeve.

Eyes red, Jens lifted his chin, and a new energy surged through him—maybe pride, maybe resolve—and he cleaned the weapon against his sleeve. "There is still work to be done, Shadebringer."

A horn sounded beyond the broken walls of the city: the full-march clarion of Junedale that brought soldiers to a brisk pace.

"No doubt, they'll attack when they see the strider," said Li. "We need to warn them."

The creature towered over us and stood strangely still under the Hollows' command.

"I'll go out to meet them," said Miriam. She tottered to the strider, brushed her hand over one of its massive claws, and giggled. It snorted, perhaps acknowledging her gesture, but didn't move. She jogged into the maze of buildings toward the approaching battalion.

CHAPTER 31

ENDS AND MEANS

You have failed to uphold your end of the bargain,
Ek Maraine, and you understand what that means for you . . .

—AZUROCUS, FIRST OF THE DAMNED

LORD OCTAVIUS AND HIS CLOSEST advisors shuffled into the room in full formal regalia and silently took their seats. We had returned to Junedale as heroes, and a feast awaited us in the lord's banquet hall, but the atmosphere in the room remained grim.

"May whatever god I eventually face judge me mercifully for what I've done," said Octavius, and he raised his chalice to us. "Especially to you, Clyde Robbins." He raised his chalice again to an empty seat with a single candle reserved for Reginald Keats.

Heat built up around my collar. "Why did you do it?"

Octavius sipped his wine and placed it on the table, eyes low and to the left as he confronted his conscience. "What I did, I did for Junedale and the future of our people." He paused and swallowed. With the dourest expression I'd seen on the man, he looked me in the eye. "We're losing this war."

"How is this *possible*?" Li sat forward in his chair. Pure consternation wracked his face. "We've heard of nothing but Junedale victories for multiple cycles. Our people eat better than they ever have before. We haven't come under siege in ages."

"Our treasury runs dry. The victories are exaggerated if not completely false. We're riddled with spies and turncoats. We haven't come to siege because the Morites have us fully blockaded. We have barely enough grob to feed our army let alone two hundred thousand citizens. We—"

"How *are* you feeding your people, Lord Octavius?" Jens stirred his food and settled on another gulp of beer.

Octavius exhaled deeply and glanced at Jens. An advisor moved her hand to his shoulder and squeezed with the most subtle shake of her head, but he pushed her hand away. "If Mother Daedrina won't provide for us, then we must provide for ourselves."

"The foraging party," said Miriam with a finger on her chin. "You sacrificed them to the Children just like the bloody Morites do."

"By gods, don't tell me!" Li shouted and shot up from his chair.

Octavius smashed a fist against the table, sending his chalice to the floor. Face red and eyes wide and white, he leveled a finger at Li. "Would you have us roll over and admit defeat? Would you rather the armies of Mora storm into Junedale and deliver us *all* to the Children at their leisure? What then? What's two hundred people for the lives of two hundred thousand? Their blood is on *my* hands—not yours!" His voice thundered about the stone room, and his arm shook.

Our muscles were taut and our spines straight; the banquet table had become a battlefield. I didn't know the old man had it in him. Li shrank into his chair. Idealism had again met its match in pragmatism. I folded my hands on the table and looked to Octavius: The great-grandfather of Junedale had become yet another mass murderer.

"Perry must have uncovered more than a means to summon a shadebringer," muttered Li, his voice barely audible. "Such heinous rituals were heretofore only possible at a waygate, but you've managed to bring this evil to Junedale."

"Perry's discoveries, thanks in large part to our brave Do here, have given us the means to carry on the fight against the Council. The Children care not where they source their souls, and we must defeat the Council at any cost."

"We have become the Council, your lordship." Li stood from his seat, bowed to Octavius, and left.

The sound of clattering silverware and dishes picked up as chatter ceased. Li's outburst had darkened Octavius, and his closest advisors fumbled with their cutlery and glanced at him every few moments.

"Ek Maraine's dead. That's a start," said Miriam, the first break in an awkward silence.

Octavius patted grob bisque from his chin. "Ah, Ek Maraine. I knew the fool long before he embraced the Council. His name was Armin Tun—not that it matters anymore. Quite wonderful our own shadebringer sent the serpent back to his masters."

"And Commander Pariseau." Miriam smiled and tore a piece of grob apart.

"Jacques Pariseau, a traitor—who would have thought?" Octavius stirred his bisque. "Though I wish we had been able to take him alive. I can only imagine what information he provided to the Morites."

"Lord Octavius," said Jens abruptly.

"Yes?"

Jens pointed at his strider-tooth weapon stowed at the entrance of the banquet hall. "I vanquished one of our traitors in the caverns and subsumed his soul. Perhaps he could provide some insight."

"Dear Visigoth, your service to Junedale is a blessing." Octavius snapped a finger, and an advisor scurried over to the weapon, removed it from its bindings, and exited the hall.

I nibbled at the various dishes of grob and other unrecognizable recipes and downed any booze put in my reach if I could grab it before Jens. Contrary to Keats's earlier assessment, the German could put it down—fast.

"Tell me about the strider attack at the gate." Octavius gulped down an advisor's wine and folded his hands in front of him.

I cleared my throat and gestured at Do.

"The Hollows have special connections with the beasts here." He fidgeted in his chair. "Especially the striders. They communicate."

"All the more reason we must seek an alliance with these Hollows."

"What makes you think they have a stake in your war?"

I turned to Do and grinned, almost proud, and awaited Octavius's reply. The kid definitely had some balls.

"Junedale is a friend of Hollows."

"You quarantine them in a windowless fortress and use them as canaries on the plains."

I burst out laughing but quickly put a hand over my mouth. I liked this kid's moxie.

"It's for the protection of all citizens of Junedale, and they are treated very well by law here."

"They live free in Hovel."

Octavius nodded and sipped his tea. "And how did you survive among them?"

"Long story," said Do, "and I would have stayed among them forever if I didn't need your help finding Nora."

"A story I would love to hear another time." Octavius smiled. "Are you certain nobody else knows the location of the enclave?"

"One of their traitors, a master diviner, may," said Do.

"Vile Giuseppe," said Miriam. "The traitor fled into the ruins, but we found no evidence of his demise, nor did we see him with Ek Maraine." She scowled.

"It's no consideration now," said Do.

We all looked to him.

"What do you mean?" said Octavius.

Do cleared his throat, and his eyes darted about the table. "Hovel is just one city, and I had them evacuate after we left."

Octavius leaned far over his plate, engrossed in Do's words. "There's another?"

"There's a whole kingdom." Do bit into a grob roll and looked away. I couldn't be sure he was relieved or ashamed to have such a secret off his chest.

* * *

"Did you see her? Hear her?" Do clamored up behind me as I sauntered, belly full, from the banquet hall.

I stopped and turned to him. The young man hid his youthful innocence behind a cold glare, or perhaps two lifetimes of war had fixed the expression upon his face. But the love in his voice was unmistakable. "I did not," I said, wishing I had a different answer for him.

"She's still here. I can feel her." He touched the locket around his neck.

"Do," I said and put my hand on the young man's shoulder, "I'll do everything in my power to see you two reunited or, at least, to give you closure."

"Thank you." He looked up at me and shook my hand.

I walked into my new quarters with two bodyguards in tow. As far as Irgendwo's standards went, these new accommodations were ritzy. Octavius insisted on the guards due to the plague of spies in Junedale. No doubt the Council would want revenge when they learned of Ek Maraine, but I felt like a prisoner again.

I kicked off my boots and fell back into the new plush bed and folded my hands behind my head. The pillows and downy-soft sheets were a vastly different experience from the austere barracks, and it wasn't long before my mind retreated to Claude and his timeless world. I envied him: He wanted for nothing and enjoyed the eternal company of his loved ones. Had I made the right decision stepping back into this shitshow? At that thought, I felt a twang of guilt, especially after Keats's death, and I thought deeply on my circumstances. Then it dawned on me: There really was no decision. I did this to myself and would have done so in any circumstance . . . every single time. *So much for free will.*

"Hands off me, snipes!" Miriam's distinct voice carried power even behind a closed door.

"Ma'am, we have orders."

I jumped from the bed and scurried over to the door and pulled it open. "It's OK, boys. If she wanted to kill me, she would have done it already."

The guards disarmed Miriam of a variety of sharp objects. She stood silently at the doorway and rolled her eyes as the two men finished their search and waved her in. If only they knew what she was capable of.

"Octavius is being a little extreme with these guards, is he not?" She adjusted her dress and patted down her disheveled hair.

"I'm told it's for my protection."

"If those two idiots are the best you've got, you're in dire straits." Miriam pulled a kris from her robes and set it down on a stately desk. The razor-sharp weapon glimmered on the smooth wooden finish of the desk.

I looked at it and shook my head. "Where were you hiding that?"

"A place where meek men fear to tread," she said and cackled. She pulled out a heavy wooden chair at the desk and sat.

"Octavius puts too much stock in me."

Miriam giggled and spun the blade on its side. "Still not convinced, are you?"

"Nope." I dug through the cabinets for a bottle of liquor.

"Ugh, for a hero, you sure are a dullard. Did you not notice only *you* were able to strike Ek Maraine?"

"I did," I said, a little bit hurt by her insult. Perhaps I was in denial.

"You defeated their cloudform magic; they are vulnerable to you . . . both of you, now that the shade and you are one."

"What exactly is the shade?" I said and palmed over my heart wondering exactly *where* this entity was joined with me.

"We're not exactly sure who or what it is, but the same being guided Uta's sword during the last cataclysm as surely as it now guides your mace. Tell me, Shadebringer, how did it happen? When you stepped through that gate?"

I sighed and pondered her question, eyes low as I tried to remember the details. I looked up and locked eyes with her. "With much difficulty and only with the help of a long dead friend. You, on the other hand, took down dozens of soldiers out on the sands, including Jacques."

Miriam blushed, and a crinkled smile appeared at her pursed lips. She looked away and brushed her hand under her chin. "Oh, the insect conjuration? Just some novice necromancy."

I stood near the bed, unsure what to say. An awkward silence passed between us, long but not unpleasant. I enjoyed her company, and I was sure she enjoyed mine.

"I'm sorry about your friend," she said and stood from the desk. Embracing me, she placed her head against my chest. Her warmth was a welcome change from the constant dull chill of Junedale.

I sighed and thought of Keats and wondered how his reality had changed. "He'll be with us until the final liberation."

"I'm glad you're with us," she said into my chest.

The warmth grew to heat, and I palmed the back of her head and drew her in closer. Electricity surged between us, and I became aware of my beating heart. I didn't want to let go, but I didn't want to go further. I knew then I loved her, and the thought of losing her lurked in the back of my mind. I breathed deeply and caressed every strand of hair; her presence energized me. In the heart of this woman, I had found a reason for existence well worth two lifetimes of struggle.

THE END

ACKNOWLEDGMENTS

WITH MANY THANKS AND GREAT APPRECIATION to those who helped me bring this book to fruition: NL, MF, SP, BD, JY, JS, BYY

ABOUT THE AUTHOR

GRAYSON W. HOOPER is an army officer and physician whose writing is inspired by the tribulations of life, death, and medicine—both at home and abroad.

CPSIA information can be obtained
at www.ICGtesting.com
Printed in the USA
LVHW051921290422
717487LV00004B/127